The Story
of Gösta Berling

SELMA LAGERLÖF

The Story
of Gösta Berling

FRITZES KUNGL. HOVBOKHANDEL

STOCKHOLM

TRANSLATED FROM SWEDISH BY

Pauline Bancroft Flach

and

W. H. Hilton-Brown

PRINTED IN SWEDEN

TRYCKT HOS

VICTOR PETTERSONS BOKINDUSTRI AKTIEBOLAG

STOCKHOLM 1959

CONTENTS

THE STORY
OF GÖSTA BERLING

Introduction

CHAPTER 1 *The Minister*

At last the minister stood in the pulpit. The heads of the congregation were lifted. Well, there he finally was. There would be no default this Sunday, as on the last and on many other Sundays before.

The minister was young, tall, slender, and strikingly handsome. With a helmet on his head, and girt with sword and shirt of mail, he could have been cut in marble and taken for an ideal of Grecian beauty.

He had a poet's deep eyes, and a general's firm, rounded chin; everything about him was beautiful, noble, full of feeling, glowing with genius and spiritual life.

The people in the church felt themselves strangely subdued to see him so. They were more used to see him come reeling out of the public house with his good friends, Beerencreutz, the Colonel with the thick, white moustaches, and the stalwart Captain Christian Bergh.

He had drunk so deeply that he had not been able to attend to his duties for many weeks, and the congregation had been obliged to complain, first to the dean, and then to the bishop and the chapter. Now the bishop had come to the parish to take him severely to task and to make an inspection. He sat in the choir with the gold cross on his breast; the school chaplains from Karlstad and the clergy of the neighbouring parishes sat round about him.

There was no doubt that the minister's conduct had gone beyond the permissible limit. At that time, in the eighteen twenties, much in the matter of drinking was overlooked, but for the sake of drink, this man had deserted his post and now he was to lose it.

He stood in the pulpit and waited while the last verse of the hymn before the sermon was sung.

As he stood there, a feeling came over him, a conviction, that he had only enemies in the church, enemies in all the pews. Among the gentry in the gallery, among the peasants in the back pews, among the little boys and girls in the choir that were to be confirmed; he had enemies, none but enemies. An enemy worked the organ-bellows, and an enemy played the organ. In the church-wardens' pews he had enemies. They all hated him, every one,— from the children in arms, who were carried into the church, to the sexton, a formal and stiff old soldier, who had fought at Leipzig.

He longed to throw himself on his knees and to appeal to their compassion.

But the next moment, he was seized by a dull rage. He remembered well what he had been when, a year ago, he first stood in this pulpit. He was then a blameless man, and now he stood there and looked down on the man with the gold cross on his breast, who had come to pass sentence on him.

While he read his text, again and again the blood surged to his face,—it was rage.

It was true enough that he had drunk, but who had a right to blame him for that? Had they seen the vicarage where he had to live? Pine forests grew dark and gloomy close up to his windows. The damp dripped from the black roofs and ran down the mouldy walls. Was not brandy needed to keep one's courgae up when rain and driving snow streamed in through the broken panes, when the neglected soil would not give bread enough to keep hunger away?

He thought that he was just such a minister as they deserved. For they all drank. Why should he alone control himself? The man who had buried his wife got drunk at the funeral repast; the father whose child had been baptized had a carouse afterwards. The congregation drank on the way back from church, so that most of them were drunk when they reached home. A drunken priest was good enough for them.

It was on his pastoral visits, when he drove in his thin cloak over miles of frozen lakes, where all the icy winds met; it was when his boat was tossed about on these very lakes in storm and pouring rain, it was when he had to climb out of his sledge in blinding snow to clear the way for his horse through drifts high as houses, or when he waded through the forests swamps,—that he learned to love brandy.

The year had dragged itself out in heavy gloom. Peasant and master had passed their days with their thoughts on the dust of the earth, but at evening their spirits, freed by brandy, had cast off their yoke. Inspiration came, the heart grew warm, life became radiant, the song rang out, roses shed their perfume. The tavern bar-room seemed to him a garden in some southern land: grapes and olives hung down over his head, marble statues shone among dark leaves, sages and poets wandered under the palms and plane-trees.

No, he, the priest, up there in the pulpit, knew that without brandy life could not be borne in this part of the country; all his congregation knew that, and yet they wished to judge him.

They wished to tear his vestments off him, because he had come drunk into God's house. Oh, all these people had they believed, or did they even want to believe, that they had any other God than brandy?

He had finished the exordium, and he kneeled down to say the Lord's Prayer.

There was a breathless silence in the church during the prayer. But suddenly, with both his hands the minister caught hold of the ribbons which held his surplice. It seemed to him as if the whole congregation, with the bishop at the head, were stealing up the pulpit steps to pluck his surplice from him. He was kneeling and his head was turned away, but he could feel how they were pulling, and he saw them so plainly, the bishop and the deans, the clergy-men, the churchwardens, the sexton, and the whole congregation in a long line, tearing and straining to get his surplice off. And he could picture to himself so vividly how all these people who were pulling so eagerly would fall over one another down the steps when the surplice gave way, and the whole row of them below, who had not got up far enough to pull at his surplice, but only at the skirts of the coats of those in front of them would also fall.

He saw it all so plainly that he had to smile as he knelt, but at the same time a cold sweat broke out on his forehead. The whole thing was too horrible.

That he should now become a reprobate for the sake of brandy! He was to be an unfrocked priest. Was there anything on God's earth more wretched?

He should be one of the beggars at the roadside, lie drunk at the edge of a ditch, go dressed in rags, with vagrants for companions.

The prayer was ended. He should read his sermon. Then a thought came to him and checked the words on his lips. He recollected that it was the last time he should stand in the pulpit and proclaim the glory of God.

For the last time—that thought seized him. He forgot the brandy and the bishop. He must take this opportunity to testify to the glory of God.

It seemed to him that the floor of the church with all his hearers sank deep, deep down; and that the roof was lifted off, so that he saw far into the sky. He stood alone, quite alone in his pulpit; his spirit took its flight to the heavens opened above him; his voice became strong and powerful, and he proclaimed the glory of God.

He was inspired. He set aside what he had written; thoughts came to him like a flock of tame doves. He felt, as if it were not he who spoke; but he felt too that this was the best earth had to give, and that no one could reach a greater height of radiance and splendour than he, who stood there and proclaimed the glory of God.

As long as the flame of inspiration burned in him he continued to speak, but when it died out, and the roof sank down over the church, and the floor came up again from far, far below, he bowed his head and wept, for he thought that for him the best of life was now over.

After the service came the inspection and the vestry meeting. The bishop asked if the congregation had any complaints to make against their minister.

The minister was no longer angry and defiant, as he had been before the sermon. He was ashamed and hung his head. Oh, all the miserable stories of his drunkenness, which would be told now.

But nothing was said. There was a deep silence about the long table in the parish-hall.

The minister looked first at the sexton,—no, he was silent; then at the churchwardens, then at the powerful peasants and mine-owners; they were all silent. They sat with their lips pressed close together; they felt embarrased and looked down on the table.

"They are waiting for somebody to begin," thought the minister.

One of the churchwardens cleared his throat.

"I think we've got a fine minister," he said.

"Your Lordship has heard how he preaches," interrupted the sexton.

The bishop spoke of repeated omissions of divine service.

"The minister has the right to be ill, as well as another," was the peasants' opinion.

The bishop hinted at their dissatisfaction with the minister's mode of life.

They defended him with one accord. He was so young, their minister; there was nothing wrong with him. No; if only he would always preach as he had done to-day they would not exchange him for the bishop himself.

There were no accusers; there could be no judge.

The minister felt how his heart swelled and how swiftly the blood flowed through his veins. Could it be that he was no longer among enemies; that he had won them over when he had least thought of it; that he should still be their priest?

After the inspection, the bishop, the clergy of the neighbour-hood, the deans and the leading men of the parish dined together at the vicarage. The wife of one of the neighbours had undertaken to arrange the dinner; for the minister was not married. She had done it all so well that it made him see that the vicarage was not so dreadful. The long dining-table was laid outside under the pines, and shone with its white cloth, with its blue and white china, its glittering glass and folded napkins. Two birches bowed over the entrance, the floor of the hall was strewn with juniper twigs, a wreath of flowers hung from the rafters, there were flowers in all the rooms; the mouldy smell was gone, and the green window-panes shone bravely in the sunshine.

The minister was so exceedingly delighted that he thought he would never tipple again.

Everyone present at that dinner-table was gratified. Those who had been generous and had forgiven were glad, and the clergy in authority were glad because they had avoided a scandal.

The good bishop raised his glass and said that he had started on this journey with a heavy heart, for he had heard many evil rumours. He had gone forth to meet Saul, but lo, Saul was already changed to a Paul, who should accomplish more than any of them. And the worthy man spoke of the rich gifts which their young brother possessed, and praised them. Not to make him proud, but so that he might strain every nerve and keep a close watch over himself, as a man must do who bears an exceedingly heavy and costly burden on his shoulders.

The minister did not get drunk at that dinner, but he was certainly intoxicated. All this great unlooked for happiness went to his head. Heaven had let the flame of inspiration burn in him, and these people had given him their love. His blood was still at fever heat and coursing through his veins, when evening came and his guests departed. Far into the night he sat awake in his room, and let the night air stream in through the open window to cool this fever of happiness, this pleasant restlessness which would not let him sleep.

Then he heard a voice.

"Are you awake?"

A man came over the lawn up to the window. The minister looked out and recognized Captain Christian Bergh, one of his trusty boon companions. He was a wayfarer without house or land, this Captain Bergh, and a giant in stature and strength; he was as big as Goliath, and as malicious and stupid as a mountain goblin.

"Of course I am up, Captain Christian," answered the minister. "Do you think I could sleep to-night?"

And hear now what this Captain Bergh says to him! The giant had guessed, he had understood, that the minister would now be afraid to drink. He would never have any peace, thought Captain Christian; for those priests from Karlstad, who had been here once, could come again and take his surplice from him if he drank.

But now Captain Christian had put his heavy hand to the good work; now he had arranged that those priests would never come again, neither they nor the bishop. Henceforth the minister and his friends could drink as much as they liked at the vicarage.

Hear what a deed he had done, he, Christian Bergh, the mighty Captain. When the bishop and the two deans had climbed into their closed carriage, and the doors had been shut tight on them, then he had mounted on the box and driven them ten miles or so in the light summer night.

And then Christian Bergh had taught the reverend gentlemen how precariously life resides in the human body. He had let the horses run at the maddest pace. That was because they would not let an honourable man get drunk in peace.

Do you suppose he kept to the roads; do you believe he spared them jolts? He drove over ditches and ploughed fields; he drove at a breakneck gallop down the hills; he drove along the water's edge, till the waves covered the wheels; he almost stuck in a bog; he drove down over bare rocks, where the horses slid with legs held stiff.

And all the time the bishop and the priests sat with blanched faces behind the leather curtains and murmured prayers. It was the worst journey they had ever made.

And think how they must have looked when they came to Rissäter's inn, alive, but shaken like shot in a leather pouch.

"What does this mean, Captain Christian?" said the bishop, when the Captain opened the carriage-door for them.

"It means that you shall think twice, my Lord Bishop, before you make a new journey of inspection to Gösta Berling," Captain Christian replied; he had thought that sentence out beforehand, so as not to get in wrong.

"Tell Gösta Berling," said the bishop, "that neither I nor any other bishop will ever come to him again."

The mighty Captain Christian stands and relates this exploit at the open window in the summer night. For Captain Christian has only just left the horses at the inn, and has come directly to the minister with his news.

"Now you can live in peace, comrade," he said.

Ah, Captain Christian, the priests sat with pale faces behind the leather curtains, but the priest at the window in the light summer night looks far, far paler still. Ah, Captain Christian!

The minister raised his arm and aimed a terrible blow at the giant's coarse, stupid face, but checked himself. He shut the window with a bang, and stood in the middle of the room, shaking his clenched fist on high.

He, in whom the fire of inspiration had flamed, he, who had been able to proclaim the glory of God, stood there and thought that God had made a fool of him.

Was not the bishop bound to believe that Captain Christian had been sent deliberately by the minister? Would not the bishop believe that he had dissembled and lied the whole day? Now he would investigate everything about him in earnest; now he would suspend him and remove him from his office.

When the dawn broke the minister was far from his home. He did not care to stay and defend himself. God had mocked at him. God would not help him. He knew that he would be dismissed. It was God's will. He might as well go at once.

All this happened in the beginning of the eighteen-twenties in a remote parish in Western Värmland.

It was the first misfortune which befell Gösta Berling; it was not the last.

For colts who cannot bear spur or whips find life hard. From any suffering which may come to them they bolt down wild ways to yawning chasms. As soon as the ground is stony and the road hard, they know no other remedy than to cast off their load and rush away in frenzy.

CHAPTER 2 *The Beggar*

One cold December day a beggar came wandering up the slopes
of Broby. He was dressed in the most miserable rags, and his
shoes were so worn that the cold snow wet his feet.

Löven is a long, narrow lake in Värmland, intersected in
several places by long narrow sounds. In the north it stretches up
to the Finn forests, in the south down to the lake Väner. There
are many parishes along its shores, but the parish of Bro is the
largest and richest. It occupies a large part of the shores of the
lake both on the east and west sides; but on the west side are the
biggest estates, such as Ekeby and Björne, known far and wide
for their wealth and beauty, and Broby, with its large village and
inn, its court-house, sherrif's-house, vicarage, and market-place.

Broby lies on a steep slope. The beggar had come past the inn,
which lies at the foot of the hill, and was struggling up towards
the vicarage, which is on the hill-top.

A little girl was going up the hill in front of him; she dragged
a sledge laden with a bag of meal. The beggar caught up with
the child and began to talk to her.

"A little horse for such a heavy load," he said.

The child turned and looked at him. She was a little creature
about twelve years old, with sharp, suspicious eyes, and lips
pressed together.

"Would to God the horse was smaller and the load larger; it
might last longer," answered the girl.

"Is it then your own food you are dragging home?"

"By God's grace it is; I have to get my own food, although I
am so small."

The beggar seized the shaft of the sledge to drag it up.

The girl turned and looked at him.

"You needn't think that you will get anything for this," she said. The beggar laughed.

"You must be the daughter of the Vicar of Broby."

"Yes, yes, I am indeed. Many have poorer fathers, but none have worse. That's the plain truth, although it's a shame that his own child should have to say it."

"I hear that your father is mean and ill-natured."

"Mean he is, and ill-natured he is, but they say his daughter will be worse if she goes on living; that's what people say."

"I believe they are right. What I should like to know is, where you found this meal-bag."

"It makes no difference if I tell you. I took the grain out of father's store-house this morning, and now I have been to the mill."

"Won't he perhaps see you dragging it home?"

"You left school too early. Father is away on his parish visits, you see."

"Somebody is driving up the hill behind us; I hear the creaking of the runners. Think if it were he who is coming!"

The girl listened and peered down, then she burst into tears.

"It is father," she sobbed. "He will kill me! He will kill me!"

"Yes, good advice is now precious, and prompt advice better than silver and gold," said the beggar.

"Look here," said the child, "you can help me. Take the rope and drag the sledge; then father will believe it is yours."

"What shall I do with it afterwards?" asked the beggar, and put he rope over his shoulders.

"Take it wherever you like for the time being, but come up to the vicarage with it when it is dark! I shall be looking out for you. You are to come with the bag and the sledge, you understand."

"I shall try."

"God help you if you don't come!" called the girl, as she ran away, hurrying to get home before her father.

The beggar turned the sledge with a heavy heart and dragged it down to the inn.

The poor fellow had had his dream, as he went in the snow half barefooted. He had thought of the great woods north of lake Löven, of the great Finn forests.

Here in the parish of Bro, where he was now wandering along the sound which connects the Upper and the Lower Löven, —in this rich and smiling country, where one estate adjoins another, where there is one factory after another,—all the roads seemed to him too heavy, the rooms too small, and the beds too hard. Here he longed for the peace of the great, eternal forests.

Here he heard them threshing in all the barns, and it seemed as if they would never cease. Loads of timber and charcoal-carts were constantly coming down from the inexhaustible forests. Endless waggons loaded with ore followed the deep ruts which the hundreds that had preceded them had cut. Here he saw sleighs filled with travellers speed from house to house, and it seemed to him as if pleasure held the reins, and beauty and love stood on the runners. Oh, how he longed for the peace of the forests!

There, where the trees rise straight and pillar-like from the even ground, where the snow rests in heavy layers on the motionless pines, and the wind is mild and only plays softly in the topmost leaves, he would wander deeper and deeper into the forests until, at last, one day his strength would fail him, and he would drop down under the great trees, dying of hunger and cold.

He longed for the great murmuring grave above Löven, where he would be overcome by the powers of annihilation; where at last hunger, cold, fatigue, and brandy should succeed in destroying his poor body, which had endured everything.

He came down to the inn to wait until it was evening. He went into the bar-room and threw himself down on a bench by the door, dreaming of the eternal forests.

The innkeeper's wife felt sorry for him and gave him a glass of brandy. She even gave him a second glass, he implored her so eagerly.

But more she would not give him, and the beggar was in despair. He must have more of the strong, sweet brandy. He must once again feel his heart dance in his body and his thoughts flame up in intoxication. Oh, this sweet corn-brandy!

The summer sun, the summer song of the birds, and the perfume and beauty of summer floated in the white wave of the spirits. Once more, before he disappeared into the night and the darkness, he would drink sunshine and happiness.

So he bartered for brandy, first the meal, then the meal-sack, and lastly the sledge. Then he got thoroughly drunk, and slept the greater part of the afternoon on a bench in the bar-room.

When he awoke he understood that there was only one thing left for him to do. Since his miserable body had taken full possession of his soul, since he had been capable of squandering in drink what a child had confided to his keeping, since he was a disgrace to the earth, he must free it of the burden of such baseness. He must give back to his soul its liberty, and let it return to its Creator.

He lay on the bench in the bar-room and passed sentence on himself: "Gösta Berling, unfrocked priest, accused of having dissipated in drink the food of a hungry child, is condemned to death. What death? Death in the snow-drifts."

He seized his cap and reeled out. He was neither quite awake nor quite sober. He wept in pity for himself, for his wretched, desecrated soul, which he must set free.

He did not go far, and did not turn from the road. At the very roadside lay a deep drift, and there he threw himself down to die. He closed his eyes and tried to sleep.

No one knows how long he lay there; but there was still life in him when the daughter of the minister of Broby came running along the road with a lantern in her hand, and found him in the drift by the roadside. She had stood for hours and waited for him; and now she had run down Broby hill to look for him.

She recognized him instantly, and she began to shake him and to scream with all her might to get him awake.

She must know what he had done with her meal-bag.

She must call him back to life; at least until he had told her what had become of her sledge and her meal-bag. Her father would kill her if she had lost his sledge. She bit the beggar's finger and scratched his face, and at the same time she screamed as if she were distracted.

Then someone came driving along the road.

"Who the devil is screaming so?" asked a harsh voice.

"I want to know what this fellow has done with my meal-bag and my sledge," sobbed the child, and beat with clenched fists on the beggar's breast.

"Are you clawing a frozen man? Away with you, wild-cat!"

The traveller was a large and coarse woman. She got out of the sleigh and came over to the drift. She took the child by the back of the neck and threw her on one side. Then she leaned over, thrust her arms under the beggar's body, and lifted him up. Then she carried him to the sleigh and laid him in it.

"Come with me to the inn, wild-cat," she called to the child, "that we may hear what you know of all this."

An hour later the beggar sat on a chair by the door in the best room of the inn, and in front of him stood the powerful woman who had rescued him from the drift.

Just as Gösta Berling now saw her, on her way home from the charcoal kilns, with sooty hands, and a clay-pipe in her mouth, dressed in a short, unlined sheepskin jacket and striped homespun skirt, with tarred shoes on her feet and a sheath-knife in her bosom, and with her gray hair combed back from her old, beautiful face, he had heard described a thousand times; and he knew that he had met the far-famed wife of the major of Ekeby.

She was the most influential woman in all Värmland, mistress of seven iron-works; accustomed to command and to be obeyed; and he was only a poor man, condemned for life, stripped of everything, who knew that every road was too heavy for him, every room too crowded. His body shook with terror, while her glance rested on him.

She stood silent and looked at the human wretchedness before her, the red, swollen hands, the emaciated form, and the splendid head, which even in its ruin and neglect shone in wild beauty.

"You are Gösta Berling, the mad priest?" she said, peering at him.

The beggar sat motionless.

"I am the mistress of Ekeby."

A shudder passed over the beggar's body. He clasped his hands and raised his eyes with a longing glance. What would she do with him? Would she force him to live? He shook before her strength. And yet he had so nearly reached the peace of the eternal forests.

She began the struggle by telling him the minister's daughter had got her sledge and her meal-sack again; and that she, the major's wife, had a shelter for him, as for so many other homeless wretches, in the bachelor's wing at Ekeby.

She offered him a life of idleness and pleasure, but he answered he must die.

Then she struck the table with her clenched fist and let him hear what she thought of him.

"So you want to die, that's what you want. That would not surprise me, if you were alive. Look, such a wasted body and such powerless limbs and such dull eyes, and you think that there is something left of you to die. Do you think that you have to lie stiff and stark with a coffin-lid nailed down over you to be dead? Don't you believe that I stand here and see how dead you are, Gösta Berling?

"I see that you have a skull for a head, and it seems to me as if the worms were creeping out of the sockets of your eyes. Do you not feel that your mouth is full of dust? Do you not hear how your bones rattle when you move?

"You have drowned yourself in brandy, Gösta Berling, and you are dead.

"It is only death spasms that now move in you, and you will not allow them to live, if you call that life. It is just as if you begrudge the dead a dance over the graves in the star-light.

"Are you ashamed that you were degraded. since you wish to die now? It would be more honourable if you used your gifts and were of some use on God's green earth, I tell you. Why did you not come directly to me? I should have arranged everything for you. Yes, now you expect to attain to much honour by being wrapped in a winding-sheet and laid on saw-dust and called a beautiful corpse."

The beggar sat calm, almost smiling, while she thundered out her angry words. He rejoiced to think that there was no danger, no danger! The eternal forests were waiting, and she had no power to turn his soul away from them.

But the major's wife was silent and walked a couple of times up and down the room; then she took a seat before the fire, put her feet on the fender, and leaned her elbows on her knees.

"Thousand devils!" she said, and laughed softly to herself. "There is more truth in what I am saying than I myself thought. Don't you believe, Gösta Berling, that most of the people in this world are dead or half-dead? Do you think that I am alive? No! No, indeed!

"Yes, look at me! I am the mistress of Ekeby, and I am the most powerful woman in Värmland. If I beckon with one finger the governor comes, if I beckon with two the bishop comes, and if I beckon with three the whole cathedral chapter and the aldermen and mine-owners in Värmland dance to my music in Karlstad's market-place. A thousand devils! Boy, I tell you that I am only a dressed-up corpse. God knows how little life there is in me."

The beggar leaned forward on his chair and listened with strained attention. The old woman sat and rocked before the fire. She did not look at him while she talked.

"Don't you believe," she continued, "that if I were a living being, and saw you sitting there, wretched and deplorable, brooding over your suicidal thoughts; don't you believe that I should relieve you of them in a single moment? I should have tears for you and prayers, which would change you entirely, and I should save your soul; but now I am dead.

"Have you heard that I was once the beautiful Margareta Celsing? That was not yesterday, but I can still sit and weep my old eyes red for her. Why should Margareta Celsing be dead, and Margareta Samzelius live? Why should the major's wife at Ekeby live?—tell me that, Gösta Berling.

"Do you know what Margareta Celsing was like? She was slender and delicate and modest and innocent, Gösta Berling. She was one over whose grave angels weep.

"She knew nothing of evil, no one had ever given her pain, she was good to all. And she was beautiful, really beautiful.

"There was a man, his name was Altringer. God knows how he happened to be travelling up there in the wilds of Älvdal, where her parents had their ironworks. Margareta Celsing saw him; he was a handsome man, and she loved him.

"But he was poor; and they agreed to wait for one another five years, as they did in the ballad. When three years had passed another suitor came. He was ugly and bad; but her parents believed that he was rich, and they forced Margareta Celsing, by fair means and foul, by blows and hard words, to take him for her husband. And that day, you see, Margareta Celsing died.

"After that there was no Margareta Celsing, only Major Samzelius's wife, and she was neither good nor modest; she believed in much evil and never thought of the good.

"You know well enough what happened afterwards. We lived at Sjö near Lake Löven, the major and I. But he was not rich, as people had said he was. I often had hard days.

"Then Altringer came again, and now he was rich. He became master of Ekeby, which lies next to Sjö; he made himself master of six other estates by Lake Löven. He was able, he was thrifty: he was a splendid man.

"He helped us in our poverty; we drove in his carriages; he sent food to our kitchen, wine to our cellar. He filled my life with feasting and pleasure. The major went off to the wars, but what did we care for that? One day I would be a guest at Ekeby, and the next day he would come to Sjö. Oh, it was like a long dance of delight around the shores of Löven.

"But there was evil talk of Altringer and me. If Margareta Celsing had been living, it would have given her much pain, but it made no difference to me. But as yet I did not understand that it was because I was dead that I had no feeling.

"At last these evil tales reached my father and mother, as they visited the charcoal kilns up in the forests of Älvdal. My mother did not stop to think; she came here to talk to me.

"One day, when the major was away and I sat dining with Altringer and several others, she arrived. I saw her come into the room, but I could not feel that she was my mother, Gösta Berling. I greeted her as if she were a stranger, and invited her to sit down at my table and take part in the meal.

"She wished to talk with me, as if I had been her daughter, but I said to her that she was mistaken, that my parents were dead, they had both died on my wedding day.

"Then she agreed to the comedy. Though she was sixty years old, a hundred and twenty miles she had driven in three days. Now she sat without ceremony at the dinner-table and ate her food; she was a strong and capable woman.

"She said that it was very sad that I had suffered such a heavy loss just on my wedding day."

" 'The saddest thing was,' I said, 'that my parents had not died a day sooner; then the wedding would never have taken place.'

" 'Is not the gracious lady pleased with her marriage?' she then asked.

" 'Oh, yes,' said I, 'I am pleased. I shall always be pleased to obey the wishes of my dear parents!'

"She asked if it had been my parents' wish that I should heap shame upon myself and them and deceive my husband. I did my parents little honour by making myself a byword in every man's mouth.

" 'As they make their beds, so they must lie on them,' I answered her. And continuing to treat her like an entire stranger, I wished her to understand that I did not intend to allow anyone to calumniate my parents' daughter.

"We two ate; but the men who were with us sat silent and could lift neither knife nor fork.

"She stayed a day to rest, then she went. But all the time I saw her, I could not understand that she was my mother. I only knew that my mother was dead.

"When she was ready to leave, Gösta Berling, and I stood beside her on the steps, and the carriage was before the door, she said to me:—

" 'I have been here twenty-four hours and never once have you treated me as befits your mother. By lonely roads I came here, a hundred and twenty miles in three days. And out of shame for you my body is trembling, as if it had been beaten with rods. May you be disowned, as I have been disowned, repudiated as I have been repudiated! May the highway be your home, the haystack your bed, the charcoal-kiln your stove! May shame and dishonour be your reward; may others strike you, as I strike you!'

"And she gave me a heavy blow on the cheek.

"But I lifted her up, carried her down the steps, and put her in her carriage.

" 'Who are you, that you curse me?' I asked; 'who are you that you strike me? I will not tolerate that from anyone.'

"And I gave her the blow again.

"The carriage drove away, but then, at that moment, Gösta Berling, I knew that Margareta Celsing was dead.

"She was good and innocent; she knew no evil. Angels had wept at her grave. If she had lived, she would not have struck her mother."

The beggar by the door had listened; and for a moment the words had drowned the sound of the alluring murmur of the eternal forests. For this great lady had made herself his equal in sin, his sister in perdition, so as to give him courage to live. Thus he was to learn that sorrow and wrong-doing weighed down other heads besides his. He rose and went over to the major's wife.

"Will you live now, Gösta Berling?" she asked in a voice broken with tears. "Why should you die? You could have been such a good minister. The man you drowned in brandy was never the Gösta Berling whose bright innocence was one with that of the Margareta Celsing whom I suffocated out of hate. Will you live?"

Gösta fell on his knees before her.

"Forgive me," he said, "I cannot."

"I am an old woman, hardened by much sorrow," answered the major's wife, "and I sit here and give myself as a prize to a beggar, whom I have found half-frozen in a snow-drift by the roadside. It serves me right. Let him go and kill himself; then at least he won't be able to tell of my folly."

"I am no suicide, I am condemned to die. Do not make the struggle too hard for me! I may not live. My body has taken possession of my soul, therefore I must let it escape and go to God."

"And so you believe you will get there?"

"Farewell, and thank you!"

"Farewell, Gösta Berling."

The beggar rose and walked with hanging head and with a shuffling gait to the door. This woman made the way up to the great forests heavy for him.

When he came to the door, he had to look back. Then he met her glance, as she sat still and looked at him. He had never seen such a change in any face, and he stood and stared at her. She, who had just been angry and threatening, sat transfigured, and her eyes shone with a pitying, compassionate love.

There was something in him, in his own wild heart, which broke down before that glance; he leaned his forehead against the door-post, stretched his arms up over his head, and wept as if his heart would break.

The major's wife tossed her clay pipe into the fire and came over to Gösta. Her movements were as tender as a mother's.

"There, there, my boy!"

And she got him down beside her on the bench by the door, so that he wept with his head on her knees.

"Do you still wish to die?"

Then he wanted to rush away. She had to hold him back by force.

"You may do as you please. But I promise you that, if you will live, I will take charge of the daughter of the minister of Broby and will make a human being of her, so that she can thank her God that you stole her meal. Now will you?"

He raised his head and looked her right in the eyes.

"Do you mean it?"

"I do, Gösta Berling."

Then he wrung his hands in anguish. He saw before him the peering eyes, the compressed lips, the wasted little hands. This young creaure would get protection and care; the marks of degradation would be effaced from her body, and her soul would be delivered from anger. Now the way up to the eternal forests was closed to him.

"I shall not kill myself as long as she is under your care," he said. "I knew well enough that you would force me to live. I felt that you were stronger than I."

"Gösta Berling," she said solemnly, "I have fought for you as for myself. I said to God: 'If there is anything of Margareta Celsing living in me, let her come forward and show herself, so that this man may not go and kill himself.' And she granted my prayer; and you saw her, and therefore you could not go. And she whispered to me that for that poor child's sake you would give up your plan, of dying. Ah, boldly you fly, you wild birds, but our Lord knows the net which will catch you."

"He is a great and wonderful God," said Gösta Berling. "He has mocked me and cast me out, but He will not let me die. May His will be done!"

From that day Gösta Berling became a cavalier at Ekeby. Twice he tried to leave and find a way of living by his own work. The first time the major's wife gave him a cottage near Ekeby; he moved into it meaning to live as a labourer. This succeeded for a while, but he soon wearied of the loneliness and the daily labour, and again returned as a cavalier. The second time was when he became the tutor of Count Henry Dohna at Borg. During this time he fell in love with young Ebba Dohna, the Count's sister; but when she died, just as he thought he had nearly won her, he gave up every thought of being anything but a cavalier at Ekeby. It seemed to him that for an unfrocked priest all ways to make amends were closed.

PART I

CHAPTER 1 *The Landscape*

I must now describe the long lake, the rich plains and the blue mountains, since they formed the background against which Gösta Berling and the other cavaliers of Ekeby passed their joyous existence.

The lake has its source far up in the north; and it is a perfect country for a lake. The forests and the mountains never cease to collect water for it; rivulets and brooks stream into it the whole year round. Its bed is of fine white sand. It has headlands and islands to mirror and to gaze at. River sprites and sea nymphs have free space to sport there; and the lake rapidly grows large and beautiful. There, in the north, it is smiling and friendly. You need only see it on a summer morning, when it lies half awake under a veil of mist, to perceive how gay it is. First it plays for a while, creeping softly, very softly, out of its light covering, so enchantingly beautiful that one can hardly recognize it; but suddenly it casts off the whole apparel and lies there bare and uncovered and rosy, glittering in the morning light.

But the lake is not content with this life of play; it contracts into a narrow strait, makes its way through the sandhills to the south, and seeks to discover a new kingdom for itself. This it succeeds in doing. The kingdom becomes larger and more powerful; there are bottomless depths to fill, and a busy landscape to adorn. And now its waters are darker, its shores less varying, its winds sharper, its whole character more severe. It has become a stately and magnificent lake. Many are the ships and the rafts of timber which pass there; only late in the year has it time to take its winter rest; but rarely before Christmas. Often it is in a sullen mood, then white with anger it can capsize sailing-boats; but it can also lie in a dreamy calm and reflect the sky.

But the lake will go still farther out into the world, although the mountains become more rugged and the intervening space is narrower; it descends still farther, so that once again it has to creep, a narrow strait between sandy shores. Then it broadens out for the third time, but no longer with the same beauty and dignity.

The shores sink down and become monotonous, gentler winds blow; the lake takes its winter rest early. It is still beautiful, but it has lost youth's levity and manhood's strength—it is now a lake like any other. With its two arms it gropes its way towards Lake Vänern, and having found it, falls, in the feebleness of old age, over the precipitous brink; and it its last roaring feat finds rest.

The plain is as long as the lake; but it is no easy matter to find any space between the hills and mountains, all the way from the valley of the basin at the northern end of the lake, where it first ventures to expand, up to the shore of Vänern where it leisurely comes to rest. There is no doubt that the plain would rather follow the shore of the lake in spite of its length; but the mountains give it no peace. The mountains are mighty granite walls, covered with woods, with many ravines, which are difficult to cross, rich in moss and lichen,—in those old days the home of many wild animals and birds.

Half way up the long line of hills, there are numerous low-lying swamps or tarns with their dark water. Here and there is a charcoal kiln or an open patch where timber and wood have been cut, or a burnt clearing; and these all show that there is work going on in the mountains. But usually the mountains are light-hearted and rest in peace. They are content to watch the lights and shadows play over their slopes.

The plain, which is upright and prosperous and loves work, wages perpetual war with these mountains, in a friendly spirit, however.

"It is quite enough," the plain says to the mountains; "if you set up your walls around me, that is safety enough for me."

But the mountains will not listen. They send out long rows of hills and barren table-lands right down to the lake. They raise magnificent outlook towers on every promontory; and so seldom do they leave the shores of the lake, that only in a few places the plain can descend to the soft sands of the wide shore. But it does not help to complain.

"You ought to be glad that we stand here," the mountains say. "Think of that time before Christmas, when the icy fogs, day after day, rolled up from the Löven. We do you good service."

The plain complains that it has no space and an ugly view.

"You are so stupid," answer the mountains; "if you could only feel how it is blowing down here by the lake. One needs at least a granite back and a fir-tree jacket to withstand it. Besides, you can be glad to have us to look at."

Yes, looking at the mountains, that is just what the plain is doing. It knows so well all the wonderful shiftings of light and shade, which pass over them. It knows how in the light of midday they sink down towards the horizon, and are low and a dim light-blue; and in the morning or evening light they raise their vener-able peaks, clear blue as the sky at the zenith.

Sometimes the light falls on them so sharply that they look green or dark-blue, and each separate fir-tree, each path and cleft, is visible for many miles.

There are places where the mountains draw back and allow the plain to come forward and gaze at the lake. But when it sees the lake either hissing and spitting in fury like a wildcat, or covered with that cold mist which comes when the seasprite is busy with brewing or washing; then it agrees that the mountains were right, and draws back to its narrow prison again.

Men have cultivated the beautiful plain from time immemorial, and have built much there. Factories and mills were erected wherever streams with foaming waterfalls rushed down the slopes to the shore. On the bright, open places, where the plain reaches to the lake, churches and parsonages were built; but along the edges of the valley, half-way up the slope, on stony ground, where grain would not grow, there are farmhouses and officers' quarters, and here and there a manor.

It must be borne in mind, however, that in the eighteen-twen-

ties, this district was not cultivated nearly as much as it is now.
Many tracts, which were then woods and lakes and swamps,
can now be cultivated. Nor were there so many people then.
They earned their living either by carting and as day-labourers
at the many factories, or by working in other districts; agriculture
could not support them. At that time the inhabitants of the plain
went dressed in homespun, ate oatcakes, and were satisfied with
a wage of ten cents a day. Many were in great want; but life was
often made easier for them by their light-hearted and joyful dis-
positions, and by an inborn handiness and capability.

And those three, the long lake, the rich plain, and the blue
mountains, made the most beautiful scenery, and still do; just as
to this day, the people are strong and brave and intelligent.
Great progress has been made, however, in prosperity and culture.

May everything go well with those who live far away by the
long lake and the blue mountains! It is some of their reminiscences
that I am now going to relate.

CHAPTER 2 *Christmas Eve*

Sintram is the name of the wicked master of the works at Fors, with his clumsy ape-body, and his long arms, with his bald head and ugly, grinning face,—whose delight is to make mischief.

Sintram it is who takes only vagrants and bullies for workmen, and has only quarrelsome, lying maids in his service; who excites dogs to madness by sticking pins in their noses, and lives happily among evil people and fierce beasts.

It is Sintram whose greatest pleasure is to dress himself up in the foul fiend's likeness, with horns, and tail, and cloven hoof, and hairy body; and to appear suddenly out of dark corners, or from behind the stove or the wood-pile, to frighten timid children and superstitious women.

It is Sintram who delights in changing old friendship into new hate, and in poisoning the heart with lies.

Sintram is his name—and one day he came to Ekeby.

Drag the great wood-sledge into the forge, put it in the middle of the floor, and lay a cart-bottom on the frame! That will serve as a table. Hurrah for the table; the table is ready!

Bring chairs, bring everything you can sit on! Bring three-legged stools and empty boxes! Bring ragged old arm-chairs without any backs, and push up the runnerless sleigh and the old coach! Ha, ha, ha, up with the old coach; it shall be the speaker's platform!

Just look; one wheel gone, and the whole bottom out! Only the coach-box is left. The cushion is thin and worn, its moss stuffing is coming through, and the leather is red with age. High as a house is the old wreck. Prop it up, prop it up, or down it will come!

Hurrah! Hurrah! It is Christmas eve at Ekeby.

Behind the board bed's silken curtains the major and his wife
are sleeping. They are asleep; and they believe that the bachelors'
wing is also asleep. The men-servants and maids can sleep,
heavy with feasting and with the bitter Christmas ale; but not
the gentlemen in the bachelors' wing. How can any one think that
the bachelors' wing is asleep? It is Christmas and the forge is
fast asleep.

Asleep! asleep! (great heavens, asleep!) when the cavaliers are
awake. The long tongs stand upright on the floor, with tallow
candles in their claws. From the mammoth kettle of burnished
copper the blue flames of the burning brandy leap high up to the dark
roof. Beerencreutz's horn-lantern hangs on the forge-hammer. The
yellow punch shines in the bowl like a bright sun. The cavaliers
are celebrating Christmas eve in the forge.

There is mirth and romping, music and song. But the noise of
the midnight feast does not waken anyone. All the noise that
comes from the forge is drowned by the mighty roar of the
waterfall.

What of it? She would probably sit down with them and empty
a bumper. She is a doughty woman; she is not afraid of a thundering drinking-song or of taking a hand at *kille*.[1] The richest woman
in Värmland, as bold as a man, proud as a queen. Songs she loves,
and sounding fiddles, and the hunting-horn. She likes wine and
card-games; and tables surrounded by merry guests are her delight. She likes to see the larder emptied, to have dancing and
merry-making in chamber and hall, and the bachelors' wing full
of cavaliers.

Look at them, round the bowl! Twelve cavaliers, twelve men.
Neither May flies nor dandies; but men whose fame will not soon
die out in Värmland; brave men and strong.

Not dried-up parchment, nor close-fisted money-bags; poor
men, without a care, gentlemen the whole day long.

No mother's darlings, no sleepy landowners living on their
own estates. Wayfaring men, cheerful men, knights of a hundred
adventures.

[1] A Swedish card game.

It is now many years that the bachelors' wing has stood empty. Ekeby is no longer the chosen refuge of homeless gentlemen. Pensioned officers and impoverished noblemen no longer drive about Värmland in shaky one-horse vehicles. But let the dead live, let them rise up in their glad, careless, eternal youth!

All these notorious men could play on one or more instruments. All where as full of wit and humour and conceits and songs as an ant-hill is full of ants; but each one had his particular great quality, his much esteemed merit as cavalier, which distinguished him from the others.

Of all those who are sitting round the bowl, I will mention first Beerencreutz, the colonel with the great white moustaches; card-player and singer of songs; and next to him, his friend and brother in arms, the silent major, the great bear-hunter, Anders Fuchs. The third is little Ruster, the drummer, who had been for many years the colonel's servant; but had been promoted to the rank of cavalier for his skill in brewing punch and his knowledge of thorough-bass. Then there was the old ensign, Rutger von Örneclou, ladykiller, dressed in stock and wig and ruffles, and painted like a woman,—he was one of the most important of the cavaliers. The next man is Christian Bergh, the mighty captain, who was a stalwart hero, but as easy to outwit as a giant in a fairy tale. Together with these two men, one often saw plump, little Master Julius, witty, merry, and gifted, an orator, painter, songster, and story-teller. He often had his joke with the gout-crippled ensign and the dull giant.

There was also the big German Kevenhüller, inventor of the self-propelling carriage and the flying-machine. His name still echoes in the murmuring forests,—a nobleman by birth and in appearance, with great curled moustaches, a pointed beard, aquiline nose, and narrow, squinting eyes set in a net of intersecting wrinkles. There sat the great warrior, Cousin Christopher, who never went outside the walls of the bachelors' wing unless there was to be a bear-hunt or some foolhardy adventure; and beside him was Uncle Eberhard, the philosopher, who had not come to Ekeby for pleasure and amusement, but in order to complete his great work in the science of sciences, without being disturbed by the worries of earning his living.

To conclude with, I will mention the best of the band: the gentle Löwenborg, an upright man, who was too good for this world and understood little of its ways; and Liljecrona, the great musician, who had a good home, and was always longing to be there, but who still remained at Ekeby, for his soul needed wealth and variety, to be able to endure life.

These eleven men were no longer young; and several of them were growing old; but among them was one who was not more than thirty years old, and who still possessed the full, undiminished vigour of his mind and body. It was Gösta Berling, the Prince of cavaliers, who was a better speaker, singer, musician, hunter, drinking companion and card-player than all of the others together. He possessed all the virtues of the cavalier. What a man the major's wife had made of him!

Look at him now on the speaker's platform! The darkness sinks from the black roof in great festoons over him. His blond head shines through this darkness like that of a young god. He stands there, slender and beautiful, and eager for adventure.

But he is speaking very seriously.

"Gentlemen and brothers, it will soon be midnight, the feast is far advanced, it is time to drink a toast to the thirteenth at the table!"

"Little brother Gösta," cries Master Julius, "there is no thirteenth; we are only twelve."

"At Ekeby a man dies every year," continues Gösta with a more and more gloomy voice. "One of the guests in the bachelors' wing dies; one of those who are joyous, carefree, and eternally young. What of that? Gentlemen ought never to grow old. If our trembling hands can no longer lift a glass; if our dull eyes can no longer distinguish the cards, what meaning has life for us, or of what use are we to life? One of the thirteen must die, who celebrate Christmas eve in the forge at Ekeby; but every year a new member comes to complete our number. A man who is experienced in the craft of pleasure, who can play the violin and understands cards, must come to complete our company. Old butterflies should know how to die while the summer sun is shining. A toast to the thirteenth!"

"But, Gösta, we are only twelve," the cavaliers protest, and do not touch their glasses.

Gösta Berling, whom they called the poet, although he never wrote verses, continues with unaltered calmness: "Gentlemen and brothers! Have you forgotten who you are? You are the men who hold pleasure captive in Värmland. You it is who ply the fiddle-bows and keep up the dance; you who make song and music resound through the land. You know how to keep your hearts from the love of gold, and your hands from work. If you did not exist, the dance would die, summer die, the roses die, card-playing die, song die, and in this whole blessed land there would be nothing but iron and foundry proprietors. Pleasure lives while you live. For six years I have celebrated Christmas eve in the Ekeby forge, and never before has any one refused to drink to the thirteenth."

"But, Gösta," they all cry, "when we are only twelve how can we drink to the thirteenth?"

An expression of profound sorrow is depicted on Gösta's face.

"Are we only twelve?" he says. "Why must we become extinct? Shall we be only eleven next year, and ten the year after. Shall our name become a legend, our company destroyed? I call upon him, the thirteenth, for I have stood up to drink his toast. From the ocean's depths, from the bowels of the earth, from heaven, from hell I call upon him who shall complete our number."

Then there was a rattling in the chimney, the furnace door was flung open, and the thirteenth came out.

He was hairy, with tail and cloven-hoof, with horns and a pointed beard, and at the sight of him the cavaliers started up with a cry.

But in uncontrollable joy Gösta Berling cries, "The thirteenth has come—a toast to the thirteenth!"

Yes, he has come, the old enemy of mankind, come to these

foolhardy men who trouble the peace of the "Holy Night". The friend of witches who ride to their Sabbaths. It is he who signs his bargains in blood on coal-black paper, he who danced with the countess at Ivarsnäs for seven days, and could not be exorcized by seven priests,—he has come.

At the sight of him, tempestuous thoughts whirl through the heads of the old adventurers. They wonder for whom he has come tonight.

Many of them were ready to hurry away in terror, but they soon saw that the horned one had not come to carry them down to his dark kingdom; but that the clinking of their glasses and their songs had attracted him. He wished to enjoy a little human happiness during this holy Christmas-night, and to lay aside his burden at this festive season.

Oh, cavaliers, cavaliers, who of you now remembers that it is the night before Christmas; that even now angels are singing for the shepherds in the fields? Children are lying in bed, and are afraid of sleeping too soundly and not waking in time for the beautiful morning service. Soon it will be time to light the Christmas candles in the church at Bro, and far away in their forest homes the young men have prepared, in the evening, resin torches to light their girls to church. In every house the mistress has placed diplights in the windows, ready to light as the people go by to church. The sexton takes up the Christmas psalm in his sleep, and the old minister lies in bed, and tries if his voice is still strong enough to sing: "Glory be to God on high, on earth peace, good-will towards men!"

Oh, cavaliers, it had been better for you to spend this peaceful night quietly in your beds than to trouble the company with the Prince of Darkness.

But they greet him with cries of welcome, as Gösta had done. A goblet filled with burning brandy is handed him. He is given the place of honour at the table; and they rejoice in his presence, as if his ugly satyr face had the delicate features of their youth's first love.

Beerencreutz invites him to a game of cards. Master Julius sings his best songs for him, and Örneclou talks to him of lovely women, those beautiful creatures who make life sweet.

He enjoys everything, the devil, as with princely bearing he leans back on the old coach-box, and with clawed hand lifts the brimming goblet to his smiling mouth.

But, of course, Gösta Berling must make a speech in his honour.

"Your Grace," he says, "we have long awaited you here at Ekeby, for you have little access, we suppose, to any other paradise. Here one can live without toiling or spinning, as your Grace perhaps knows. Here roasted ortolans fly into one's mouth, and the bitter ale and the sweet brandy flow in brooks and rivulets. This is a good place, your Grace! We cavaliers have waited for you, I tell you, for our number has never been complete before. Mark you, we are somewhat finer than we seem; we are the mighty twelve of the poets; we are of all time. For we were twelve when we ruled the world, up there on the cloud-veiled summit of Olympus; and twelve when we lived like birds in Ygdrasil's green crown. Wherever poetry flourished, we were to be found. Did we not sit twelve valiant men about King Arthur's Round Table, and were there not twelve paladins at Charlemagne's court? One of us has been a Thor, a Jupiter; any one can see that in us now. They can perceive the divine splendour under our rags, the lion's mane under the ass's head. Times are bad with us; but if we are present, a forge becomes Olympus, and the bachelors' wing Valhalla.

"But, your Grace, our number has not been complete. Every one knows that in the poets' Band of Twelve there must always be a Loki, a Prometheus. It is he, who was missing.

"Your Grace, I wish you welcome!"

"Hear, hear, hear!" says the evil one; "such a fine speech, a fine speech indeed! And I, who have no time to answer. Business, boys, business. I must be off, otherwise I should so gladly be at your service in any rôle you like. Thanks for a pleasant evening, old gossips. We shall meet again."

The cavaliers then ask where he is going; and he tells them that the noble major's wife, mistress of Ekeby, is waiting for him to renew her pact.

The cavaliers are greatly astonished.

A strict and capable woman, the major's wife at Ekeby. She can lift a barrel of flour on her broad shoulders. She accompanies the orecars from the Bergslagen mines, on the long road to Ekeby. She sleeps like a waggoner on the stable floor, with a meal-bag under her head. In the winter she will watch by a charcoal kiln, in the summer she goes on a timber-raft along lake Löven. She is a powerful woman. She swears like a trooper, and rules over her seven estates like a king; rules her own parish and all the neighbouring parishes; yes, the whole of lovely Värmland. But for homeless gentlemen she has been like a mother, and therefore they have closed their ears when slander whispered to them that she was in league with the devil.

In amazement, they ask him what kind of a pact she has made with him.

And he answers them, the black pact, according to which he had given the major's wife her seven estates on condition that she sent him, every year, a human soul.

Oh! the horror which then conctracted the hearts of the cavaliers!

Of course they knew it, but they had not understood before.

At Ekeby, every year a man dies; one of the guests in the bachelors' wing dies, one of the joyful, the carefree, the ever young, dies. What of that?—gentlemen may not grow old! If their trembling fingers cannot lift the glass, if their dulled eyes cannot see the cards, what has life for them, and what are they to life? Butterflies should know how to die while the sun is shining.

But now, now for the first time, they grasp its real meaning.

Woe to that woman! That is why she had given them so many good meals, why she had let them drink her bitter ale and her sweet brandy, that they might reel from the drinking-halls and the card-tables at Ekeby down to the king of hell,—one a year, one for each passing year.

Woe to the woman, the witch! Strong men had come to this Ekeby, had come hither to perish. For she had destroyed them here. Their brains were like sponges, their lungs dry ashes, and their spirits darkened, when they sank back on their death-beds and were ready for their long journey without hope, without soul, and without virtue.

Woe to the woman! That is how better men than they had died; and that is how they would die.

But the cavaliers were not paralyzed by terror for long.

"You king of perdition!" they cry, "never again shall you make a blood-signed pact with that witch; she shall die! Christian Bergh, the mighty captain, has thrown over his shoulder the heaviest sledge-hammer in the forge. He will bury it right up to the handle in the hag's head. No more souls shall she sacrifice to you.

"And you, you horned thing, we shall lay you on the anvil and let the forge-hammer loose. We shall hold you quiet with tongs under the hammer's blows and teach you to go a-hunting for gentlemen's souls."

He is a coward, the devil, as every one knows of old, and all this talk of the forge-hammer does not please him at all. He calls Christian Bergh back and begins to bargain with the cavaliers.

"Take the seven estates; take them for yourselves, gentlemen, and give me the major's wife!"

"Do you think we are as base as she?" cries Master Julius. "We will have Ekeby and all the rest, but you must look after the major's wife yourself."

"What does Gösta say? what does Gösta say?" asks the gentle Löwenborg. "Gösta Berling must speak. We must hear what he thinks of this important matter."

"It is madness," says Gösta Berling. "Gentlemen, don't let him make fools of you! Are we all against the major's wife? Come what may to our souls, but I shall never consent to our becoming such ungrateful wretches as to act like rascals and traitors. I have eaten her food for too many years to desert her now."

"Yes, you can go to hell, Gösta, if you wish! We would rather rule at Ekeby."

"But are you all raving, or have you drunk away your wits? Do you believe it is true? Do you believe that thing is the devil? Don't you see that it's all a confounded lie?"

"Tut, tut, tut," says the black Gentleman; "he does not see that he will soon be ready, and yet he has been seven years at Ekeby. He does not see how far gone he is."

"Clear out, man! I myself helped to shove you into the oven there."

"As if that made any difference; as if I were not as good a devil as another. Yes, yes, Gösta Berling, you are in for it. You have improved, indeed, under her treatment."

"It was she who saved me," says Gösta. "What would I have been without her?"

"As if she did not know what she was about when she kept you here at Ekeby. You can lure others into the trap; you have great gifts. Once you tried to get away from her; you let her give you a cottage, and you became a labourer; you wished to earn your own living. Every day she passed your cottage, and she had lovely young girls with her. Once it was Marianne Sinclair; then you threw aside your spade and apron, Gösta Berling, and came back as a cavalier."

"The cottage was on the highroad; she had to pass that way, you fool."

"Yes, yes, of course; it was on the highroad. Then you came to Borg, were tutor there to Henrik Dohna, and might have been Countess Märta's son-in-law. Who was it that contrived to let young Ebba Dohna hear that you were only an unfrocked priest, so that she refused you? It was the major's wife, Gösta Berling. She wanted you back again."

"That is of no consequence!" says Gösta. "Ebba Dohna died soon afterwards. I would never have got her anyway."

Then the devil came close up to him and hissed right in his face: "Died! yes, of course she died. Killed herself for your sake; but they never told you that before."

"You are not such a bad devil," says Gösta.

"It was the major's wife who arranged it all, I tell you. She wanted to have you back in the bachelors' wing."

Gösta burst out laughing.

"You are not such a bad devil," he cried wildly. "Why should we not make a pact with you? I'm sure you can get us the seven estates if you have a mind to."

"It is well that you no longer stand in the way of your own good fortune."

The cavaliers drew a sigh of relief. They had reached the stage where they could do nothing without Gösta. If he had not agreed to the arrangement it could never have come to anything. And it was no small matter for destitute gentlemen to acquire seven estates.

"Remember, now," says Gösta, "that we take the seven estates in order to save our souls, but not to be foundry proprietors who count their money and weigh their iron. We will not become like dried-up parchment, nor will we be purse-proud money-bags; gentlemen we are, and gentlemen we will remain."

"The very words of wisdom," murmurs the black Devil.

"If you will give us the seven estates for one year we will accept them; but remember, that if we do anything during that time which is not worthy of a gentleman; if we do anything which is sensible, or useful, or effeminate, then you may take the whole twelve of us when the year is out, and give the estates to anyone you like."

The devil rubbed his hands with delight.

"But if we always behave like true gentlemen," continues Gösta, "then you may never again make any pact about Ekeby, and no pay do you get for this year, either from us or from the major's wife."

"That is hard," says the devil. "Oh, dear Gösta, I must have one soul, just one little, poor soul. Couldn't I have the major's wife? Why should you spare the major's wife?"

"I do not drive any bargains with such wares," roars Gösta; "but if you must have some one, you can take old Sintram at Fors; he is ready, I can answer for that."

"Well, well, that will do," says the devil, without blinking. "The cavaliers or Sintram, they can counterbalance each other. This will be a good year."

And so the pact was written, with blood from Gösta's little finger, on the devil's black paper and with his quill-pen.

And when it was done the cavaliers rejoiced. Now the world would belong to them for a whole year, and afterwards there would always be some way out.

They push aside the chairs, make a ring about the kettle, which stands in the middle of the black floor, and whirl in a wild dance. Innermost in the circle dances the devil, with wild bounds; and at last he falls flat beside the kettle, rolls it over, and drinks.

Then Beerencreutz throws himself down beside him, and also Gösta Berling; and after them, all the others lie down in a circle round the kettle, which is rolled from mouth to mouth. At last it is tipped over by a push, and the hot, sticky drink pours over them.

When they get up, swearing, the devil is gone; but his golden promises float like shining crowns over the cavaliers' heads.

CHAPTER 3 *Christmas Day*

On Christmas day the major's wife gives a great dinner at Ekeby.

She sits as hostess at a table laid for fifty guests. She sits there in splendour and magnificence. Here she does not appear in her short sheepskin jacket and striped woolen skirt, and her clay-pipe is laid aside. She rustles in silk, heavy gold ornaments adorn her bare arms, and pearls cool her white neck.

Where are the cavaliers? Where are they, who on the black floor of the forge, drank a toast, out of the burnished copper kettle, to the new masters of Ekeby?

In the corner by the stove the cavaliers are sitting at a separate table; to-day there is no room for them at the big table. To them the food comes late, the wine sparingly; beautiful women do not cast glances in their direction; and no one listens to Gösta's jokes.

But the cavaliers are like tamed birds, like satiated wild beasts. They had scarcely slept an hour the previous night; then they had driven to morning service, lighted by torches and the stars. They saw the Christmas candles, they heard the Christmas hymns, their faces were like those of smiling children. They forgot the night in the forge as one forgets an evil dream.

Great and powerful is the major's wife at Ekeby. Who would dare lift his hand against her; who would venture to give evidence against her? Certainly not poor gentlemen who for many years have eaten her bread and slept under her roof. She can put them where she likes; she can shut her door to them when she feels so inclined; and they have not the strength to escape from her power. God be merciful to their souls! Far from Ekeby they cannot live.

At the big table there was rejoicing: Marianne Sinclair's beautiful eyes were shining, and gay Countess Dohna's low laugh was clearly heard.

But the cavaliers are gloomy. Was it not just as easy to have put them at the same table with the other guests? What a degrading position there in the corner by the stove. As if cavaliers were not fit to associate with fine people!

The major's wife is proud to sit between Count Borg and the dean of Bro. The cavaliers hang their heads like shamefaced children, and gradually the thoughts of the previous night awaken in them.

Like shy guests the gay sallies, the merry mendacious stories make their way to the table in the corner by the stove. Then the rage they had felt in the night, and the promises that had been made, began to penetrate the minds of the cavaliers. Master Julius makes the mighty captain, Christian Berg, believe that the roasted grouse, which are being served at the big table, will be insufficient for all the guests; but it amuses no one.

"They won't go round," he says. "I know how many there are. But they'll manage in spite of that, Captain Christian; they have some roasted crows for us here at the little table."

But Colonel Beerencreutz's lips are curved by only a very faint smile, under the fierce moustaches, and Gösta has looked the whole day as if he was contemplating somebody's death.

"Any food is good enough for cavaliers," he says.

At last the dish heaped up with magnificent grouse reaches the little table.

But Captain Christian is angry. Has he not had a life-long hatred of crows,—those odious, cawing, winged things?

He hated them so bitterly, that last autumn he had put on a woman's trailing dress, and had fastened a cloth on his head and made himself a general laughing-stock, only so as to get within range when they ate the grain in the fields.

He sought them out when they danced in the mating season in the bare fields in the spring and killed them. He looked for their nests in the summer, and threw out the screaming, featherless young ones, or smashed the half-hatched eggs.

Now he seizes the dish of grouse.

"Do you think I don't know them?" he cries to the servant.

"Do I need to hear them caw to recognize them? Shame on you, to offer Christian Berg crows! Shame on you!"

Thereupon he takes the grouse, one by one, and throws them against the wall.

"Confound it!" he shouts, so that the whole room rings,—"to offer Christian Berg crows! Shame!"

And just as he used to hurl the helpless young crows against the cliffs, so now he sends grouse after grouse whizzing against the wall.

Sauce and grease spatter about him, the crushed birds rebound from the wall onto the floor.

And the bachelor's wing rejoices.

Then the angry voice of the major's wife penetrates to the cavaliers' ears.

"Turn him out!" she calls to the servants.

But they do not dare to touch him. He is still Christian Bergh, the mighty captain.

"Turn him out!"

He hears the command, and, terrible in his rage, he now turns upon the major's wife as a bear turns from a fallen enemy to meet a new attack. He marches up to the horse-shoe table. His heavy tread resounds through the hall. He stands opposite her, with the table between them.

"Turn him out!" cries the major's wife again.

But he is raging; none dare face his frowning brow and great clenched fist. He is as big and as strong as a giant. The guests and servants tremble, and dare not approach him. Who would dare to touch him now, when rage has deprived him of his reason?

He stands opposite the major's wife and threatens her.

"I took the crow and threw it against the wall. And I did right."

"Out with you, Captain!"

"Shame, woman! To offer Christian Bergh crows! If I were to do what is right, I would take you and your seven hell's—"

"Thousand devils, Christian Bergh! don't swear! No one swears here, but I."

"Do you think I am afraid of you, hag? Don't you think I know how you got your seven estates?"

"Silence, Captain!"

"When Altringer died he gave them to your husband because you had been his mistress."

"Will you be silent?"

"Because you had been such a faithful wife, Margareta Samzelius. And the major took the seven estates and let you manage them and pretended not to know. And the devil arranged it all; but now comes the end for you."

The major's wife sits down; she is pale and trembling. She assents in a strange, low voice.

"Yes, now it is the end for me, and it is your doing, Christian Bergh."

At her voice Captain Christian trembles, his face works, and his eyes are filled with tears of anguish.

"I am drunk," he cries. "I don't know what I am saying; I haven't said anything. Dog and slave, dog and slave, and nothing more have I been for her for forty years. She is Margareta Celsing, whom I have served my whole life. I say nothing against her. What should I have to say against the beautiful Margareta Celsing! I am the dog which guards her door, the slave who bears her burdens. She may strike me, she may kick me! You see how I hold my tongue and bear it. I have loved her for forty years. How could I say anything against her?"

And a wonderful sight it is to see how he kneels and begs for forgiveness. And as she is sitting on the other side of the table, he goes on his knees round the table till he comes to her; then he bends down and kisses the hem of her dress, and the floor is wet with his tears.

But not far from the major's wife sits a small, strong man. He has shaggy hair, small, squinting eyes, and a protruding under-jaw. He looks like a bear. He is a man of few words, who likes to go his own quiet way and let the world take care of itself. He is Major Samzelius.

He rises when he hears Captain Christian's accusing words;

and the major's wife rises, and all the fifty guests with her. The women are weeping in terror of what is coming; the men stand dejected; and at the feet of the major's wife lies Captain Christian, kissing the hem of her dress, wetting the floor with his tears.

The major slowly clenches his broad, hairy fists, and lifts his arm.

But the woman speaks first. Her voice sounds hollow and unfamiliar.

"You stole me," she cried. "You came like a thief and took me. They forced me, in my home, by blows, by hunger, and hard words to be your wife. I have treated you as you deserved."

The major's broad fist is clenched. His wife gives way a couple of steps. Then she speaks again.

"Living eels twist under the knife; an unwilling wife takes a lover. Will you strike me now for what happened twenty years ago? Do you not remember how he lived at Ekeby, and we at Sjö? Do you not remember how he helped us in our poverty? We drove in his carriages, we drank his wine. Did we hide anything from you? Were not his servants your servants? Did not his gold weigh heavy in your pocket? Did you not accept the seven estates? You held your tongue and took them; that is when you should have struck, Berndt Samzelius,—you should have struck then."

The man turns from her and looks on all those present. He reads in their faces that they think she is right, that they all believe he took the estates in return for his silence.

"I never knew it!" he says, and stamps on the floor.

"It is well that you know it now!" she cries, in a shrill, ringing voice. "Was I not afraid lest you should die without knowing it? It is well that you know it now, so that I can speak out to you who have been my master and jailer. You now know that, in spite of all, I was his, although you stole me from him. I tell you all now, you who have slandered me!"

It is the old love which exults in her voice and shines from her eyes. Her husband stands before her with lifted hand. She reads horror and scorn on the fifty faces about her. She feels that it is the last hour of her power. But she cannot help rejoicing that she may speak openly of the tenderest memory of her life.

"He was a man, a fine man. Who were you, to come between us? I have never seen his equal. He gave me happiness, he gave me riches. Blessed be his memory!"

Then the major lets his lifted arm fall without striking her; now he knows how he shall punish her.

"Away!" he cries; "out of my house!"

She stands motionless.

But the cavaliers stand with pale faces and stare at one another. Everything was going as the devil had prophesied. They now saw the consequences of the pact not being renewed. If that is true, then it is also true that for more than twenty years she had sent cavaliers to perdition, and that this was also to be their destiny. Oh, the witch!

"Out with you!" continues the major. "Beg your bread on the highway! You shall have no pleasure of his money, you shall not live on his lands. There is no longer a mistress of Ekeby. The day you set your foot in my house I will kill you."

"Do you drive me from my home?"

"You have no home. Ekeby is mine."

A feeling of despair comes over the major's wife. She retreats to the door, and he keeps close to her.

"You who have been the misfortune of my whole life," she laments, "will you have power to do also this to me now?"

"Out, out!"

She leans against the door-post, clasps her hands, and holds them before her face. She thinks of her mother and murmurs to herself:—

" 'May you be disowned, as I have been disowned; may the highway be your home, the hay-stack your bed!' It is all coming true."

The good old dean of Bro and the judge from Munkerud came forward now to Major Samzelius and tried to calm him. They said to him that it would be best to let all those old stories rest, to let everything be as it was, to forget and forgive.

He shakes the mild old hands from his shoulder. He is terrible to approach, just as Christian Bergh had been.

"It is no old story," he cries. "I never knew anything till to-day. I have never before been able to punish the adulteress."

At that word the major's wife lifts her head and regains her old courage.

"You shall go out before I do. Do you think that I shall give in to you?" she says. And she comes forward from the door.

The major does not answer, but he watches every movement she makes; ready to strike, if he finds no better way to revenge himself.

"Help me, good gentlemen," she cries, "to get this man bound and carried out, until he regains the use of his senses. Remember who I am and who he is! Think of it, before I have to give in to him! I see to all the work at Ekeby, while he sits the whole day long and feeds his bears. Help me, good friends and neighbours! There will be boundless misey if I am no longer here. The peasant gets his living by cutting my wood and carting my iron. The charcoal burner lives by getting me charcoal, the lumber man by bringing down my timber. It is I who give the work which brings prosperity. Smiths, mechanics, and carpenters live by serving me. Do you think that man can keep my wotk going? I tell you that if you drive me away, you will let famine in."

Many hands are lifted to help the major's wife; again mild, persuading hands are laid on the major's shoulders.

"No," he says, "away with you. Who will defend an adulteress? I tell you that if she does not go of her own accord, I shall take her in my arms and carry her down to my bears."

At these words the raised hands are lowered.

Then, as a last resource, she turns to the cavaliers.

"Will also you allow me to be driven from my home? Have I let you freeze in the snow in winter? Have I denied you bitter ale and sweet brandy? Did I demand payment or work from you because I gave you food and clothes? Have you not played at my feet, safe as children at their mother's side? Has there not been dancing in my halls? Have not merriment and laughter been your daily bread? Do not let this man, who has been my life's misfortune, drive me from my home, gentlemen! Do not let me become a beggar on the highway!"

At these words Gösta Berling had stolen away to a beautiful dark-haired girl who sat at the big table.

"You were much at Borg five years ago, Anna," he says. "Do you know if it was the major's wife who told Ebba Dohna that I was an unfrocked priest?"

"Help her, Gösta!" is the girl's only answer.

"You must understand that I will first know if she has made me a murderer."

"Oh, Gösta, what a terrible thought! Help her, Gösta!"

"You won't answer, I see. Then Sintram told the truth." And Gösta goes back to the other cavaliers. He does not lift a finger to help the major's wife.

Oh, if she had only not put the cavaliers at a separate table there in the corner by the stove! Now the thoughts that came to them during the night, awake in their minds; and a rage no less fierce than the major's burns in their faces.

They remain silent; pitiless, obdurate and unmoved by her entreaties.

Did not everything they saw confirm the events of the night?

"One can see that she did not get her pact renewed," murmurs one.

"Go to hell, hag!" screams another. "By rights we ought to hunt you from the door."

"Fools," cries gentle old Uncle Eberhard to the cavaliers. "Don't you understand it was Sintram?"

"Of course we understand; of course we know it," answers Julius; "but what of that? May it not be true, all the same? Does not Sintram go on the devil's errands? Don't they understand one another?"

"Go yourself, Eberhard; go and help her!" they mock. "You don't believe in hell. You can go!"

And Gösta Berling stands, without a word, motionless.

No, from the threatening, murmuring, struggling bachelors' wing she will get no help.

Then once again she retreats to the door and raises her clasped hands to her eyes.

" 'May you be disowned, as I have been disowned,' " she cries to herself in her bitter sorrow. " 'May the highway be your home, the hay-stack your bed!' "

Then she lays one hand on the door latch, but the other she lifts high above her head.

Know! all of you who now let me fall, know! that your hour is soon coming! You shall be scattered, and your place shall remain empty. How shall you stand when I am not there to support you? You, Melchior Sinclair, who have a heavy hand and let your wife feel it, beware! You, vicar of Broby, your punishment is coming! Madame Uggla, look to your house; poverty is coming! You young, beautiful women—Elizabeth Dohna, Marianne Sinclair, Anna Stjärnhök—do not think that I am the only one who must flee from her home. Beware cavaliers! a storm is coming over the land. You will be swept away from the earth; your day is over, it is indeed over! I do not lament for myself, it is for you that I grieve; for the storm shall break over your heads, and who shall be able to stand, now that I have fallen? And my heart bleeds for my poor people. Who will give them work when I am gone?"

She opens the door; but then Captain Christian lifts his head and says:—

"How long must I lie here at your feet, Margareta Celsing? Will you not forgive me, so that I may stand up and fight for you?"

Then the major's wife has a hard struggle with herself, for she realizes that if she forgives him he will rise up and attack her husband; and this man, who has loved her faithfully for forty years, will become a murderer.

"Must I forgive, too? she says. "Are you not the cause of all my misfortune, Christian Bergh? Go to the cavaliers and rejoice over your work."

Thus she went. She went calmly; leaving terror and dismay behind her. She fell, but she was not without greatness in her fall. She did not demean herself by grieving weakly; but in her old age she still exulted over the love of her youth. She did not demean herself by lamenting and pitiable weeping, when she left everything. She did not shrink from wandering about the land with beggar's wallet and crutch-stick. She pitied only the poor peasants and the happy, carefree people on the shores of lake Löven; she grieved for the penniless cavaliers,—and for all those whom she had protected and cared for.

She was abandoned by all; and yet she had sufficient strength to turn away her last friend, so that he should not be a murderer.

She was a woman of great strength, and loved activity. We shall not soon see her like again.

The next day Major Samzelius moved from Ekeby to his own farm of Sjö, which lies next to the large estate.

In Altringer's will, the estates had been bequeathed to the major; but it was clearly stated that none of them was to be sold or given away, but that after the major's death, his wife and her heirs should inherit all the estates. Since he was thus prevented from dissipating this hated inheritance, he put the cavaliers in charge of the properties, thinking that by this means he would succeed in doing the greatest possible damage to Ekeby and the other six estates.

As no one in the whole countryside now doubted that the evil-doer Sintram went on the devil's errands, and as everything he had promised had been so brilliantly fulfilled, the cavaliers were quite sure that the pact would be carried out in every detail; and they were firmly decided not to do anything sensible, or useful, or effeminate, during the year. So fully convinced were they that the major's wife was an abominable witch who sought their ruin.

The old philosopher, Eberhard, ridiculed their belief. But who paid any attention to a man so obstinate in his unbelief, that if he had lain in the midst of the fires of hell and had seen all the devils standing and grinning at him, he would still have insisted that they did not exist, because they could not exist?—for Uncle Eberhard was a great philosopher.

Gösta Berling told no one what he thought. It is certain that he did not feel that he owed the major's wife much gratitude for making him a cavalier at Ekeby; it seemed to him better to be dead than to have the guilt of Ebba Dohna's suicide on his conscience.

He did nothing either to be revenged on the major's wife, or to help her. He could not. But the cavaliers had attained great power and magnificence. Christmas was at hand, with its feasts and pleasures. The hearts of the cavaliers were filled with rejoicing; and whatever sorrow Gösta Berling may have felt in his heart, was not revealed either in his face or by his speech.

CHAPTER 4 *Gösta Berling as Poet*

It was Christmas, and there was to be a ball at Borg.

At that time, and it is soon sixty years ago, a young Count Dohna lived at Borg; he was newly married; and the countess was young and beautiful. It was sure to be gay at the old castle.

An invitation had come to Ekeby; but it so happened that of all those who were spending Christmas there that year, it was only Gösta Berling, whom they called "the poet", who wished to go.

Borg and Ekeby are both situated by lake Löven, but on opposite shores. Borg is in Svartsjö parish, Ekeby in Bro. When the lake is impassable, it is a ten or twelve miles' journey from Ekeby to Borg.

The pauper, Gösta Berling, was fitted out for the festival by the old men, as if he had been a king's son, and had the honour of a kingdom to keep up.

His coat with the glittering buttons was new, his ruffles were stiff, and his buckled shoes shone. He wore a cloak of the finest beaver, and a sable cap on his yellow, curling hair. They spread a bear-skin with silver claws over his sledge, and gave him black Don Juan, the pride of the stable, to drive.

He whistled to his white Tancred, and seized the braided reins. He drove exulting in being surrounded by the lustre and splendour of riches. And yet he was resplendent in his physical beauty and in the playful brilliance of his genius.

He left early in the forenoon. It was Sunday, and he heard the organ in the church at Bro as he drove by. He followed the lonely forest road which led to Berga, where Captain Uggla then lived. He meant to stop there for dinner.

Berga was not a rich man's home. Hunger knew the way to that turf-roofed house; but he was met with jests, charmed with song and games as the other guests were; and he went away as unwillingly as they.

The old Mamselle Ulrika Dillner, who looked after everything at Berga, stood on the steps and wished Gösta Berling welcome. She courtesied to him, and the false curls, which hung down over her brown face with its thousand wrinkles, danced with joy. She led him into the dining-room, and began to tell him about the family, and their changing fortunes.

Distress stood at the door, she said; they were hard times for Berga. They would not have had even any horse-radish with their corned beef for dinner, if Ferdinand and the girls had not harnessed Disa to a sledge and driven down to Munkerud to borrow some.

The captain was off in the woods again, and would, of course, come home with a tough old hare, to cook which more butter had to be used than it was worth. That's what he called getting food for the house. Still, it would do, if only he did not come with a miserable fox, the worst beast our Lord ever created; no use, dead or alive.

And the captain's wife, yes, she was not up yet. She lay abed and read novels, just as she had always done. She, God's angel, was not made for work.

No, that could be done by some one who was old and gray like Ulrika Dillner, working night and day to keep the whole miserable place together. And it wasn't always so easy; for it was the truth, that for one whole winter, they had not had any other meat, in that house, than bear-hams. Big wages she did not expect; so far she had never had any; but they would not turn her out on the road, when she couldn't work any longer for her food. They treated a house-maid like a human being, in that house; and one of these days they would give old Ulrika a good burial, if they had anything to buy the coffin with.

"For who knows how it will be?" she bursts out, and wipes her eyes, which are always so quick to shed tears. "We have debts to the wicked Sintram, and he can take everything from us. Of course Ferdinand is engaged to the rich Anna Stjärnhök; but she is tired,—she is tired of him. And what will become of us, of our three cows, and our nine horses, of our gay young ladies who want to go from one ball to another, of our parched fields where nothing grows, and of our dear Ferdinand, who will never be a real man? What will become of the whole blessed house, where everything thrives except work?"

But dinner-time came, and the family assembled. The good Ferdinand, the gentle son of the house, and the lively daughters came home with the borrowed horse-radish. The captain came, reinvigorated by a bath in an ice-hole and a tramp through the woods. He threw up the window to get more air, and shook Gösta's hand with a strong grip. And his wife came, dressed in silk, with wide laces hanging over the white hands, which Gösta was allowed to kiss.

They all greeted Gösta with joy; they were all very jovial; gayly they asked him:—

"How are you all at Ekeby; how is it in that promised land?"

"Milk and honey flow there," he answered. "We empty the mountains of iron and fill our cellar with wine. The fields bear gold, with which we gild life's misery, and we cut down our woods to make bowling-alleys and build summer houses."

The captain's wife sighed and smiled at his answer, and her lips murmured the word,—

"Poet!"

"Many sins have I on my conscience," answered Gösta, "but I have never written a line of poetry."

"You are nevertheless a poet, Gösta; that name you must put up with. You have lived through more poems than all our poets have written."

Then she spoke, tenderly as a mother, of his wasted life. "I shall live to see you become a man," she said. And he felt it sweet to be urged on by this gentle woman, who was such a faithful friend, and whose romantic heart burned with the love of great deeds.

But just as they had finished their cheerful meal and had enjoyed the corned beef and horse-radish and cabbage and apple fritters and Christmas ale, and Gösta had made them laugh and cry by telling them of the major and his wife and the vicar of Broby, they heard sleigh-bells outside, and immediately afterward the malevolent Sintram walked in.

He beamed with satisfaction, from the top of his bald head down to his long, flat feet. He swung his long arms, and his face was twisted. It was easy to see that he brought bad news.

"Have you heard," he asked,—"have you heard that the banns have been called to-day for Anna Stjärnhök and the rich Dahlberg in the Svartsjö church? She must have forgotten that she was engaged to Ferdinand."

They had not heard a word of it. They were amazed and grieved.

Already they could see their home pillaged to pay the debt to this wicked man; the beloved horses sold, as well as the worn furniture, which had come from the home of the captain's wife. They saw an end to the gay life with feasts and going from one ball to another. Bear-hams would again adorn the board, and the young people would be forced to go out into the world and work for strangers.

The captain's wife caressed her son, and let him feel the comfort of a never-failing love.

But—there sat the invincible Gösta Berling in their midst, and turned over a thousand plans in his head.

"Listen," he cried, "it is not yet time to give way to grief. It is the vicar's wife at Svartsjö who has arranged all this. She has got a hold on Anna, since she has been living with her at the vicarage. It is she who has persuaded her to forsake Ferdinand and take old Dahlberg; but they're not married yet, and never will be either. I am on my way to Borg, and shall meet Anna there. I shall talk to her; I shall get her away from the vicar, from her fiancé,—I shall bring her with me here to-night. And afterwards old Dahlberg will never make any headway with her."

And so it was arranged. Gösta started for Borg alone, without taking any of the gay young ladies, but with hearty good wishes for his return. And Sintram, who rejoiced that old Dahlberg should be cheated, decided to stop at Berga to see Gösta come back with the faithless girl. In a burst of good-will he even wrapt round him his green plaid, a present from Mamselle Ulrika.

The captain's wife came out on the steps with three little books, bound in red leather, in her hand.

"Take them," she said to Gösta, who already sat in the sledge; "take them, if you fail! It is 'Corinne', Madame de Staël's 'Corinne'. I do not want them to go by auction."

"I shall not fail."

"Ah, Gösta, Gösta," she said, and passed her hand over his bared head, "strongest and weakest of men! How long will you remember that a few poor people's happiness lies in your hand?"

Once more Gösta flew along the road, drawn by the black Don Juan, followed by the white Tancred, and the joy of adventure filled his soul. He felt like a young conqueror, the spirit was in him.

His way took him past the vicarage at Svartsjö. He turned in there and asked if he might drive Anna Stjärnhök to the ball. And he was permitted to do so.

The girl who sat in his sledge was beautiful and self-willed. Who would not want to drive with black Don Juan?

The young people were silent at first, but then she began the conversation, audaciousness personified.

"Have you heard what the minister read out in church to-day?"

"Did he say that you were the prettiest girl between lake Löven and the Klar River?"

"How stupid you are! but every one knows that. He called the banns for me and old Dahlberg."

"Never would I have let you sit in my sledge nor would I have sat here myself, if I had known that. Never would I have wished to drive you at all."

And the proud heiress answered:—

"I could have got there well enough without you, Gösta Berling."

"It is a pity for you, Anna," said Gösta, thoughtfully, "that your father and mother are not alive. You are your own mistress, and no one can hold you to account."

"It is a much greater pity that you did not say that before, so that I might have driven with some one else."

"The vicar's wife thinks as I do, that you need some one to take your father's place; otherwise she never would have harnessed you together with such an old nag."

"It is not she who has decided it."

"Ah, Heaven preserve us!—have you yourself chosen such a fine man?"

"He does not take me for my money."

"No, the old ones, they only run after blue eyes and red cheeks; and awfully nice they are, when they do that."

"Oh, Gösta, are you not ashamed?"

"But remember that you are not to play with young men any longer. No more dancing and games. Your place is in the corner of the sofa—or perhaps you mean to play cribbage with old Dahlberg?"

They were silent, till they drove up the steep hill to Borg.

"Thanks for the drive! It will be long before I drive again with you, Gösta Berling."

"Thanks for the promise! I know many who will be sorry to-day they ever drove you to a party."

It was little to the haughty beauty's liking when she entered the ball-room and looked at the guests assembled there.

First of all she saw little, bald Dahlberg beside tall, slender, golden-haired Gösta Berling. She wished she could have driven them both out of the room.

Her fiancé came to ask her to dance, but she received him with crushing astonishment.

"Are you going to dance? You never do!"

And the girls came to congratulate her.

"Don't give yourselves the trouble, girls. You don't suppose that any one could be in love with old Dahlberg. But he is rich, and I am rich; that is why we go well together."

The old ladies went up to her, pressed her white hand, and spoke of life's greatest happiness.

"Congratulate the vicar's wife," she said. "She is happier about it than I am."

But there stood Gösta Berling, the gay cavalier, who was greeted with joy for his cheerful smile and his pleasant words, which sprinkled gold-dust over life's gray web. Never before had she seen him as he was that night. He was no outcast, no homeless jester; no, a king among men, a born king.

He and the other young men conspired against her. She should be made to feel how badly she had behaved, when she gave herself, with her lovely face and her great fortune, to an old man. And they let her sit out ten dances.

She was boiling with rage.

At the eleventh dance came a man, the most insignificant of all, a poor thing, whom nobody would dance with, and invited her to dance.

"There is no more bread, bring on the crusts," she said.

They played a game of forfeits. The fair-haired girls put their heads together and condemned her to kiss the one she loved best. And with smiling lips they waited to see the proud beauty kiss old Dahlberg.

But she rose, stately in her anger, and said:—

"May I not just as well strike the one I like the least"!

The moment after Gösta's cheek burned under her firm hand. He flushed a flaming red, but he conquered himself; seized her hand, held it fast a second, and whispered:—

"Meet me in half an hour in the red drawing-room on the lower floor!"

His blue eyes flashed on her, radiating a magical enchantment, which appeared to encircle her. She felt that she must obey.

She met him there with proud and angry words.

"What concern of yours is it whom I marry?"

He was not ready to speak gently to her, nor did it seem to him fitting to speak of Ferdinand yet.

"I thought it was not too severe a punishment for you to sit out ten dances. But you want to be allowed to break vows and promises with impunity. If a better man than I had sentenced you, he could have imposed harder punishment."

"What have I done to you and all the others, that I may not be left in peace? It is because of my money that you persecute me. I shall throw it into the Löven, and any one who wants it can fish it up."

She put her hands before her eyes and wept in anger.

That moved the poet's heart. He was ashamed of his harshness. He spoke in caressing tones.

"Ah, child, child, forgive me! Forgive poor Gösta Berling! Nobody cares what such a poor wretch says or does, you know that. Nobody weeps for his anger, one might just as well weep over a mosquito's bite. It was madness in me to hope that I could prevent our loveliest and richest girl marrying that old man. And now I have only distressed you."

He sat down on the sofa beside her. Gently he put his arm about her waist, with caressing tenderness, to support and raise her.

She did not move away. She pressed closer to him, threw her arms round his neck, and wept with her beautiful head on his shoulder.

O poet. strongest and weakest of men, it was not about your neck those white arms should rest.

"If I had known that," she whispered, "never would I have taken the old man. I have watched you this evening; there is no one like you."

From between pale lips Gösta forced out,—

"Ferdinand."

She silenced him with a kiss.

"He is nothing; no one but you is anything. To you I will be faithful."

"I am Gösta Berling," he said gloomily; "you cannot marry me."

"You are the man I love, the noblest of men. You do not have to do anything or be anything. You are born a king."

Then the poet's blood seethed. She was beautiful and tender in her love. He took her in his arms.

"If you will be mine, you cannot remain at the vicarage. Let me drive you to Ekeby to-night; there I shall know how to defend you till we can be married."

That was a wild drive through the night. Absorbed in their love, they let Don Juan take his own pace. The noise of the runners was like the lamentations of those whom they had deceived. What did they care about that? She hung on his neck, and he leaned forward and whispered in her ear.

"Can any happiness be compared in sweetness to stolen pleasures?"

What did the banns matter? They had love. And the anger of men! Gösta Berling believed in fate; fate had mastered them: no one can resist fate.

If the stars had been the candles which had been lighted for her wedding, if Don Juan's sleigh-bells had been the church bells, calling the people to witness her marriage to old Dahlberg, still she must have fled with Gösta Berling. So powerful is fate.

They had passed the vicarage and Munkerud. They had three miles to Berga and three miles more to Ekeby. The road skirted the edge of the wood; on their right lay dark hills, on their left a long, white valley.

Then they saw Tancred rushing towards them. He ran so fast that his whole body appeared to be very close to the ground. Howling with fright, he sprang into the sledge and crept under Anna's feet.

Don Juan shied and bolted.

"Wolves!" said Gösta Berling.

They saw a long, gray line running by the fence. There were at least a dozen of them.

Anna was not afraid. The day had been richly blessed with adventure, and the night promised to be equally so. It was life,— to speed over the sparkling snow, defying wild beasts and men.

Gösta uttered an oath, leaned forward, and struck Don Juan a heavy blow with the whip.

"Are you afraid?" he asked. "They mean to cut us off there, where the road turns."

Don Juan ran, racing with the wild beasts of the forest, and Tancred howled in rage and terror. They reached the turn of the road at the same time as the wolves, and Gösta drove back the foremost with the whip.

"Ah, Don Juan, my boy, how easily you could get away from twelve wolves, if you did not have us to carry."

They tied the green plaid behind them. The wolves were afraid of it, and fell back for a while. But when they had overcome their fright, one of them ran, panting, with hanging tongue and open mouth up to the sledge. Then Gösta took Madame de Staël's "Corinne" and threw it into his mouth.

Once more they had gained a breathing-space, while the brutes tore their booty to pieces; and then again they felt the jerks as the wolves bit the green plaid, and they heard their panting breath. They knew that they would not pass any human dwelling before Berga; but to Gösta it appeared to be worse than death to have to meet those whom he had deceived. But he knew that the horse would tire, and what would become of them then?

They saw the house at Berga at the edge of the forest. Candles burned in the windows. Gösta knew only too well for whose sake they were lighted.

But now the wolves drew back, fearing the presence of men, and Gösta drove past Berga. He came no further than to the place where the road once again buried itself in the wood; there he saw a dark group in front of him,—the wolves were waiting for him.

"Let us turn back to the vicarage and say that we just took a little drive in the starlight. We can't go on."

They turned, but in the next moment the sledge was surrounded by wolves. Gray forms brushed by them, their white teeth glittered in their gaping mounths, and their glowing eyes shone. They howled with hunger and thirst for blood. The glittering teeth were ready to seize the soft human flesh. The wolves leaped up on Don Juan, and hung on the saddle-cloth. Anna sat and wondered if the wolves would eat them up entirely, or if there would be something left, so that next morning people would find their mangled limbs on the trampled, bloody snow.

"It's a question of our lives," she said, and leaned down and seized Tancred by the nape of the neck.

"Don't,—that won't help! It is not for the dog that the wolves are out to-night."

Thereupon Gösta drove into the yard at Berga, but the wolves hunted him up to the very steps. He had to beat them off with the whip.

"Anna," he said, as they drew up, "God would not have it. Keep a good countenance; if you are the woman I take you for, keep a good countenance!"

In the house, they had heard the sleigh-bells, and they now came out.

"He has her!" they cried, "he has her! Long live Gösta Berling!" and the new-comers were embraced by all in turn.

Few questions were asked. The night was far advanced, the travellers were agitated by their terrible drive and needed rest. It was enough that Anna had come.

All was well. Only "Corinne" and the green plaid, Mamselle Ulrika's highly prized gift, were destroyed.

The whole house slept. But Gösta rose, dressed himself, and stole out. Unnoticed he led Don Juan out of the stable, harnessed him to the sledge, and meant to set out. But Anna Stjärnhök came out from the house.

"I heard you go out," she said. "So I got up, too. I am ready to go with you."

He went up to her and took her hand.

"Don't you understand it yet? It cannot be. God does not wish it. Listen now and try to understand. I was here to dinner and saw their grief over your faithlessness. I went to Borg to bring you back to Ferdinand. But I have always been a good-for-nothing, and will never be anything else. I betrayed him, and kept you for myself. There is an old woman here who believes that I shall become a man. I betrayed her. And another poor old thing will freeze and starve here for the sake of dying among friends, but I was ready to let the wicked Sintram take her home. You were beautiful, and sin is sweet. It is so easy to tempt Gösta Berling. Oh, what a miserable wretch I am! I know how they love their home, all those in there, but I was ready just now to leave it to be pillaged. I forgot everything for your sake, you were so sweet in your love. But now, Anna, now, since I have seen their joy, I will not keep you; no, I will not. You could have made a man of me, but I may not keep you. Oh, my beloved! He who is above mocks at our desires. We must bow under His chastening hand. Tell me that from this day you will take up your burden! All of them rely upon you. Say that you will stay with them and be their support and their help! If you love me, if you will lighten my deep sorrow, promise me this! My beloved, is your heart so great that you can conquer yourself, and smile in doing it?"

She accepted the renunciation in a sort of ecstasy.

"I shall do as you wish,—sacrifice myself and smile."

"And not hate my poor friends?"

She smiled sadly.

"As long as I love you, I shall love them."

"Now for the first time I know what you are. It is hard to leave you."

"Farewell, Gösta! Go, and God be with you! My love shall not tempt you to sin."

She turned to go in. He followed her.

"Will you soon forget me?"

"Go, Gösta! We are only human."

He threw himself down in the sledge; but then she came back again.

"Do you not think of the wolves?"

"Just of them I am thinking, but they have done their work. From me they have nothing more to get this night."

Once more he stretched his arms towards her, but Don Juan became impatient and set off. He did not take the reins. He sat backwards and looked after her. Then he leaned against the seat and wept despairingly.

"I have possessed happiness and have driven her from me; I myself drove her from me. Why did I not keep her?"

Ah, Gösta Berling, strongest and weakest of men!

CHAPTER 5 *La Cachucha*

War-horse! war-horse! Old friend, who now stand tethered in the pasture, do you remember your youth?

Do you remember the day of the battle? You sprang forward, as if you had been borne on wings, your mane fluttered about you like waving flames, on your black haunches shone drops of blood and foam. In your harness of gold you bounded forward; the ground thundered under you. You trembled with joy. Ah, how beautiful you were!

It is the gray hour of twilight in the cavaliers' wing. In the big room the cavaliers' red-painted chests stand against the walls, and their holiday clothes hang on hooks in the corner. The fire-light plays on the whitewashed walls and on the yellow-striped curtains which conceal the beds. The cavaliers' wing is not a princely dwelling,—no seraglio with cushioned divans and soft pillows.

But Lilliecrona's violin is heard there. He is playing the cachucha in the dusk of the evening. And he plays it over again.

Cut the strings, break his bow! Why does he play that cursed dance? Why does he play it, when Örneclou, the ensign, is laid up with the gout; the attack is so severe that he cannot move in his bed? No; snatch the violin away from him and throw it against the wall if he will not stop.

La cachucha, is it for us, master? Shall it be danced over the shaking floor of the cavaliers' wing, between the narrow walls, black with smoke and greasy with dirt, under that low ceiling? Woe to you, to play in this way!

La cachucha, is it for us,—for us cavaliers'? Outside the snow-storm howls. Do you intend to teach the snow-flakes to dance in time? Are you playing for the light-footed children of the storm?

Women's bodies that tremble with the throbbing of hot blood, small sooty hands, which have thrown aside the pot to seize the castanets, bare feet under tucked-up skirts, courts paved with marble slabs, crouching gypsies with bagpipe and tambourine, Moorish arcades, moonlight, and black eyes,—have you these, master? If not, let the violin rest.

The cavaliers are drying their wet clothes by the fire. Shall they dance in high boots with iron-shod heels and inch-thick soles? Through snow a yard deep they have waded the whole day to reach the bear's lair. Do you think they will dance in wet, reeking homespun clothes, with shaggy bruin for a partner?

An evening sky glittering with stars, red roses in dark hair, tremulous sweetness in the air, natural grace in their movements, love rising from the ground, love falling from the sky like rain, floating in the air,—have you all that to give, master? If not, why do you compel us to long for such things?

Most cruel of men, are you summoning the tethered war-horse to the combat? Rutger von Örneclou is lying in his bed, imprisoned by gout. Spare him the pain of tender memories, master! He too has worn a sombrero and a bright-coloured hair-net: he too has owned a velvet jacket and a belted poniard. Spare old Örneclou, master!

But Lilliecrona plays the cachucha, always the cachucha; and Örneclou is tortured like the lover when he sees the swallow fly away to his beloved's distant dwelling; like the hunted hart when it must run past the cooling spring.

Lilliecrona takes the violin for a second from his chin.

"Ensign, do you remember Rosalie von Berger?"

Örneclou swears a solemn oath.

"She was as light as a candle-flame. She sparkled and danced like the diamond set in the tip of the fiddle bow. You must remember her in the theatre at Karlstad. We saw her when we were young; do you remember?"

And the ensign remembered. She was small and ardent. She was like a sparkling flame. She could dance la cachucha. She taught all the young men in Karlstad to dance the cachucha and to play the castanets. At the governor's ball a *pas de deux* was danced by the ensign and Mlle. von Berger, dressed as Spaniards.

And he had danced as one dances under fig-trees and magnolias, like a Spaniard,—a real Spaniard.

No one in the whole of Värmland could dance the cachucha as he could. Only he could dance it so that it was worth talking about.

What a cavalier Värmland lost when the gout stiffened his legs and great nodes grew around his joints! What a cavalier he had been, so slender, so handsome, so courtly! "The handsome Örneclou" he had been called by the young girls who were ready to come to blows in order to dance with him.

Then Lilliecrona begins the cachucha again, always the cachucha, and Örneclou is taken back to old times.

There he stands, and there she stands, Rosalie von Berger. Just now they were alone in the dressing-room. She was a Spaniard, and so was he. He was allowed to kiss her, but carefully, for she was afraid of his blackened moustache. Now they dance. Ah, as one dances under fig-trees and magnolias! She draws away, he follows; he is bold, she proud; he wounded, she conciliatory. When at the end he falls on his knees and receives her in his outstretched arms, a sigh goes through the ball-room, a sigh of rapture.

He had been like a Spaniard, a real Spaniard.

Just at that stroke of the bow, he had bent so, stretched his arms so, and put out his foot to glide forward. What grace! He might have been hewn in marble.

He does not know how it has happened, but he has got his foot over the edge of the bed, he stands upright, he bends, he raises his arms, snaps his fingers, and wishes to glide forward over the floor in the same way as he did long ago, when he wore such tight patent leather shoes that the foot of his stockings had to be cut off.

"Bravo, Örneclou! Bravo, Lilliecrona!"

His foot gives way; he cannot rise on his toes. He makes one or two movements with one leg; he can do no more, he falls back on the bed.

Handsome señor, you have grown old.

Perhaps the señorita has too.

It is only under the plane-trees of Granada that the cachucha is danced by eternally young gipsies. Eternally young, because, like the roses, each spring brings new ones.

So now the time has come to cut the strings.

No, play on, Lilliecrona, play the cachucha, always the cachucha!

Teach us that! Although we have got slow bodies and stiff joints, in our feelings we are always the same, always Spaniards.

War-horse, war-horse!

Say that you love the trumpet-blast, which beguiles you into a gallop, even if by doing so the iron chain of the tether cuts your leg to the bone.

CHAPTER 6 *The Ball at Ekeby*

Ah, women of former times!

To speak of you is to speak of the kingdom of heaven; you were all beauties, ever bright, ever young, ever lovely and gentle as a mother's eyes when she looks down on her child. Soft as young squirrels you hung on your husbands' necks. Your voices never trembled with anger, no frowns ruffled your brows, your white hands were never rough and hard. You, sweet saints, stood like adored images in the temple of the home. Incense and prayers were offered you, through you love worked its wonders, and poetry crowned your heads with golden radiance.

Ah, women of former times, this is the story of how one of you gave Gösta Berling her love.

Two weeks after the ball at Borg there was one at Ekeby.

What a feast it was! Old men and women could become young again, could smile and rejoice just by speaking about it.

The cavaliers were masters at Ekeby at that time. The major's wife went about the country with a beggar's wallet and a crutch-stick; and the major lived at Sjö. He could not even be present at the ball, for small-pox had broken out at Sjö; and he was afraid to spread the infection.

What a wealth of pleasure those twelve hours contained, from the pop of the first cork at the dinner-table to the last wail of the violins long after midnight.

They have sunk down into the abyss of time, those crowned hours, made magical by the most fiery wines, by the most delicate food, by the most inspiring music, by the wittiest of theatricals, by the most beautiful tableaux. They have sunk down, dizzy with the dizziest dance. Where are to be found such polished floors, such courtly knights, such lovely women?

Ah, women of former times, you knew well how to adorn a ball. The fire of life, genius, and youthful vigour thrilled one and all who approached you. It was worth wasting one's gold on wax-candles to light up your loveliness, on wine to instil gayety into your hearts; it was worth dancing the soles of one's shoes to dust and having to rub arms grown stiff in playing the violin for you.

Ah, women of former times, it was you who had the key to the door of Paradise.

The halls of Ekeby are crowded with the loveliest of your lovely throng. There is young Countess Dohna, sparkling with gayety and eager for fun and dancing as befits her twenty years; there are the lovely daughters of the county-court judge at Munkerud, and the lively young ladies from Berga; there is Anna Stjärnhök, a thousand times more beautiful than ever before, with that gentle dreaminess which had come over her ever since the night she had been hunted by wolves; there are many more, who are not yet forgotten, but soon will be; and there is the beautiful Marianne Sinclair.

She was famous; for she had shone at the royal court, and had travelled throughout the country and had received homage everywhere; she lighted the spark of love wherever she showed herself,—and now she had deigned to come to the cavaliers' ball.

At that time Värmland's glory was at its height, borne up by many proud names. The happy children of this beautiful land had much to be proud of; but when they named their glories they never neglected to speak of Marianne Sinclair.

The tales of her conquests filled the land.

They spoke of the coronets which had floated above her head, of the millions which had been laid at her feet, of the warriors' swords and the poets' wreaths whose splendour had tempted her.

And she possessed not only beauty. She was witty and learned. The cleverest men of the day enjoyed talking to her. She was not an author herself; but many of her ideas, with which she had inspired her friends who were poets, lived again in song.

She seldom stayed in Värmland, the land frequented by bears.

Her life was spent in constant travel. Her father, the rich Melchior Sinclair, remained at home at Björne and let Marianne go to her noble friends in the large towns or at the great country-seats. He had his pleasure in telling of all the money she wasted, and both the old people lived happily in the splendour of Marianne's brilliant existence.

Her life was a life of pleasure and admiration. The very air about her was love—love her light and her lamp, and love her daily bread.

She, too, had often loved, often, often; but never had that fire lasted long enough to forge the bonds which bind for life.

"I wait for him, the irresistible," she used to say of love. "Hitherto he has neither climbed over several ramparts, nor swum across several moats. He has come tamely, without wildness in his eye and madness in his heart. I wait for the conqueror, who shall take me out of myself. I will feel love so strong within me that I must tremble before him; now I know only the love at which my good sense laughs."

Her presence gave fire to the talk, and life to the wine. Her ardent spirit set the fiddle-bows going, and the dance floated in sweeter ecstasy after her little feet had touched the floor. She was brilliant in the tableux, she gave genius to the comedy, her lovely lips—

Ah, hush, it was not her fault, she never meant to do it! It was the balcony, it was the moonlight, the lace veil, the knightly dress, the song, which were to blame. The poor young creatures were innocent.

All that led to so much unhappiness was done, however, with the best intentions. Master Julius, who could do anything, had arranged a tableau especially in order that Marianne might shine in her full glory.

In the theatre, which was set up in the great drawing-room at Ekeby, the hundred guests sat and watched the performance. In Spain the yellow moon was seen wandering across the dark night sky. A Don Juan came stealing along a street in Seville and stopped under an ivy-clad balcony. He was disguised as a monk, but one could see an embroidered cuff under the sleeve, and a gleaming sword-point under the hem of his cowl.

He raised his voice and sang:—

> "I kiss the lips of no fair maid,
> Nor wet mine with the foaming wine
>   Within the beaker's gold.
> A cheek upon whose rose-leaf shade
> Mine eyes have lit a glow divine,
> A look which shyly seeketh mine,—
> These leave me still and cold.
>
> "Ah, come not in thy beauty's glow,
> Señora, through yon terrace-door;
>   I fear when thou art nigh!
> Cope and stole my shoulders know,
> The Virgin only I adore,
> And water-jugs hold comfort's store;
>   For ease to them I fly."

As he finished, Marianne came out on the balcony, dressed in black velvet and a lace veil. She leaned over the balustrade and sang slowly and ironically:

> "Why tarry thus, thou holy man
> Beneath my window late or long?
> Dost pray for my soul's weal?"

Then suddenly, animatedly and eagerly:—

> "Ah, flee, begone while yet you can!
> Your gleaming sword sticks forth so long.
> And plainly, spite your holy song,
> The spurs clank on your heel."

At these words the monk cast off his disguise, and Gösta Berling stood under the balcony in a knight's garb of silk and gold. He did not heed the beauty's warning, but climbed up one of the balcony-pillars, swung himself over the balustrade, and, just as Master Julius had arranged it, fell on his knees at the lovely Marianne's feet.

Graciously she smiled on him, and gave him her hand to kiss, and while the two young people gazed at one another, absorbed in their love, the curtain fell.

And before her knelt Gösta Berling, eith a face tender as a poet's, and bold as a soldier's with deep eyes, which glowed with wit and genius, and which both implored and constrained. He was supple and full of strength, and fiery and captivating.

While the curtain rose and fell, the two stood always in the same position. Gösta's eyes held lovely Marianne fast; they implored; they constrained.

Then the applause ceased; the curtain hung quiet; no one saw them.

The beautiful Marianne bent down and kissed Gösta Berling. She did not know why,—she had to. He streched up his arms about her head and held her fast. She kissed him again and again.

But it was the balcony, it was the moonlight, it was the lace veil, the knight's garb, the song, and the applause, which were to blame. They had not wished it. She had not thrust aside the coronets which had floated above her head, and spurned the millions which lay at her feet, out of love for Gösta Berling; nor had he already forgotten Anna Stjärnhök. No; they were blameless; neither of them had wished it.

It was the gentle Löwenborg,—who had tears in his eyes and a smile on his lips,—who was curtain-raiser that day. Distracted by the memory of many sorrows, he noticed little of the things of this world, and had never learned to look after them properly. When he now saw that Gösta and Marianne had taken up a new position, he thought that it also belonged to the tableau, and so he began to pull the rope of the curtain.

The two on the balcony observed nothing until thunders of applause greeted them.

Marianne started back and wanted to run away, but Göta held her fast, and whispered:—

"Stand still; they think it belongs to the tableau."

He felt how her body was shaken with shuddering, and how the fire of her kisses died out on her lips.

"Do not be afraid," he whispered; "lovely lips have a right to kiss."

They had to stand while the curtain rose and fell; and each time hundreds of eyes saw them, hundreds of hands thundered out a stormy applause.

For it was beautiful to see two fair young people represent love's happiness. No one could think that those kisses were anything but stage illusion. No one guessed that the señora trembled with embarrassment and the knight with uneasiness. No one could think that it did not all belong to the tableau.

At last Marianne and Gösta stood behind the scenes.

She pushed her hair back from her forehead.

"I don't understand myself," she said.

"Fie! for shame, Miss Marianne," said he, grimacing, and stretched out his hands. "To kiss Gösta Berling; shame on you!"

Marianne had to laugh.

"Every one knows that Gösta Berling is irresistible. My fault is no greater than that of others."

And they agreed to put a good face on it, so that no one should suspect the truth.

"Can I be sure that the truth will never come out, *Herr* Gösta?" she asked, before they joined the guests.

"Absolutely! Gentlemen can hold their tongues, I promise you that."

She dropped her eyes. A strange smile curved her lips.

"If the truth should come out, what would people think of me, Herr Gösta?"

"They would not think anything. They would know that it meant nothing. They would think that we entered into our parts and were going on with the play."

Yet another question, with lowered lids and with the same forced smile,—

"But you yourself? What do you think about it, Herr Gösta?"

"I think that you are in love with me," he jested.

"Think no such thing," she smiled, "for then I must run you through with my stiletto to show you that you are wrong."

"Women's kisses are precious," said Gösta. "Does it cost one's life to be kissed by Marianne Sinclair?"

A glance flashed on him from Marianne's eyes, so sharp that it felt like a blow.

"I could wish to see you dead, Gösta Berling! dead! dead!"

These words revived the old longing in the poet's blood.

"Ah," he said, "would that those words were more than words!—that they were arrows which came whistling from some dark ambush; that they were daggers or poison, and had the power to destroy this wretched body and set my soul free!"

She was calm and smiling now.

"Childishness!" she said, and took his arm to join the guests.

They kept their costumes, and their triumphs were renewed when they once again appeared together off the stage. Every one complimented them. No one suspected anything.

The ball began again, but Gösta escaped from the ballroom.

His heart ached from Marianne's glance, as if it had been wounded by sharp steel. He understood too well the meaning of her words.

It was a disgrace to love him; it was a disgrace to be loved by him; a disgrace far worse than death itself.

He would never dance again. He wished never to see them again, those lovely women.

He knew it only too well. Those beautiful eyes, those red cheeks did not glow for him. The light feet did not glide for him, the low laughter was not to charm him.

Yes, dance with him, flirt with him, that they could do, but not one of them would be his in earnest.

The poet went into the smoking-room to the old men, and sat down by one of the card-tables. He happened to seat himself

at the table where the powerful master of Björne sat and alternately played "baccarat", and had the bank, with a great pile of
silver in front of him.

The play was already high. Gösta gave it an even greater impulse. Green bank-notes appeared; and all the time the pile of
money continued to grow in front of the powerful Melchior
Sinclair.

But Gösta was also accumulating both coins and notes, and soon
he was the only one who held out in the struggle against the great
landowner at Björne. Soon the great pile of money changed over
from Melchior Sinclair to Gösta Berling.

"Gösta, my boy," cried the landowner, laughing, when he had
gambled away everything he had in his wallet and purse, "what
shall we do now? I am bankrupt, and I never play with borrowed
money. I promised my wife that."

He discovered a way. He gambled away his watch and his beaver
coat, and was just going to stake his horse and sledge, when
Sintram checked him.

"Stake something to win on," he advised him. "Stake something to turn the luck."

"What the devil have I got?"

"Play for your reddest heart's blood, brother Melchior. Stake
your daughter!"

"You would never venture that," said Gösta, laughing. "That
prize I would never get under my roof."

Melchior could not help laughing also. He could not endure
that Marianne's name should be mentioned at the card-tables,
but this was so insanely ridiculous that he could not be angry. To
gamble away Marianne to Gösta, yes, that he certainly could
venture.

"That is to say," he explained, "if you can win her consent,
Gösta, I will stake my blessing to the marriage, on this card."

Gösta staked all his winnings and the play began. He won, and
Sinclair stopped playing. He could not fight against such bad
luck; he saw that.

The night slipped by; it was past midnight. The lovely women's cheeks began to grow pale; curls hung straight, ruffles were crumpled. The old ladies rose up from the sofa-corners and said that as they had been there twelve hours, it was about time for them to be thinking of home.

And the beautiful ball would have ended, had not Lilliecrona himself seized the fiddle and struck up the last polka. The horses stood at the door; the old ladies were dressed in their cloaks and shawls; the old men wound their plaids about them and buckled their galoches.

But the young people could not tear themselves from the dance. They danced in their outdoor wraps, and a mad dance it was. As soon as a girl stopped dancing with one partner, another came and dragged her away with him.

And even the sorrowful Gösta was dragged into the whirl. He hoped to dance away grief and humiliation; he wished to have the love of life in his blood again; he longed to be gay, he, as well as the others. And he danced till the walls went round, and he no longer knew what he was doing.

Who was it he had got hold of in the crowd? She was light and supple, and he felt that firey currents passed between them. Ah, Marianne!

While Gösta danced with Marianne, Sintram sat in his sledge before the door, and beside him stood Melchior Sinclair.

The great landowner was impatient at having to wait for Marianne. He stamped in the snow with his great snow-boots and beat himself with his arms, for it was bitter cold.

"Perhaps you ought not to have gambled Marianne away to Gösta," said Sintram.

"What do you mean?"

Sintram arranged his reins and lifted his whip, before he answered:—

"It did not belong to the tableau, that kissing."

The powerful landowner raised his arm for a death-blow, but Sintram was already gone. He drove away, whipping the horse to a wild gallop without daring to look back, for Melchior Sinclair had a heavy hand and little patience.

He then went into the ballroom to look for his daughter, and saw how Gösta and Marianne were dancing.

That last polka appeared to be wild and giddy.

Some of the couples were pale, others were all aglow; in the ballroom the dust was like smoke; the wax-candles, which had burned down to the sockets, gleamed, and in the midst of all the ghostly ruin, Gösta and Marianne flew on, royal in their tireless strength, no blemish on their beauty, and happy in the glorious motion.

Melchior Sinclair watched them for a while; but then he went away and left Marianne to her dancing. He slammed the door, tramped down the stairs, and got into the sledge, where his wife was already waiting, and drove home.

When Marianne stopped dancing, and asked where her parents were; she found they had gone.

When she was certain of this, she showed no surprise. She dressed herself quietly and went out into the yard. The ladies in the dressing-room thought that she was driving in her own sledge.

She hurried along the road, in her thin satin shoes without telling anyone of her distress.

In the darkness no one recognized her, as she went by the edge of the road; no one could think that this late wanderer, who was forced into the high snow drifts by the passing sledges, was beautiful Marianne Sinclair.

When she could go in the middle of the road she began to run. She ran as long as she was able, then walked for a while, then ran again. A hideous, torturing fear drove her on.

It cannot be more than two miles at most, from Ekeby to Björne. Marianne soon reached her home; but she almost believed that she had come the wrong way. For when she came to the house, all the doors were closed, all the lights out; she wondered if her parents had not come home.

She went forward and twice knocked loudly on the front door. She seized the door-handle and shook it till the noise resounded through the whole house. No one came and opened the door;

but when she let go of the iron handle, which she had grasped with her bare hands, the skin of her hands, which had frozen onto the iron, was torn off.

Melchior Sinclair had driven home in order to shut his door on his only child.

He was drunk with much drinking; and wild with rage. He hated his daughter, because she liked Gösta Berling. He had shut the servants up in the kitchen, and his wife in the bedroom. With solemn oaths he told them that anyone who attempted to let Marianne in, he would beat to a jelly. And they knew that he would keep his word.

No one had ever seen him so angry. He had never known such grief before. Had his daughter come into his presence, he would perhaps have killed her.

He had given her golden ornaments, silken dresses; knowledge and book-learning had been procured her. She had been his pride, his glory. He had been as proud of her as if she had worn a crown. Oh, his queen, his goddess, his honoured, beautiful, proud Marianne! Had he ever denied her anything? Had he not always considered himself too common to be her father? Oh, Marianne, Marianne!

Ought he not to hate her, when she is in love with Gösta Berling and kisses him? Was he not right in casting her out, in shuting his door against her, when she insisted on disgracing her greatness by loving such a man? Let her stay at Ekeby, let her run to the neighbours for shelter, let her sleep in the snow-drifts; it's all the same, she has already been dragged in the dirt, lovely Marianne. The bloom is gone. The lustre of her life is gone.

He lies there in his bed, and hears how she beats on the door. What does that matter to him? He is asleep. Outside stands one who will marry an unfrocked priest; he has no home for such a person. If he had loved her less, if he had been less proud of her, he could have let her come in.

Yes, he could not refuse them his blessing. He had gambled it away. But to open the door for her, that he would not do. Ah, Marianne!

The beautiful young woman still stood outside the door of her home. One moment she shook the lock in powerless rage, the next she fell on her knees, clasped her mangled hands, and begged for forgiveness.

But no one heard her, no one answered, no one opened to her.

Oh! was it not terrible? I am filled with horror as I tell of it. She came from a ball where she had been the queen! She had been proud, rich, happy; and in a single instant she was cast into such an endless misery. Shut out from her home, exposed to the cold,— not scorned, not beaten, not cursed, but shut out with cold, inexorable, insensibility.

Think of the cold, starlit night, which spread its arch above her; the great wide night with the empty, desolate snow-fields, with the silent woods. Everything slept, everything was sunk in painless sleep; only one living point in all that sleeping whiteness. All the sorrow and pain and horror, which otherwise had been spread over the world, crept forward towards that one lonely point. O God, to suffer alone in the midst of this sleeping, ice-bound world!

For the first time in her life she met with mercilessness and hardness. Her mother would not take the trouble to leave her bed to save her. The old servants, who had guided her first steps, heard her and did not move a finger for her sake. For what crime was she punished?

Where should she find compassion, if not at this door? If she had been a murderess, she would still have knocked on it, knowing that they would forgive her. If she had sunk to being the basest of creatures; if she had come wasted and in rags, she would still have confidently gone up to that door, and would have expected a loving welcome. That door was the entrance to her home; behind it she could only meet with love.

Had not her father tried her enough? Would they not soon open to her?

"Father, father!" she called. "Let me come in! I am freezing, I am trembling. It is terrible out here!

"Mother, mother! You who have done so much for me, you

who have watched over me for so many nights, why do you sleep now? Mother, mother, wake just this one night, and I will never cause you pain again!"

She calls, and remains breathlessly silent to listen for an answer. But no one heard her, no one listened to her, no one answered.

Then she wrings her hands in despair, but there are no tears in her eyes.

The long, dark house with its closed doors and darkened windows lay weirdly motionless in the night. What would become of her, now that she was homeless? She was branded and dishonoured for as long as she continued to encumber the earth. And it was her father himself who pressed the red-hot branding iron deeper into her shoulders.

"Father," she called once more, "what will become of me? People will believe the worst of me."

She wept and suffered agonies; her body was stiff with cold.

Alas, that such misery can come to one who but lately stood so high! That conditions change so easily, plunging us into the deepest suffering! Ought we not to fear life? Who can be sure that the ship in which he sails is safe? Round about us sorrows surge like a heaving ocean; see! how the hungry waves lick the ship's sides; see how they rage mountainous about her. Ah, there is no safe anchorage, no solid ground, no steady ship, as far as the eye can see; only an unknown sky over an ocean of sorrow!

But hush! At last, at last! A light step comes through the hall.

"Is it mother?" asked Marianne.

"Yes, my child."

"May I come in now?"

"Father will not let you come in."

"I have run through the snow-drifts in my thin shoes all the way from Ekeby. I have stood here an hour knocking and calling. I am freezing to death out here. Why did you drive away and leave me?"

"My child, my child, why did you kiss Gösta Berling?"

"But father must have seen that I do not like him because of that. It was only in fun. Does he think that I want marry Gösta?"

"Go to the farm-foreman's house, Marianne, and ask to be allowed to spend the night there. Your father is drunk. He will not listen to reason. He has kept me a prisoner up there. I crept out when I thought he was asleep. He will kill me, if you come in."

"Mother, mother, am I to go to strangers when I have a home? Are you as hard as father? How can you allow me to be shut out? I will lie down in the snow-drift out here, if you do not let me in."

Then Marianne's mother took hold of the lock to open the door, but at the same moment a heavy step was heard on the stair, and a harsh voice called her.

Marianne listened: her mother hurried away, the harsh voice cursed her and then—

Marianne heard something terrible,—she could hear every sound in the silent house.

She heard the thud of a blow, a blow with a stick or a box on the ear; then she heard a fint noise, and then again a blow.

He struck her mother, the terrible brutal Melchior Sinclair struck his wife!

And pale with horror, Marianne threw herself down on the threshold and writhed in anguish. Now she wept, and her tears froze to ice on the threshold of her home.

Mercy! pity! Open, open, that she might bend her own back under the blows! Oh, that he could strike her mother; strike her, because she did not want to see her daughter lying dead in the snow-drift next morning; because she had wished to comfort her child!

That night Marianne had suffered great humiliation. She had fancied herself a queen, and she lay there little better than a whipped slave.

But she rose up in cold rage. Once more she struck the door with her blood-stained hand and called:—

"Hear what I say to you,—you, who beat my mother. You shall weep for this, Melchior Sinclair, you shall weep!"

Then she went and laid down to rest in the snow-drift. She threw off her fur cloak and lay in her black velvet dress. She was clearly visible against the white snow. She lay and thought of how her father would come out the next day on his early morning tour of inspection and find her there. She only hoped that he himself might find her.

O Death, pale friend, is it as true as it is consoling, that I never can escape meeting you? You will come even to me, the lowliest of earth's labourers, to remove the torn leather shoes from my feet, to take the tools from my hand, and to take off my working-clothes. With gentle strength you lay me out on a lace-trimmed bed; you adorn me with draped linen sheets. My feet need no more shoes, my hands are clad in snow-white gloves, which no more work shall soil. Consecrated by thee to the sweetness of rest, I shall sleep; I shall sleep for a thousand years. Oh, deliverer! I am the lowliest of earth's labourers; and I dream with a thrill of pleasure of the hour when I shall be received into your kingdom.

Pale friend, on me you can easily try your strength; but I tell you that your fight was harder against those women of former times. Life's strength was mighty in their slender bodies; no cold could cool their hot blood. You had laid Marianne on your bed, O Death, and you sat by her side, as an old nurse sits by the cradle to lull the child to sleep. You faithful old nurse, who knows what is good for the children of men, how angry you must be when noisy, romping playmates come and wake your sleeping child. How vexed you must have been when the cavaliers lifted lovely Marianne out of the bed; and a man laid her against his breast, and warm tears fell from his eyes on to her face.

At Ekeby all lights were out, and all the guests had gone. The cavaliers stood alone in the bachelors' wing, around the last, half-emptied punch bowl.

Then Gösta tapped the edge of the bowl and made a speech for you, women of former times. To speak of you, he said, was to speak of the kingdom of heaven: you were all beauties, ever bright, ever young, ever lovely and gentle as a mother's eyes when she looks down on her child. Soft as young squirrels you hung on your husband's necks, your voices never trembled with anger, no frowns ruffled your brows, your white hands were never rough and hard. Sweet saints, you were adored images in the temple of home. Men knelt at your feet, offering you incense and prayers. Through you, love worked its wonders, and poetry crowned your heads with golden radiance.

And the cavaliers sprang up, wild with wine, wild with his words, and with their blood surging with festive mirth. Even old Eberhard and lazy Christopher joined in the sport. In the wildest haste the cavaliers harnessed the horses to their sledges, and hurried out into the cold night to pay homage to those who never could be honoured enough; to sing a serenade to each and all of them who possessed the rosy cheeks and bright eyes which had just lighted up the halls of Ekeby.

But the cavaliers did not get far on their happy way; for when they came to Björne, they found Marianne lying in the snow-drift, just by the door of her home.

They trembled and were incensed at seeing her there. It was like finding an adored saint lying mangled and stripped outside the churchdoor.

Gösta shook his clenched fist at the dark house. "You children of hate," he cried, "you northern storms, you ravagers of God's garden!"

Beerencreutz lighted his horn lantern and let it shine on the livid face. Then the cavaliers saw Marianne's mangled hands, and the tears which had frozen to ice on her eyelashes; and they wailed like women; for she was not merely a saintly image, but a beautiful woman, who had been a joy to their old hearts.

Gösta Berling threw himself on his knees beside her.

"She is lying here, my bride," he said. "She gave me the betrothal kiss a few hours ago, and her father has promised me his blessing. She lies and waits for me to come and share her white bed."

And Gösta lifted up the lifeless form in his strong arms.

"Let us take her home to Ekeby!" he cried. "Now she is mine. In the snow-drift I have found her; no one shall take her from me.

We will not wake them in there. What has she to do within those doors, against which she has beaten and bruised her bloodstained hands?"

He was allowed to do as he wished. He laid Marianne in the foremost sledge and sat down at her side. Beerencreutz sat behind and took the reins.

"Take snow and rub her, Gösta!" he commanded.

The cold had paralyzed her limbs, nothing more. The wildly agitated heart still beat. She had not even lost consciousness; she knew all about the cavaliers and how they had found her; but she could not move. So she lay stiff and stark in the sledge, while Gösta Berling rubbed her with snow, and alternately wept over her and kissed her; and she felt an infinite longing to be able to lift only a hand, that she might give a caress in return.

She remembered everything. She lay there stiff and motionless and thought more clearly than ever before. Was she in love with Gösta Berling? Yes, she was. Was it merely a passing whim? No, it had lasted for many years. She compared herself with him and the other people in Värmland. They were all just like children. They followed whatever impulse came to them. They only lived superficially; they had never looked deep into their souls. But she had become what one grows to be by living in the world; she could never really devote herself to anything. If she loved; yes, whatever she did, one half of her stood and looked on with a cold scornful smile. She had longed for a passion which should carry her away in wild recklessness; and now it had come. When she kissed Gösta Berling on the balcony, for the first time she had forgotten herself.

And now the passion came over her again, her heart throbbed so that she heard it beat. Would she not soon be mistress of her limbs? She felt a wild joy that she had been thrust out from her home. Now she could be Gösta's without hesitation. How stupid she had been, in subduing her love for so many years. Ah, it is so sweet to yield to love. But shall she never, never be free from these icy chains? She has been ice within and fire on the surface; now it is the opposite, a soul of fire in a body of ice.

Then Gösta feels how she gently raises her arms and puts them round his neck in a weak, nerveless embrace.

He could only just feel them; but Marianne imagined that she had given vent to her suppressed passion by an overwhelmingly strong embrace.

But when Beerencreutz saw it, he let the horse go as it would along the familiar road. He raised his eyes and looked obstinately and unceasingly at the Pleiades.

CHAPTER 7 *The Old Vehicles*

Friends! If you should happen to be sitting or lying and reading this at night, as I am writing it during the silent hours of the night, then do not draw a sigh of relief here and think that the good cavaliers were allowed to sleep undisturbed, after they had come back with Marianne and made her a good bed in the best guest-room beyond the big drawing-room.

They went to bed and went to sleep; but it was not their lot to sleep in peace and quiet till noon, as you and I, dear reader, might have done, if we had been awake till four in the morning and our limbs ached with fatigue.

It must not be forgotten that the major's old wife went about the country with beggar's wallet and stick, and that it never was her way, when she had anything to do, to think of a poor tired sinner's convenience. And now she would do so even less, as she had decided to drive the cavaliers that very night from Ekeby.

Gone was the day when she sat in splendour and magnificence at Ekeby and dispensed happiness over the earth, as God sows stars over the skies. And while she wandered homeless about the land, the welfare and honour of the great estate were left in the cavaliers' hands to be guarded by them, as the wind guards ashes, as the spring sun guards the snow-drift.

It sometimes happened that the cavaliers drove out, six or eight of them, in a long sledge drawn by four horses, with jingling sleigh-bells and braided reins. If they chanced to meet the major's wife, as she went by as a beggar, they did not look away.

Clenched fists were raised threateningly against her. By a violent swing of the sledge, she was forced to go into the snow-drifts by the roadside; and Major Fuchs, the bear-killer, always took pains to spit three times to take away the evil effects of meeting the old woman.

They had no pity on her. She was as odious as a witch to them as she went along the road. If any mishap had befallen her, they would no more have felt sorry for her than a man, who shoots off his gun on Easter Eve, when it is loaded with brass hooks, would care if he were to hit a witch who was flying by.

It was in order to win their salvation that these unhappy cavaliers persecuted the major's wife. People have often been cruel to, and tortured, one another with the greatest harshness, when they have trembled for their own souls.

When, late at night, the cavaliers reeled from the tables at which they had been drinking to the window to see if the night was calm and clear, they often noticed a dark shadow, which glided over the grass, and knew that the major's wife had come to see her beloved home; then the bachelors' wing rang with the cavaliers' scornful laughter, and from the open windows gibes were hurled at her.

Indeed, insensibility and arrogance began to take possession of the penniless adventures' hearts. Sintram had planted hate. Their souls could not have been in greater danger if the major's wife had remained at Ekeby. More die in flight than in battle.

The major's wife cherished no great anger against the cavaliers.

If she had had the power, she would have whipped them like naughty boys, and would then have again granted them her grace and favour.

But she now feared for the land she loved so well, which was in the cavaliers hands, who were guarding it as wolves guard the sheep, as crows guard the spring grain.

There are many who have suffered the same sorrow. She is not the only one who has seen a beloved home ruined, and well-kept fields fall into decay. They have seen their childhood's home look at them like a wounded animal. Many feel like culprits when they see the trees there wither away, and the paths covered with tufts of grass. They wish to throw themselves on their knees in those fields, which once boasted of rich harvests, and beg them not to blame them for the disgrace which has befallen them. And they turn away from the poor old horses; they have not the courage to meet their gaze. And they dare not stand by the gate and see the cattle come home from the pasture. There is no place on earth, which is so sad to visit, as an old home in ruin. Oh, I would beg you, all of you, who have fields and meadows and parks and well loved flower-gardens that bring joy, in your keeping, to look after them well! Cherish them with love, work for them! It is not good that nature should have to grieve for what men have done.

When I think, what proud Ekeby must have suffered under the cavaliers' rule, I wish that the major's wife had succeeded in her plan to take Ekeby from them.

It was not at all her intention to regain possession of her estates.

She had only one object,—to rid her home of these madmen, these wild brigands, these locusts, who left nothing growing in their path.

While she went about the country begging and lived on alms, she continually thought of her mother; and the thought bit deep into her heart, that there could be no improvement for her until her mother lifted the curse from her.

No one had ever mentioned the old woman's death; so she must be still living up there by the ironworks in the forest. At ninety years of age she still worked unceasingly; watching over her milk-pans in the summer, and her charcoal-kilns in the winter; working till she died; longing for the day when she would have completed her life's duties.

And the major's wife thought that her mother had lived so long in order that she might lift the curse from her life. That mother could not die who had called down such misery on her child.

So the major's wife wanted to go to the old woman, that they both might find rest. She wished to make her way through the dark woods by the long river to the home of her childhood.

Until she had done this, she could find no rest. There were many who offered her a comfortable home and all the consolations of faithful friendship, but she would not stay anywhere. Grim and fierce, she went from house to house, for she was weighed down by the curse.

She was going up to her mother; but first she wanted to provide for her beloved home. She would not go and leave it in the hands of wanton spendthrifts, of worthless drunkards, of good-for-nothing squanderers of God's gifts.

Was she to go, only to find on her return her inheritance wasted, her hammers silent, her horses starving, and her servants scattered? Ah, no, once more she would gather strength, and drive out the cavaliers.

She was fully aware that her husband saw with joy how her inheritance was being squandered. But she knew him well enough to realize, that if she drove away his devouring locusts, he would be too lazy to get new ones. If the cavaliers were removed, then her old bailiff and overseer could carry on the work at Ekeby in the old way.

An consequently, for many nights her dark shadow had glided along the black lanes. She had stolen in and out of the crofters' cottages; she had whispered with the miller and the mill-hands on the lower floor of the great mill; she had conferred with the smith in the dark coal-house.

They had all sworn to help her. The honour of the great estate would no longer be left in the hands of reckless cavaliers, to be guarded as the wind guards the ashes, as the wolf guards a flock of sheep.

And this night, when the merry gentlemen had danced, played, and drunk until they had sunk down on their beds in a dead sleep, this very night they must go. She has let them have their good time. She had sat in the forge and waited until the ball had ended. She waited still longer, until the cavaliers returned from their nocturnal drive. She sat silent, waiting until the message was brought her that the last light was out in the bachelors' wing and that the great house slept. Then she rose and went out.

The major's wife ordered that all the workmen on the estate should be assembled by the bachelors' wing; she herself went to the house. She knocked at the main building and was let in. The young daughter of the vicar of Broby, whom she had trained to be a capable maidservant, was there to meet her.

"You are very welcome, madame," said the maid, and kissed her hand.

"Put out the light!" said the major's wife. "Do you think I cannot find my way without a candle?"

Then she wandered through the silent house. She went from the cellar to the attic, and said farewell. With stealthy steps they passed from room to room.

The major's wife communed with old memories. The maid neither sighed nor sobbed, but the tears flowed unchecked from her eyes, while she followed her mistress. The major's wife told her to open the linen-closet and the silver-chest, and passed her hand over the fine damask table-cloths and the magnificent silver service. She felt caressingly the mighty pile of pillows in the store-closet. She touched all the implements, the looms, the spinning-wheels, and winding-bobbins. She thrust her hand into the spice-box, and felt the rows of tallow candles which hung from the rafters.

"The candles are dry," she said. "They can be taken down and put away."

When she was down in the cellar, she carefully lifted the beer-casks, and gropingly checked the rows of wine bottles.

She went into the pantry and kitchen; she felt everything, examined everything. She stretched out her hand and said farewell to everything in her house.

Finally, she went through the rooms. She found the long broad sofas in their places; she laid her hands on the cool slabs of the marble tables, and on the mirrors with their frames of gilded dancing nymphs.

"This is a rich house," she said. "He was a fine man who entrusted all this to me."

In the great drawing-room, where the ball had taken place, the stiff-backed arm-chairs already stood in prim order against the walls.

She went over to the piano, and very gently struck a chord.

"Joy and gladness were no strangers here in my time, either," she said.

She went also to the guest-room beyond. It was pitch dark. The major's wife groped with her hands and happened to touch the maid's face.

"Are you weeping?" she said, for she felt that her hands were wet with tears.

Then the young girl burst out sobbing.

"Madame," she cried, "madame, they will destroy everything. Why do you leave us and let the cavaliers ruin your house?"

The major's wife drew back the curtain and pointed out into the yard.

"It is I who have taught you to weep and lament?" she cried. "Look out! the place is full of people; to-morrow there will not be one cavalier left at Ekeby."

"Are you coming back?" asked the maid.

"My time has not yet come," said the major's wife. "The highway is my home, and the haystack my bed. But you shall watch over Ekeby for me, child, while I am away."

And they went on. Neither of them knew or thought that Marianne slept in that very room. But she did not sleep. She was wide awake, heard everything, and understood it all. She had lain there in bed and had sung a hymn to Love.

"You conqueror, you have taken me out of myself," she said, "I lay in unfathomable misery and you have changed it to a paradise. My hands stuck fast to the iron latch of the closed door and were torn and wounded; on the threshold of my home my tears lie frozen to pearls of ice. Anger froze my heart when I heard the blows on my mother's' back. In the cold snow-drift I hoped to sleep away my anger, but you came. O Love, child of fire, you came to one who was frozen by a great cold. When I compare my sufferings to the glory that they have brought me, they seem to me as nothing, I am free of all ties. I have no father, no mother, no home. People will believe all evil of me and will turn away from me. It has pleased you to do this, O Love, for why should I stand higher than my beloved? Hand in hand we will wander out into the world. Gösta Berling's bride is penniless; he found her in a snow-drift. We shall not live in lofty halls, but in a cottage at the edge of the wood. I shall help him to watch the kiln, I shall help him to set snares for partridges and hares, I shall cook his food and mend his chlothes. Oh, my beloved, how I shall long and mourn, while I sit there alone by the edge of the wood and wait for you! But not for the days of riches, only for you; only for you shall I yearn, only for you shall I keep watch, —your footstep on the forest path, your joyous song, as you come with your axe on your shoulder. Oh, my beloved, my beloved! As long as my life lasts, I could sit and wait for you."

So she lay and sang hymns to the all-conquering god of human hearts; and had not been asleep, when the major's wife came in.

As soon as she had gone, Marianne got up and dressed herself. Once more she had to wear the black velvet dress and the thin satin slippers. She wrapped a blanket about her like a shawl, and hurried out once again into the terrible night.

Calm, starlit, and bitterly cold, the February night lay over the earth; it seemed as if the night would never end. And the darkness and the cold that came of this long night persisted on the earth, long, long after the sun had risen, and long after the snow-drifts through which Marianne wandered had been melted away.

Marianne hurried away from Ekeby to get help. She could not let those men, who had rescued her from the snow-drift and had opened their hearts and their home to her, be hunted away. She went down to Sjö to Major Samzelius. It would be an hour before she could return.

When the major's wife had said farewell to her home, she went out into the yard, where her people were waiting, and the struggle for the bachelors' wing began.

She placed them round the high, narrow house, the upper story of which was the cavaliers' far-famed home,—the great room with the whitewashed walls, the red-painted chests, and the great folding-table, where playing-cards swim in the spilled brandy; where the broad beds, on which the cavaliers sleep, are hidden by yellow-striped curtains.

And in the stable, before full mangers, the cavaliers' horses sleep and dream of the journeys of their youth. It is sweet to dream when they know that they shall never again leave the filled cribs, the warm stalls of Ekeby.

In a musty old carriage-house, where all the broken-down coaches and worn-out sledges were stored, was a wonderful collection of old vehicles.

Many are the cavaliers who have lived and died at Ekeby. Their names are forgotten on the earth, and they have no longer a place in men's hearts; but the major's wife has kept the vehicles in which they came to Ekeby; she has collected them all in the old carriage-house.

And there they stand and sleep, and dust falls thick, thick over them.

But now in this February night the major's wife has the door opened to the carriage-house, and with lanterns and torches she seeks out the vehicles which belong to the cavaliers who are now living in Ekeby;—Beerencreutz's old gig, and Örneclou's coach, painted with his coat of arms, and the narrow cutter which had brought Cousin Christopher.

She does not care if the vehicles are for summer or winter use, she only sees that each one gets his own.

And in the stable they are now awake, all the cavalier's old horses, who had so lately been dreaming before full mangers. The dream shall come true.

You shall again climb the steep hills, and eat the musty hay in the sheds of wayside inns, and feel the drunken horse-dealers' sharp whips, and take part in the mad races on ice so slippery that you tremble only to walk on it.

The old beasts mouth and snort when the bit is put into their toothless jaws; the old vehicles creak and crack. Pitiful infirmity, which should have been allowed to sleep in peace till the end of the world, was now dragged out before all eyes; stiff joints, halting forelegs, spavin, and broken-wind are revealed.

The stable grooms succeed, however, in getting the horses harnessed; then they go and ask the major's wife in what Gösta

Berling shall be put, for, as every one knows, he came to Ekeby in the coal-sledge belonging to the major's wife.

"Put Don Juan in our best sledge," she says, "and spread over it the bear-skin with the silver claws!" And when the grooms grumble, she continues: "There is not a horse in my stable which I would not give to be rid of that man, remember that!"

Well, now the vehicles are waked and the horses too, but the cavaliers still sleep. It is now their time to be brought out in the winter night; but it is a more perilous deed to seize them in their beds than to bring out stiff-legged horses and shaky old carriages. They are bold, strong men, tried in a hundred adventures; they are ready to defend themselves unto death; it is no easy matter to take them out their beds, against their will, and to get them into the vehicles in which they shall drive away.

The major's wife has her men set fire to a hay-stack, which stands so near the house that the flames must shine in to where the cavaliers are sleeping.

"The hay-stack is mine, all Ekeby is mine," she says.

And when the stack is in flames, she cries: "Wake them now!"

But the cavaliers sleep behind well-closed doors. All the people begin to shout that terrible word "Fire, fire!" but the cavaliers sleep on.

The master-smith's heavy sledge-hammer thunders against the door, but the cavaliers sleep on.

A hard snowball breaks the window-pane and flies into the room, rebounding against the bed-curtains, but the cavaliers are still asleep.

They dream that a lovely girl throws a handkerchief at them; they dream of applause from behind fallen curtains; they dream of gay laughter and the deafening noise of midnight feasts.

Only the noise of cannon firing close to their ears, or an ocean of ice-cold water could have woken them.

They have bowed, danced, played, acted, and sung. They are heavy with wine, exhausted, and they sleep like the dead.

This blessed sleep almost saves them.

The people begin to think that danger may be lurking behind

this silence. What if it means that the cavaliers are already out to get help? What if it means that they are awake, and have their fingers on their triggers; on guard behind windows or door, ready to fall upon the first who enters?

These men are crafty, ready to fight; they must mean something by their silence. Who could imagine that they would let themselves be surprised in their lairs like bears?

The people bawl "Fire, fire!" time after time, but nothing comes of it.

Then, when all are trembling, the major's wife takes an axe and bursts open the outer door.

Then she rushes alone up the stairs, throws open the door to the bachelors' wing, and shouts into the room: "Fire!"

Her voice awakens a deeper echo in the cavaliers' ears than the people's outcry. Accustomed to obey that voice, twelve men at the same moment spring from their beds, see the flames, throw on their clothes, and rush down the stairs out into the yard.

But at the door stands the great master-smith and two stout mill-hands, and great disgrace then befalls the cavaliers. Each cavalier, as he comes down, is seized, thrown to the ground, and his feet bound; therupon he is carried without ceremony to the vehicle prepared for him.

None escaped; they were all caught. Beerencreutz, the grim colonel, was bound and carried away; also Christian Bergh, the mighty captain, and Eberhard, the philosopher.

Even the invincible, the terrible Gösta Berling was caught. The major's wife had succeeded.

She is more powerful than all the cavaliers.

They are a pitiful sight, as they sit with bounds limbs in the mouldy old vehicles. There are hanging heads and angry glances, and the yard rings with oaths and wild bursts of powerless rage.

The major's wife goes from one to the other.

"You shall swear," she says, "never to come back to Ekeby."

"Begone, hag!"

"You shall swear," she says, "otherwise I will throw you into the bachelors' wing, bound as you are, and you shall burn to death there; for to-night I am going to burn down the bachelors' wing."

"You dare not do that."

"Dare not! Is not Ekeby mine? Ah, you villain! Do you think I do not remember how you spat at me on the highway? Do you not think that I longed to set fire to your quarters and let you all burn? Did you lift a finger to defend me when I was driven from my home? No, swear now!"

She appears so terrible as she stands there; although she pretends perhaps to be more angry than she really is; and so many men armed with axes stand about her, that they are obliged to swear, that no worse misfortune may befall them.

The major's wife has their clothes and boxes brought down and has their handcuffs loosened; then the reins are put in their hands.

But this has taken much time; and Marianne has reached Sjö.

The major was always up early of a morning; he was dressed when she came. She met him in the yard; he had been out to feed his bears.

He did not say anything when he heard her story. He only went in to the bears, put muzzles on them, led them out, and hurried away to Ekeby.

Marianne followed him at a distance. She was dropping with fatigue; but then she saw a bright light of fire in the sky and was frightened nearly to death.

What a night it was! A man beats his wife and leaves his child to freeze to death outside his door. Did a woman now mean to burn her enemies; did the old major mean to let the bears loose on his own people?

She overcame her weariness, hurried past the major, and ran madly up to Ekeby.

She had a good start. When she reached the yard, she made her way through the crowd. When she stood in the middle of the ring, face to face with the major's wife, she cried as loud as she could,—

"The major, the major is coming with the bears!"

There was consternation among the people; all eyes turned to the major's wife.

"You fetched him," she said to Marianne.

"Run!" cried the latter, more earnestly. "Away, for God's sake! I do not know what the major intends to do, but he has the bears with him."

All stood still and looked at the major's wife.

"I thank you for your help, children," she said quietly to the people. "Everything which has happened to-night has been so arranged that none of you can be prosecuted or can get into trouble for it. Go home now! I do not want to see any af my people murder or be murdered. Go now!"

Still the people waited.

The major's wife turned to Marianne.

"I know that you are in love," she said. "You act in the madness of love. May the day never come when you must look on powerless at the ruin of your home! May you always be mistress of your tongue and your hands when anger fills your soul!"

"Dear children, come now, come!" she continued, turning to the people. "May God protect Ekeby! I must go to my mother. Oh, Marianne, when you have got back your senses, when Ekeby is ravaged, and the land groans in distress, think of what you have done this night, and look after the people!"

Thereupon she went, followed by her people.

When the major reached the yard, he found there no living thing but Marianne and a long line of horses with sledges and carriages,—a long dismal line, where the horses were not worse than the vehicles, nor the vehicles worse than their owners. They had all been badly knocked about in the struggle of life.

Marianne went forward and freed them.

She noticed how they bit their lips and looked away. They were ashamed as never before. A great disgrace had befallen them.

"I was not better off when I knelt on the steps at Björne a couple of hours ago," said Marianne.

And so, dear reader, what happened afterwards that night— how the old vehicles were put into the carriage-house, and the horses into the stable, and the cavaliers went back into their house—I shall not try to relate. Dawn began to break over the eastern hills, and the day came clear and calm. How much quieter the bright, sunny days are than the dark nights, under whose protecting wings beasts of prey hunt and owls hoot!

I will only add that when the cavaliers had gone in again and had found a few drops in the last punchbowl to fill their glasses, a sudden ecstasy came over them.

"A toast for the major's wife!" they cried.

Ah, she is a peerless woman! What better could they wish for than to serve her, and to worship her?

Was it not sad that the devil had got her in his power, and that all she could strive for was to send poor gentlemen's souls to hell?

CHAPTER 8 *The Great Bear on Gurlitta Cliff*

In the darkness of the forests dwell unholy creatures, whose jaws
are armed with horrible, glittering teeth or sharp beaks, whose
feet have pointed claws, which long to sink into a throat filled
with blood, and whose eyes shine with murderous desires.

There the wolves live, who come out at night and hunt the
peasant's sledge until the wife must take her little child, which
sits upon her knee, and throw it to them, to save her own and
her husband's life.

There the lynx lives, which the people call "göpa", for in the
woods at least it is dangerous to call it by its right name. He who
speaks of it during the day had best see that the doors and windows of the sheepcote are well closed towards night, for otherwise
it will come. It climbs right up the walls, for its claws are as strong
as steel nails; it glides in through the smallest hole, and throws
itself on the sheep. And the "göpa" hangs on their throats, and
drinks their blood, and kills and tears, till every sheep is dead.
He does not cease his wild death-dance among the terrified animals
as long as any of them show a sign of life.

And in the morning the peasant finds all the sheep lying dead
with torn throats, for the "göpa" leaves nothing living where he
ravages.

There the great owl lives, which hoots at dusk. If one mimics
him, he comes whizzing down with outspread wings and strikes
out one's eyes, for he is no real bird, but an evil spirit.

And there lives the most terrible of them all, the bear, who has
the strength of twelve men, and who, when he has become a
full-grown ravenous bear, can be killed only with a silver bullet.

And if one should chance to meet him in the wood, big and
high as a wandering cliff, one must not run, or defend oneself;

one must throw oneself down on the ground and pretend to be dead. Many small children have imagined themselves lying on the ground with the bear over them. He has rolled them over with his paw, and they have felt his hot breath on their faces, but they have lain quiet, until he has gone away to dig a hole to bury them in. Then they have got up slowly and stolen away, slowly at first, then in mad haste.

But imagine, imagine if the bear had not thought that they were really dead, but had bitten them; or if he had been very hungry and had wanted to eat them right up, or if he had seen them when they moved and had run after them. O God!

Terror is a witch. She sits in the dimness of the forest, sings magic songs to people, and fills their hearts with frightful thoughts. From her comes that deadly fear which weighs down life and darkens the beauty of smiling landscapes. Nature is malignant, treacherous as a sleeping snake; one can believe nothing. There lies lake Löven in superb beauty; but do not trust it, for it will lure you to destruction. Every year it must gather its tribute of the drowned. There lies the wood temptingly peaceful; but trust it not! The wood is full of unholy things, bewitched by evil spirits and bloodthirsty vagrants' souls.

Trust not the brook with its gliding waters. It will bring sudden sickness and death to wade in it after sunset. Trust not the cuckoo, who sings so gayly in the spring. In the autumn he becomes a hawk with fierce eyes and terrible claws. Trust not the moss, nor the heather, nor the rock. Nature is evil, full of invisible powers, who hate man. There is no spot where you can set your foot in safety; it is wonderful that your weak race can withstand so much persecution.

Terror is a witch. Does she still sit in the darkness of the woods of Värmland? Does she still darken the beauty of smiling places, does she still paralyze the joy of living? Her power has been great. How well I know it, for I have had steel put in my cradle and a red-hot coal in the bath; I know it, I who have felt her iron hand around my heart.

But no one must think that I am now going to relate anything

terrible or dreadful. It is only an old story of the great bear on
Gurlitta Cliff which I must tell; and any one can believe it or not,
as is customary with hunting stories.

The great bear has its home on the beautiful mountain crest
which is called Gurlitta Cliff, and which rises precipitously from
the shores of lake Löven.

The roots of a fallen pine, between which tufts of moss are
hanging, make the walls and roof of his dwelling; branches and
twigs protect it; and the snow keeps it warm. He can lie there and
sleep a good quiet sleep from one summer to another.

Is he, then, a poet, a dreamer, this hairy monarch of the forest?
Does he wish to sleep through the bleak nights and the gray days
of the cold winter so as to be waked by purling brooks and the
song of birds? Will he lie there and dream of reddening cranberry
bogs, and of ant-hills full of brown delicious insects, and of the
white lambs which graze on the green slopes? Does he, the happy
creature, wish to escape the winter of life?

Outside the snow-storm rages; wolves and foxes wander about,
mad with hunger. Why shall the bear alone sleep? Let him get up
and feel how the cold bites, how heavy it is to wade in deep snow.

He has bedded himself in so well. He is like the sleeping princess
in the fairy tale; and as she was waked by love, so will he be waked
by the spring. He will be waked by a ray of sunlight which
penetrates the twigs and warms his nose, by the drops of melting
snow which wet his fur. Woe to him who disturbs him at an
untimely moment!

He suddenly hears, shouts, noise, and shots. He shakes the sleep
out of his joints, and pushes aside the branches to see what it is.
It is not spring, which rattles and roars outside his lair, or the
wind, which uproots pine-trees and drives the whirling snow; but
the cavaliers, the cavaliers from Ekeby; old acquaintances of the
monarch of the forest. He remembered well the night when Fuchs
and Beerencreutz sat and dozed in a Nygård peasant's barn, where
they awaited a visit from him. They had just fallen asleep over
their brandy-bottle, when he swung himself in through the peat-

roof; but they awoke, when he was trying to lift the cow, which he had killed, out of the stall, and attacked him with their guns and knives. They took the cow from him and blinded one of his eyes; but he managed to save his life.

Yes, to be sure, he and the cavaliers are old acquaintances. He remembered how they had come across him another time, when he and his queen consort had just laid themselves down for their winter sleep in the old lair here on Gurlitta Cliff and had cubs with them. He remembered well how they came upon them unawares. He got away all right, throwing to either side everything that stood in his path; but he must limp for life from a bullet in his thigh, and when he came back at night to the royal lair, the snow was red with his queen consort's blood, and the royal children had been carried away to the plain, to grow up there and be man's servants and friends.

Yes, now the ground trembles; now the snow-drift which hides his lair shakes; now he bursts out, the great bear, the cavaliers' old enemy. Look out, Fuchs, old bear-killer; look out now, Beerencreutz; look out, Gösta Berling, hero of a hundred adventures!

Woe to all poets, all dreamers, all heroes of romance! There stands Gösta Berling with his finger on the trigger, and the bear comes straight towards him. Why does he not shoot? What is he thinking about?

Why does he not send a bullet straight into the broad breast? He stands in just the place to do it. The others are not in the right position to shoot. Does he think he is on parade before the forest monarch?

Gösta of course stood and dreamed of the lovely Marianne, who is lying at Ekeby dangerously ill, from the chill she caught that night when she slept in the snow-drift.

He thinks of her, who is also a victim of the curse of hatred which lies upon the earth; and he shudders to think that he has come out to persecute and to kill.

And there comes the great bear straight towards him; blind in one eye from the stab of a cavalier's knife; lame in one leg from a bullet from a cavalier's gun; fierce and shaggy; alone, since they had killed his wife and carried away his children. And Gösta sees him as he is,—a poor, persecuted beast, whom he will not deprive of life, which is all that he has left; since people have taken from him everything else.

"He may kill me," thinks Gösta, "but I will not shoot."

And while the bear plunges towards him, he stands quite still as if on parade; and when the forest monarch stands directly in front of him, he presents arms and takes a step to one side.

The bear continues on his way, knowing too well that he has no time to waste, breaks into the wood, ploughs his way through drifts the height of a man, rolls down the steep slopes, and escapes; while all of them, who had stood with cocked guns and had waited for Gösta's shot, fire their guns at him.

But it is of no avail; the ring is broken, and the bear gone. Fuchs scolds, and Beerencreutz swears, but Gösta only laughs.

How could they ask that anyone as happy as he should harm one of God's creatures?

Thus the great bear of Gurlitta Cliff got away with his life; he has been waked from his winter sleep; as the peasants will discover. No bear has greater skill than he to tear apart the roofs of their low, cellar-like cowsheds; none can so cunningly evade an ambush.

The people about the upper Löven soon were at their wits' end about him. Message after message was sent down to the cavaliers that they should come and kill the bear.

Day after day, night after night, during the whole of February, the cavaliers scour the upper Löven to find the bear, but he always escapes them. Has he learned cunning from the fox, and swiftness from the wolf? If they lie in wait at one place, he is ravaging the neighbouring farmyard; if they seek him in the wood, he is pursuing the peasant, who comes driving over the ice. He has become the boldest of marauders: he creeps into the garret and empties the housewife's honey-jar; he kills the horse in the peasant's sledge.

But gradually they begin to understand what kind of a bear he is and why Gösta could not shoot him. It is terrible to have to say it, and dreadful to have to believe it; but this is no ordinary bear. No one can hope to kill him if he does not have a silver bullet in his gun. A bullet of silver and bell-metal, cast, at new moon, on a Thursday evening, in the church-tower, without the priest or the sexton or anybody knowing about it, would certainly kill him; but such a bullet is not easy to get.

There is one man at Ekeby, who, more than all the rest, grieves over all this. It is, as one can easily guess, Anders Fuchs, the bear-killer. He loses both his appetite and his sleep in his anger at not being able to kill the great bear of Gurlitta Cliff. At last even he understands that the bear can only be killed with a silver bullet.

Grim Major Anders Fuchs was not handsome. He had a heavy, clumsy body, and a broad, red face, with hanging pouches under his cheeks and several double chins. His small black moustache was stiff as a brush above his thick lips, and his black hair stood out rough and thick from his head. Moreover, he was a man of few words and a glutton. He was not a person whom women meet with a sunny smile and open arms, nor did he give them tender glances in return. One could not believe that he would ever meet a woman whom he could tolerate; and everything which concerned love and infatuation was foreign to him.

One Thursday evening, when the moon, just two fingers wide, lingers above the horizon an hour or two after the sun has gone down, Major Fuchs leaves Ekeby without telling anyone where he means to go. He has flint and steel and a bullet-mould in his hunting-bag, and his gun on his back, and goes up towards the church at Bro to see what luck there may be for an honest man.

The church lies on the eastern shore of the narrow sound between the upper and lower Löven; and Major Fuchs must go over a bridge to get there. He makes his way towards it, deep in thought; without looking up towards Broby hill, where the houses stand out against the clear evening sky; he only looks on the ground, and wonders how he shall get hold of the key of the church without anybody's knowing it.

When he comes down to the bridge, he hears some one screaming so despairingly that he has to look up.

At that time the little German, Faber, was organist at Bro. He was a slender man, small in body and mind. And the sexton was Jan Larsson, an energetic peasant, but poor; for the clergyman at Broby had cheated him out of his patrimony, five hundred rix-dollars.

The sexton wanted to marry the organist's sister, a little, delicate maiden, but the organist would not let him have her; and therefore the two were not good friends. That evening the sexton has met the organist as he crossed the bridge and has fallen upon him. He seizes him by the shoulder, and holding him at arm's length out over the railing tells him solemnly that he will drop him into the sound if he does not give him the little maiden. The small German will not give in; he struggles and screams, and continues to shout "No," although far below him he sees the black water rushing between the white banks.

"No, no," he screams; "no, no!"

And it is uncertain if the sexton in his rage would have let him fall into the cold black water if Major Fuchs had not just then come over the bridge. The sexton is afraid, puts Faber down on solid ground, and runs away as fast as he can.

Little Faber falls on the major's neck in gratitude for saving his life; but the major pushes him away, and says that there is nothing to thank him for. The major has no love for Germans, ever since he had his quarters at Putbus on the Rügen during the Pomeranian war. He had never been so near starving to death, as in those days.

Then little Faber wants to run up to the bailiff Scharling and accuse the sexton of attempting to murder him; but the major informs him that it is of no use doing so in this country; no one can be convicted for killing a German.

Little Faber grows calmer and asks the major to come home with him to eat a bit of sausage and to taste his home-brewed ale.

The major accompanies him, for he thinks that the organist must have a key to the church-door; and so they go up the hill, where the Bro church stands, with the vicarage, the sexton's cottage and the organist's house around it.

"You must excuse us," says little Faber, as he and the major enter the house. "The place is not really in good order to-day. We have had much to do, my sister and I. We have killed a cock."

"The devil!" cries the major.

Little miss Faber has just come in with the ale in great earthen mugs. Now, everyone knows that the major did not look upon women with a tender glance, but this little maiden he had to gaze upon with delight, as she came in so neat in lace and cap. Her light hair lay combed so smoothly above her forehead; the home-woven dress was so pretty and so dazzlingly clean, her little hands were so busy and eager, and her little face so rosy and round, that he could not help thinking that if he had seen such a little woman twenty-five years ago, he must have come forward and proposed.

She is so pretty and rosy and nimble, but her eyes are quite red with weeping. It is that which suggests such tender thoughts.

While the men eat and drink, she goes in and out of the room. Once she comes to her brother, courtesies, and says,—

"How do you wish me to place the cows in the stable?"

"Put twelve on the left and eleven on the right, then they can't gore one another."

"Have you so many cows, Faber?" bursts out the major.

The fact was that the organist had only two cows, but he called one eleven and the other twelve, so that it should make a good impression, when he spoke of them.

And then the major hears that Faber's cow-house is being re-built; so that the cows are out all day, and at night they are put into the woodshed.

The little maiden comes again to her brother, courtesies to him, and says that the carpenter had asked how high the cow-house was to be built.

"According to the size of the cows," says the organist, "let him measure the cows!"

Major Fuchs thinks that is a good answer. However, the major asks the organist why his sister's eyes are so red; and learns that she weeps because he will not let her marry the penniless sexton, who is in debt and without any inheritance.

Major Fuchs grows more and more thoughtful. He empties

tankard after tankard, and eats sausage after sausage, without noticing it. Little Faber is appalled at such an appetite and such a thirst; but the more the major eats and drinks, the clearer and more determined his mind grows. The more firmly he resolves to do something for the little maiden.

He has kept his eyes fixed on the great key which hangs on a knob by the door, and as soon as little Faber, who has had to keep up with the major in drinking the home-brewed ale, lays his head on the table and snores, Major Fuchs has seized the key, put on his cap, and hurried away.

A minute later he is groping his way up the tower stairs, lighted by his little horn lantern, and comes at last to the bellroom, where the bells open their wide throats above him. He scrapes off a little of the bell-metal with a file, and is just going to take the bullet-mould and melting-ladle out of his hunting-bag, when he finds that he has forgotten what is most important of all: he has no silver with him. If the bullet is to have any power, it must be cast in the tower. Everything is in order: it is Thursday evening, and there is a new moon, and no one has any idea he is there; and now he cannot do anything. In the silence of the night he swears so vehemently, that his oath sets the bells humming.

Then he hears a slight noise down in the church and thinks he hears steps on the stairs. Yes, it is true, heavy steps are coming up the stairs.

Major Fuchs, who stands there and swears so that the bells vibrate, now becomes a little wary. He wonders who can be coming to help him cast the bullet. The steps come nearer and nearer. Whoever it is, is coming all the way up to the bell-room.

The major creeps far in among the beams and rafters, and puts out his lantern. He is not exactly afraid, but the whole thing would be spoiled if anyone should see him there. He has scarcely had time to hide before the new-comer's head appears above the floor.

The major knows him well; it is the miserly vicar of Broby. He is nearly mad with greed; and has the habit of hiding his treasures in the strangest places. He comes now with a roll of bank-notes which he is going to hide in the tower-room. He does not know that anyone sees him. He lifts up a board in the floor, conceals the money, and then goes away again.

The major does not waste any time: he lifts up the same board. Oh, what a lot of money! Bundle after bundle of bank-notes, and among them brown leather bags, full of silver. The major takes just enough silver to make a bullet; the rest he leaves.

When he comes down, he has the silver bullet in his gun. He wonders what luck has in store for him this night. Strange things happen on Thursday nights, as everyone knows. He goes up towards the organist's house. Fancy if the bear knew that Faber's cows are in a miserable shed that offers no better protection than if they were under the open sky.

What! surely he sees something big and black coming over the field towards the woodshed; it must be the bear. He puts the gun to his cheek and is just going to shoot; but then he changes his mind.

In the darkness, he sees in front of him the eyes of the litttle maid, which are red with weeping; he thinks that he will help her and the sexton a little; but this will mean that he will not be able to kill the great bear. He said afterwards that nothing in the world had ever entailed so greater a sacrifice for him; but as the little maiden was so dear and sweet, it had to be done.

He goes up to the sexton's house, wakes him, drags him out, half dressed and half naked, and says that the sexton must shoot the bear, which is creeping about outside of Faber's woodshed.

"If you shoot the bear, Faber will surely let you marry his sister," he says, "for then you will be a famous man. That is no ordinary bear, and the best men in the country would consider it an honour to kill it."

And he gives him his own gun, loaded with a bullet of silver and bell-metal cast in a church-tower on a Thursday evening at the new moon; and he cannot help trembling with envy that another man, and not he, is to shoot the great monarch of the forest, the old bear of Gurlitta Cliff.

The sexton aims,—God help us! aims, as if he meant to hit the Great Bear, which high up in the sky wanders about the North

Star, and not a bear wandering on the plain,—and the gun goes off with a bang which can be heard all the way to Gurlitta Cliff.

But regardless of how he has aimed, the bear is killed. That's what happens when one shoots with a silver bullet. One shoots the bear through the heart, even if one aims at the Dipper.

People come rushing out from all the neighbouring farmyards and wonder what is going on; for never had a shot sounded so loud nor waked so many sleeping echoes as this one; and the sexton wins much praise, for the bear had been a real pest.

Little Faber comes out too, but now is Major Fuchs sadly disappointed. There stands the sexton covered with glory, besides having saved Faber's cows; but the little organist is neither touched nor grateful. He does not open his arms to him and greet him as his brother-in-law and a hero.

The major stands and frowns and stamps his foot in rage over such meanness. He wants to explain to the covetous, narrow-minded little fellow what a feat this is; but he begins to stammer, so that he cannot get a word out. And he becomes more and more angry at the thought that he has given up the glory of killing the great bear in vain.

Oh, it is quite impossible for him to grasp that the man who has performed such a deed should not be worthy to win the proudest of brides.

The sexton and some of the young men are going to skin the bear; they go to the grindstone and sharpen the knives. Others go home to bed. Major Fuchs stands alone by the dead bear.

Then he goes to the church once more, puts the key again in the lock, climbs up the narrow stairs and the twisted ladder, wakes the sleeping pigeons, and once more comes up to the tower-room.

Afterwards, when the bear is skinned under the major's inspection, they find between his jaws a bundle of notes of five hundred rix-dollars. It is impossible to say how it came there, but of course he was a strange bear; and as the sexton had killed him, the money is his, that is quite clear.

When it is made known, little Faber understands too what a

glorious deed the sexton has performed; and he declares that he would be proud to be his brother-in-law.

On Friday evening Major Anders Fuchs returns to Ekeby from a feast at the sexton's house in honour of the lucky shot, and from festivities at the organist's in celebration of the engagement. He follows the road with a heavy heart; he feels no joy that his enemy is dead, and no pleasure in the magnificent bear-skin which the sexton has given him.

Many will believe that perhaps he is grieving because the sweet little maid is betrothed to another. Oh no, that causes him no sorrow. But what goes to his very heart is that the old, one-eyed forest king is dead, and it was not he who shot the silver bullet at him.

So he comes into the cavaliers' wing, where the cavaliers are sitting round the fire, and without a word throws the bear-skin down among them. Let no one think that he talked about that expedition; it was not until long, long afterwards that anyone could get the truth out of him. Nor did he betray where the vicar of Broby hid his money; the latter perhaps never noticed the theft.

The cavaliers examine the skin.

"It is a fine skin," says Beerencreutz. "I should like to kown why this fellow left his hibernating-den, or perhaps you shot him in his winter lair?"

"He was shot at Bro."

"He was not as big as the Gurlitta bear," says Gösta, "but he was a fine beast all the same."

"If he had had only one eye," says Kevenhüller, "I would have thought that you had killed the old fellow himself, he is so big; but this one has no wound or inflammation about his eyes, so it cannot be the same."

Fuchs swears at his stupidity; but then his face lights up so that he is really handsome. The great bear has not been killed by another man's bullet.

"Lord God, how good thou art!" he says, and folds his hands.

CHAPTER 9 *The Auction at Björne*

We young people have often had to wonder at the old people's tales. "Was there a ball every night, as long as your radiant youth lasted?" we asked them. "Was life then one long adventure?"

"Were all young women beautiful and lovely in those days, and did every feast end by Gösta Berling carrying off one of them?"

Then the old people shook their worthy heads, and began to tell of the whirring of the spinning-wheel and the clatter of the loom, of work in the kitchen, of the thud of the flail and the clearings made in the forest; but it was not long before they harked back to the old theme. Then sledges drove up to the door, horses speeded away through the dark woods with the joyous young people; then the dance whirled and the violin-strings snapped. The wild chase for adventure rushed along the shores of lake Löven. The noise it made could be heard far away. The forest tottered and fell; all the powers of destruction were let loose. Fire broke out, floods laid waste the land, starving wild beasts roamed about the farmyards. Under the horses' hoofs all quiet happiness was trampled to dust. Wherever the hunt rushed by, men's hearts grew fierce, and the women, blanched by terror, had to flee from their homes.

And we youngsters sat wondering, silent, troubled in mind, and yet happy. "What people!" we thought. "We shall never see their like."

"Did the people of those days never *think* of what they were doing?" we asked.

"Of course they did, children," the old people answered.

"But not as we think," we insisted.

But the old people did not understand what we meant.

But we thought of the strange spirit of self-consciousness which

had already taken possession of us. We thought of him, with his
eyes of ice and his long, bent fingers,—who sits there in the
darkest corner of the soul and picks to pieces our being; just as
old women pick bits of silk and wool to pieces.

Bit by bit the long, hard, crooked fingers had picked, until our
whole self lay there like a pile of rags, and our best impulses, our
most original thoughts, everything which we had done and said,
had been examined, scrutinized, and picked to pieces; and the icy
eyes had looked on, and the toothless mouth had laughed in de-
rision and whispered,—

"See, they are all rags, only rags."

There was one person, however, who belonged to the people of
that time who had opened her soul to the spirit with the eyes of
ice. In this person the spirit sat, watching the sources of action,
sneering at both good and evil, understanding everything, con-
demning nothing, examining, seeking out, picking to pieces, para-
lyzing the emotions of the heart and the power of the mind by
sneering unceasingly.

Beautiful Marianne carried the spirit of introspection within her.
She felt his icy eyes and his sneers following every step she took,
every word she uttered. Her life had become a drama where she
was the only spectator. She had ceased to be a human being; she
did not suffer, nor was she happy, nor did she love; she played
beautiful Marianne Sinclair's rôle; and self-consciousness sat there
with staring, icy eyes and busy, picking fingers, and watched her
performance.

She was divided into two halves. Pale, unsympathetic, and
sneering, one half sat and watched what the other half was doing;
and the strange spirit who picked her being to pieces, never had
any feeling or a word of sympathy for her.

But where had he been, the pale watcher of the sources of action,
that night, when she had learned to know the fulness of life?
Where had he been, when she, the sensible Marianne, kissed Gösta
Berling before a hundred pairs of eyes, and when in a fit of anger
she had thrown herself down in the snow-drift to die? Then the
icy eyes were blinded, then the sneer was powerless, for passion

had raged in her soul. The roar of adventure's wild hunt had thundered in her ears. She had been an integrated personality during that one terrible night.

Oh, you god of self-mockery, when, with the greatest effort, Marianne had succeeded in lifting her stiffened arms and putting them about Gösta's neck, you too, like old Beerencreutz, had to turn away your eyes from the earth and look at the stars.

That night you had no power. You were dead while she sang her love-song, dead while she hurried down to Sjö fetch the major, dead when she saw the flames redden the sky over the tops of the trees.

For they had come, the mighty storm-birds, the griffins of demoniac passions. With wings of fire and claws of steel they had come swooping down over you, you spirit with the eyes of ice; they had struck their claws into your neck and flung you far into the unknown. You were crushed and dead.

But now they, whose course no sage can predict, no observer can follow, had rushed on; and out of the depths of the unknown the strange spirit of self-consciousness had again arisen and had once more taken possession of Marianne's soul.

During the whole of February Marianne lay ill at Ekeby. When she went to the major at Sjö she had been infected with small-pox. The terrible illness had been very severe, coming, as it did, after she had been so chilled and exhausted. Death had been very near to her, but at the end of the month she had recovered. She was still very weak and much disfigured. She would never again be called beautiful Marianne.

As yet, however, this was known only to Marianne and her nurse. The cavaliers themselves did not know it. For very few persons were allowed to visit her sick-room.

But when is the power of introspection greater than during the long hours of convalescence? Then the fiend sits and stares and stares with his icy eyes, and picks and picks with his bony, hard fingers. And if one looks carefully, behind him sits a still paler creature, who stares and sneers, and behind him another and still another, sneering at one another and at the whole world.

And while Marianne lay and looked at herself with all these staring eyes, all natural feelings died within her.

She lay there and acted that she was ill; she lay there and acted that she was unhappy, in love, and longing for revenge.

She was all of these things; and nevertheless it was only acting. Everything became a mere play and unreal under the gaze of those icy eyes, which watched her, while they in turn were watched by a pair behind them, and these again, were watched by other pairs of eyes in an infinite perspective.

All the energy of life had died within her. She had found sufficient strength for fierce hatred and ardent love for a single night, and no longer.

She did not even know if she loved Gösta Berling. She longed to see him to know if he could take her out of herself.

During her illness, she had only thought of one thing clearly: she did not want people to know about her illness. She did not wish to see her parents; she did not wish to be reconciled to her father, and she knew that he would repent if he should know how ill she was. Consequently, she gave orders that her parents and everyone else should be told that the troublesome irritation of the eyes, from which she invariably suffered when she visited her native place, forced her to sit in a darkened room. She forbade her nurse to say how ill she was; she forbade the cavaliers to get the doctor from Karlstad. She had of course small-pox, but only very mildly. In the medicine-chest at Ekeby there were remedies enough to save her life.

She never thought of death; she only lay and waited until she was well enough to be able to go to the clergyman with Gösta and have the banns published.

The fever now left her and her illness was over. She was once more cold and sensible. It seemed to her as if she alone was sensible in this world of fools. She neither hated nor loved. She understood her father; she understood them all. He who understands does not hate.

She had heard that Melchior Sinclair meant to have an auction at Björne and get rid of his property, so that she should not inherit anything from him. People said that what he intended to do would be devastating. First he would sell the furniture and household utensils, then the cattle and implements, and finally, the house itself with all its lands. He would then put the money in a bag and let it sink to the bottom of lake Löven. Dissipation, confusion, and devastation should be her inheritance. Marianne smiled approvingly when she heard it; such was his character, and so he must act.

It seemed strange to her that she had composed that great hymn to love. She had dreamed of love in a cottage, as others have done. Now it seemed odd to her that she had ever had a dream.

She sighed for naturalness. She was tired of this continual acting. She had never felt any strong emotion. She only grieved for her beauty; but she shuddered at the compassion of strangers.

Oh, that she might for an instant forget herself! Oh, for one gesture, one word, one act which was not premeditated!

One day, when the rooms had been disinfected and she lay dressed on a sofa, she had Gösta Berling called. They told her that he had gone to the auction at Björne.

There was indeed a big auction at Björne. It was a rich, old home. People had come long distances to be present at the sale.

Melchior Sinclair had flung all the property in the house into the great drawing-room. There lay thousands of articles in piles, which reached from floor to ceiling.

He had himself gone about the house like an angel of destruction on the day of judgment, and dragged out what he wanted to sell. Everything in the kitchen,—the black pots, the wooden chairs, the pewter dishes, the copper kettles, all were left in peace, for among them there was nothing which recalled Marianne; but they were the only things which escaped his anger.

He burst into Marianne's room, turning everything out. Her dollshouse stood there, and her book-case, the little chair he had had made for her, her trinkets and clothes, her sofa and bed; verything must go.

And then he went from room to room. He tore down everything that did not please him, and carried great loads down to the auction-room. He panted under the weight of sofas and marble slabs; but he went on. He had thrown open the sideboards and taken out the magnificent family silver. Away with it! Marianne had touched it. He filled his arms with snow-white damask and with shining linen sheets with hem-stitching as wide as one's hand,—honest home-made work, the fruit of many years of labour,—and flung them down together on the piles. Away with them! Marianne was not worthy to own them. He stormed through the rooms with piles of china, not caring if he broke the plates by the dozen; he seized the hand-painted cups with the family coat-of-arms. Away with them! Let anyone who wants use them! He staggered under mountains of bedding from the attic: bolsters and pillows so soft that one sunk down in them as in a wave. Away with them! Marianne had slept on them.

He cast fierce glances at the old, familiar furniture. Was there a chair where she had not sat, or a sofa which she had not used, or a picture which she had not looked at, a candlestick which had not lighted her, a mirror which had not reflected her features? Gloomily he shook his fist at this world of memories. He would have liked to have rushed at them with a club and to have smashed everything to fragments.

But it seemed to him a still more splendid revenge to sell them all at auction. They should go to strangers! Away to be soiled in the cottagers' huts, to be in the care of indifferent strangers. Did he not know them, the dented pieces of furniture, bought at auctions, in the peasants' houses, fallen into dishonour like his beautiful daughter? Away with them! May they stand with torn-out stuffing and worn-off gilding, with cracked legs and stained leaves, and long for their former home! Away with them to the ends of the earth, so that no eye can find them, no hand collect them!

When the auction began, he had filled half the hall with an incredible confusion of piled-up articles.

Right across the room he had placed a long counter. Behind it stood the auctioneer who cried the goods; there the clerks sat and kept the record, and there Melchior Sinclair had a keg of brandy standing. In the other half of the room, in the hall, and in the yard were the buyers. There were many people, and much noise and gayety. The bids followed close on one another, and the auction was lively. But by the keg of brandy, with all his possessions in endless confusion behind him, sat Melchior Sinclair, half drunk and half mad. His hair stood up in rough tufts above his red face; his eyes were rolling, fierce, and bloodshot. He shouted and laughed, as if he had been in the best of moods; and everyone who had made a good bid he called up to him and offered him a dram.

Among those who saw him there was Gösta Berling, who had stolen in with the crowd of buyers, but who endeavoured to keep out of Melchior Sinclair's sight. What he saw there made Gösta Berling thoughtful; and his heart stood still, as if he had had a presentiment of calamity.

He wondered where Marianne's mother could be while all this was happening. And he went out, against his will, but driven by fate, to find Madame Gustava Sinclair.

He had to go through many doors before he found her. Her husband had short patience and little fondness for wailing and for women's complaints. He had wearied of seeing her tears flow over the fate which had befallen her household treasures. He was furious that she could weep over table and bed linen, when, what was worse, his beautiful daughter was lost; and so, with clenched fists, he had driven her before him through the house, out into the kitchen, and all the way to the pantry.

She could not go any farther, and he had rejoiced at seeing her there, cowering behind the step-ladder, awaiting heavy blows, perhaps death. He let her stay there, but he locked the door and stuffed the key in his pocket. She could sit there as long as the auction lasted. She did not need to starve, and his ears had rest from her laments.

There she still sat, imprisoned in her own pantry, when Gösta came through the corridor between the kitchen and the dining-room. He saw her face at a little window high up in the wall. She had climbed up on the step-ladder, and stood staring out of her prison.

"What are you doing up there?" asked Gösta.

"He has shut me in," she wispered.

"Your husband?"

"Yes. I thought he was going to kill me. But listen, Gösta, take the key of the dining-room door, and go into the kitchen and unlock the pantry door with it, so that I can come out. That key fits here."

Gösta obeyed, and in a couple of minutes the little woman stood in the kitchen, which was quite deserted.

"You should have let one of the maids open the door with the dining-room key," said Gösta.

"Do you think I want to teach them that trick? Then I should never have any peace in the pantry. And, besides, I took this chance to put the upper shelves in order. They needed it, indeed. I cannot understand how I could have let so much rubbish collect there."

"You have so much to attend to," said Gösta.

"Yes, that's true enough. If I were not everywhere, neither the loom nor the spinning-wheel would be going right. And if—"

Here she stopped and wiped away a tear from the corner of her eye.

"God help me, how I do talk!" she said; "they say I won't have anything more to look after. He is selling everything we have."

"Yes, it is a wretched business," said Gösta.

"You know that big mirror in the drawing-room, Gösta. It was such a beauty, the glass was perfect, without a flaw, and there was no blemish at all on the gilding. I got it from my mother, and now he wants to sell it."

"He is mad."

"You may well say so. He is not far from it. He won't stop until we have to go and beg on the highway, just as the major's wife does."

"It will never be as bad as that," answered Gösta.

"Yes, Gösta. When the major's wife went away from Ekeby, she foretold that misfortune would befall us; and now it is coming. She would never have allowed him to sell Björne. And think, his own china, the old Canton cups from his own home, are to be sold. The major's wife would never have let it happen."

"But what is the matter with him?" asked Gösta.

"Oh, it is only because Marianne has not come back again. He has waited and waited. He has gone up and down the avenue the whole day and waited for her. He is driving himself mad with longing, but I do not dare to say anything."

"Marianne believes that he is angry with her."

"She does not believe that. She knows him well enough; but she is proud and will not take the first step. They are inflexible and hard, both of them, and I have to stand between them."

"You must know that Marianne is going to marry me?"

"Alas, Gösta, she will never do that. She says that only to make him angry. She is both too spoiled and too proud to marry a poor man. Go home and tell her that if she does not come home soon, all her inheritance will be lost. He will throw everything away, without getting anything for it."

Gösta was really angry with her. There she sat on a big kitchen table, and could think only of her mirrors and her china.

"You ought to be ashamed!" he burst out. "You first throw your daughter out into a snow-drift, and then you presume that it is only malice on her part that prevents her from coming back. And you even believe that she is capable of forsaking a person she cares for, for fear of being disinherited."

"Dear Gösta, don't be angry! I don't know what I am saying. I tried my best to open the door for Marianne, but he seized hold of me and dragged me away. They all say here that I don't understand anything. I shall not grudge you Marianne, Gösta, if you can make her happy. It is not so easy to make a woman happy, Gösta."

Gösta looked at her. How could he too have raised his voice in anger against such a person as she was,—terrified and cowed, but with such a good heart!

"You do not ask how Marianne is," he said gently.

She burst into tears.

"Will you not be angry with me if I ask you?" she said. "I have longed to ask you the whole time. All I know is that she is alive! All this time I have not had a word of greeting from her; not even when I sent her clothes; and so I thought that you and she did not want me to know anything about her."

Gösta could bear it no longer. He was wild, he was out of his senses,—sometimes God had to send his wolves after him to force him to obey—but this old woman's tears, this old woman's grief was harder for him to bear than the howling of the wolves. He told her the truth.

"Marianne has been ill the whole time," he said. "She has had small-pox. She was to get up to-day and lie on the sofa. I have not seen her since the first night."

Madame Gustava jumped down at once. She left Gösta standing there, and rushed away without another word to her husband.

The people in the auction-room saw her come up to him and eagerly whisper something in his ear. They saw how his face grew still more flushed, and his hand, which rested on the tap, turned it so that the brandy streamed over the floor.

It seemed to all as if Madame Gustava had come with such important news that the auction must end immediately. The auctioneer's hammer no longer fell, the clerks' pens stopped, there were no new bids.

Melchior Sinclair roused himself from his thoughts.

"Well," he cried, "what is the matter?"

And once more the auction was in full swing.

Gösta still sat in the kitchen, and Madame Gustava returned to him.

"It's no use," she said. "I thought he would stop when he heard that Marianne had been ill; but he is letting the auction go on. He would like to stop it; but now he feels ashamed."

Gösta shrugged his shoulders and bade her farewell.

In the hall he met Sintram.

"This is a funny show," exclaimed Sintram, and rubbed his hands. "You are a marvel, Gösta! Lord, what you have brought to pass!"

"It will be funnier in a little while," whispered Gösta. "The vicar of Broby is here with a sledge full of money. They say that he wants to buy the whole of Björne and pay for it in cash. Then I should like to see Melchior Sinclair, Sintram."

Sintram drew his head down between his shoulders and laughed inwardly a long time. And then he made his way into the auction-room and went up to Melchior Sinclair.

"If you want a drink, Sintram, you must make a bid first."

Sintram came close up to him.

"You are in luck to-day as always," he said. "A fellow has come to the house with a sledge full of money. He is going to buy Björne and everything both inside and out. He has told a lot of people to bid for him. He does not want to show himself yet for a while."

"You may as well tell me who he is, then I will give you a drink for your pains."

Sintram took the dram and moved a couple of steps back before he answered,—

"They say it is the vicar of Broby, Melchior."

There were few people that Melchior Sinclair liked less than the vicar of Broby. There had been a life-long feud netween them. It was said that on dark nights he had lain in wait on the road where the vicar was to pass, and had given him many an honest drubbing, the old fawner and oppressor of the peasants.

It was well for Sintram that he had drawn back a step or two, but he did not entirely escape the big man's anger. He got a brandy glass between his eyes and the whole brandy keg on his feet. But then followed a scene which rejoiced his heart for a long time to come.

"Does the vicar of Broby want to get my house?" roared Melchior Sinclair. "Are you bidding for my things on his behalf? Oh, you ought to be ashamed of yourselves! You ought to know better!"

He seized a candlestick, and an inkstand, and slung them at the crowd of people.

All the bitterness of his poor heart at last found expression. Roaring like a wild beast, he clenched his fist at those standing about, and slung at them whatever he could lay his hands on.

Brandy glasses and bottles flew across the room. He did not know what he was doing in his rage.

"It's the end of the auction," he cried. "Out with you! Never while I live shall the vicar of Broby have Björne. Out! I'll teach you to bid for the vicar of Broby!"

He rushed at the auctioneer and the clerks. They hurried away. In the confusion they overturned the desk, and Sinclair with indescribable fury burst into the crowd of peaceful people.

They fled in the wildest confusion. A couple of hundred people were crowding towards the door, running away from one man. And he stood still, roaring "Out with you!" He sent curses after them, and now and again he swept about him with a chair, which he brandished like a club.

He pursued them out into the hall, but no farther. When the last stranger had left the house, he went back into the drawing-room and bolted the door after him. Then he dragged together a mattress and a couple of pillows, laid himself down on them, and went to sleep in the midst of all the havoc, and never woke till the next day.

When Gösta got home, he heard that Marianne wished to speak to him. That was just what he wanted. He had been wondering how he could get a word with her.

When he came into the dim room where she lay, he had to stand for a moment at the door. He could not see where she was.

"Stay where you are, Gösta," Marianne said to him. "It may be dangerous to come near me."

But Gösta had come up the stairs in two bounds, trembling with eagerness and longing. What did he care for the contagion? He wished to have the bliss of seeing her.

For she was so beautiful, his beloved! No one had such soft hair, such an open, radiant brow. Her whole face was composed of exquisite lines.

He thought of her eyebrows, sharply and clearly drawn like the honey-guides of a lily, and of the bold curve of her nose, and of her lips, softly curving like rolling waves, and of her oval cheeks and the perfect shape of her chin.

And he thought of the rosy hue of her skin, of the magical effect

of her coal-black eyebrows and her light hair, and of her blue
irises swimming in clear white, and of the light in her eyes.

She was beautiful, his beloved! He thought of the warm heart
which she hid under a proud exterior. She had strength for devotion
and self-sacrifice concealed under that fine skin and under her
proud words. It was bliss to see her.

He had rushed up the stairs in two bounds, and she thought that
he would stop at the door. He stormed through the room and fell
on his knees at the head of her bed.

But he meant to see her, to kiss her, and to bid her farewell.

He loved her. He would certainly never cease to love her, but
his heart was used to being trampled on. Oh, where should he find
her, that rose without support or roots, which he could take and
call his own? He might not keep even her, whom he had found
disowned and half dead at the roadside.

When would his love sing a song so loud and clear that no dis-
sonance would be heard? When would his palace of happiness be
built on ground for which no other heart longed restlessly and
with regret?

He thought of how he would bid her farewell.

"There is great sorrow in your home," he would say. "My heart
is torn at the thought of it. You must go home so that your father
may recover his reason. Your mother is in continual danger of
losing her life. You must go home, my beloved."

These were the words he had on his lips, but they were never
spoken.

He fell on his knees at the head of her bed, and took her face
between his hands and kissed her; but then he could not speak.
His heart began to beat so fiercely, as if it would burst.

Small-pox had passed over that lovely face. Her skin had become
coarse and scarred. Never again would the red blood glow in her
cheeks, or the fine blue veins show on her temples. Under her
swollen lids, her eyes were dull. Her eyebrows had fallen out, and
the lustre of the whites of her eyes had changed to yellow.

Everything was laid waste. The bold lines had become coarse
and heavy.

They were not few who mourned over Marianne Sinclair's lost beauty. In the whole of Värmland, people lamented the change in her bright colour, her sparkling eyes, and blond hair. For there beauty is prized as nowhere else. The joyful people grieved, as if the country had lost one of the jewels from the crown of its honour; as if the splendour of their lives had been tarnished.

But the first man who saw her after she had lost her beauty did not indulge in sorrow.

Inexpressible emotion filled his soul. The more he looked at her, the more animated he became. His love grew and grew, like a river in spring. In waves of fire it welled up in his heart, it filled his whole being, it rose to his eyes as tears; it sighed on his lips, trembled in his hands, and in his whole body.

Oh, to love her, to protect her, to keep her from all harm!

To be her slave, her protector!

Love is strong when it has gone through the baptismal fire of pain. He could not speak to Marianne of parting and renunciation. He could not leave her—he owed her his life. He could commit mortal sin for her sake.

He could not speak a coherent word; he only wept, and kissed her; until at last the old nurse thought it was time to lead him out.

When he had gone, Marianne lay and thought of him and his emotion. "It is good to be loved so much," she thought.

Yes, it was good to be loved; but what about herself? What did she feel? Oh, nothing, less than nothing!

Was it dead, her love, or where had it taken flight? Where had it hidden itself, the child of her heart?

Did it still live? Had it crept into the darkest corner of her heart and sat there freezing under the icy eyes; frightened by the pale sneer; and half suffocated by the bony fingers?

"Ah, my love," she sighed, "child of my heart! Are you alive, or are you dead, dead as my beauty?"

The next day Melchior Sinclair went into his wife's room.

"See to it that there is order in the house again, Gustava!" he said. "I am going to bring Marianne home."

"Yes, dear Melchior, of course, I will put things in order," she answered.

Thereupon there was peace between them.

An hour afterwards he was on his way to Ekeby.

It was impossible to find a nobler and more kindly old gentleman than Melchior Sinclair, as he sat in the open sledge in his best fur coat and his best rug. His hair lay smooth on his head, but his face was pale and his eyes were sunken in their sockets.

The bright light of the clear sky illimitable on that February day. The snow sparkled like a young girl's eyes when she hears the music of the first waltz. The birches stretched the delicate tracery of their reddish-brown twigs against the sky; and on some of them hung a fringe of little icicles.

The day was full of a splendour and a festive glow. The horses pranced; and the coachman cracked his whip in the sheer joy of living.

After a short drive the sledge drew up before the great steps at Ekeby.

The footman came out.

"Where are the gentlemen?" asked Melchior.

"They are hunting the great bear on Gurlitta Cliff."

"All of them?"

"All of them, sir. Those who do not go for the sake of the bear go for the sake of the luncheon."

Melchior laughed so that it echoed through the silent yard. He gave the man a crown for his answer.

"Go and tell my daughter that I have come to take her home. She need not be afraid of the cold. I have the big sledge and a wolfskin cloak to wrap her in."

"Will you not come in, sir?"

"Thank you! I am quite all right where I am."

The man disappeared, and Melchior waited.

He was in such a genial mood that day that nothing could irritate him. He had expected to have to wait a little for Marianne; perhaps she was not even up. He would have to amuse himself by looking about him for a while.

From the cornice hung a long icicle, with which the sun was having considerable trouble. It began its work at the upper end of the icicle, where the ice melted and formed drops of water. The sun wanted these to run down the icicle and fall to the ground. But before a drop had gone half the way, it would freeze again. And the sun made one attempt after another, which always failed. But at last a freebooter of a ray attached itself to the tip of the icicle, which shone and sparkled with eagerness; and as was only proper, it accomplished its object,—a drop fell tinkling to the ground.

Melchior looked on and laughed. "You were not such a fool," he said to the ray of sunlight.

The yard was quiet and deserted. Not a sound was heard in the big house. But he was not impatient. He knew that women needed plenty of time to make themselves ready.

He sat and looked at the dove-cote. The birds had a grating before the door. They were shut in, as long as the winter lasted, lest hawks should exterminate them. Time efter time a pigeon came and stuck out its white head through the meshes.

"She is waiting for the spring," said Melchior Sinclair, "but she must have patience for a while."

The pigeon came so regularly that he took out his watch, and holding it in his hand, he timed her. Exactly every third minute she stuck out her head.

"No, my little friend," he said, "do you think spring will be here in three minutes? You must learn to wait."

And he had to wait himself; but he had plenty of time.

The horses first pawed impatiently in the snow, but then they grew sleepy by standing and blinking in the sun. They laid their heads together and slept.

The coachman sat straight on his box, with whip and reins in his hand and his face turned directly towards the sun, and slept, slept so that he snored.

But Melchior did not sleep. He had never felt less like sleeping. He had seldom passed pleasanter hours than during this joyful time of waiting. Marianne had been ill. She had not been able to come before, but now she would come. Oh, of course she would. And everything would be well again.

She must understand that he was not angry with her. He had come himself with two horses and the big sledge.

It is nothing to have to wait when one is sure of oneself; and when there is so much to distract one's mind.

There comes the great watch-dog. He creeps forward on the tips of his toes, keeps his eyes on the ground, and wags his tail gently, as if he meant to set out on the most indifferent errand. All at once he begins to burrow eagerly in the snow. The old rascal must have hidden some stolen goods there. But just as he lifts his head to see if he can eat it now undisturbed, he is quite astonished to see two magpies right in front of him.

"You old thief!" say the magpies, and look like conscience itself. "We are police officers. Give up your stolen goods!"

"Oh, be quiet with your noise! I am the steward—"

"Just the right one," they sneer.

The dog throws himself on them, and they fly away with slow flaps. The dog rushes after them, jumps, and barks. But while he is chasing one, the other is already back. She flies down into the hole, tears at the piece of meat, but cannot lift it. The dog snatches away the meat, holds it between his paws, and bites into it. The magpies place themselves close in front of him, and make disagreeable remarks. He glares fiercely at them, while he eats, and when they get too impertinent, he jumps up and drives them away.

The sun began to sink towards the western hills. Melchior looked at his watch. It is three o'clock. His wife had had dinner ready for twelve!

At the same moment the footman came out and announced that Miss Marianne wished to speak to him.

Melchior laid the wolfskin cloak over his arm and went beaming up the steps.

When Marianne heard his heavy tread on the stairs, she did not even then know if she should go home with him or not. She only knew that she must put an end to this long waiting.

She had hoped that the cavaliers would come home; but they

did not come. So she had to do something to put an end to it all.
She could bear it no longer.

She had thought that he would have driven away, in a fit of
anger, after he had waited five minutes, or that he would break the
door in or try to set the house on fire.

But there he sat calm and smiling, and only waited. She cherished neither hatred nor love for him. But there was a voice in her
which seemed to warn her against putting herself in his power
again, and moreover, she wished to keep her promise to Gösta.

If he had slept, if he had spoken, if he had been restless, if he had
shown any sign of doubt, if he had had the carriage driven into the
shade! But he was all patience and assurance.

His assurance! His assurance was infectious that she would come
if he only waited!

Her head ached. Every nerve quivered. She could get no rest as
long as she knew that he sat there. It was as if his will dragged
her bound down the stairs.

So she thought she would at least talk with him.

Before he came, she had all the curtains drawn up, and she placed
herself so that the light fell full on her face.

For she intended to test him in a way; but Melchior Sinclair was
a wonderful man that day.

When he saw her, he did not make a sign, or give vent to any
exclamation. It was as if he had not seen any change in her. She
knew how highly he prized her beauty. But he showed no sorrow.
He controlled himself so as not to wound her. That touched her.
She began to understand why her mother had loved him in spite
of everything.

He showed no hesitation. He came with neither reproaches nor
excuses.

"I will wrap the wolfskin about you, Marianne; it is not cold.
It has been on my knees the whole time."

To make sure, he went up to the fire and warmed it.

Then he helped her to raise herself from the sofa, wrapped the
cloak about her, put a shawl over her head, drew it down under
her arms, and knotted it behind her back.

She let him do it. She was helpless. It was good to have every-thing arranged; it was good not to have to decide anything; especially good for one who had been so picked to pieces as she, for one who did not possess a single thought or feeling which was her own.

Melchior lifted her up, carried her down to the sleigh, closed the top, tucked the furs in about her, and drove away from Ekeby.

She shut her eyes and sighed, partly from pleasure, partly from regret. She was leaving life, the real life; but it did not make so much difference to her,—for she was incapable of really living; she could only act her role.

A few days later her mother arranged that she should meet Gösta. She sent for him while her husband was out taking his long walk to inspect his timber. When Gösta arrived, she took him in to Marianne.

Gösta came in; but he neither bowed nor spoke. He stood at the door and looked on the ground like an obstinate boy.

"But, Gösta!" cried Marianne. She sat in her arm-chair and looked at him half amused.

"Yes, that is my name."

"Come here, come to me, Gösta!"

He went slowly forward to her, but did not raise his eyes.

"Come nearer! Kneel down here!"

"Lord God, what is the use of all that?" he cried; but he obeyed.

"Gösta, I want to tell you that I think it was best that I came home."

"Let us hope that they will not throw you out in the snow-drift again."

"Oh, Gösta, do you not care for me any longer? Do you think that I am too ugly?"

He drew her head down and kissed her, but looked as cold as ever.

She was almost amused. If he wanted to be jealous of her parents, what did it matter? It would pass. It amused her to try and win him back. She did not know why she wished to keep him, but she did. She thought that it was he who had succeeded for once in freeing her from herself. He was the only one who would be able to do it again.

And now she began to speak, eager to win him back. She said that she had not intended to desert him for good; but, so as to keep up appearances, they must for a time break off their relationship. He must have seen, that her father was on the verge of insanity; that her mother was in constant danger of her life. He must understand that she had been forced to come home.

Then his anger burst out in words. She need not give herself so much trouble. He would be her plaything no longer. She had given him up when she had gone home, and he could not love her any more. When he came home the day before yesterday from his hunting-trip and found her gone without a message, without a word, his blood ran cold in his veins, he had nearly died of grief. He could not love anyone who had caused him such pain. Besides, she had never loved him. She was a coquette, who wanted to have someone to kiss and caress her when she was here in the country, that was all.

Did he think that she was in the habit of allowing young men to caress her?

Oh yes, he was sure of it. Women were not so saintly as they seemed. Selfishness and coquetry from beginning to end! No, if she only knew how he had felt when he came home from the hunt. It was as though he had waded in icy water. He would never get over that pain. It would be with him for the whole of his life. He would never be the same person again.

She tried to explain to him how it had all happened. She tried to convince him that she was still faithful. Well, it did not matter, for now he did not love her any more. He had seen through her. She was selfish. She did not love him. She had gone without leaving him a message.

He kept on coming back to that. She really enjoyed the performance. She could not feel annoyed; she understood his anger so well. She did not fear any real break between them. But at last she became uneasy. Had there really been such a change in him that he could no longer care for her?

"Gösta," she said, "was I selfish when I went to Sjö to fetch the major; I knew that they had small-pox there. Nor is it pleasant to go out in satin slippers in the cold and snow."

"Love lives by love, and not by services and deeds," said Gösta.

"Do you wish us to be as strangers from now on, Gösta?"

"That is what I wish."

"You are very changeable, Gösta Berling."

"People often accuse me of being so."

He was cold; it was impossible to make him more animated; and she was still colder. Self-consciousness sat and sneered at her attempt to act being in love.

"Gösta," she said, making a last effort, "I have never intentionally wronged you, even if it may seem so. I beg you to forgive me!"

"I cannot forgive you."

She knew that if her feeling for him had been genuine, she could have won him back. And she strove to simulate passion. The icy eyes mocked at her, but she tried nevertheless. She did not want to lose him.

"Do not go, Gösta! Do not go in anger! Think how ugly I have become! No one will ever love me again."

"Nor will I," he said. "You will have to bear seeing your heart trampled on, just as other people have to."

"Gösta, I have never loved any one but you. Forgive me. Do not forsake me! You are the only one who can save me from myself."

He thrust her from him.

"You do not speak the truth," he said with icy calmness. "I do not know what you want of me, but I see that you are lying. Why do you want to keep me? You are so rich that you will never lack suitors."

Then he went.

And not until he had closed the door, did regret and pain in all their strength take possession of Marianne's heart.

It was love, dear child of her heart, who came out of the corner where the cold eyes had banished him. He, for whom she had so longed, came, now that it was too late.

When Marianne became fully aware that Gösta Berling had forsaken her, she felt a purely physical pain so terrible that she was almost stupified. She pressed her hands against her heart, and sat for hours in the same place, struggling with a tearless grief.

It was she herself who was suffering; not a stranger, nor an actress. It was she herself. Why had her father come and separated them? Her love had never been dead. It was only that in her weak condition, after her illness, she had been unable to realize his influence on her.

O God, O God, that she had lost him! O God, that awareness had come so late!

Ah, he was the only one; he had vanquished her heart! From him she could accept anything. Hardness and angry words from him aroused only humble love in her. If he had beaten her, she would have crept to him like a dog, and kissed his hand.

She did not know what to do to get relief from this dull pain.

She seized pen and paper and wrote with terrible eagerness. First she wrote of her love and her regret. Then she would ask, not for his love, but only for his pity. It was a kind of poem that she wrote.

When she had finished, she thought that if he saw the letter he must believe that she loved him. Well, why should she not send what she had written to him? She would send it the next day, and she was sure that it would bring him back to her.

The next day she spent in an agonizing struggle with herself. What she had written seemed to her paltry and stupid. It had neither rhyme nor metre. It was only prose. He would only laugh at such verses.

Her pride was roused too. If he no longer cared for her, it was such a terrible humiliation to beg for his love.

Sometimes her good sense told her that she ought to be glad to escape from her connection with Gösta, and all the deplorable circumstances which it had entailed.

She suffered such agonies, that finally she gave way to her

emotions. Three days after she had become conscious of her love, she enclosed the verses and wrote Gösta Berling's name on the envelope. But they were never sent. Before she could find a suitable messenger, such information reached her concerning Gösta Berling that she understood it was too late to win him back.

But it was the sorrow of her life that she had not sent the verses in time, while she still could have won him back.

All her pain was centred on that one point: "If only I had not waited so long, if I had not waited so many days!"

She would have obtained the happiness, or at any rate the reality of life, by those written words. She was sure they would have brought him back to her.

Grief, however, rendered her the same service as love. It made her a whole being; capable of devoting herself to both good and evil. Passionate feelings filled her soul, unrestrained by the icy chill of self-consciousness. And she was, in spite of her plainness, much loved.

But they say that she never forgot Gösta Berling. She mourned for him as one mourns for a wasted life.

Her poor verses, which at one time were much read, are forgotten long ago. I would ask you to read them and to think of them. Who knows what power they might have had, if they had been sent? They are impassioned enough to bear witness to a real feeling. Perhaps they would have brought him back to her.

They are touching enough, tender enough in their awkward formlessness. No one could wish them to be different. No one could possibly want to see them restrained by rhyme and metre; and yet it is so sad to think that it was perhaps just this imperfection which prevented her from sending them in time.

I would ask you to read them and to love them. It is a person in great anguish who has written them.

"Child, thou hast loved once, but nevermore
 Shalt thou taste of the joys of love!
 A passionate storm has raged through thy soul
 Rejoice, thou hast gone to thy rest!
 No more in wild joy shalt thou soar up on high
 Rejoice, thou hast gone to thy rest!
 No more shalt thou sink in abysses of pain,
 Oh, nevermore.

"Child, thou hast loved once, but nevermore
 Shall thy soul burn and scorch in the flames.
 Thou wert as a field of brown, sun-dried grass
 Flaming with fire for a moment's space;
 From the whirling smoke-clouds the fiery sparks
 Drove the birds of heaven with piercing cries.
 Let them return! Thou burnest no more!—
 Wilt burn nevermore.

"Child, thou hast loved, but now nevermore
 Shalt thou hear love's murmuring voice.
 Thy young heart's strength, like a weary child
 That sits and tired on the hard school-bench,
 Yearns for freedom and pleasure.
 But no man calleth it more like a forgotten song;
 No one sings it more,—nevermore.

"Child, the end has now come!
 And with it gone love and love's joy.
 He whom thou didst love as if he had taught thee
 With wings to hover through space,
 He, whom thou didst love as if he had given thee
 Safety and home when the village was flooded,
 Is gone, who alone understood
 The key to the door of thy heart.

"I ask but one thing of thee, O my beloved:
'Lay not upon me the load of thy hate!'
That weakest of all things, the poor human heart,
How can it live with the pang and the thought
That it gave pain to another?

"O my beloved, if thou wilt kill me,
Use neither dagger nor poison nor rope!
Say only you wish me to vanish
From the green earth and the kingdom of life,
And I shall sink to my grave.

"From thee came all life in living; thou gavest me love,
And now thou recallest thy gift, I know it too well.
But do not give thy hate!
I still have love of living! Oh, remember that;
But under a load of hate I have but to die."

CHAPTER 10 *The Young Countess*

The young countess sleeps till ten o'clock in the morning, and wants to have fresh bread on the breakfast-table every day. The young countess embroiders, and reads poetry. She knows nothing about weaving and cooking. The young countess is spoiled.

But the young countess is gay, and lets her gaiety light on everyone and everything. One is happy to forgive her sleeping late of a morning and demanding fresh bread, for she is lavish in her kindness to the poor and is friendly to everyone.

The young countess's father is a Swedish nobleman, who has lived in Italy all his life; for he has been held captive by the loveliness of Italy and by one of her beautiful daughters. When Count Henrik Dohna travelled in Italy he had been received in this nobleman's house; and had made the acquaintance of his daughters. Subsequently, he had married one of these ladies; and brought her with him to Sweden.

Since she had always spoken Swedish and had been brought up to love everything Swedish, she was happy to live in Sweden. She moves so merrily in the long dance of pleasure, that circles around the shores of lake Löven, that one could well believe she had always lived there. Little does she understand what it means to be a countess. There is no display, no stiffness, no condescending dignity in that young, joyous creature.

It was the old men who liked the young countess best. It was wonderful, what a success she had with old men. When they had seen her at a ball, one could be sure that all of them, the judge at Munkerud and the dean of Bro and Melchior Sinclair and the captain at Berga, would tell their wives in the greatest confidence that if they had met the young countess thirty or forty years ago—

"Yes, she was not born then," the old ladies reply.

And the next time they meet the young countess, they joke with her about winning from them the old men's hearts.

The old ladies look at her with a certain anxiety. They remember so well Countess Märta. She had been just as joyous and good and well beloved when she first came to Borg. And she had become a vain and pleasure-seeking coquette, who never could think of anything but her amusements. "If only she had a husband who could keep her occupied!" say the old ladies. "If she only could learn to weave!" For weaving was a consolation for everything; it absorbed all other interests, and had been the saving of many a woman.

The young countess wants to be a good housekeeper. She can conceive of nothing better than to live, as a happy wife, in a comfortable home; and she often goes to balls, and sits down beside the old people.

"Henrik wants me to learn to be a good housekeeper," she says, "just as his mother is. Teach me how to weave!"

Then the old people heave a sigh: first, over Count Henrik, who can think that his mother was a good housekeeper; and then over the difficulty of initiating this young, ignorant creature in such a complicated matter. It was enough to speak to her of heddles, and harnesses, and warps, and woofs,[1] to make her head spin.

No one who sees the young countess can help wondering why she married stupid Count Henrik. A stupid person needs to be pitied wherever he may be; but he is most to be pitied if he lives in Värmland.

There are already many stories of Count Henrik's stupidity, and he is only a little over twenty years old. People speak about how he entertained Anna Stjärnhök on a sleighing party a few years ago.

"You are very pretty, Anna," he said.

"How you talk, Henrik!"

"You are the prettiest girl in the whole of Värmland."

"That I certainly am not."

"The prettiest in this sleighing party at any rate."

"Alas, Henrik, I am not that either."

[1] Terms used in weaving.

"Well, you are the prettiest in this sledge, that you can't deny."

No, she could not deny it.

For Count Henrik is no beauty. He is as ugly as he is stupid. They say of him that the head supported by his thin neck has been inherited by members of the family for a couple of hundred years. That is why the last heir's brain is so worn out.

"It is perfectly plain that he has no head of his own," they say. "He has borrowed his father's. He does not dare to bend it; he is afraid of losing it—he is already yellow and wrinkled. Both his grandfather and his father used that head. How can one otherwise account for the hair being so thin and the lips so bloodless and the chin so pointed?"

He is always surrounded by people who ridicule him, and who encourage him to say stupid things, which they record, circulate and even embellish.

It is lucky for him that he does not notice it. He is solemn and dignified in everything he does. He moves formally, he walks very erect; he never turns his head without turning his whole body.

He had been at Munkerud on a visit to the judge a few years ago. He had ridden there in a top-hat, yellow breeches, and polished boots, and had sat stiff and proud in the saddle. When he arrived everything went well, but when he was to ride away again it so happened that one of the low-hanging branches of a birch-tree knocked off his hat. He got off, put on his hat, and rode again under the same branch. His hat was again knocked off; this was repeated four times.

The judge at last went out to him and said: "Why not ride on one side of the branch the next time?"

The fifth time he got safely by.

But still the young countess cared for him in spite of his old man's head. She, of course, did not know that he was crowned with such a halo of stupidity in his own country, when she saw him in Rome. Then, there had been something of the glory of youth about him, and they had met under such romantic circumstances. You ought to hear the countess tell how Count Henrik had to elope with her. The priests and the cardinals had been wild with

rage that she wished to give up her mother's religion and become
a Protestant. The mob had been in an uproar. Her father's palace
was besieged. Henrik was pursued by bandits. Her mother and
sisters implored her to give up the marriage. But her father was
furious that the Italian rabble should attempt to prevent him from
giving his daughter in marriage to whomsoever he might wish.
He commanded Count Henrik to carry her off. Since it was impossible for them to be married at home, without its being discovered, Henrik and she stole away through back streets and all
sorts of dark alleys to the Swedish consulate. And when she had
abjured the Catholic faith and had become a Protestant; they were
immediately married and sent north in a swift travelling-carriage.
"There was no time for banns, you see. It was quite impossible,"
the young countess used to say. "And of course it was gloomy to
be married at a consulate, and not in one of the beautiful churches,
but if we had not done that, Henrik would have had to do without
me. Everyone is so impetuous down there, both papa and mamma,
and the cardinals and the priests, all are so impetuous. That was
why everything had to be done so secretly, and if the people had
seen us steal out of the house, they would certainly have killed us
both—so as to save my soul; Henrik was of course already lost."

The young countess loves her husband, even since they came
home to Borg and live a quieter life. She loves in him the glory of
the old name and the famous ancestors. She likes to see how her
presence softens the stiffness of his manner, and to hear how his
voice grows tender when he speaks to her. And besides, he cares
for her and spoils her, and she is married to him. The young
countess cannot imagine that a married woman should not care
for her husband.

In a certain way he represents her ideal of manliness. He is
honest and loves the truth. He had never broken his word. She
considers him a true nobleman.

On the 18th of March Bailiff Scharling celebrates his birthday,
and many people then drive up Broby Hill. People from east and
west, known and unknown, invited and uninvited, come to the
bailiff's house on that day. All are welcome, all find plenty of food

and drink, and in the ballroom there is room for dancers from seven parishes.

The young countess is coming too, as she always does where there is to be dancing and merry-making.

But she is not happy in coming. It is as if she has a presentiment that it is now her turn to be dragged into the wild hunt for adventure.

On the way she sat and watched the sinking sun. It set in a cloudless sky and left no gold edges on the light clouds. A pale, gray, twilight, swept by cold squalls, settled down over the country.

The young countess saw how day and night struggled, and how fear seized all living things at the mighty contest. The horses quickened their pace with the last load to come under shelter. The wood-cutters hurried home from the woods, the maids from the farmyard. Wild creatures howled at the edge of the wood. The day, beloved of man, was defeated.

The light grew dim, the colours faded. She only saw chillness and ugliness. What she had hoped, what she had loved, what she had done, seemed to her to be also wrapped in the gray light of twilight. It was the hour of weariness, of depression, of impotence, for her as for the whole of nature.

She thought that a time might come when her own heart, which in its playful gladness decked existence in purple and gold, would perhaps lose its power to light up her world.

"Oh, impotence, my own heart's impotence!" she said to herself. "Goddess of the stifling, gray twilight. You will one day be mistress of my soul. Then life will appear ugly and gray, as perhaps it is in reality; then my hair will grow white, my back be bent, my brain be paralyzed."

At the same moment the sledge turned in at the bailiff's gate, and as the young countess looked up, her eyes fell on a grated window in the wing, and on a fierce, staring face behind the grating.

It was the face of the major's wife from Ekeby; and the young woman knew that her pleasure for the evening was now spoiled.

It is possible to be joyful when one does not see sorrow, but only hears it spoken of. But it is harder to be gay when one stands face to face with black, fierce, staring need.

The countess knows, of course, that Bailiff Scharling had put the major's wife in prison, and that she is to be tried for the damage she had caused at Ekeby on the night of the great ball. But the countess never thought that the major's wife would be kept in custody there at the bailiff's house, so near the ballroom, that from it, one could look into her room; so near that she must hear the dance music and the noise of merry-making. And the thought takes away all her pleasure.

The young countess dances both the waltz and the quadrille. She takes part in the minuet and the contra-dance; but after each dance she steals to the window in the wing. There is a light there and she can see how the major's wife walks up and down in her room. She never seems to rest, but always goes on walking.

The countess takes no pleasure in the dance. She only thinks of the major's wife going backwards and forwards in her prison like a caged wild beast. She wonders how all the others can dance. She is sure there are many there who are as deeply moved as she is by the knowledge that the major's wife is so near; and yet not one of them shows it.

But every time she looks out her feet grow heavier in the dance, and her laughter sticks in her throat.

The bailiff's wife notices her as she wipes the moisture from the window-pane to see out, and comes to her.

"Such misery! Oh, it is such suffering!" she whispers to the countess.

"I think it is almost impossible to dance to-night," the countess whispers in reply.

"It is not with my consent that we dance here, while she is sitting up there," answers Madame Scharling. "She has been in Karlstad since she was arrested. But there is soon to be a trial now, and that is why she was brought here to-day. We could not put her in that miserable cell in the court-house; so she was allowed to stay in the weaving-room in the wing. She would have had my drawing-room, countess, if all these people had not come to-day."

You hardly know her, but she has been like a mother and queen for us all. What will she think of us, who are dancing here, while she is in such great distress. It is as well that most of them do not know that she is sitting there."

"She ought never to have been arrested," says the young countess, sternly.

"No, that is true enough, countess, but there was nothing else that could be done, if a worse misfortune was to be avoided. No one blamed her for setting fire to her own hay-stack and driving out the cavaliers; but the major was scouring the country for her. God knows what he would have done if she had not been put in prison. Scharling has given much offence because he arrested the major's wife, countess. Even in Karlstad they were greatly displeased with him, because he did not shut his eyes to everything that happened at Ekeby; but he did what he thought was best."

"But now I suppose she will be sentenced?" says the countess.

"Oh, no, countess, she will not be sentenced. She will be acquitted, but all that she has to bear these days is too much for her. She is going mad. You can well understand it; such a proud woman, how can she bear to be treated like a criminal! I think that it would have been best if she had been allowed to go free. She might have been able to escape by herself."

"Let her go," says the countess.

"Anyone can do that but the bailiff and his wife," whispers Madame Scharling. "We have to guard her. Especially to-night, when so many of her friends are here. There are two men on guard outside her door, and it is locked and barred so that no one can come in. But if anyone got her out, countess, we should be so glad, both Scharling and I."

"Can I not go to her?" says the young countess. Madame Scharling seizes her eagerly by the wrist and leads her out. In the hall they throw a couple of shawls about them, and hurry across the yard.

"It is not certain that she will even speak to us," says the bailiff's wife. "But she will see that we have not forgotten her."

They come into the first room in the wing, where the two men sit and guard the barred door, and, without being stopped, they go into the room where the major's wife was. It was a large room crowded with looms and other implements. It was used mostly as a weaving-room, but it had bars in the window and a strong lock on the door, so that, in case of need, it could be used as a cell.

The major's wife continues to walk up and down, without paying any attention to them.

She has set out on a long journey these days. She cannot remember anything except that she is going the hundred and twenty miles to her mother, who is up in the Älfdal forests, and is waiting for her. She never has time to rest. She must go. A restless haste has taken possession of her. Her mother is over ninety years old. She will soon be dead.

She has measured the floor in yards, and she is now adding up the yards to furlongs and the furlongs to half-miles and miles.

Her way seems heavy and long, but she dare not rest. She wades through deep drifts. She hears the forests murmuring above her as she goes. She rests in Finn huts and in the charcoal-burners' log cabins. Sometimes, when she does not meet anyone for many miles, she has to break branches for a bed and to rest under the roots of a fallen pine.

And at last she has reached her journey's end, the hundred and twenty miles have been traversed; the wood opens out, and the red house stands in a snow-covered yard. The Klar River rushes foaming through a succession of little waterfalls, and by that well-known sound she knows that she is at home. And her mother, who must have seen her coming as a beggar, just as she had wished would happen, comes to meet her.

When the major's wife has got so far she always looks up, glances about her, sees the closed door, and knows where she is.

Then she wonders if she is going mad, and sits down to think and to rest. But after a time she sets out again, calculates the yards and the furlongs, the half-miles and the miles, rests for a short time in Finn huts, and does not sleep by night or day until she has again traversed the hundred and twenty miles.

During all the time she has been in prison she has hardly ever slept.

And the two women who had come to see her looked at her with anguish.

The young countess will always remember her, as she walked in that room. She sees her often in her dreams, and wakes with eyes filled with tears and a moan on her lips.

The old woman is so pitifully changed; her hair is so thin, and loose ends stick out from the narrow braid. Her face is flabby and sunken; her dress is disordered and ragged. But in spite of it all, she has retained so much of her lofty bearing that she inspires not only sympathy but also respect.

But what the countess remembered most distinctly were her eyes, sunken, turned inward, not yet wholly deprived of the light of reason, but almost on the point of extinction, with a spark of wildness lurking in their depths, so that one was compelled to shudder and to fear that the next moment the old woman would be upon one, with teeth ready to bite, and with fingers ready to claw.

They had been there quite a while when the major's wife suddenly stopped before the young woman and looked at her with a stern glance. The countess took a step backwards and seized Madame Scharling's arm.

All at once, the features of the major's wife become vital and expressive; her eyes look out into the world with full intelligence.

"Oh, no; oh, no," she says and smiles; "as yet it is not so bad, my dear young lady."

She asks them to sit down, and sits down herself. She assumes an air of old-time stateliness, reminiscent of the days of festivity at Ekeby and of the royal balls at the governor's house at Karlstad. They forget the rags and the prison and only see the proudest and richest woman in Värmland.

"My dear countess," she says, "what possessed you to leave the dance to visit a lonely old woman? You must be very good."

Countess Elizabeth cannot answer. Her voice is choking with emotion. Madame Scharling replies on her behalf: that the countess had not been able to dance for thinking of the major's wife.

"Dear Madame Scharling," answers the major's wife, "have I got to such a state that I disturb the young people in their pleasure? You must not weep for me, my dear young countess," she continued. "I am a wicked old woman, who deserves all I get. You do not think it right to strike one's mother?"

"No, but—"

The major's wife interrupts her and strokes the curly, light hair back from her forehead.

"Child, child," she says, "how could you marry that stupid Henrik Dohna?"

"But I love him."

"I see how it is, I see how it is," says the major's wife. "A kind child and nothing more; weeps with those in sorrow, and laughs with those who are joyful. And feels obliged to say 'yes' to the first man who says, 'I love you.' Yes, of course. Go back now and dance, my dear young countess. Dance and be happy! There is nothing bad in you."

"But I want to do something for you."

"Child," says the major's wife, solemnly, "an old woman lived at Ekeby who held the winds of heaven prisoners. Now she is caught and the winds are free. Is it strange that a storm goes over the land?

"I, who am old, have seen it before, countess. I recognize it. I know that the storm of the God of thunder is coming. Sometimes it rushes over great kingdoms, sometimes over small out-of-the-way communities. God's storm forgets no one. It comes over the great as well as the small. It is grand to see God's storm coming.

"Anguish shall spread itself over the land. The small birds' nests shall fall from the branches. The hawk's nest in the crown of the pine-tree shall be shaken down to the earth with a great noise; and even the eagle's nest in the mountain cleft shall be caused to hiss by the dragon-tongue of the wind.

"We thought that here all was well with us; but it was not. God's storm is needed. I understand that, and I do not complain. I only wish that I might be permitted go to my mother."

She suddenly sinks back.

"Go now, young woman," she says. "I have no more time. I must proceed. Go now, and be on your guard against those who ride on the storm-cloud!"

Thereupon she resumes her journey. Her features become expressionless; and her glance turns inward. The countess and Madame Scharling have to leave her.

As soon as they are back again among the dancers the young countess goes straight to Gösta Berling.

"I can greet you from the major's wife," she says. "She is waiting for you to get her out of prison."

"Then she must go on waiting, countess."

"Oh, help her, Herr Berling!"

Gösta stares gloomily before him. "No," he says, "why should I help her? What thanks do I owe her? Everything she has done for me has been to my ruin."

"But Herr Berling—"

"If she had not existed," he says angrily, "I would now be sleeping up there in the forest. Is it my duty to risk my life for her, because she has made me a cavalier at Ekeby? Do you think much credit is attached to that profession?"

The young countess turns away from him without answering. She is angry.

She goes back to her place with bitter thoughts of the cavaliers. They have come to-night with horns and fiddles, and mean to let the bows play on the strings until the horse-hair is worn out, without thinking that the merry tunes can be heard in the prisoner's miserable room. They come here to dance until their shoes fall to pieces, and do not remember that their old benefactress can see their shadows whirling across the misty window-panes. Alas, how gray and ugly the world was! Alas, what a shadow trouble and hardness had cast over the young countess's soul!

After a while Gösta comes to ask her to dance.

She refuses curtly.

"Will you not dance with me, countess?" he asks, and grows very red.

"Neither with you nor with any other of the Ekeby cavaliers" she says.

"We are not worthy of such an honour."

"It is no honour, Herr Berling. But it gives me no pleasure to dance with those who forget the precepts of gratitude."

Gösta has already turned on his heel.

This scene is heard and seen by many. All think the countess is right. The cavaliers' ingratitude and heartlessness had caused general indignation.

But in these days Gösta Berling is more dangerous than a wild beast in the forest. Ever since he came home from the hunt and found Marianne gone, his heart has been like an aching wound. He longs to do someone a great injury and to spread sorrow and pain far around.

If that is her wish, he says to himself, it shall be as she wishes. But she shall not save her own skin. The young countess likes elopements. She shall have her fill. He has nothing against adventure. For eight days he has mourned on account of a woman. It is long enough. He calls Beerencreutz the colonel, and Christian Bergh the great captain, and the slow Cousin Christopher, who never hesitates at any mad adventure, and consults with them how he shall avenge the insult to the honour of the cavaliers.

It is the end of the party. A long line of sledges drive up into the courtyard. The men are putting on their fur cloaks. The ladies look for their wraps in the dreadful confusion of the dressing-room.

The young countess has been in great haste to leave this hateful ball. She is the first of all the ladies to be ready. She stands smiling in the middle of the room and looks at the confusion, when the door is thrown open, and Gösta Berling appears on the threshold.

No man has a right to enter this room. The old ladies stand there with their thin hair no longer adorned with becoming caps; and the young ones have turned up their skirts under their cloaks, that the stiff ruffles may not be crushed on the way home.

But without paying any attention to the warning cries, Gösta Berling rushes up to the countess and seizes her.

He lifts her in his arms and rushes with her out of the room, into the hall and then on to the steps.

The screams of the astonished women could not check him. When they hurry after him, they only see how he throws himself into a sledge with the countess in his arms.

They hear the driver crack his whip and see the horse set off. They know the driver: it is Beerencreutz. They know the horse: it is Don Juan. And in deep distress over the countess's fate they call their husbands.

And these waste no time in questions, but hasten to their sledges. And with the count at their head they pursue the abductor.

But he lies in the sledge, holding the young countess fast. He has forgotten all his grief, and intoxicated by the joy of adventure, he sings at the top of his voice a song of love and roses.

He presses her close to him; but she makes no attempt to escape. Her face lies, white and petrified, against his breast.

Ah, what shall a man do when he has a pale, helpless face so near his own, when he sees the fair hair which usually shades the white, gleaming forehead, pushed to one side, and when the eyelids have closed heavily over the roguish glance of the gray eyes?

What shall a man do when red lips he is gazing at grow pale?

Kiss, of course, kiss the fading lips, the closed eyes, the white forehead.

But then the young woman awakes. She throws herself back. She is like a bent spring. And he has to struggle with her with his whole strength to keep her from throwing herself out of the sledge, until finally he forces her, subdued and trembling, into the corner of the sledge.

"See," says Gösta quite calmly to Beerencreutz, "the countess is the third whom Don Juan and I have carried off this winter. But the others hung about my neck with kisses, and she will neither be kissed by me nor dance with me. Can you understand these women, Beerencreutz?"

But when Gösta drove away from the house, when the women screamed and the men swore, when the sleigh-bells rang and the whips cracked, and there was nothing but cries and confusion, the men who guarded the major's wife began to wonder what was happening.

"What is going on?" they thought. "Why are they screaming?"

Suddenly the door is thrown open, and a voice calls to them.

"She is gone. He is driving away with her."

They rush out, running like mad, without waiting to see whether it was the major's wife or some other person who was gone. Luck was with them; and they caught up with a sledge that was racing away. They had to drive a long way and go very fast before they discovered whom they were pursuing.

But Berg and Cousin Christopher went quietly to the door, burst the lock, and opened it for the major's wife.

"You are free," they said.

She came out. They stood straight as ramrods on either side of the door and did not look at her.

"There is a horse and sledge waiting for you outside."

She went out, got into the sledge, and drove away. No one followed her. No one knew where she went.

Down Broby hill Don Juan races towards the frozen surface of lake Löven. The proud courser flies on. Strong, ice-cold breezes whistle by their cheeks. The bells jingle. The stars and the moon are shining. The snow is blue-white and glitters from its own brightness.

Gösta becomes aware that poetical thoughts are awaking in him.

"Beerencreutz," he says, "that is life. Just as Don Juan is speeding away with this young woman, so time speeds away with man. You are necessity, who steers the course. I am desire, who fetters the will, and she, who is helpless, is dragged always deeper and deeper down."

"Don't talk!" cries Beerencreutz. "They are coming after us."

And with a whistling cut of the whip he urges Don Juan to still wilder speed.

There are the wolves, here is the prey," cries Gösta. "Don Juan, my boy, imagine that you are a young elk. Rush through the brushwood, wade through the swamps, leap from the mountain top down into the clear lake, swim across it with bravely lifted head, and vanish, vanish in the thick darkness of the pine forest where lies our salvation! Run, Don Juan! Run like a young elk!"

The speed at which they were driving fills his wild heart with joy. The cries of the pursuers are to him a song af victory. Joy fills his wild heart when he feels the countess's body shake with fright, when he hears her teeth chatter.

Suddenly he loosens the grip of iron with which he has held her. He stands up in the sledge and waves his cap.

"I am Gösta Berling," he cries, "lord of ten thousand kisses and thirteen thousand love-letters! Hurrah for Gösta Berling! Take him who can!"

And in the next instant he whispers in the countess's ear:—

"Is not the pace splendid? Is it not a royal drive? Beyond Löven lies Lake Väner. Beyond Väner lies the sea, everywhere endless stretches of clear blue-black ice, and beyond all a glowing world. The rolling thunder of the ice; shrill cries behind us, shooting stars above us, and the jingling bells in front of us! Forward! Always forward! Have you a mind to try the journey, my beautiful, young lady?"

He had let her go. She pushes him roughly away. The next instant finds him on his knees at her feet.

"I am a wretch, a wretch. You ought not to have angered me, countess. You stood there so proud and fair, and never thought that a cavalier's hand could reach you. Heaven and earth love you. You ought not to add to the burden of those whom heaven and earth scorn."

He draws her hands to him and lifts them to his face.

"If you only knew," he says, "what it means to be an outcast. One does not stop to think what one does. No, indeed not."

At the same moment he notices that she has nothing on her hands. He draws a pair of big fur gloves from his pocket and puts them on her hands.

All at once he has become quite quiet. He sits in the sledge, as far from the young countess as possible.

"You need not be afraid," he says. "Do you not see where we

are driving? You must understand that we do not dare to do you any harm."

She had been almost out of her mind with fright; but now she sees that they have driven across the lake and that Don Juan is struggling up the steep hill to Borg.

They stop the horse before the steps of the castle, and let the young countess get out of the sledge at the door of her own home.

When she is surrounded by attentive servants, she regains her courage and presence of mind.

"Take care of the horse, Andersson!" she says to the coachman. "These gentlemen who have driven me home will be kind enough to come in for a while. The count will soon be here."

"As you wish, countess," says Gösta, and instantly gets out of the sledge. Beerencreutz throws the reins to the groom without a moment's hesitation. And the young countess goes before them and ushers them into the hall with ill-concealed malicious joy.

The countess had expected that the cavaliers would hesitate to accept her proposal to wait until her husband arrived.

They did not know perhaps what a stern and upright man he was. They were not afraid of the interrogation he would subject them to for having seized her by force and compelled her to drive with them. She longed to hear him forbid them ever again to set foot in her house.

She wished to see him call in the servants to point out the cavaliers to them as men who henceforth should never be admitted within the doors of Borg. She wished to hear him express his scorn not only of what they had done to her, but also of their conduct toward the major's wife, their benefactress.

He, who showed her only tenderness and consideration, would rise in just wrath against her presecutors. Love would give fire to his speech. He, who guarded and looked after her as a being of a finer mould than any other, would not tolerate that rough men had fallen upon her like birds of prey upon a sparrow. She was aglow with a thirst for revenge.

Beerencreutz, however, walked undaunted into the dining-

room, and up to the fire, which was always lighted when the
countess came home from a ball.

Gösta remained in the darkness by the door and silently watched
the countess, while the servant removed her outer wraps. As he
sat and looked at the young woman, he rejoiced as he had not done
for many years. He saw so clearly, it was like a revelation, although
he did not understand how he had discovered it, that she had a
most beautiful spirit.

As yet it lay bound and sleeping; but one day it would manifest
itself. He rejoiced at having discovered all the purity and gentleness and innocence which was hidden in her. He was almost ready
to laugh at her, because she looked so angry and stood with flushed
cheeks and frowning brows.

"You do not know how gentle and good you are," he thought.

That side of her which was turned towards the external world
would never do justice to her essential personality, he concluded.
But from that hour, Gösta Berling must become her servant; since
one must serve everything that is beautiful and godlike. Yes, there
was no reason to regret that he had been so violent with her. If she
had not been so afraid, if she had not thrust him from her so angrily,
if he had not felt how her whole being was shaken by his roughness,
he would never have realized what a fine and noble spirit she had.

He could not have believed this before. She had only cared for
dancing and amusement. And she had married that stupid Count
Henrik.

Yes, now he would be her slave until he died; dog and slave as
Captain Bergh used to say, and nothing more.

Gösta Berling sat by the door, and with clasped hands he held
a kind of divine service. Since the day, when for the first time he
had felt the flame of inspiration burn in him, he had not experienced such a feeling of holiness in his soul. He did not move, even
when Count Dohna came in with a crowd of people, who swore
and upbraided the prank the cavaliers had played.

He let Beerencreutz weather the storm. With indolent calm,
hardened by many adventures, the latter stood by the fireplace. He
had put one foot up on the fender, rested his elbow on his knee,

and his chin on his hand, and looked at the excited company.

"What is the meaning of all this?" roared the little count at him.

"The meaning is," he said, "that as long as there are women on earth, there will be fools to dance after their piping."

The young count's face grew red.

"I ask what this means!" he repeated.

"That's also what I want to know," sneered Beerencreutz. "I ask what it means that Henrik Dohna's countess will not dance with Gösta Berling."

The count turned questioningly to his wife.

"I could not, Henrik," she cried. "I could not dance with him or any of them. I thought of the major's wife, whom they allowed to languish in prison."

The little count straightened his stiff body and drew up his old-man's head.

"We cavaliers," said Beerencreutz, "permit no one to insult us. She who will not dance with us, must drive with us. No harm has come to the countess, and there the matter can end."

"No," said the count. "It cannot be concluded in this manner. It is I who am responsible for my wife's actions. I wish to know why Gösta Berling did not turn to me to get satisfaction when my wife had insulted him."

Beerencreutz smiled.

"That's what I want to know," repeated the count.

"One does not ask leave of the fox to take his skin from him," said Beerencreutz.

The count laid his hand on his narrow chest.

"I am known to be a just man," he cried. "I can pass sentence on my servants. Why should I not be able to pass sentence on my wife? The cavaliers have no right to judge her. The punishment they have inflicted on her, I annul. It has never been executed, do you understand, gentlemen. It has never been executed."

The count screamed out the words in a high falsetto. Beerencreutz cast a swift glance about the people who had assembled there. There was not one of those present—Sintram and Daniel Bendix and Dahlberg and all the others who had come in—who did not stand and smile at the way he had outwitted stupid Henrik Dohna.

The young countess did not understand at first. What was it that should be considered as annulled? Her anguish, the violence her tender body had suffered from the cavaliers, the wild song, the wild words, the wild kisses, had they never existed? Had that evening never been, over which the goddess of the gray twilight had reigned?

"But, Henrik—"

"Silence!" he said. And he drew himself up to chide her. "Alas, that you, who are a woman, have wished to set yourself up as a judge of men," he says. "That you, who are my wife, should dare to insult a person whose hand I gladly shake. What is it to you if the cavaliers have had the major's wife put in prison? Were they not right? You can never know how angry a man is in the depth of his soul when he hears of a woman's infidelity. Do you also mean to go that evil way, that you take such a woman's part?

"But, Henrik—"

She wailed like a child, and stretched out her arms to ward off the angry words. She had never before heard such hard words addressed to her. She was so helpless among these hard men, and now her only defender turned against her. Never again would her heart have power to light up the world.

"But, Henrik, it is you who ought to protect me."

Now that it was too late, Gösta Berling paid attention to what was happening. He did not know what to do. He wished to do his utmost to help her. But he did not dare to thrust himself between man and wife.

"Where is Gösta Berling?" asked the count.

"Here," said Gösta. And he made a pitiable attempt to make a jest of the matter. "You were making a speech, I think, count, and I fell asleep. I should like to propose that we drive home and let you all go to bed."

"Gösta Berling, since my countess has refused to dance with you, I command her to kiss your hand and to ask you for forgiveness."

"My dear Count Henrik," says Gösta, smiling, "it is not a fit hand for a young woman to kiss. Yesterday it was red with blood from killing an elk, to-day black with soot from a fight with a charcoal-burner. You have given a noble and high-minded sentence. That is satisfaction enough. Come, Beerencreutz!"

The count barred in his way.

"Do not go," he said. "My wife must obey me. I wish my countess to know where it leads to be self-willed."

Gösta stood helpless. The countess was quite white; but she did not move.

"Go," said the count.

"Henrik, I cannot."

"You can," said the count, harshly. "You can. But I know what you want. You will force me to fight this man, because it is your whim not to like him. Well, if you will not make him amends, I shall do so. You women love to have a man killed for your sake. You have done wrong, but will not atone for it. Therefore I must do it. I shall fight the duel, countess. In a few hours I shall be a bloody corpse."

She looked at him intently. She saw what he was,—stupid, cowardly, puffed up with pride and vanity, the most pitiful of men.

"Be calm," she said. And she became as cold as ice. "I will do it."

But now Gösta Berling was quite beside himself.

"You shall not, countess! No, you shall not! You are only a child, a poor, innocent child, and you would kiss my hand. You have such a beautiful, white soul. I will never again come near you. Oh, never again! I bring death and destruction to everything good and blameless. You shall not touch me. I shudder for you, as fire does for water. You shall not do it!"

He put his hands behind his back.

"It is all the same to me, Herr Berling. Nothing makes any difference to me any more. I ask your forgiveness. I ask you to let me kiss your hand!"

Gösta kept his hands behind his back. He approached the door.

"If you do not accept the amends my wife offers, I must fight you, Gösta Berling, and moreover I shall then be compelled to impose upon her another, severer, punishment."

The countess shrugged her shoulders. "He is mad with fear," she wispered. "Let me do it! It does not matter if I am humbled. After all, it is what you wanted the whole time."

"Did I want that? Do you think I wanted that? Well, if I have no hands to kiss, you must see that I did not want it," he cried.

He ran to the fire and stretched out his hands into it. The flames closed over them, the skin shrivelled up, the nails crackled. But in the same second Beerencreutz seized him by the neck and threw him across the floor. He tripped against a chair and sat down. He sat and almost blushed for such a foolish performance. Would she think that he did it only by way of boasting? To do such a thing in the crowded room must seem like foolish swaggering. There had not been a vestige of danger.

Before he could raise himself, the countess was kneeling beside him. She seized his red, sooty hands and looked at them.

"I will kiss them, kiss them," she cried, "as soon as they are not too painful and sore!" And the tears streamed from her eyes as she saw the blisters rising under the schorched skin.

For he had been like a revelation to her of an unknown glory. That such things could happen here on earth, that they could be done for her! What a man this was, ready for everything, mighty in good as in evil, a man of great deeds, of strong words, of splendid actions! A hero, a hero, made of different stuff from others! Slave of a whim, of the desire of the moment, wild and terrible, but possessor of a tremendous power, fearless of everything.

She had been so depressed the whole evening; she had seen only pain and cruelty and cowardice. Now everything was forgotten. The young countess was glad once again to be alive. The goddess of the twilight was conquered. The young countess saw light and colour enlighten the world.

The same night in the cavaliers' wing they scolded and swore at Gösta Berling. The old men wanted to sleep; but it was impossible. He let them get no rest. It was in vain that they drew the bed-curtains and put out the light. He only talked.

He let them know what an angel the young countess was, and

how he adored her. He would serve her, worship her. He was glad that everyone had forsaken him. He could devote his life to her service. She despised him of course. But he would be satisfied to lie at her feet like a dog.

Had they ever noticed an island out in lake Löven? Had they seen it from the south side, where the rugged cliff rises precipitously from the water? Had they seen it from the north, where it sinks down to the sea in a gentle slope, and where the narrow shoals, covered with great pines, wind their way above the surface of the water, and form the most wonderful little lakes? There, on the steep cliff, where the ruins of an old viking fortress still remain, he would build a palace for the young countess, a palace of marble. Broad steps, at which boats decked with flags should land, would be hewn in the cliff and would lead down to the sea. There would be glowing halls and lofty towers with gilded pinnacles. It should be a suitable dwelling for the young countess. That old wooden house at Borg was not fit for her to enter.

When he had gone on like this for a while, first one snore and then another began to sound behind the yellow-striped curtains. But most of them swore and bewailed his foolishness.

"Friends," he then says solemnly, "I see the green earth covered with the works of man or with the ruins of his work. The pyramids weigh down the earth, the tower of Babel has bored through the sky; the beautiful temples and the gray castles have fallen into ruins. But of all that has been built by human hands, what is it that has not fallen, nor ever shall fall? Ah, friends, throw away the trowel and the mortar! Spread your mason's aprons over your heads and lay you down to build bright palaces of dreams! What has the soul to do with temples of stone and clay? Learn to build everlasting palaces of dreams and visions!"

Thereupon he went laughing to bed.

Shortly afterwards, when the countess heard that the major's wife had been set free, she gave a dinner for the cavaliers.

And this was the beginning of her long friendship with Gösta Berling.

CHAPTER 11 *Ghost-Stories*

Oh, children of the present day!

I have nothing new to tell you, only what is old and almost forgotten. I have legends from the nursery, where the little ones sat on low stools about the old nurse with white hair; or from the log-fire in the cottage, where the labourers sat and talked, while the steam reeked from their wet clothes, and they drew knives from leather sheaths, which they wore around their necks, to spread the butter on thick, soft bread; or from the hall, where old men sat in their rocking-chairs, and, cheered by the steaming toddy, talked of old times.

If a child, who had listened to the old nurse, to the labourers, and to the old men, stood at the window on a winter's evening, and saw any clouds on the horizon they were bound to be the cavaliers; the stars were wax-candles, which were lighted at the old house at Borg; and the spinning-wheel which hummed in the next room was driven by old Ulrika Dillner. For the child's head would be full of the stories of the people of those old days: it adored those people and lived for them.

But if such a child, whose whole mind was filled with stories, should be sent through the dark attic to the store-room for flax or biscuits, then the little feet scurried; then it came flying down the stairs, through the passage to the kitchen. For up there in the dark it could not help thinking of the wicked mill-owner at Fors,—who was in league with the devil.

Sintram's ashes have been resting long in Svartsjö churchyard, but no one believes that his soul has been called to God, as is inscribed on his tombstone.

While he was alive, he was one of those to whose home, on long, rainy Sunday afternoons, a heavy coach, drawn by black horses, used to come. A gentleman richly but plainly dressed gets out of the carriage, and helps, with cards and dice, to while away the long hours which, with their monotony, have driven the master of the house to despair. The game is carried on far into the night; and when the stranger departs at dawn he always leaves behind some baleful parting gift.

As long as Sintram was here on earth he was one of those beings whose coming is made known by spirits. They are heralded by visions. Their carriages roll into the yard, their whips crack, their voices sound on the stairs, the door of the entry is opened and shut. The dogs and people are awakened by the noise, it is so loud: but in reality no one has come; it is only an hallucination which precedes them.

Ugh, those horrible people, whom evil spirits seek out! What kind of a big black dog was it that appeared at Fors in Sintram's time? He had terrible, shining eyes, and a long tongue which dripped blood and hung far out of his panting throat. One day, when the men-servants had been in the kitchen and had eaten their dinner, he had scratched at the kitchen door, and all the maids had screamed with fright; but the biggest and strongest of the men had taken a burning log from the fire, thrown open the door, and hurled it into the dog's gaping mouth.

Then he had fled with terrible howls, flames and smoke had burst from his throat, sparks whirled about him, and his footprints on the path shone like fire.

And was it not dreadful that every time Sintram came home from a journey he had changed his draught-animals? He set out with horses, but when he came home at night his carriage was always drawn by black bulls. The people who lived near the road saw their great black horns against the sky when he drove by, and heard their bellowing. These people were terrified by the line of sparks which the hoofs and wheels struck in the dry gravel.

Yes, the little feet needed to hurry, indeed, to come across the big, dark attic. Think if something awful, if he, whose name one may not mention, should come out of a dark corner! Who can be sure? It was not only to wicked people that he revealed himself.

Had not Ulrika Dillner seen him? Both she and Anna Stjärnhök could vouch that they had seen him.

Friends, you who dance, you who laugh! I beg you most earnestly to dance carefully, to laugh gently, for there can be so much unhappiness if your thin slippers tread on sensitive hearts instead of on hard boards; and your merry silvery laughter can drive a soul to despair.

It was indeed so; the young people's feet had trodden too hard on old Ulrika Dillner, and the young people's laughter had rung too arrogantly in her ears; for there suddenly came over her an irresistible longing for a married woman's titles and dignities. At last she said "yes" to wicked Sintram's long courtship, accompanied him to Fors as his wife; and was thus parted from her old friends at Berga; and no longer attended to the dear old work, or felt the old anxiety for their daily bread.

It was a match which went quickly and gayly. Sintram proposed at Christmas, and in February they were married. That year Anna Stjärnhök was living in Captain Uggla's home. She was a good substitute for old Ulrika, and the latter could leave without compunction, and enjoy the privileges of a married woman.

Without compunction, but not without regret. It was not a pleasant place she had come to; the big, empty rooms were filled with dreadful terrors. As soon as it was dark she began to tremble and be afraid. She almost died of homesickness.

The long Sunday afternoons were the hardest of all. They never came to an end, neither they nor the long succession of torturing thoughts which crawled through her brain.

So it happened one day in March, when Sintram had not come home to dinner, after going to church, that she went into the drawing-room, on the second floor, and sat down at the piano. It was her last consolation. The old piano, with a fluteplayer and a shepherdess painted on the white cover, was her own, it had been in her parents' home. To it she could confide her troubles; it understood her.

But is it not both pitiful and ridiculous? Do you know what she is playing? Only a polka, and she who is so heart-broken!

She cannot play anything else. Before her fingers stiffened holding brooms and carving-knives, she had learned just this one polka. She feels it in her fingers; but she does not know any other piece,— no funeral march, no impassioned sonata, not even a wailing ballad,—only the polka.

She plays it whenever she has anything to confide to the old piano. She plays it when she feels like either weeping or smiling. When she was married she played it, and when she first came to her own home, and also now.

The old chords understand her; she is unhappy, unhappy.

A traveller passing by and hearing the polka being played could well believe that Sintram was having a ball for neighbours and friends, it sounds so gay. It is such a gallant and joyful melody. With it, in the old days, she has introduced a carefree spirit at Berga and has banished hunger; when they heard it everyone had to dance. It burst the fetters of rheumatism about the joints, and lured cavaliers who were eighty years of age to dance. The whole world would gladly dance to that polka, it sounds so gay—but old Ulrika weeps. Sintram has sulky, morose servants about him, and savage animals. She longs for friendly faces and smiling mouths. It is this despairing longing which the lively polka is intended to interpret.

People find it hard to remember that she is Madame Sintram. Everybody calls her Mamselle Dillner. She wants the polka tune to express her sorrow for the vanity which tempted her to seek the privileges of married life.

Old Ulrika plays as if she would break the chords. There is so much to drown; the lamentations of the poor peasants, the curses of overworked cottagers, the sneers of insolent servants, and, above all, the shame,—the shame of being the wife of a bad man.

To those notes Gösta Berling has led young Countess Dohna to the dance. Marianne Sinclair and her many admirers have danced to them, and the major's wife at Ekeby has moved to their measure when Altringer was still alive. She can see them, couple after couple, in their youth and beauty, whirl by. There was a stream of

gayety from them to her, from her to them. It was her polka which
made their cheeks glow, their eyes shine. She is separated from all
that now. Let the polka resound, there are so many memories, so
many tender memories to drown!

She plays to deaden her anguish. Her heart is ready to burst
with terror when she sees the black dog, when she hears the
servants whispering of the black bulls. She plays the polka over
and over again to deaden her anguish.

Then she perceives that her husband has come home. She hears
that he has come into the room and sits down in the rocking-chair.
She knows so well the sound of the rockers creaking on the deal
floor that she does not even look round.

All the time she is playing the rocking continues; soon she no
longer hears the music, only the rocking.

Poor old Ulrika, so tortured, so lonely, so helpless, astray in a
hostile country, without a friend to complain to, without anyone to
console her except a cracked piano, which answers her with a polka.

It is like loud laughter at a funeral, a drinking song in a church.

While the rocking-chair is still rocking she hears suddenly how
the piano is laughing at her sorrows, and she stops in the middle
of a bar. She rises and turns to the rocking-chair.

But the next instant she is lying in a swoon on the floor. It was
not her husband who sat in the rocking-chair, but another,—he, to
whom little children do not dare to give a name, he who would
frighten them to death if they should meet him in the deserted attic.

Can anyone whose mind has been filled with legends ever free
himself from their dominion? The night wind howls outside, the
trees whip the pillars of the balcony with their stiff branches, the
sky arches darkly over the far-stretching hills, and I, who sit alone
in the night and write, with the lamp lighted and the curtains
drawn, I, who am old and ought to be sensible, feel the same
shudder creeping up my back as when I first heard this story; and
I have to keep lifting my eyes from my work to be certain that no
one has come in and hidden himself in that further corner; I have
to look out on the balcony to see if there is not a black head look-

ing over the railing. This fright never leaves me when the night is dark and my solitude complete; and finally, it becomes so overwhelming that I have to throw aside my pen, and get into my bed and draw the blanket up over my eyes.

It was the great, secret wonder of my childhood that Ulrika Dillner survived that afternoon. I should never have done so.

It was fortunate that shortly after this had occured, Anna Stjärnhök happened to drive up to Fors and found Ulrika lying unconscious on the drawing-room floor. She succeeded in helping her to regain consciousness. If it had been me, things would not have gone so well, for I should have been dead already.

I hope, dear friends, that you may never see the tears in old eyes; may you not have to stand helpess when a gray head leans against your breast for support, or when old hands are clasped about yours in a silent prayer. May you never see the old sunk in a sorrow which you cannot comfort.

What is the grief of the young? They have strength, they have hope. But what suffering it is when the old weep; what despair when they, who have always been the support of your young days, sink into helpless repining.

There sat Anna Stjärnhök and listened to old Ulrika, and she saw no way out for her.

The old woman wept and trembled. Her eyes were wild. She talked and talked, sometimes quite incoherently, as if she did not know where she was. The thousand wrinkles which crossed her face were twice as deep as usual, the false curls, which hung down over her eyes, were straightened by her tears, and her whole long, thin body was shaken with sobs.

At last Anna had to put an end to the lamentations. She had made up her mind. She was going to take her back with her to Berga. Of course, she was Sintram's wife, but she could not remain at Fors. He would drive her mad if she stayed with him. Anna Stjärnhök had decided to take old Ulrika away.

Ah, how the poor thing rejoiced, and yet trembled at this decision! But she never would dare to leave her husband and her home. He would perhaps send the big black dog after her.

But Anna Stjärnhök overcame her resistance, partly by jests, partly by threats, and in half an hour she had her beside her in the sledge. Anna was driving herself, and old Disa was in the shafts. The road was wretched, for it was late in March; but it did old Ulrika good to drive once more in the well-known sledge, behind the old horse who had been a faithful servant at Berga almost as long as she had.

As by nature she had a cheerful disposition, she stopped crying by the time they passed Arvidstorp; at Högberg she was already laughing, and when they passed Munkeby she was describing how things were in her youth, when she lived with the countess at Svaneholm.

They drove up a steep and stony road in the lonely and deserted region north of Munkeby. The road sought out all the hills it possibly could find; it crept up to their summits by a process of slowly winding, rushed down them in a steep descent, and hurried across the level valley to find a new hill to climb over.

They were just driving down Vestratorp hill, when old Ulrika stopped short in what she was saying, and seized Anna by the arm. She was staring at a big black dog at the roadside.

"Look!" she said.

The dog set off into the wood. Anna did not see much of him.

"Drive on," said Ulrika; "drive as fast as you can! Now Sintram will hear that I have gone."

Anna tried to overcome her fear by laughing at her, but she stuck to her idea.

"We shall soon hear his sleigh-bells, you will see. We shall hear them before we reach the top of the next hill."

And when Disa drew breath for a second at the top of Elofs hill sleigh-bells could be heard behind them.

Old Ulrika became quite mad with fright. She trembled, sobbed, and wailed as she had done in the drawing-room at Fors. Anna tried to urge Disa on, but she only turned her head and gave her a glance of unspeakable surprise. Did she think that Disa had forgotten when it was time to trot and when it was time to walk? Did she want to teach her how to drag a sledge, to teach her, who had known every stone, every bridge, every gate, every hill for more than twenty years?

All this went on while the sleigh-bells were coming nearer.

"It is he, it is he! I know his bells," wails old Ulrika.

The sound comes ever nearer. Sometimes it seems so unnaturally loud that Anna turns to see if Sintram's horse has not got his head in her sledge; sometimes it dies away. They hear it now on the right, now on the left of the road, but they see no one. It is as if the jingling of the bells were alone pursuing them.

What they hear now, is just the same as is heard at night on going home from a party. These bells ring out a tune; they sing, speak, answer. The woods echo with their sound.

Anna Stjärnhök almost wishes that their pursuer would come near enough for her to see Sintram himself and his red horse. The dreadful sleigh-bells anger her.

"Those bells torture me," she says.

The word is taken up by the bells. "Torture me," they ring. "Torture me, torture, torture me," they sing to all possible tunes.

It was not so long ago that she had driven the same way, hunted by wolves. She had seen their white teeth, in the darkness, gleam in their gaping mouths; she had thought that her body would soon be torn to pieces by the wild beasts of the forest; but then she had not been afraid. She had never lived through a more glorious night. The horse who had drawn the sledge had been strong and beautiful, and the man who shared the adventure with her had also been strong and beautiful.

Ah, this old horse, this old, helpless, trembling companion. She feels so powerless that she longs to cry. She cannot escape from those terrible, irritating bells.

So she stops and gets out of the sledge. There must be an end to it all. Why should she run away as if she were afraid of that wicked, contemptible wretch?

At last she sees a horse's head come out of the deepening twilight, and after the head a whole horse, a whole sledge, and in the sledge sits Sintram himself.

She notices, however, that it is not as if they had come along the road—this sledge, and this horse, and their driver—but rather as if they had been conjured up just there before her eyes, and had come forward out of the twilight as soon as they had materialized.

Anna threw the reins to Ulrika and went to meet Sintram.

He stops the horse.

"Well, well," he says; "what a piece of luck! Dear Miss Stjärn-hök; let me move my companion over to your sledge. He is going to Berga to-night, and I am in a hurry to get home."

"Where is your companion?"

Sintram lifts his blanket, and shows Anna a man who is lying asleep on the bottom of the sledge. "He is a little drunk," he says; "but what does that matter? He will sleep. Moreover, it's an old acquaintance; it is Gösta Berling."

Anna shudders.

"Well, I will tell you," continues Sintram, "that she who forsakes the man she loves sells him to the devil. That was the way I got into his claws. People think that they are acting for the best, of course; to renounce is virtuous, and to love is evil."

"What do you mean? What are you talking about?" asks Anna, quite disturbed.

"I mean that you should not have let Gösta Berling go from you, Miss Anna."

"It was God's will."

"Yes, yes, that's the way it is; to renounce is virtuous and to love is evil. The good God does not like to see people happy. He sends wolves after them. But if it was not God who did it, Miss Anna? Could it not just as well have been I who called my little gray lambs from the Dovre mountains to hunt the young man and the young girl? Think, if it was I who sent the wolves, because I did not wish to lose one of my own! Think, if it was not God who did it!"

"You must not tempt me to doubt that," says Anna, in a weak voice, "for then I am lost."

"Look here," says Sintram, and bends down over the sleeping Gösta Berling; "look at his little finger. That little sore never heals. We took the blood there when he signed the contract. He is mine.

There is a peculiar power in blood. He is mine, and it is only love which can free him; but if I am allowed to keep him he will be a fine thing."

Anna Stjärnhök struggles and struggles to shake off the fascination which has seized her. It is all madness, madness. No one can swear away his soul to the odious tempter. But she has no power over her thoughts; the twilight lies so heavy over her, the woods stand so dark and silent. She cannot escape the dreadful terror of the moment.

"You think, perhaps," continues Sintram, "that there is not much left in him to ruin. But don't think that! Has he ground down the peasants, has he deceived poor friends, has he cheated at cards? Has he, Miss Anna, has he been a married woman's lover?"

"I think you are the devil himself!"

"Let us exchange. You take Gösta Berling, take him and marry him. Keep him, and give them at Berga the money. I surrender him to you, and you know that he is mine. Think that it was not God who sent the wolves after you the other night, and let us exchange!"

"What do you want as compensation?"

Sintram grinned.

"I—what do I want? Oh, I am satisfied with little. I only want that old woman there in your sledge, Miss Anna."

"Satan, tempter," cries Anna, "leave me! Shall I betray an old friend who relies on me? Shall I leave her to you, that you may torture her to madness?"

"There, there, there; quietly, Miss Anna! Think what you are doing! Here is a fine young man, and there an old, worn-out woman. One of them I must have. Which of them will you let me keep?"

Anna Stjärnhök laughed wildly.

"Do you think that we can stand here and exchange souls as they exchange horses at the market at Broby?"

"That's right, yes. But if you wish, we can consider it from another point of view. We shall think of the honour of the Stjärnhöks."

Thereupon he begins to call in a loud voice to his wife, who is sitting in Anna's sledge; and, to the girl's unspeakable horror, she obeys the summons instantly, gets out of the sledge, and comes, trembling and shaking, to them.

"See, see, see!—such an obedient wife," says Sintram. "You cannot prevent her coming when her husband calls. Now, I shall lift Gösta out of my sledge and leave him here,—leave him for *good*, Miss Anna. Whoever wants to can pick him up."

He bends down to lift Gösta up; but Anna leans forward, fixes him with her eyes, and hisses like an angry animal:—

"In God's name, go home! Do you not know who is sitting in the rocking-chair in the drawing-room waiting for you? Do you dare to let him wait?"

It was for Anna almost the climax of the horrors of the day to see how these words affect him. He pulls the reins, turns, and drives homewards, urging the horse to gallop down the dreadful hill, with blows and wild cries, while a long line of sparks crackle under the runners and hoofs in the thin March snow.

Anna Stjärnhök and Ulrika Dillner stand alone in the road, but they do not say a word. Ulrika trembles before Anna's wild eyes, and Anna has nothing to say to the poor old thing, for whose sake she has sacrificed her beloved.

She would have liked to weep, to rave, to roll on the ground and strew snow and sand on her head.

Formerly, she had known the sweetness of renunciation, now she knew its bitterness. What was it to sacrifice her love compared with sacrificing her beloved's soul? They drove on to Berga in the same silence: but when they arrived, and the hall-door was opened, Anna Stjärnhök fainted for the first and only time in her life. There sat both Sintram and Gösta Berling, and chatted quietly. The tray with toddy had been brought in; they had been there at least an hour.

Anna Stjärnhök fainted, but old Ulrika remained calm. She had noticed that all was not well with him who had pursued them on the road.

Afterwards the captain and his wife came to an arrangement

with Sintram that old Ulrika should be allowed to stay at Berga. He agreed good-naturedly.

"He did not want to drive her mad," he said.

I do not ask anyone to believe these old stories. They cannot be anything but lies and fiction. But the anguish which sways the heart backwards and forwards, until it groans as the floor boards in Sintram's room groaned under the swaying rockers; and the questions which ring in the ears, as the sleigh-bells rang for Anna Stjärnhök in the lonely forest,—when will they be merely lies and fiction?

Oh, that this could be so!

CHAPTER 12 *Ebba Dohna's Story*

The fair headland on the eastern shore of lake Löven, around which the bays glide with lapping waves, the proud headland on which the manor of Borg stands, beware of approaching it.

Löven never looks more glorious than from its crown.

No one can know how lovely is the lake of my dreams, until from the headland of Borg, he has seen the morning mist glide away from its smooth surface; until, from the windows of the little blue cabinet, where so many memories dwell, he has seen it reflect a pink sunset.

But I still say, do not go there!

For perhaps you will be seized with a desire to remain in the mournful halls of the old manor; perhaps you will make yourself the owner of those fair lands; and if you are young, rich, and happy, you will make your home there with a young wife.

No, it is better never to see the beautiful headland, for at Borg no one can live and be happy. No matter how rich, how happy you may be, when you move in, those old tear-drenched floors would soon drink *your* tears as well, and those walls, which could re-echo so many plaintive sounds, would also gather *your* sighs.

An implacable fate is connected with this lovely spot. It is as if misfortune were buried there, but finding no rest in its grave, continually rises from it to terrify the living. If I were master of Borg I would search the grounds, both in the park and under the cellar floor in the house, and in the fertile soil out in the meadows, until I had found the witch's worm-eaten corpse, and then I would have her buried in consecrated ground in the Svartsjö churchyard. And at the burial I would not stint the ringer's pay, but let the bells sound long and loud over her; and to the clergyman and the sexton I would send rich gifts, that with redoubled strength, with speech and song, they might consecrate her to ever-lasting rest.

Or, if that did not help, some stormy night I would set fire to the wooden walls, and let it destroy everything; so that no one might be tempted any more to live in the home of misfortune. Afterwards no one should be allowed to approach that doomed spot; only the black jackdaws of the church-tower should build in the great chimney, which, blackened and gruesome, would rise above the deserted foundations.

Still, I should certainly mourn when I saw the flames close over the roof, when thick smoke, reddened by the fire and flecked with sparks, rolled out from the old manor-house. In the crackling and the roaring I should fancy I heard the complaint of homeless memories; on the blue points of the flames I should see disturbed spirits floating. I should think how sorrow beautifies, how misfortune adorns; and I should weep as if a temple to the old gods had been condemned to destruction.

But why croak of unhappiness? As yet Borg stands resplendent on the crown of the headland; it is shaded by its park of great pines, and the snow-covered fields glitter in the burning sun of March; as yet, the gay laughter of young countess Elizabeth is still heard within those walls.

Every Sunday she goes to church at Svartsjö, which lies near Borg, and invites a few friends for dinner. The judge and his family from Munkerud used to come, and the Ugglas from Berga, and even Sintram. If Gösta Berling happens to be in Svartsjö, wandering over the ice of lake Löven, she invites him too. Why should she not invite Gösta Berling?

She probably does not know that the gossips are beginning to whisper that Gösta comes over very often to the east shore to see her. Perhaps he also comes to drink and play cards with Sintram; but no one thinks so much of that; everyone knows that his body is of steel; but it is another matter with his heart. No one believes that he can see a pair of shining eyes, and fair hair which curls about a white brow, without falling in love.

The young countess is good to him. But there is nothing strange

in that; she is good to all. She takes ragged beggar children on
her knee, and when she drives by some poor old creature on the
highroad she has the coachman stop, and takes the poor wanderer
into her sledge.

Gösta used to sit in the little blue cabinet, where there is such a
glorious view over the lake, and read poetry to her. There can be
no harm in that. He does not forget that she is a countess, and he a
homeless adventurer; and it is good for him to be with someone
whom he venerates and looks upon as holy. He could just as well
be in love with the Queen of Sheba as with her.

He only asks to be allowed to wait on her as a page waits on his
noble mistress; to fasten her skates, to hold her skeins, to steer
her sled. There cannot be any question of love between them;
he is just the man to find his happiness in a romantic, innocent
adoration.

The young count is silent and serious, and Gösta is playfully gay.
He is just such a companion as the young countess likes. No one
who sees her, imagines that she is hiding a forbidden love. She
thinks of dancing,—of dancing and merrymaking. She would like
the earth to be quite flat, without stones, without hills or seas, so
that she could dance everywhere. From the cradle to the grave she
would like to dance in her small, thin-soled, satin slippers.

But rumour is not very merciful to young women.

When the guests come to dinner at Borg, after the meal, the men
generally go into the count's room to sleep and smoke; the old
ladies sink down in the easy-chairs in the drawing-room, and lean
their venerable heads against the high backs; but the countess and
Anna Stjärnhök go into the blue cabinet and exchange endless
confidences.

The Sunday after the one on which Anna Stjärnhök took Ulrika
Dillner back to Berga, they are sitting there again.

No one on earth is so unhappy as the young girl. All her gayety
has departed, and gone is the joyful defiance which she showed
everything and everybody who wished to come too near her.

Everything which had happened to her that day has sunk back
into the twilight out of which it was conjured forth; she has only

one distinct impression left,—yes, one, which is poisoning her soul.

"If it really was not God who did it," she used to whisper to herself. "If it was not God, who sent the wolves?"

She asks for a sign, she longs for a miracle. She searches heaven and earth. But she sees no finger stretched from the sky to point out her way.

As she sits now opposite the countess in the blue cabinet, her eyes fall on a little bunch of hepaticas which the countess holds in her white hand. Like a bolt it strikes her that she knows where the flowers have grown, that she knows who has picked them.

She does not need to ask. Where else in the whole countryside do hepaticas bloom in the beginning of April, except in the birch grove which lies on the slopes of Ekeby?

She stares and stares at the little blue stars; those happy flowers which possess all hearts; those little prophets who, beautiful in themselves, are also glorified by the splendour of all the beauty which they foretell. And as she watches them a storm of anger rises in her soul, rumbling like thunder, and blinding like lightning. "By what right," she thinks, "does Countess Dohna hold this bunch of hepaticas, picked by the shore at Ekeby?"

They were all tempters: Sintram, the countess, everybody wanted to allure Gösta Berling to what was evil. But she would protect him; she would protect him against all. Even if it should cost her heart's blood, she would do it.

She thinks that she must see those flowers torn out of the countess's hand, and thrown aside, trampled, crushed, before she leaves the little blue cabinet.

She thinks that, and begins to struggle with the little blue stars. Out in the drawing-room the old ladies lean their venerable heads against the chair-backs and suspect nothing; the men smoke their pipes in calm and quiet in the count's room; peace is everywhere; only in the little blue cabinet rages a terrible struggle.

Ah, how well they do, who keep their hands from the sword, who understand how to wait quietly, how to lay their hearts to rest and let God direct! The restless heart always goes astray. Evil always increases evil.

But Anna Stjärnhök believes that at last she has seen a finger in the sky.

"Anna," says the countess, "tell me a story!"

"About what?"

"Oh," says the countess, and caresses the flowers with her white hand. "Don't you know something about love, something about loving?"

"No, I know nothing of love."

"That's what you say! But is there not a place here which is called Ekeby,—a place full of cavaliers?"

"Yes," says Anna, "there is a place which is called Ekeby, and there are men there who suck the marrow out of the land, who make us incapable of serious work, who ruin our youth, and lead our geniuses astray. Do you want to hear about them? Do you want to hear love-stories about them?"

"Yes. I like the cavaliers."

So Anna Stjärnhök speaks,—speaks in short strophes, like those of an old hymn-book; for she is nearly choking with tempestuous emotions. Suppressed suffering trembles in each word, and the countess was both frightened and interested to hear her.

"What is a cavalier's love, what is a cavalier's faith?—one sweet-heart to-day, another to-morrow, one in the east, another in the west. Nothing is too high for him, nothing too low; one day a count's daughter, the next day a beggar girl. Nothing on earth is so capacious as his heart. But alas, alas for her who loves a cavalier. She must look for him where he lies drunk at the wayside. She must silently look on while at the card-table he gambols away the home of her childhood. She must put up with him doting on other women. Oh, Elizabeth, if a cavalier asks an honourable woman for a dance she ought to refuse to dance with him; if he gives her a bunch of flowers she ought to throw the flowers on the ground and trample on them; if she loves him she ought rather to die than to marry him. There was one among the cavaliers who was an un-frocked priest; he was deprived of his office because of drunken-ness. He was drunk in the church. He drank up the communion wine. Have you ever heard of him?"

"No."

"After he had been dismissed from his office he wandered about the country as a beggar. He drank like a madman. He would steal to get brandy."

"What is his name?"

"He is no longer at Ekeby. The major's wife took him in hand; she gave him clothes, and persuaded your mother-in-law, Countess Dohna, to employ him as young count Henrik's, your husband's, tutor."

An unfrocked priest!"

"Oh, he was a young, powerful man, of good intelligence. There was no harm in him, if he only did not drink. Countess Märta was not particular. It amused her to quarrel with the neighbouring clergy. Still, she ordered him to say nothing of his past life to her children. Otherwise, her son would have lost his respect for him, and her daughter would not have been able to tolerate him, for she was a saint.

"So he came here to Borg. He always sat just inside the door, on the very edge of his chair, never said a word at table, and fled into the park when any visitors came.

"But there along the lonely paths he used to meet young Ebba Dohna. She did not care for the noisy feasts which resounded in the halls at Borg after the countess became a widow. She was so gentle, so shy. Although seventeen, she was still only an impressionable child; but she was very lovely, with her brown eyes, and the faint, delicate colour in her cheeks. Her thin, slender body bent slightly forward. Her little hand would creep into yours with a shy pressure. Her little mouth was very silent and extremely serious. Ah, her voice, her sweet little voice, which pronounced the words so slowly and so well, but never rang with the freshness and warmth of youth,—its languid cadence resembled a weary musician's last chord.

"She was not like others. Her step so light, so soft, as if she were a frightened fugitive. She kept her eyelids lowered in order not to be disturbed in her contemplation of the beauty of her inner visions. Her spirit had turned away from the world when she was but a child.

"When she was little her grandmother used to tell her stories; and one evening they both sat by the fire; but the stories had come to an end. But still the little girl's hand lay on the old woman's dress, and she gently stroked the silk,—that jolly material which sounded like a little bird. And this stroking was her entreaty, for she was one of those children who never ask by using words.

"Then the old lady began to tell her of a little child in the land of Judah; of a little child who was born to become a great King. The angels had filled the earth with songs of praise when he was born. The kings of the East came, guided by the star of heaven, and gave him gold and incense; and old men and women foretold his glory. This child grew up to possess greater beauty and wisdom than all other children. When he was only twelve years old, his wisdom was greater than that of the chief-priests and the scribes.

"Then the old woman told her of the most beautiful thing the earth has ever seen: of that child's life while he remained among men,—those wicked men who would not acknowledge him as their King.

"She told her how the child became a man, but that the glory still surrounded him.

"Everything on the earth served him and loved him, except mankind. The fishes let themselves be caught in his net, bread filled his baskets, water changed itself to wine when he wished it.

"But the people gave the great King no golden crown, no shining throne. He had no bowing courtiers about him. They let him go among them like a beggar.

"Nevertheless the great King was so good to them! He cured their sicknesses, restored the sight of the blind, and waked the dead.

"'But,' said the grandmother, 'the people would not have the great King for their Lord.

"'They sent their soldiers against him, and took him prisoner; in mockery, they dressed him in a silken cloak, with crown and sceptre; and made him go out to the place of execution, bearing a heavy cross. Oh, my child, the good King loved the high mountains. At night he used to climb them to talk with those who dwelt in heaven, and by day he liked to sit on the mountain-side and talk to the listening people. But now they led him up a hill to crucify him. They drove nails through his hands and feet, and hung the good King on a cross, as if he had been a robber or a malefactor.

"'And the people mocked at him. Only his mother and his friends wept, that he should die before he had been a King.

"'Oh, how the dead things mourned his death!

"'The sun lost its light, and the mountains trembled; the curtain in the temple was rent asunder, and the graves opened, that the dead might rise up and show their grief.'

"The little one lay with her head on her grandmother's knee, and sobbed as if her heart would break.

"'Do not weep, little one; the good King rose from his grave and went up to his Father in heaven.'

"'Grandmother,' sobbed the poor little thing, 'did he ever get any kingdom?'

"'He sits on God's right hand in heaven.'

"But that did not comfort her. She wept helplessly and unrestrainedly, as only a child can weep.

"'Why were they so cruel to him? Why were they allowed to be so cruel to him?'

"Her grandmother was almost frightened at her overwhelming sorrow.

"Oh, grandmother, do say that you have not told the true story! Say that it did not end so! Say that they were not so cruel to the good King! Say that he got a kingdom on earth!'

"She threw her arms around the old woman and beseeched her while the tears streamed down her cheeks.

"'Child, child,' said her grandmother, to console her. There are some who believe that he will come again. Then he will have power over the earth and will rule the world. The beautiful earth will be a glorious kingdom. It shall last a thousand years. Then the fierce animals will become gentle; little children will play by the viper's nest, and bears and cows will eat together. No creature shall injure or destroy another; the spears shall be beaten into pruninghooks, and the swords into plowshares. And everything shall be joy and happiness, for the good will possess the earth.'

"Then the little one's face brightened in spite of her tears.

"'Will the good King then get a throne, grandmother?'

"'A throne of gold.'

"'And servants, and courtiers, and a golden crown?'

"'Yes.'

"'Will he come soon, grandmother?'

"'No one knows when he will come.'

"'May I sit on a stool at his feet?'

"'You may.'

"'Grandmother, I am so happy,' says the little one.

"Evening after evening, through many winters, they both sat by the fire and talked of the good King and his kingdom. The little one dreamed both by night and by day of the kingdom which should last a thousand years. She never wearied of adorning it with everything beautiful which she could think of.

"Ebba Dohna never dared to speak of it to anyone; but from that evening she only lived for the Lord's kingdom, and to await his coming.

"When the evening sunset glow threw open the gates of the western sky, she wondered if he would ever appear there, glowing with a mild splendour, followed by a host of millions of angels, and march by her, allowing her to touch the hem of his garment.

"She often thought, too, of those pious women who had hung a veil over their heads, and never lifted their eyes from the ground, but shut themselves in the calm of gray cloisters, in the darkness of little cells, in order always to contemplate the radiant visions which rise from the night of the soul.

"This was how she had grown up; this was what she was like when she and the new tutor met in the lonely paths of the park.

"I will not speak more harshly of him than I must. I wish to believe that he loved that child, who soon chose him for her companion in her lonely wanderings. I think that his soul regained her wings when he walked by the side of that quiet girl, who had never confided in any other. I think that he felt himself a child again, good, gentle, virtuous.

"But if he really loved her, why did he not remember that he could not give her a worse gift than his love? He who was one of the world's outcasts, what did he want, what did he think of when he walked beside the count's daughter? What did the unfrocked priest think when she confided to him her gentle dreams? What did he want, he who had been a drunkard, and would be one again when he got the chance, of a girl who dreamed of a bridegroom in heaven? Why did he not go far, far away from her? Would it not have been better for him to wander about the land begging and stealing, than to walk under the silent pines and again be good, gentle, and virtuous, when it could not change the life he had led, nor make it right that Ebba Dohna should love him?

"Do not think that he looked like a drunkard, with livid cheeks and red eyes. He was always a fine-looking man, handsome and unimpaired in body and mind. He had the bearing of a king and a body of steel, which was not injured by the wildest way of living."

"Is he still living?" asks the countess.

"Oh, no, he must be dead now. All that happened so long ago."

There is something in Anna Stjärnhök which begins to tremble at what she is doing. She begins to think that she will never tell the countess who the man is of whom she speaks; that she will let her believe that he is dead.

"At that time he was still young"; and she begins her story again. "Once again he was animated by the joy of living. He had the gift of eloquence, and a fiery, impulsive heart.

"One evening he spoke to Ebba Dohna of love. She did not answer; she only told him what her grandmother had told her that winter evening, and described to him the land of her dreams. Then she exacted a promise from him. She made him swear that he would be a preacher of the word of God; one of those who prepare the way for the Lord, so that his coming may be hastened.

"What could he do? He was an unfrocked priest, and no way was so firmly barred against him as that on which she wanted him to embark. But he did not dare to tell her the truth. He did not have the heart to grieve that gentle child whom he loved. He promised to do everything she wished.

"After that, few words were needed. It went without saying, that some day she would be his wife. It was not a love of kisses and caresses. He hardly dared come near her. She was as sensitive as a fragile flower. But her brown eyes were sometimes raised from the ground to seek his. On moonlit evenings, when they sat on the veranda, she would creep close to him, and then he would kiss her hair without her noticing it.

"But you understand that his sin consisted in his forgetting both the past and the future. It did not matter that he could forget that he was poor and humble; but he ought always to have remembered that a day must come when in her soul love would rise against love, earth against heaven; when she would be obliged to choose between him and the resplendent Lord of the millennial kingdom. And she was not one who could endure such a struggle.

"A summer went by, autumn and winter passed. When the spring came, and the ice melted, Ebba Dohna fell ill. It was thawing in the valleys; streams were running down all the hills, the ice was unsafe, the roads almost impassable both for sledges and carts.

"Countess Dohna wanted to get a doctor from Karlstad; there was none nearer. But all her orders were in vain. Neither by entreaties nor threats could she induce a servant to go. She threw herself on her knees before the coachman, but he refused. She went into hysterics of grief over her daughter—Countess Märta always went to extremes, both in sorrow and in joy.

"Ebba Dohna had pneumonia, and her life was in danger; but no doctor could be got.

"Then the tutor drove to Karlstad. To make that journey in the condition the roads were in, was to risk his life; but he did it. It took him over ice that bent as he passed over it, and through break-neck freshets. Sometimes he had to cut steps for the horse in the ice; sometimes he had to drag him out of the deep clay in the road. It was said that the doctor refused to go with him, and that he forced the doctor to accompany him at the point of a pistol.

"When he came back the countess was ready to throw herself at his feet. 'Take everything!' she said. 'Say what you want, what you desire,—my daughter, my lands, my money!'

"'Your daughter,' answered the tutor."

Anna Stjärnhök suddenly stops.

"Well, what then, what then?" asks Countess Elizabeth.

"That's enough for the present," answers Anna, for she is one of those unhappy people who live in the anguish of doubt. She has felt it a whole week. She does not know what she wants. What seems right to her one moment appears wrong the next. Now she wishes that she had never begun this story.

"I begin to think that you want to deceive me, Anna. Do you not understand that I *must* hear the end of this story?"

"There is not much more to tell.—The hour of conflict had come for Ebba Dohna. Love raised itself against love, earth against heaven.

"Countess Märta told her of the wonderful journey the young man had made for her sake; and added, that, as a reward, she had promised that Ebba would marry him.

"Ebba was so much better that she lay dressed on a sofa. She was weak and pale, and even more silent than usual.

"When she heard those words she lifted her brown eyes reproachfully to her mother, and said to her:—

"'Mamma, have you given me to an unfrocked priest, to one who has forfeited his right to serve God, to a man who has been a thief, and a beggar?'

"'But, child, who has told you that? I thought you knew nothing about it.'

"'I heard your guests speaking of him the day I was taken ill.'

"'But, child, remember that he has saved your life!'

"'I remember that he has deceived me. He should have told me who he was.'

"'He says that you love him.'

"'I have done so. I cannot love anyone who has deceived me.'

"'How has he deceived you?'

"'You would not understand, mamma.'

"She did not wish to speak to her mother of the kingdom of her dreams, which her beloved was to have helped her to realize.

"'Ebba,' said the countess, 'if you love him you must not ask what he has been, you must marry him. The husband of a Countess Dohna will be rich enough, powerful enough, to excuse all the follies of his youth.'

"'I care nothing for his youthful follies, mamma; it is because he can never be what I want him to be that I cannot marry him.'

"Ebba, remember that I have given him my promise!'

"The girl became as pale as death.

"'Mamma, I tell you that if you marry me to him you part me from God.'

"'I have decided to act for your happiness,' says the countess. 'I am certain that you will be happy with this man. You have already succeeded in making a saint of him. I have decided to overlook the claims of birth and to forget that he is poor and despised, in order to give you a chance to raise him. I feel that I am doing right. You know that I scorn all old prejudices.'

"The young girl lay quiet on her sofa for a while after the countess had left her. She was fighting her battle. Earth raised itself against heaven, love against love; but her childhood's love won the victory. As she lay there on the sofa, she saw the western sky glow in a magnificent sunset. She thought that it was a greeting from the good King; and as she could not be faithful to him if she lived, she decided to die. There was nothing else for her to do, since her mother wished her to belong to one who never could be the good King's servant.

"She went over to the window, opened it, and let the cold, damp air of twilight chill her poor, weak body.

"It was easily done. The illness was certain to begin again, and it did.

"It is only I who know that she sought death, Elizabeth. I found her at the window. I heard her delirium. She liked to have me near her during those last days.

"It was I who saw her die; who saw how one evening she stretched out her arms towards the glowing west, and died, smiling, as if she had seen someone advance out of the glory of the sunset to meet her. It was also I who had to take her last greeting to the man she loved. I was to ask him to forgive her, that she could not be his wife. The good King would not permit it.

"But I have never dared to say to that man that he was her murderer. I have not dared to lay the burden of such torment on his shoulders. And yet he who won her love by lies, was he not her murderer? Wasn't he, Elizabeth?"

Countess Dohna had long ago stopped caressing the blue flowers. Now she rises, and the bouquet falls to the floor.

"Anna, you are deceiving me. You say that the story is old, and that the man has been dead a long time. But I know that it is scarcely five years since Ebba Dohna died, and you say that you yourself were there through it all. You are not old. Tell me who the man is!"

Anna Stjärnhök begins to laugh.

"You wanted a love-story. Now you have had one which has cost both tears and pain."

"Do you mean that you have lied?"

"Nothing but romance and lies, the whole thing!"

"You are too bad, Anna."

"Maybe. I am not so happy, either.—But the ladies are awake, and the men are coming into the drawing-room. Let us join them!"

On the threshold she is stopped by Gösta Berling, who is looking for the young ladies.

"You must have patience with me," he says, laughing. "I shall only torment you for ten minutes: but you must hear my verses."

He tells them that in the night he had had a dream more vivid than ever before: he had dreamt that he had written verse. He, whom the world called "poet," although he had always been undeserving of the title, had got up in the middle of the night, and, half asleep, half awake, had begun to write. It was a whole poem, which he had found the next morning on his writing-table. He could never have believed it of himself. Now the ladies must hear it.

And he reads;—

"The moon rose, and with her came the sweetest hour of the day.
From the clear, pale-blue, lofty vault
She flooded the leafy veranda with her light.
On the broad steps we were sitting, both old and young,
Silent at first to let the emotions sing
The heart's old song in that tender hour.

"From the mignonette rose a sweet perfume,
And from dark thickets shadows crept over the dewy grass.
Oh, who can be safe from emotion
When the night's shadows play, when the mignonette sheds its
   heavy perfume?

"The last faded petal dropped from the rose,
Although the offering was not sought by the wind.
So—we thought—will we give up our life,
Vanish into space like a sound,
Like autumn's yellowed leaf go without a moan.
Death is the reward of life; may we meet it quietly,
Just as a rose lets its last faded petal fall.

"On its fluttering wing a bat flew by us,
Flew and was seen, wherever the moon shone;
Then the question arose in our oppressed hearts,—

"The question which none can answer,
The question, heavy as sorrow, old as pain:
'Oh, whither go we, what paths shall we wander
When we no longer walk on earth's green pastures?'
Is there no one to show our spirits the way?
Easier were it to show a way to the bat who fluttered by us.

"She laid her head on my shoulder, her soft hair,
She, who loved me, and whispered softly:
'Think not that souls fly to far-distant places;
When I am dead, think not that I am far away.

Into my beloved's soul my homeless spirit will glide
And I will come and live in thee.'

"Oh what anguish! With sorrow my heart will break.
Was she to die, die soon? Was this night to be her last?
Did I press my last kiss on my beloved's waving hair?

"Years have gone by since then. I still sit many times
In the old place, when the night is dark and silent.
But I tremble when the moon shines on the leafy veranda,
For her who alone knows how often I kissed my darling there,
For her who blended her quivering light with my tears,
Which fell on my darling's hair.
Alas, for memory's pain! Oh, 'tis the grief of my poor, sinful
  soul
That it should be her home! What punishment may he not
  await
Who has bound to himself a soul so pure, so innocent."

"Gösta," says Anna, jestingly, while her throat contracts with
pain, "people say that you have lived more poems than others
have written, who have not done anything else all their lives; but
do you know, you will do best to compose poems in your own
way. Those were nocturnal imaginings, as you well know."

"You are not kind."

"To come and read such a thing, on death and suffering—you
ought to be ashamed!"

Gösta is not listening to her. His eyes are fixed on the young
countess. She sits quite stiff, motionless as a statue. He thinks she
is going to faint.

But with infinite difficulty her lips form one word.

"Go!" she says.

"Who shall go? Shall *I* go?"

"The priest shall go," she stammers out.

"Elizabeth, be silent!"

"The drunken priest shall leave my house!"

"Anna, Anna," Gösta asks, "what does she mean?"

"You had better go, Gösta."

"Why shall I go? What does all this mean?"

"Anna," says Countess Elizabeth, "tell him, tell him!"

"No countess, tell him yourself!"

The countess sets her teeth, and masters her emotion.

"Herr Berling," she says, and goes up to him, "you have a wonderful power of making people forget who you are. I did not know it till to-day. I have just heard the story of Ebba Dohna's death, and that it was the discovery that she loved one who was unworthy, that killed her. Your poem has made me understand that you are that man. I cannot understand how anyone with your antecedents can show himself in the presence of an honourable woman. I cannot understand it, Herr Berling. Do I speak plainly enough?"

"You do, Countess. I will only say one word in my defence. I was convinced, all the time I was convinced that you knew everything about me. I have never tried to hide anything; but it is not so pleasant to cry the bitterest sorrow of one's life on the highways."

He goes.

And in the same instant Countess Dohna sets her little foot on the bunch of blue stars.

"You have now done what I wished," says Anna Stjärnhök sternly to the countess; "but it is also the end of our friendship. You need not think that I can forgive you for having been cruel to him. You have turned him away, scorned, and wounded him, and I—I will follow him into captivity; to the scaffold if need be. I will watch over him, protect him. You have done what I wished, but I shall never forgive you."

"But Anna, Anna!"

"Because I told you all that, do you think that I did it joyfully? Have I not sat here and bit by bit torn my heart out of my breast?"

"Why did you do it?"

"Why? Because I did not wish—that he should be a married woman's lover.

CHAPTER 13 *Mamselle Marie*

There is a buzzing over my head. It must be a bumble-bee. And such a perfume! As true as I am alive, it is sweet marjoram and lavender and hawthorn and lilacs and Easter lilies. It is glorious to smell it on a gray autumn evening in the midst of the town. I have only to think of that blessed little corner of the earth to become aware of humming and to smell fragrance around me; and I am transported to a little square rose-garden, filled with flowers and protected by a privet hedge. In the corners are lilac arbours with small wooden benches, and round about the flower-beds, which are heart-shaped and star-shaped, wind narrow paths strewed with white sea-sand. On three sides the rose-garden is enclosed by the dark and silent forest.

On the fourth side lies a little gray cottage.

The rose-garden of which I am thinking, was owned, sixty years ago, by an old Madame Moreus in Svartsjö, who made her living by knitting blankets for the peasants, and by cooking their feasts.

Old Madame Moreus was, in her day, the possessor of many things. She had three lively and industrious daughters and a little cottage by the roadside. She had a store of pennies at the bottom of a chest, stiff silk shawls, and straight-backed chairs. She could turn her hand to everything; which is useful for a person who has to earn her living. But the best that she had was the rose-garden, which gave her joy as long as the summer lasted.

Now I must tell you that in Madame Moreus' little cottage there was a boarder, a little wizened old maid, about forty years of age, who lived in a gable-room in the attic. Mamselle Marie, as she was always called, had her own ideas about many things, as people always do who sit much alone and let their thoughts dwell on what they have seen.

Mamselle Marie thought that love was the root and source of all evil in this sorrowful world.

Every evening, before she fell asleep, she used to clasp her hands and say her evening prayers. After she had said "Our Father" and "The Lord bless us" she always ended by praying that God would preserve her from love.

"It causes only misery," she said. "I am old and ugly and poor. No, may I never be in love!"

She sat day after day in her attic room in Madame Moreus' little cottage, and knitted curtains and table-covers. All these she subsequently sold to the peasants and the gentry. She had knitted so much that she could almost afford a little cottage of her own.

For a little cottage on the side of the hill opposite Svartsjö church was what she wanted to have. But love she would never hear of.

When on summer evenings she heard the sound of the fiddle from the cross roads, where the fiddler sat on the stile, and the young people danced the polka till the dust whirled, she went a long way round through the woods to avoid hearing and seeing these things.

The day after Christmas, when the peasant brides came, five or six of them, to be dressed by Madame Moreus and her daughters; when they were adorned with wreaths of myrtle, and high crowns of silk and glass beads, with gorgeous silk sashes and bunches of artificial roses, and with skirts edged with garlands of taffeta flowers, she stayed up in her room to avoid seeing how they were being decked out in Love's honour.

But she knew of Love's misdeeds, and of these she could tell. She wondered that he dared to show himself on earth, that he was not frightened away by the complaints of the forsaken, by the curses of those whom he had made criminals, by the lamentations of those whom he had thrown into hateful fetters. She wondered that his wings could bear him so easily and lightly; and that he did that his wings could bear him so easily and lightly; and that weighed down by pain and shame, he did not fall into the unfathomable abyss.

Of course, she, as well as the others, had been young, but she had never loved. She had never let herself be tempted by dancing and caresses. Her mother's guitar hung dusty and unstrung in the attic; she had never played sentimental love-ditties on it.

Her mother's rose bushes stood in her window. She gave them scarcely any water. She did not like flowers, those children of love. The dusty leaves drooped, spiders played among the branches, and the buds never opened.

There came a time when the Svartsjö congregation had an organ installed in their church. It was the summer before the year when the cavaliers reigned at Ekeby. A young organ-builder came there. He too became a boarder at Madame Moreus'.

Whether the young organ-builder was a master of his profession may readily be doubted. But he was a gay young blade, with sunshine in his eyes. He had a friendly word for everyone, for rich and poor, for old and young.

When he came home from his work in the evening, he held Madame Moreus' skeins, and worked together with the young girls in the rose-garden. He also recited "Axel" and sang "Frithiof." He picked up Mamselle Marie's ball of thread as often as she dropped it, and repaired her clock.

He never left a ball until he had danced with everybody, from the oldest woman to the youngest girl; and if any adversity befell him, he sat down next to the first woman he met, and made her his *confidante*. He was the kind of man women create in their dreams! It cannot be said that he spoke of love to anyone. But when he had lived a few weeks in Madame Moreus' gable-room, all the girls were in love with him, and poor Mamselle Marie knew that she had said her prayers in vain.

That was a time both of sorrow and of joy. In the evening a pale dreamer often sat in the lilac arbour, and up in Mamselle Marie's little room the newly strung guitar twanged to old love-songs, which she had learned from her mother.

The young organ-builder was just as careless and gay as ever, and doled out smiles and services to all these languishing women, who quarrelled over him when he was away at his work. And at last the day came when he had to leave.

The carriage stood before the door. His bag had been tied on behind, and the young man said farewell. He kissed Madame Moreus' hand and took the weeping girls in his arms and kissed them on the cheek. He too wept at being obliged to go, for he had had a pleasant summer in the little gray cottage. At last he looked for Mamselle Marie.

She came down the narrow attic-stairs in her best array. The guitar hung about her neck on a broad, green-silk ribbon, and in her hand she held a bunch of damask roses, for this year her mother's rose-bushes had blossomed. She stood before the young man, struck the guitar and sang;—

> "Thou goest far from us. Ah! welcome again!
> Hear the voice of my friendship, which greets thee.
> Be happy: forget not a true, loving friend
> Who in Värmland's forests awaits thee!"

Thereupon she put the flowers in his buttonhole and kissed him full on the lips. Yes, and then she vanished up the attic stairs again, the old apparition.

Love had revenged himself on her and made her a spectacle for all men. But she never again complained of him. She never put away the guitar, and never forgot to water her mother's rosebushes.

She had learned to cherish Love in spite of all the pain and tears and yearning that he brings.

"Better to be sorrowful with him than happy without him," she said.

The time passed. The major's wife was driven out of Ekeby, the cavaliers came into power, and, as has been described, one Sunday evening Gösta Berling happened to read a poem aloud to the countess at Borg, and was afterwards forbidden by her to show himself in her house.

It is said that when Gösta shut the hall-door after him, he saw several sledges driving up to Borg. He cast a glance on the little lady who sat in the first sledge. Gloomy as the hour was for him, it became still more gloomy at the sight. He hurried away not to be recognized, but forebodings of disaster filled his mind. Had the conversation in there conjured up this woman? One misfortune always brings another.

But the servants hurried out, the shawls and furs were thrown on one side. Who had come? Who was the little lady who stood up in the sledge? Ah, it was indeed Märta Dohna, the famous Countess Dohna.

She was the gayest and most foolish of women. Worldly joy had taken her as his queen and placed her on his throne. Festivity and laughter were her loyal subjects. Music and dancing and adventure had been her prize, when the lottery of life was drawn.

She was nearly fifty now; but she was one of the wise, who do not count the years. She used to say, "he who is not ready to dance, or to laugh, is old. He knows the terrible weight of years, not I."

The reign of pleasure did not remain unchallenged in the days of her youth, but change and uncertainty only increased the delight of his joyful presence. His Majesty with the butterfly wings would one day have afternoon tea in the rooms of the Court ladies at the palace in Stockholm, and the next day would dance in Paris. He visited Napoleon's camps; he went on board Nelson's fleet in the blue Mediterranean; he attended a congress at Vienna; and he risked his life at Brussels at a ball the night before a famous battle.

And wherever Pleasure was, there too was Märta Dohna, his chosen queen. Dancing, playing, jesting, Countess Märta rushed round the whole world. What had she not seen, what had she not lived through? Her dancing had caused thrones to fall; she had played écarté for principalities, and had caused devastating wars by her jests! Her life had been full of gayety and folly, and would continue to be so. Her body was not too old for dancing, nor her heart for love. When did she weary of masquerades and comedies, of merry stories and plaintive ballads?

When sometimes Pleasure could find no home out in the world which had been converted into a battlefield she would drive up to the old manor by the shores of lake Löven,—just as she had done when the princes and their court had become too gloomy for her in the time of the Holy Alliance. It was then she had thought expedient to make Gösta Berling her son's tutor. She always enjoyed staying at Borg. Pleasure had never had a pleasanter kingdom. There was song and card-playing; and men who loved adventure, and gay, lovely women. There were dances and balls, boating-parties over moonlit lakes, sledging tours through dark forests, and appalling adventures and the sorrow and pain of love.

But after her daughter's death she had ceased to come to Borg. She had not been there for five years. Now she had come to see how her daughter-in-law could stand the life up among the pine forests, and the bears, and the snow-drifts. She thought it her duty to come and see if stupid Henrik had not bored her to death with his tediousness. She meant to be the gentle angel of domestic peace. Sunshine and happiness were packed in her forty leather trunks, Gayety was her waiting-maid, Jest her coachman, Festivity her companion.

And when she ran up the steps she was met with open arms. Her old rooms on the lower floor had been prepared for her. Her man-servant, her lady's companion, and her maid, her forty leather trunks, her thirty hat-boxes, her bags and shawls and furs, everything was brought by degrees into the house. There was bustle and noise everywhere. There was a slamming of doors and a running on the stairs. It was plain enough that Countess Märta had come.

It was a spring evening, a really beautiful spring evening, although it was only April and the ice had not broken up. Mamselle Marie had opened her window. She sat in her room, played on the guitar, and sang.

She was so engrossed in her guitar and her memories that she did not hear that a carriage came driving up the road and stopped at the cottage. Countess Märta sat in the carriage; and it amused her to see Mamselle Marie, who sat at the window with her guitar on her lap, and with eyes turned towards heaven, sang forgotten love-songs.

At last the countess got out of the carriage and went into the cottage, where the girls were sitting at their work. She was never haughty; the wind of revolution had whistled over her and blown fresh air into her lungs.

It was not her fault that she was a countess, she used to say; but at all events she wanted to live the life she liked best. She enjoyed herself just as much at peasant weddings as at court balls. She acted a part with her maids when there was no other spectators; and wherever she went; brought joy with her, with her beautiful little face and her overflowing love of life.

She ordered a blanket from Madame Moreus and praised the girls. She looked about the rose-garden and told her adventures on the journey. She always was having adventures. And finally, she ventured up the attic stairs, which were dreadfully steep and narrow, and sought out Mamselle Marie in her gable-room.

She bought curtains from her. She could not live at Borg without having knitted curtains for all her windows, and on every table she wished to have one of Mamselle Marie's table-covers.

She borrowed her guitar and sang to her of pleasure and love. And she told her stories, so that Mamselle Marie found herself transported into the gay, rushing world. And the countess's laughter was so musical that the freezing birds in the rose-garden began to sing when they heard it; and her face, which was hardly pretty now,—for her complexion was ruined by paint; and there was such an expression of sensuality about the mouth,—seemed to Mamselle Marie so lovely that she wondered how the little mirror could let it vanish when it had once caught it on its shining surface.

When she left, she kissed Mamselle Marie and asked her to come to Borg.

Mamselle Marie's heart was as empty as a swallow's nest at Christmas. She was free, but she sighed for her fetters like a slave who has been set free in his old age.

Now there began again for Mamselle Marie a time both of joy and of sorrow; but it did not last long,—only one short week.

The countess sent continually for her to come to Borg. She acted her part and told about all her lovers, and Mamselle Marie laughed as she had never laughed before. They became the best of friends. The countess soon knew all about the young organ-builder and about the parting. And in the twilight she made Mamselle Marie sit on the window-seat in the little blue cabinet. Then she hung the guitar ribbon round her neck and got her to sing love-songs. And the countess sat and watched how the old maid's dry, thin figure and little plain head were outlined against the red evening sky, and she said that the poor old Mamselle was like a languishing maiden of the Middle Ages. All the songs were of tender shepherds and cruel shepherdesses, and Mamselle Marie's voice was the thinnest voice in the world, and it is easy to understand how the countess was amused at such a comedy.

There was a party at Borg, as was natural, when the count's mother had come home. And it was gay as always. There were not so many present, as only members of the parish were invited.

The dining-room was on the lower floor; and after supper the guests did not go upstairs again, but sat in Countess Märta's room, which was situated on the other side of the dining-room. The countess got hold of Mamselle Marie's guitar and began to sing for the company. She was a merry person, Countess Märta, and she could mimic anyone. It now came into her head to mimic Mamselle Marie. She looked up at the sky and sang in a thin, shrill, childish voice.

"Oh no, oh no, countess!" begged Mamselle Marie.

But the countess was enjoying herself, and no one could help laughing, although they all thought that it was hard on Mamselle Marie.

The countess took a handful of dried rose-leaves out of a pot-pourri jar, went with tragic gestures up to Mamselle Marie, and sang with deep emotion:—

"Thou goest far from us. Ah! welcome again!
Hear the voice of my friendship, which greets thee.
Be happy: forget not a true, loving friend
Who in Värmland's forests awaits thee!"

Then she strewed the rose-leaves over her head. Everybody laughed; but Mamselle Marie was wild with rage. She looked as if she could have torn out the countess's eyes.

"You are a bad woman, Märta Dohna," she said. "No decent woman ought to speak to you."

Countess Märta lost her temper too.

"Out with you, mamselle!" she said. "I have had enough of your folly."

"Yes, I shall go," said Mamselle Marie; "but first I want to be paid for my covers and curtains which you have put up here."

"The old rags!" cried the countess. "Do you want to be paid for such rags? Take them away with you! I never want to see them again! Take them away immediately!"

Thereupon the countess threw the table-covers at her and tore down the curtains, for she was beside herself.

The next day the young countess begged her mother-in-law to make her peace with Mamselle Marie; but the countess would not. She was tired of her.

Countess Elizabeth then bought the whole set of curtains from Mamselle Marie, and put them up in the upper floor. Whereupon Mamselle Marie felt herself redressed.

Countess Märta made great fun of her daughter-in-law for her love of knitted curtains. Although countess Märta was capable of concealing her anger; she could also keep it alive and preserve its freshness and newness for years. Her's was a richly gifted personality.

PART II

CHAPTER 1 *Cousin Christopher*

They had an old bird of prey up in the cavaliers' wing. He always sat in the corner by the fire and saw that it did not go out. He was rough and gray. His little head, with the big beak and the sunken eyes, hung sorrowfully on the long, thin neck which stuck out of a fluffy fur collar. For the bird of prey wore "furs" both winter and summer.

Formerly, he had belonged to the swarm of people who had swept over Europe in the train of the great Emperor; but what name and title he then bore no one now can say. In Värmland they only knew that he had taken part in the great wars, that he had risen to high power in the mighty struggle, and that after 1815 he had been compelled to fly from the ungrateful land of his fathers. He found a refuge with the Swedish Crown Prince, and the latter advised him to disappear in far away Värmland.

Such were the times, that one, whose name had caused the world to tremble, was now glad that no one even knew that once dreaded name.

He had given the Crown Prince his word of honour not to leave Värmland and not to reveal his identity. He had been sent to Ekeby with a letter from the Crown Prince to the major. In the letter, he had been given the best of recommendations. It was then the cavaliers' wing opened its doors to him.

In the beginning, people wondered very much who it was who concealed his identity under an assumed name. But gradually he was transformed into a cavalier. Everybody called him Cousin Christopher, without knowing exactly how he had acquired the name.

But it is not good for a bird of prey to live in a cage. One can understand that he is accustomed to something different from hopping from perch to perch and taking food from his keeper's hand. The excitement of battle and deadly peril had set his pulse on fire. Drowsy peace disgusts him.

It is true that none of the cavaliers were exactly tame birds; but none of them had such hot blood as Cousin Christopher. A bear hunt was the only thing which could put life into him, a bear hunt or a woman, but only one particular woman.

He had come to life when, ten years ago, he saw Countess Märta for the first time. She was then a widow,—a woman as changeable as war, as alluring as danger, a startling, audacious creature; he loved her.

And now he sat there and grew old and gray without being able to ask her to be his wife. He had not seen her for five years. He was withering and dying by degrees, as caged eagles do. Every year he became more dried up and frozen. He had to get down deeper into his furs and move nearer the fire.

So there he is sitting and shivering; shaggy and gray, on the morning of the day, when the Easter bullets should be shot off in the evening, and the Easter witch burned. The cavaliers have all gone out: but he sits in the corner by the fire.

Oh, Cousin Christopher, Cousin Christopher, do you not know?

Smiling she has come, the enchanting spring.

Nature starts up from her drowsy sleep; and in the blue sky, spirits with butterfly-wings, frolic in lively play. Close as roses on the sweet brier, their faces shine between the clouds.

Earth, the great mother, begins to live. Romping like a child she rises from her bath in the floods and the rains of spring.

But Cousin Christopher sits still and does not understand. He leans his head on his stiffened fingers and dreams of a rain of bullets and of honours won on the field of battle.

One pities the lonely old warrior who sits there by the fire, without compatriots, without a country. He never hears the sound of his native language; and finally, he will be laid in a nameless grave in the churchyard at Bro. Is it his fault that he is an eagle, and was born to persecute and to kill?

Oh, Cousin Christopher, you have sat and dreamed long enough in the cavaliers' wing! Up and drink the sparkling wine of life. You must know, Cousin Christopher, that a letter has come to the major this day, a royal letter adorned with the seal of Sweden. It is addressed to the major, but the contents concern you. It is strange to see you, when you read the letter, old eagle. Your eye regains its brightness, and you lift your head. You see the cage door open and free space for the wings of your longing.

Cousin Christopher is burrowing deep down to the bottom of his chest. He pulls out the gold-laced uniform, which has been carefully laid away, and dresses himself in it. He presses the plumed hat on his head and is soon hastening away from Ekeby on his fine white horse.

This is a different life from sitting shivering by the fire; he too now sees that spring has come.

He straightens himself in his saddle and sets off at a gallop. The fur-lined dolman flutters. The plumes on his hat wave. The man has grown young like the earth itself. He has awaked from a long winter. The old gold can still shine. The bold face of the warrior under the cocked hat is a proud sight.

It is a wonderful ride. Brooks gush from the ground, and flowers shoot forth, as he rides by. The birds cry and rejoice for the prisoner who has been set free. All nature shares in his joy.

He is like a victor. Spring rides before on a floating cloud. And round about Cousin Christopher rides a staff of old brothers-in-arms: there is Happiness, who stands on tiptoe in the saddle, and Honour on his stately charger, and Love on his fiery Arab. The ride is wonderful; and wonderful is the rider. The thrush calls to him:—

"Cousin Christopher, Cousin Christopher, whither are you riding? Whither are you riding?"

"To Borg to propose, to Borg to propose," answers Cousin Christopher.

"Do not go to Borg, do not go to Borg! An unmarried man has no sorrow," screams the thrush after him.

But he does not listen to the warning. Up hill and down dale he rides, until at last he is there. He leaps from the saddle and is shown in to the countess.

Everything goes well. The countess is gracious to him. Cousin Christopher feels sure that she will not refuse to bear his glorious name or to reign in his palace. He sits and puts off the moment of rapture, when he will show her the royal letter. He enjoys the waiting.

She talks and entertains him with a thousand stories. He laughs at everything, enjoys everything. But as they are sitting in one of the rooms where Countess Elizabeth has hung up Mamselle Marie's curtains, the countess begins to tell him their story. And she makes it as funny as she can.

"See," she says at last, "see how bad I am. Here the curtains are hanging now, that I may think daily and hourly of my sin. It is an unprecedented penance. Oh, those dreadful knitted curtains!"

The great warrior, Cousin Christopher, looks at her with burning eyes.

"I, too, am old and poor," he says, "and I have sat for ten years by the fire and longed for my beloved. Do you laugh at that too, countess?"

"Oh, that is another matter," cries the countess.

"God has taken from me happiness and my fatherland, and forced me to eat the bread of charity," says Cousin Christopher, earnestly. "I have learned to have respect for poverty."

"You, too," cries the countess, and holds up her hands. "How virtuous every one is getting!"

"Yes," he says, "and let me tell you, countess, that if some day God were to give me back riches and power, I should make better use of them than to share them with such a wordly woman, such a painted, heartless monkey, who makes fun of poverty."

"You would be right in doing so, Cousin Christopher."

Then Cousin Christopher marches out of the room and rides home to Ekeby; but the spirits do not follow him, the thrush does not call to him, and he no longer sees the smiling spring.

He came to Ekeby just as the Easter witch was to be burned.

She is a big straw doll, with a rag face, on which eyes, nose, and mouth are drawn with charcoal. She is dressed in old cast-off clothes. The long-handled oven-rake and broom are placed beside her, and she has a horn of oil hung round her neck. She is quite ready for the journey to hell.

Major Fuchs loads his gun and shoots it off into the air time after time. A pile of dried branches is lighted, the witch is thrown on it and is soon burning gayly. The cavaliers do all they can, according to the old, approved customs, to destroy the power of the evil one.

Cousin Christopher stands and looks on with gloomy mien. Suddenly he takes the great royal letter from his cuff and throws it on the fire. God alone knows what he thought. Perhaps he imagined that it was Countess Märta herself who was burning there on the pile. Perhaps he thought that, since, in reality, she consisted only of rags and straw, there was nothing of any value left on earth.

He goes once more into the cavaliers' wing, lights the fire, and puts away his uniform. Again he sits down at the fire, and every day he gets more rough and more gray. He is dying by degrees, as old eagles do in captivity.

He is no longer a prisoner; but he does not care to make use of his freedom. The world stands open to him. The battle-field, honour, life, await him. But he has not the strength to spread his wings in flight.

CHAPTER 2 *The Paths of Life*

Burdensome are the ways men have to follow here on earth.

They lead through deserts, and through marshes, and over mountains.

Why is so much sorrow allowed to go on without interruption, until it loses itself in the desert or sinks in the bog, or is killed in the mountains? Where are the little flower-pickers, where are the little princesses of the fairy tale about whose feet roses grow; where are they who should strew flowers on the weary path?

Gösta Berling has decided to get married. He is searching for a bride who is poor enough, humble enough for a mad priest.

Beautiful and high-born women have loved him, but they may not compete for his hand. The outcast shall choose among outcasts.

Whom shall he choose, whom shall he seek out?

There is a poor girl who sometimes comes to Ekeby from a lonely forest hamlet far away among the mountains, in order to sell brooms. In that hamlet, where poverty and great misery exist, there are many who are not in full possession of their mental faculties; the girl with the brooms is one of them.

But she is beautiful. She has a wealth of black hair, which forms such thick braids that there is scarcely room for them on her head. Her cheeks are delicately rounded, her nose straight and not too large, her eyes blue. She is of a melancholy, Madonna-like type, such as is still found among the lovely girls by the shores of lake Löven.

Well, Gösta has found his sweetheart; a half-crazy broom-girl is just the wife for a mad priest. Nothing can be more suitable.

All he has to do is to go to Karlstad for the rings, and then they can once more have a merry day by the shores of the lake. Let them laugh at Gösta Berling when he gets engaged to the broom-girl, and when he marries her! Let them laugh! Has he ever had a merrier idea?

Must not the outcast go the way of the outcasts,—the way of anger, the way of sorrow, the way of unhappiness? What does it matter if he falls, if he is ruined? Is there anyone who cares sufficiently for him to stop him? Is there anyone who would give him a helping hand or offer him a cooling drink? Where are the little flower-pickers, where are the little princesses of the fairy-tale, where are they who should strew roses on the stony path?

No, no, the gentle young countess at Borg will not interfere with Gösta Berling's plans. She must think of her reputation, she must think of her husband's anger and her mother-in-law's hate, she must not do anything to restrain him.

All through the long service in the Svartsjö church, she must bend her head, fold her hands, and only pray for him. During sleepless nights she can weep and grieve over him, but she has no flowers to strew on the way of the outcast, not a drop of water to give one who is thirsting. She does not stretch out her hand to lead him back from the edge of the precipice.

Gösta Berling does not care to clothe his chosen bride in silk and jewels. He lets her go from farm to farm with brooms, as her habit is, but when he has gathered together all the chief men and women of the place at a great feast at Ekeby, he will make his engagement known. Then he will summon her from the kitchen, just as she is on her return from her long tramps; with the dust and dirt of the road on her clothes; perhaps ragged, perhaps with dishevelled hair, with wild eyes, with an incoherent stream of words on her lips. And he will ask the guests if he has not chosen a suitable bride, if the mad priest ought not to be proud of such a lovely sweetheart, of that gentle Madonna face, of those blue, dreamy eyes.

He intended that no one should know anything about it beforehand; but he did not succeed in keeping the secret; and one of those who heard of it was young Countess Dohna.

But what can she do to stop him? It is the late evening of the

engagement day. The countess stands at the window in the blue
cabinet and looks out towards the north. She thinks that she can
almost see Ekeby, although her eyes are dim with tears. She can
see how the big three-storied house shines with three rows of
lighted windows; she thinks how the champagne flows in the
glasses, how the toast resounds and how Gösta Berling proclaims
his engagement to the broom-girl.

If she were only near him and could quite gently lay her hand on
his arm, or only give him a friendly look, would he not turn back
from the evil path? If a word from her had driven him to such a
desperate deed, would not also a word from her check him?

She shudders at the sin he is going to commit against that poor,
half-witted child. She shudders at his sin against the unfortunate
creature, who shall be enticed to love him, perhaps only for the
jest of a single day. Perhaps too—and then she shudders even more
at the sin he is committing against himself—to fetter his life
with such a galling burden, which would always rob his spirit of
the strength to reach the highest.

And the fault was chiefly hers. She had, by her condemnation,
driven him on the evil way. She, who had come to bless, to alle-
viate suffering, why had she twisted one more thorn into the
sinner's crown.

Yes, now she knows what she will do. She will have the black
horses harnessed to the sledge; she will drive quickly over lake
Löven and on to Ekeby; she will sit opposite to Gösta Berling, and
tell him that she does not despise him; that she did not know what
she was saying when she drove him from her house. No, she could
never do such a thing; she would be ashamed and would not dare
to say a word. Now that she was married, she must take care.
There would be such a scandal if she did such a thing. But if she
did not do it, what would become of him?

She must go.

Then she remembers that such a plan is impossible. No horse can
go again this year over the ice. The ice is melting, it has already
broken away from the land. It is lose, cracked, terrible to look at.
Water bubbles up through it, in some places it has gathered in

black pools, in other places the ice is dazzlingly white. It is mostly gray, dirty with melting snow, and the roads look like long, black streaks on its surface.

How can she think of going? Old Countess Märta, her mother-in-law, would never permit such a thing. She must sit beside her the whole evening in the drawing-room and listen to those old stories which are the older woman's delight.

At last the night comes, and her husband is away; she is free.

She cannot drive, she does not dare to call the servants, but her anxiety drives her out of her home. There is nothing else for her to do.

Weary are the ways along which men wander on earth; they lead through deserts, through marshes and over mountains.

But that way by night over the melting ice, with what shall I compare it? Is it not the way which the little flower-pickers have to go, an uncertain, shaking, slippery way, the way of those who wish to make amends, the way of the light foot, the quick eye, and the brave, loving heart?

It was past midnight when the countess reached the shore at Ekeby. She had fallen on the ice, she had leaped over wide fissures, she had hurried across places where her footprints were filled with bubbling water, she had slipped, she had crept on all fours.

It had been a weary journey; she had wept while walking. She was wet and tired, and out there on the ice, the darkness and the loneliness had given her terrible thoughts.

Finally, she had had to wade in water over her ankles to reach land. And when she had come to the shore, she had not had the courage to do more that sit down on a rock and weep from fatigue and helplessness.

This young, high-born lady was, however, a brave little heroine. She had never gone such ways in her bright mother country. She may well sit by the edge of that terrible lake, wet, tired, unhappy as she is, and think of the fair, flowery paths of her Southern mother country.

Ah, for her it is not a question of South or North. She is not weeping because she is homesick. She is weeping because she is so tired, because she will not come in time. She thinks that she has come too late.

Then people come running along the shore. They hurry by her without seeing her, but she hears what they say.

"If the dam gives way, the forge will go," one says. "And the mill and the workshops and the smith's house," adds another.

Then she gets new courage; rises, and follows them.

Ekeby mill and forge lay on a narrow headland around which the Björksjö river rushes. It comes roaring down towards the headland, whipped white by the great waterfall above. At that time, there was a large breakwater in front of the headland to protect the land, on which the buildings stood, from the water. But the dam was old now, and the cavaliers managed the estate. In their day the dance of life was all they thought about; and no one took the trouble to see how the current, the cold, and time itself had affected the old stone-dam.

Now with the spring-floods the dam begins to yield.

The falls at Ekeby are like mighty granite stairs, down which tha waves come rushing. Giddy with their speed, they tumble over one another and rush together. They rise up in anger and dash in spray over one another, fall again, over a rock, over a log, and rise up again, again to fall, again and again, foaming, hissing, roaring.

And now these wild, raging waves, drunken with the spring air, dizzy with their newly won freedom, storm against the old stone-wall. They come, hissing and tearing; they leap high up on to the dam, and then fall back again, as if they had hit their white heads. They use logs as battering-rams, they strain, they beat, they rush against that poor wall, until suddenly, just as if someone had called to them, "Look out!" they rush backwards, and after them comes a big stone, which has broken away from the dam and with a noise like thunder, sinks down in the stream.

But why are these wild waves allowed to rage without meeting any resistance? Is everyone dead at Ekeby?

No, there are people enough there,—a wild, perplexed, helpless crowd of people. The night is dark, they can see neither one another, nor where they are going. Loud roars the waterfall, terrible is the din of the breaking ice and the pounding logs; they cannot hear their own voices. The wild delirium by which the roaring waves are possessed affects also the brains of the people present; they become incapable of thought and are deprived of their intelligence. They feel that the end is coming. The dam is trembling, the forge is in danger, the mill is in danger, and their own poor houses, which they love in spite of their inferior quality.

Message after message is sent up to the house to the cavaliers. Are they in a mood to think of the forge or the mill? A hundred guests are assembled in the spacious halls. The broom-girl is waiting in the kitchen. The hour has come. The champagne bubbles in the glasses. Julius rises to make his speech. All the old adventurers at Ekeby are rejoicing at the petrifying amazement which will fall upon the assembly.

Out on the ice young Countess Dohna is wandering along a terrible, perilous way in order to whisper a word of warning to Gösta Berling. Down at the waterfall the waves are storming the honour and might of Ekeby; but in the wide halls only joy and eager expectation reign; wax-candles are shining, wine is flowing; no one thinks of what is happening in the dark, stormy spring night.

The crucial moment has now come. Gösta rises and goes out to bring in his sweetheart. He has to go through the hall, and its great doors are standing open; he stops, he looks out into the pitch dark night—and listens; he hears something!

He hears the bells ringing, the roaring of the waterfall. He hears the thunder of the breaking ice, the noise of the pounding logs, the rushing and threatening voice of the rebellious waves.

He hastens out into the night, forgetting everything. Let them stand there with lifted glasses till the Day of Judgment; he cares nothing for them. The broom-girl can wait, Julius's speech may die on his lips. There will be no rings exchanged tonight, no shock of amazement will paralyze the brilliant assembly.

Now the waves must indeed fight for their freedom, for Gösta Berling has come, the people have found a leader. Terrified hearts take courage, a terrible struggle begins.

Hear how he calls to the people; he commands, he sets all to work.

"First of all, we must have light; the miller's horn-lantern is not enough. See all those piles of branches; carry them up on the cliff and set fire to them. That is what the women and children can do. Only be quick; build up a great flaming brush-pile and set fire to it! That will light up our work; that will be seen far and wide and bring more to help us. Do not let your fire go out! Bring straw, bring branches, let the flames mount up to the sky!"

"Look, look, you men, here is work for you. Here is timber, here are planks; make a temporary dam, which we can sink in front of this wall, which is giving way. Quick, quick to work; make it firm and solid! Get stones and sandbags ready to sink it with! Quick! Swing your axes! To work! to work!"

"And where are the boys? Get poles, get boat-hooks, and come out here in the midst of the struggle. Out on the dam with you, boys, right in the waves. Ward off, reduce and drive back their attacks, which are causing the wall to crack. Push aside the logs and pieces of ice; get down into the water yourselves, if nothing else helps, and hold up the loosening stones with your hands; bite into them, seize them with claws of iron. Out on the wall, boys! We shall fight for every inch of land."

Gösta himself takes his stand farthest out on the dam and stands there covered with spray; the ground shakes under him, the waves thunder and rage, but his wild heart rejoices at the danger, the anxiety, the struggle. He laughs. He jokes with the boys beside him on the dam; he has never had a merrier night.

The rescue work makes rapid progress; the fire flames, the axes resound, and the dam stands firm.

The other cavaliers and the hundred guests have come down to the waterfall. People come rushing from near and far; all are working, at the fires, at the temporary dam, at the sandbags, out on the tottering, trembling stone-wall.

Now the temporary dam is ready, and is to be sunk in front of the breakwater, which is giving way. Have the stones and sandbags ready, and boat-hooks and rops, so that the dam may not be carried away; so that the people may prove victorious, and the cowed waves return to their bondage.

Just before the decisive moment, Gösta happens to catch sight of a woman who is sitting on a stone at the water's edge. The flames from the bonfire light up the place where she sits staring out over the waves; he cannot see her clearly and distinctly through the mist and spray, but his eyes are continually drawn to her. Again and again he has to look at her. He feels as if that woman had a special errand in connection with him.

Among all these hundreds of people who are busily working, she is the only one who sits still; and to her his eyes keep turning, he can see nothing else.

She is sitting so far out that the waves break at her feet, and the spray dashes over her. She must be dripping wet. Her dress is dark, she has a black shawl over head, she sits shrunk together, her chin on her hand, and stares persistently at him out on the dam. He feels as if those staring eyes were drawing and calling him, although he cannot even distinguish her face, he thinks only of the woman who sits on the shore by the white waves.

"It is the sea-nymph from lake Löven who has come up the river to lure me to destruction," he thinks. "She sits there and calls and calls. I must go and drive her away."

All these waves with their white crests seem to him the dark woman's hair; it was she who incited them, she who led them in their attack on him.

"I really must drive her away," he says.

He seizes a boat-hook, runs to the shore, and hurries towards the woman.

He leaves his place on the end of the dam to drive the sea nymph away. He felt, in that moment of excitement, as if the evil powers of the deep were fighting against him. He did not know what he thought, what he believed, but he must drive that black thing away from the stone by the river's edge.

Alas, Gösta, why is your place empty in the decisive moment? They are coming with the temporary dam, a long line of men station themselves on the break-water; they have ropes and stones and sand-bags ready to weight it down and hold it in place; they stand ready, they wait, they listen. Where is their leader? Is there no one who can take charge?

No, Gösta Berling is chasing the sea-nymph, his voice is silent, he does not lead anyone.

So the temporary dam has to be sunk without him. The waves rush back, it sinks into the water and after it come the stones and sand-bags. But how is the work carried out without a leader? No proper care is taken, and there is no order. The waves dash up again, they break with renewed rage against this new obstacle, they begin to roll the sand-bags over, tear the ropes, loosen the stones; and they succeed, they succeed. Threatening, rejoicing, they lift the whole dam on their strong shoulders, they tear and wrench it, and then they have it in their power. Away with the miserable defence, down to lake Löven with it! Then they renew their attack on the tottering, helpless stone-wall.

But Gösta is chasing the sea-nymph. She saw him as he came towards her swinging the boat-hook. She was frightened. It looked as if she was going to throw herself into the water, but she changed her mind and ran to the land.

"Sea-nymph!" cries Gösta, and brandishes the boat-hook. She runs in among the alder-bushes, gets entangled in their thick branches, and stops.

Then Gösta throws away the boat-hook, goes forward, and lays his hand on her shoulder.

"You are out late to-night, Countess Elizabeth," he says.

"Let me alone, Herr Berling, let me go home!"

He obeys instantly and turns away from her.

But since she is not only a high-born lady, but a really kind little woman, who cannot bear the thought that she has driven anyone to despair; since she is a little flower-picker, who always has roses enough in her basket to adorn the most barren path, she repents, goes after him and seizes his hand.

"I came," she says, and stammers, "I came to—Oh, Herr Berling, you have not done it? Say that you have not done it! I was so frightened when you came running after me, but it was you I wanted to meet. I wanted to ask you not to think of what I said the other day, and to come to see me as usual."

"How have you come here, countess?"

She laughs nervously. "I knew that I should come too late, but I did not like to tell anyone that I was going; and besides, you know, it is impossible to drive over the ice now."

"Have you walked across the lake, countess?"

"Yes, yes, of course; but, Herr Berling, tell me. Are you engaged? You understand; I wish so much that you were not. It is so wrong, you see; and I felt as if the whole thing was my fault. You should not have minded what I said so much. I am a stranger, who does not know the customs of the country. It is so dull at Borg since you have stopped coming, Herr Berling."

It seems to Gösta Berling, as he stands among the wet alder-bushes on the marshy ground, as if someone were throwing arm-fuls of roses over him. He wades in roses up to his knees, they shine before his eyes in the darkness, he eagerly drinks in their fragrance.

"Have you done that?" she repeats.

He must make up his mind to answer her and to put an end to her anxiety, although he greatly rejoices because of it. He feels so warm and bright when he thinks of the way she has come, of how wet and frozen she is, and how frightened she must have been, and how broken with weeping her voice sounds.

"No," he says, "I am not engaged."

Then she takes his hand again and strokes it. "I am so glad, I am so glad," she says, and her voice is shaken with sobs.

There are flowers enough now on the poet's path, everything dark, evil, and hateful melts from his heart.

"How good you are, how good you are!" he says.

At their side the waves are rushing against the whole honour and glory of Ekeby. The people have no leader, no one to instil courage and hope into their hearts; the dam gives way, the waves close over it, and then rush forward in triumph to the headland where the mill and the forge stand. No one tries any longer to resist the waves; no one thinks of anything but of saving life and property.

It seems quite natural to both the young people that Gösta should escort the countess home; he cannot leave her alone on this dark night, or let her again wander alone over the melting ice. They never think that he is needed up at the forge; they are so happy that they are friends again.

One might easily believe that these young people cherish an ardent love for one another, but who can be sure? In broken fragments the glowing adventures of their lives have come to me. I know nothing, or next to nothing, of what took place in the depths of their spirits. What can I say about the motives of their actions. All I know is: that night a beautiful young woman risked her life, her honour, her reputation, and her health, to help a poor wretch to regain the right way of living. I only know: that night Gösta Berling let the power and the splendour of his beloved Ekeby perish, in order to follow the woman who, for his sake, had conquered the fear of death, the fear of shame, and the fear of punishment.

Often in my thoughts I have followed them over the ice that terrible night, which ended so well for them. I do not think that there was anything hidden or forbidden in their hearts, as they wandered over the ice, gay and talking of everything which had happened during their separation.

He is once more her slave, her page, who lies at her feet; and she is his lady.

They are only happy, only joyous. Neither of them speaks a word which can denote love.

Laughing they splash through the water, they laugh when they find the path or when they lose it; when they slip, when they fall, and when they get up again; they laugh all the time.

This blessed life is once more a merry game; and they are children who had been cross and had quarrelled. Oh, how good it is to be reconciled and to begin playing again.

Rumour came, and rumour went. In time the story of the countess's exploit reached Anna Stjärnhök.

"I see," she said, "that God has not one string only to his bow. I can rest, and stay where I am needed. He can make a man of Gösta Berling without my help."

CHAPTER 3 *Penitence*

Dear friends, if you should ever chance to meet a pitiful wretch on your way, a little distressed creature, who lets his hat hang on his back and holds his shoes in his hand, so as not to have any protection against the heat of the sun and the stones of the road, who is defenceless, who voluntarily calls down destruction on his head,—well, pass him by in silent fear! It is a penitent, do you understand? —a penitent on his way to the holy sepulchre.

The penitent must wear a coarse cloak and live on water and dry bread, even if he were a king. He must walk and not ride. He must beg. He must sleep among thistles. He must wear down the hard graveslabs with kneeling. He must lash his back with the thorny scourge. He can know no sweetness except in suffering, no tenderness except in grief.

Young Countess Elizabeth was once one of those who wore the heavy cloak and trod the thorny paths. Her heart accused her of sin. It longed for pain as a weary person longs for a warm bath. She brought down dire disaster on herself while she descended rejoicing into the night of suffering.

Her husband, the young count with the old-man's head, came home to Borg the morning after the mill and forge at Ekeby were destroyed during the night by the spring flood. He had hardly arrived before Countess Märta sent a message asking him to come to her; she had a wonderful story to tell him.

"Your wife was out last night, Henrik. She was gone many hours. She came home with a man. I heard how he said good-night to her. I also know who he is. I heard when she went out and when she returned. She is deceiving you, Henrik. She is deceiving you, the hypocritical creature, who hangs knitted curtains in all the windows only to cause me discomfort. She has never loved you, my poor boy. Her father only wanted to have her well married. She took you because you could support her.

She stated her case so well that Count Henrik became furious. He wished to get a divorce. He wished to send his wife home to her father.

"No, my friend," said Countess Märta, "that would mean abandoning her entirely to evil. She is spoiled and badly brought up. But let me take her in hand, let me lead her into the path of duty."

And the count summoned his countess to inform her that she was now to obey his mother in everything.

The young man spoke many angry words to the young woman. He lifted his hands toward heaven and accused it of having let his name be dragged in the dirt by a shameless woman. He shook his clenched fist in front of her face and asked her what punishment she thought was severe enough for such a crime as she had committed.

She was not at all afraid. She thought that she had done right. She said that she had already caught a heavy cold, and that might prove sufficient punishment.

"Elizabeth," says Countess Märta, "this is not a matter to joke about."

"We two," answers the young woman, "have never been able to agree about when it was the right time to joke and when to be serious."

"But you ought to understand, Elizabeth, that no honourable woman leaves her home to roam about in the middle of the night with a man who is known to be an adventurer."

Then Elizabeth Dohna saw that her mother-in-law intended to bring about her ruin. She saw that she must fight with all her strength, lest Countess Märta should succeed in bringing upon her a terrible misfortune.

"Henrik," she implores, "do not let your mother come between us! Let me tell you how it all happened. You are just, you will not condemn me unheard. Let me tell you all, and you will see that I only acted as you have taught me."

The count nodded a silent consent, and Countess Elizabeth told him how she had come to drive Gösta Berling into evil. She related everything that had happened in the little blue cabinet; and how she had felt herself driven by her conscience to go and save the man she had wronged. "I had no right to judge him," she said, "and you, my husband, have yourself taught me that no sacrifice is too great when one desires to make amends for a wrong. Isn't that so, Henrik?"

The count turned to his mother.

"What have you to say to this, mother?" he asked. His little body was now quite stiff with dignity; and there were majestic furrows on his high, narrow forehead.

"I," answered the countess,—"I say that Anna Stjärnhök is a clever girl, and she knew what she was doing when she told Elizabeth that story."

"You are pleased to misunderstand me," said the count. "I ask what you think of this story. Did Countess Märta Dohna try to persuade her daughter, my sister, to marry an unfrocked priest?"

Countess Märta was silent an instant. It is indeed a misfortune that Henrik is so stupid, so very stupid! Now he was quite on the wrong track. Her hound was pursuing the hunter himself and letting the hare get away. But if Märta Dohna was without an answer, it was only for an instant.

"Dear friend," she said with a shrug, "there is a reason for letting all those old stories about that unhappy man rest,—the same reason which makes me beg you to suppress all public scandal. It is most probable that he has perished in the night."

She spoke in a gentle, commiserating tone, but there was not a word of truth in what she said.

"Elizabeth has slept late to-day and therefore has not heard that people have already been sent all round the lake to look for Herr Berling. He has not returned to Ekeby, and they fear that he has been drowned. The ice broke up this morning. See, the storm has split it into a thousand pieces."

Countess Elizabeth looked out. The lake was almost open.

Then in despair she threw herself on her knees before her husband and her confession burst from her lips. She had wished to escape God's justice. She had lied and dissembled. She had thrown the white mantle of innocence over her.

"Condemn me, turn me out! I have loved him. You may be sure that I have loved him! I tear my hair, I rend my clothes with grief. I do not care for anything when he is dead. I do not care to shield myself. You shall know the whole truth. My deepest love I have taken from my husband and given it to a stranger. Oh, I am one of those who have been allured by an illicit love."

You desperate young creature, lie there at your judges' feet and tell them everything! Welcome, martyrdom! Welcome, disgrace! Welcome! Oh, how shall you bring down the bolt from heaven on to your young head!

Tell your husband how frightened you were when this overwhelming and irresistible passion took possession of you; how you shuddered over the wretchedness that gripped your heart. You would rather have faced the ghosts in the churchyard than the demons in your own soul.

Tell them how you, when banished by God, felt that you were unworthy to live! You have struggled against these things with prayers and tears.

You have prayed: "O God, save me! O Son of God, who cast the devils out, save me!"

Tell them how you thought it best to conceal it all. No one should know your wretchedness. You thought that it was God's pleasure to act in this way. You thought, too, that you were obeying God's will when you wished to save the man you loved. He knew nothing of your love. He must not be lost for your sake. Did you know what was right? Did you know what was wrong? God alone knew it, and he had passed sentence upon you. He had destroyed the idol of your heart. He had led you on to the great, healing way of penitence.

Tell them that you know that salvation is not to be found in concealment. Devils love darkness. Let your judges' hands close on the scourge! The punishment shall be like soothing balm on the wounds caused by sin. Your heart longs for suffering.

Tell them all that, while you kneel on the floor and wring your hands in turbulent sorrow, speaking in the wild accents of despair; greeting with a shrill laugh the thought of punishment and dishonour, until at last your husband seizes you and pulls you up from the floor.

"Behave yourself as befits a Countess Dohna, or I must ask my mother to chastise you as if you were a child."

"Do with me what you will!"

Then the count pronounced his sentence:—

"My mother has interceded for you. Therefore you may stay in my house. But henceforth she will give the orders, and you will obey."

See the way of penitence! The young countess has become the most humble of servants. How long? Oh, how long?

How long will a proud heart be able to humble itself? How long can impatient lips keep silent; how long a violent hand be restrained?

Sweet is the misery of humiliation. When the back aches from the heavy work accomplished, the heart is at peace. To one who sleeps a few short hours on a hard bed of straw, sleep comes uncalled.

Let the older woman change herself into an evil spirit to torture the younger. She thanks her benefactress. As yet the evil is not dead in her. Hunt her up at four o'clock every morning when she is famished for sleep! Exact from the inexperienced worker an unreasonable day's work at the heavy weaving-loom! That is as it should be. The penitent may not have sufficient strength to apply the scourge with the required force.

When the time for the great spring washing comes,[1] Countess Märta has her stand at the tub in the wash-house. She comes herself to supervise her work. "The water is too cold in your tub," she says, and takes boiling water from a kettle and pours it over her bare arms.

The day is cold; the washerwomen have to stand by the lake and rinse the clothes. Squalls rush by and drench them with sleet. The washerwomen's skirts are dripping wet and as heavy as lead.

[1] It was formerly the custom, in the rural districts of Sweden, for housewives to have a "big wash" twice a year, namely, in spring and autumn.

It is hard to work with the wooden clapper. The blood runs from under the delicate nails.

But Countess Elizabeth does not complain. Praised be the goodness of God! The scourge's thorny knots fall softly, as if they were rose-leaves, on the penitent's back.

The young woman soon hears that Gösta Berling is alive. Her mother-in-law had only wanted to cheat her into a confession. Well, what of it? See the hand of God! He had won over the sinner to the path of atonement.

She grieves for only one thing. What will happen to her mother-in-law, whose heart God has hardened for her sake? Ah, he will judge her leniently. She must show anger so as to help the sinner to regain God's love.

She did not know that often a soul that has tried all other sensual pleasures endeavours to find delight in cruelty. The suffering of men and animals is a source of pleasure for enervated emotion.

The older woman is not conscious of any malice. She thinks she is only chastening a wanton wife. Consequently, she sometimes lies awake at night brooding over new methods of torture.

One evening she goes through the house and has the countess light her way with a candle. She holds it in her hand without a candle-stick.

"The candle is burnt out," says the young woman.

"When the candle is burnt out, the candle-stick must burn," answers Countess Märta.

And they go on, until the reeking wick goes out in the scorched hand.

But that is childishness. There are mental tortures which are greater than any bodily suffering. Countess Märta invites guests and makes the mistress of the house wait on them at her own table.

That is the penitent's great day. Strangers shall see her in her humiliation. They shall see that she is no longer worthy to sit at her husband's table. Oh with what scorn their cold eyes will rest on her!

It is worse, far worse. Not any eye meet hers. Everybody at the table sits silent and depressed; both men and women are equally dejected.

But she gathers all these experiences to lay like coals of fire on her head. Is her sin so dreadful? Is it a disgrace to be near her?

Then temptation comes. Anna Stjärnhök, who has been her friend, and the judge at Munkerud, who sits next to Anna at the table, take hold of her when she comes, snatch the dish from her, push up a chair, and will not let her escape.

"Sit there, child, sit there!" says the judge. "You have done no wrong."

And with one voice all the guests declare that if she does not sit down at the table, they must all go. They are not executioners. They will not do Märta Dohna's bidding. They are not so easily deceived as that sheep-like count.

"Oh, kind gentlemen! Oh, beloved friends! Do not be so charitable. You force me to cry out my sin. There is some one whom I have loved too dearly."

"Child, you do not know what sin is. You do not understand how guiltless you are. Gösta Berling did not even know that you liked him. Take your proper place in your home! You have done no wrong."

They keep up her courage for a while; and suddenly they become gay as children. Laughter and jests resound at the table.

These impetuous, emotional people, they are so good; but still they are sent by the tempter. They want to make her think that she is a martyr, and they openly scoff at Countess Märta as if she were a witch. But they do not understand. They do not know how the soul longs for purity, or how the penitent is driven by his own heart to expose himself to the stones on the way and the heat of the sun.

Sometimes Countess Märta forces her to sit quietly the whole day long in the bay window, and then she tells her endless stories of Gösta Berling, the priest and adventurer. If her memory proves inadequate, she makes things up; her one concern is that his name shall sound in the young woman's ears the whole day long. That is what the penitent fears most. On those days she feels that her penance will never end. Her love will not die. She thinks that she herself will die before it does. Her strength begins to give way. She is often very ill.

"But where is your hero tarrying?" asks the countess, spitefully. "From day to day I have expected him at the head of the cavaliers. Why does he not take Borg by storm, and set you on a throne, and having bound us, throw me and your husband into a dungeon? Are you already forgotten?"

She is almost ready to defend him and say that she herself had forbidden him to give her any help. But no, it is best to be silent, to be silent and to suffer.

Day by day she is more and more consumed by the fire of irritation. She has incessant fever and is so weak that she can scarcely remain up. She longs to die. Life's strongest forces are subdued. Love and joy do not dare to move. She no longer fears pain.

It is as if her husband no longer knew that she existed. He sits shut up in his room almost the whole day and studies indecipherable manuscripts, and essays in old, blurred print.

He reads charters of nobility written on parchment, from which the great seal of Sweden is suspended; a large and potent emblem stamped in red wax, and kept in a carved wooden box. He examines old coats of arms with lilies on a white field and griffins on a blue. Such things he understands, and can interpret with ease. And he reads over and over again speeches by, and obituary notices of, the noble counts Dohna, where their exploits are compared to those of the heroes of Israel and the gods of Greece.

These old things have always given him pleasure. But he does not trouble to think any more about his young wife.

Countess Märta said something which killed all his love: "She took you for your money." No man can bear to hear such a thing. It quenches all love. Now it was all the same to him what happened to the young woman. If his mother succeeded in leading her into the path of duty, so much the better. Count Henrik greatly admired his mother.

This misery went on for a month. Still it was not such a stormy and agitated time as it may sound when it is all compressed into a few written pages. Countess Elizabeth was always outwardly calm.

Once only, when she heard that Gösta Berling might be dead, emotion overcame her.

But so great was her grief because she had failed in preserving her love for her husband, that she would probably have let Countess Märta torture her to death, if her old housekeeper had not spoken to her one evening.

"You must speak to the count, countess," she said. "Good heavens, you are such a child! Perhaps you yourself do not know, countess, what you have to expect; but I see well enough what the matter is."

But that was exactly what she could not do, while he harboured such a grave suspicion of her.

That night she dressed herself quietly, and went out. She wore an ordinary peasant-girl's dress, and had a bundle in her hand. She meant to run away from her home and never come back.

She did not go to escape pain and suffering. But now she believed that God had given her a sign that she might go, that she must preserve her bodily health and strength.

She did not turn to the west across the lake, for there lived one whom she loved very dearly; nor did she go to the north, for there many of her friends lived; nor towards the south, for, far, far to the south lay her father's home, and she did not wish to come a step nearer to it; but she went to the east, for there she knew she had no home, no beloved friend, no acquaintance, no help or comfort.

She did not go with a light step, for she thought that she had not yet appeased God. But still she was glad that in future she could bear the burden of her sin among strangers. They would look at her indifferently, which would be as soothing as cold steel laid on a swollen limb.

She meant to continue her wandering until she found a lowly cottage at the edge of the wood, where no one knew her. "You can see what has happened to me, and my parents have turned me out," she intended to say. "Let me have food and a roof over my head here, until I can earn my bread. I have some money."

So she went into the bright June night, for the month of May had passed during the time she had suffered greatly. Alas, the month of

May, that fair season when the birches mingle their pale green with the darkness of the pine forest, and when the southwind comes again filled with warmth.

Ah, May, you dear, bright month, have you ever seen a child sitting on its mother's knee listening to fairy stories? As long as the child is told about cruel giants and bitter suffering and beautiful princesses, it holds its head up and its eyes open; but if the mother begins to speak of happiness and sunshine, the little one closes its eyes and falls asleep with its head against her breast.

Fair month of May, I am such a child. Others may listen to tales of flowers and sunshine; but for myself I choose the dark nights, full of visions and adventures, cruel destinies, and the passion of wild hearts which is filled with tribulation.

Spring had come, and the iron from all the mines in Värmland was to be sent to Gothenburg.

But at Ekeby they had no iron to send. In the autumn there had been a scarcity of water; and in the spring the cavaliers had been running the estate.

In their time, strong, bitter ale foamed down the broad granite slope of Björksjö falls, and the long lake of Löven was filled not with water, but with brandy. In their time, no iron was brought to the forge; the smiths stood in shirt-sleeves and clogs by the hearth and turned enormous roasts on long spits, while the boys held larded capons with long tongs over the coals. In those days, they slept on the carpenter's bench and played cards on the anvil. In those days, no iron was forged.

But the spring came and in the wholesale office in Gothenburg they began to expect the iron from Ekeby. They looked up the contract made with the major and his wife, where the delivery of many hundreds of tons was stipulated.

But what did the cavaliers care about the contract? They thought only of pleasure, music and feasting.

Iron came from Stömne, from Sölje, from Uddeholm, from Munkfors, and from all of the many mines. But where is the iron from Ekeby?

Is Ekeby no longer the principal ironworks in Värmland? Is there no one to maintain the honour of the old estate? Like ashes strewn in the wind, it is left in the hands of shiftless cavaliers.

Even if the Ekeby hammers have not been working, they must have worked at our six subsidiary works. These must have enough and more than enough iron.

So Gösta Berling sets out to talk with the managers of the six mines.

He travelled ten miles or so to the north, till he came to Löta-fors. It is a pretty place; there can be no doubt of that. The upper Löven lies spread out before it, and close behind is Gurlitta cliff, with steeply rising top and with its wild and romantic aspect, which well befits an old mountain. But the forge is not as it ought to be: the swing-wheel is broken, and has been so a whole year.

"Well, why has it not been mended?"

"The carpenter, my dear friend, the carpenter, the only one in the whole district who could mend it, has been busy somewhere else. We have not been able to forge a single ton."

"Why did you not send for the carpenter?"

"Send for him! As if we had not sent for him every day, but he has not been able to come. He was busy building bowling-alleys and summer-houses at Ekeby."

He goes further to the north to Björnidet. Also a beautiful spot; but iron, is there any iron?

No, of course not. They had no coal, and they had not been able to get any money from Ekeby to pay charcoal-burners and teamsters. There had been no work all winter.

Then Gösta turns to the south. He comes to Hån, and to Lövsta-fors, far in in the forests; but he fares no better there. Nowhere have they any iron; and everywhere it seems to be the cavaliers' own fault.

So Gösta turns back to Ekeby; and with gloomy looks the cavaliers consider the fifty tons or so of iron, which are in stock; and their heads are weighed down with grief, for they hear how the whole of nature sneers at Ekeby; and they think that the ground shakes with sobs; that the trees threaten them with angry gestures, and the grass and the plants lament that the honour of Ekeby is lost.

But why so many words and so much perplexity? There is the iron from Ekeby.

There it is, loaded on barges on the River Klar, ready to sail down the stream, ready to be weighed at Karlstad, ready to be conveyed to Gothenburg. So the honour of Ekeby is saved.

But how is it possible? At Ekeby there were not more than fifty tons of iron; at the six other mines there was no iron at all. How is it possible that fully loaded barges shall now carry such an enormous amount of iron to the weighing-machines at Karlstad? Yes, one may well ask the cavaliers.

The cavaliers themselves are on board the heavy, ugly vessels; they mean to escort the iron from Ekeby to Gothenburg. They are going to do everything for their beloved iron, and they will not forsake it until it is unloaded on the wharf in Gothenburg. They are going to load and unload; they will see to the sails and the rudder. They are the right men for such an undertaking. Is there a shoal in the River Klar or a reef in Vänern which they do not know?

If they love anything in the world, it is the iron on those barges. They treat it like the most delicate glass, they spread cloths over it. Not a bit may lie bare. It is those heavy, gray bars which are going to retrieve the honour of Ekeby. No stranger may cast indifferent glances on them.

None of the cavaliers have remained at home. Uncle Eberhard has left his desk, and Cousin Christopher has come out of his corner. No one can hold back when the honour of Ekeby is at stake.

Everyone knows that such coincidences often occur in life as that which now followed. Whoever is still capable of feeling surprised may wonder how it happened that the cavaliers should be lying with their barges at the ferry over the River Klar on the very morning after Countess Elizabeth had started out on her way towards the east. But it would certainly have been still more remarkable if the young woman had found no help in her need. It now chanced that she, after walking the whole night, was coming along the highway which led down to the ferry, just as the cavaliers intended to put off; they stood and looked at her while she talked to the ferryman and he untied his boat. She was dressed like a peasant girl, and they never guessed who she was.

But still they stood and stared at her, because there was something familiar about her. As she stood and talked to the ferryyman, a cloud of dust appeared on the highway, and in that cloud of dust they could catch a glimpse of a big yellow coach. She knew that it was from Borg, that they were out to look for her, and that she would now be discovered. She could no longer hope to escape in the ferryman's boat, and the only hiding-place she could see was the cavaliers' barges. She rushed down to them without seeing who was on board. And well it was that she did not see, for otherwise she would rather have thrown herself under the horses' feet than have sought refuge in those barges.

When she came on board she only screamed, "Hide me, hide me!" And then she tripped and fell on the piles of iron. But the cavaliers bade her be calm. They pushed off hurriedly from the land, so that the barge came out into the current and bore down towards Karlstad, just as the coach reached the ferry.

In the carriage sat Count Henrik and Countess Märta. The count ran forward to ask the ferryman if he had seen his countess. But as Count Henrik was a little embarrassed at having to ask about a runaway wife, he only said;—

"Something has been lost!"

"Really?" said the ferryman.

"Something has been lost. I am asking you if you have seen anything?"

"What are you asking about?"

"Yes, it makes no difference, but something has been lost. I am asking if you have ferried anything over the river to-day?"

In this way he could find out nothing; and Countess Märta had to go and speak to the man. She knew in a moment that the person whom they were looking for was on board one of the heavy barges that were gliding away.

"Who are the people on those barges?"

"Oh, they are the cavaliers, as we call them."

"Ah," said the countess. "Yes, then your wife is in safe keeping, Henrik. We might as well go straight home."

On the barge there was no such feeling of great joy as Countess

Märta believed. As long as the yellow coach was in sight, the frightened young woman lay huddled on the cargo, motionless and silent, staring at the shore.

Probably, she first recognized the cavaliers when she had seen the yellow coach drive away. She started up. It was as if she wanted to escape again, but she was stopped by the man standing nearest to her, and she sank back on the cargo with a faint moan.

The cavaliers did not dare to speak to her or ask her any questions. She looked as if she were on the verge of madness.

Their carefree heads began to feel heavy with responsibility. This iron was already a heavy load for unaccustomed shoulders, and now they had to look after a young, high-born lady, who had run away from her husband.

When they had met this young woman at the balls during the winter, some of them had thought of a little sister whom he had once loved. When he had played and romped with that sister he had had to be gentle to her; when he talked to her he had learned to be careful not to use bad words. If a strange boy had chased her too wildly in their play or had sung coarse songs for her, he had attacked him furiously and almost pounded the life out of him; for his little sister should never hear anything bad nor suffer any pain nor ever be met with anger and hate.

Countess Elizabeth had been like a happy sister to them all. When she had laid her little hands in their hard fists, it had been as if she had said: "Feel how fragile I am, but you are my big brother; you shall protect me both from others and from yourself." And they had been courtly knights as long as they had been with her.

Now the cavaliers looked upon her with terror, and did not quite recognize her. She was worn and thin, her neck had lost its beautiful shape, her face was transparent. She must have knocked herself against something while she was wandering about during the night, for blood was trickling from a little wound on her temple, and her curly, light hair, which shaded her brow, was sticky with it. Her dress was soiled from her long walk on the wet paths, and her shoes were muddy. The cavaliers had a dreadful feeling that this was a stranger. The Countess Elizabeth whom they knew never had had such wild, glittering eyes. Their poor little sister had been driven nearly mad. It was as if a spirit who had descended from some other region was struggling with her true spirit for the mastery of her tortured body.

But there was no need for them to worry about what they should do with her. The old thoughts soon awoke in her again. She was being tempted. God wished to try her once more. See, she is among friends; does she intend to leave the path of the penitent?

She rises and cries out that she must go.

The cavaliers tried to calm her. They told her that she was safe. They would protect her from all persecution.

She only begged to be allowed to get into the little boat which was being towed after the barge, and to row to the land, to continue her wandering.

But they could not let her go. What would become of her? It was better to remain with them. They were only poor old men, but they would surely find some way of helping her.

Then she wrung her hands and begged them to let her go. But they could not grant her request. She was so exhausted and weak that they thought she would only die by the roadside.

Gösta Berling stood a short distance away and looked down into the water. Perhaps the young woman would not wish to see him. He could not tell; but his thoughts played and smiled. "Nobody knows where she is," he thought; "we can take her with us to Ekeby. We will keep her hidden there, we cavaliers, and we will be good to her. She shall be our queen, our lady, but no one shall know that she is there. We will guard her with the greatest care. Perhaps she would be happy with us; she would be cherished like a daughter by all the old men."

He had never dared to ask himself if he loved her. She could not be his without sin, and he knew that he would not drag her down to anything low and wretched. But to keep her concealed at Ekeby; to be good to her after others had been so cruel, and to let her enjoy everything that was pleasant in life, ah, what a dream, what a blissful dream that was!

But he awakened out of his dream, for the young countess was in dire distress, and her words had the piercing accents of despair. She had thrown herself on her knees in the midst of the cavaliers and was begging them to let her go.

"God has not yet pardoned me," she cried. "Let me go!"

Gösta saw that none of the others meant to obey her, and he understood that he must do so. He, who loved her, had to comply with her wishes.

He felt a difficulty in walking, as if all his limbs resisted his will, but he dragged himself to her and said that he would take her on shore.

She rose instantly. He lifted her down into the boat and rowed her to the east shore. He landed at a little pathway and helped her out of the boat.

"What is to become of you, Countess?" he said.

She lifted her finger solemnly and pointed towards heaven.

"If you are in need, Countess—"

He could not speak, his voice failed him, but she understood him and answered;—

"I will send you word when I need you."

"I would have liked to protect you from all evil," he said.

She gave him her hand in farewell, and he was not able to say anything more. Her hand lay cold and limp in his.

She was not conscious of anything but those inward voices which forced her to go among strangers. She hardly knew that it was the man she loved whom she now left.

So he let her go; and rowed out to the cavaliers again. When he came up on the barge he was trembling with fatigue and seemed exhausted and faint. It seemed to him that he had performed the hardest task in his life.

For a few more days he kept up his courage, until the honour of Ekeby was saved. He brought the iron to the weighing-office on Kanike point; then for a long time he lost all his strength and love of life departed from him.

The cavaliers noticed no change in him as long as they were on board. He strained every nerve to keep his hold on gaiety and

light-heartedness, for it was by gaiety and light-heartedness that
the honour of Ekeby was to be saved. How should their venture
at the weighing-office succeed if they came with anxious faces
and dejected hearts?

If it is true, as rumour has it, that the cavaliers had more sand
than iron in their barges, if it is true that they kept bringing the
same bars to the weighing-office at Kanike point, until the many
hundred tons were weighed; if it is true that all this could happen
because the keeper of the public scales and his men were so well
entertained out of the hampers and wine cases brought from
Ekeby, one must remember that they had to be gay on the iron
barges.

Who can know the truth now? But if it was so, it is certain
that Gösta Berling had no time to grieve. He felt nothing, however,
of the joy of adventure and danger. As soon as he dared, he sank
into a condition of despair.

As soon as the cavaliers had obtained the weighing-master's
receipt, they loaded their iron on a bark. It was the general custom
that the captain of the vessel took charge of the cargo to Gothenburg, and the Värmland ironworks had no more responsibility
for their iron once they had got their certificate from the weighing-
master that delivery had been completed. But the cavaliers would
do nothing by halves, they were going to take the iron all the
way to Gothenburg.

On the way they met with misfortune. A storm broke out in
the night, the vessel was disabled, was driven on a reef, and sank
with all her precious cargo. But if one gave it a second thought,
what did it matter if the iron was lost? The honour of Ekeby was
saved. The iron had been weighed at the weighing-office at Kanike
point. And even if the major had to sit down and in a curt letter
inform the waiting merchants in the big town that he was not
going to accept their money, as they had not got his iron, that
made no difference either. Ekeby was so rich, and its honour was
saved.

But what if harbours and locks, mines and charcoal-kilns,
schooners and barges begin to whisper of strange things? If a

gentle murmur goes through the forests that the journey was a fraud? If it is asserted through the whole of Värmland that there were never more than fifty miserable tons on the barges and that the shipwreck had been prearranged? A bold exploit had been carried out, and a trick characteristic of the cavaliers had been played. Such things, however, do not sully the honour of the old estate.

But it is so long ago now. It is quite possible that the cavaliers bought the iron or that they found it in some hitherto unknown storehouse. We shall never know the truth of the matter. The weighing-master, at any rate, will never admit that there was any possibility of fraud, and he, after all, ought to know.

When the cavaliers reached home they heard that Count Dohna's marriage was to be annulled. The count had sent his steward to Italy to obtain evidence that the marriage had not been legal. He had come back late in the summer with satisfactory reports. What these were,—well, that I do not know with any certainty. One must treat old tales with care; they are like faded roses. They easily drop their petals if one comes too near to them. People say that the marriage-ceremony in Italy had not been performed by a real priest. I do not know, but it is certainly true that the court at Borg declared that a marriage between Count Dohna and Elizabeth von Thurn had never taken place.

The young woman knew nothing of all this. If she was still alive, she was living among peasants in some out-of-the-way place.

I have often mentioned that one of the cavaliers was a great musician. He was a tall, heavily built man, with a big head and bushy, black hair. He was certainly not more than forty years old at that time, but he had an ugly, large-featured face and a pompous manner. This made many think him old. He was a good man, but low-spirited.

One afternoon he took his violin under his arm and went away from Ekeby. He bade no one farewell, although he never meant to return. He loathed the life there ever since he had seen the misfortune that had befallen Countess Elizabeth. He walked the whole evening and the whole night without resting, until at early sunrise he came to a little farm, called Lövdala, which belonged to him.

It was so early that nobody was awake yet. Lilliecrona sat down on the green bench outside the main building and looked at his estate. A more beautiful place did not exist. The lawn in front of the house sloped gently and was covered with fine, light-green grass. Never had there been another lawn to compare with it! The sheep were allowed to graze there and the children to romp and play their games, but it always remained as smooth and green as ever. The scythe never passed over it, but at least once a week the mistress of the house had all sticks and straws and dry leaves swept from the fresh grass. He looked at the gravel walk in front of the house and suddenly drew his feet back. The children had raked it late in the evening, and his big feet had done great harm to their fine work. How everything grew there! The six mountain ashes which guarded the place were as high as beeches and as widespreading as oaks. Such trees had never been seen before. They were beautiful with their thick trunks covered with yellow lichens, and with big, white flower-clusters protruding from the dark foliage. It made him think of the sky and its stars. It was indeed wonderful how the trees grew here. There stood an old willow, so thick that two men could not encircle it with their arms. It was now rotten and hollow, and the lightning had taken the top off it, but it would not die. Every spring a cluster of green shoots came up out of the shattered trunk to show that it was alive. That hawthorn by the east gable had become such a big tree that it overshadowed the whole house. The roof was white with its dropping petals, for the hawthorn had already blossomed. And the birches, which stood in small clumps here and there in the pastures, had certainly found their paradise on his farm. They grew there in so many different ways, as if they meant to imitate all the other trees. One was like a linden, thick and leafy with a wide-spreading arch; another stood close and tall like a poplar, and a third drooped its branches like a weeping-willow. They were all different, and they were all beautiful.

Then he rose and went round the house. There lay the garden, so wonderfully beautiful that he had to stop and draw a long breath. The apple-trees were in bloom. Yes, of course, he knew that. He had seen it on all the other farms; but in no other place did they bloom as they did in that garden, where he had seen them blossom since he was a child. He walked with clasped hands very carefully up and down the gravel path. The ground was white, and the trees were white, here and there with a touch of pink. He had never seen anything so beautiful. He knew every tree, as one knows one's brothers and sisters and playmates. The astrachan trees and the winter fruit-trees were quite white. But the blossoms of the russets were pink, and those of the crab-apple were almost red. The most beautiful was the old wild apple-tree, whose little, bitter apples nobody could eat. It was not stingy with its blossoms; it looked like a great snow-drift in the morning light.

Remember that it was early in the morning! The dew made every leaf shine, all dust was washed away. Behind the forest-clad hills, close under which the farm lay, came the first rays of the sun. It was as if the tops of the pines had been set on fire by them. Over the clover meadows, over rye and corn fields, and over the sprouting oat-shoots, lay the lightest of mists, like a thin veil, and the shadows fell sharp as in moonlight.

He stood and looked at the big vegetable beds between the paths. He knew that mistress and maids had been at work here. They had dug, raked, pulled up weeds and turned the earth, until it had become fine and light. After they had made the beds even and the edges straight, they had taken tapes and pegs and had marked out rows and squares. Then they had sowed, and had set out plants until all the rows and squares had been filled. And the children had been with them and had been so happy and eager to be allowed to help, although it had been hard work for them to stand bent and to stretch their arms out over the broad beds. And it is unlikely that they were of great assistance, as everyone can understand.

Now what they had sowed was beginning to come up.

God bless them! they stood there so bravely, both peas and beans with their two thick seed-lobes; and how thick and nice both carrots and beets had come up! The funniest of all were the little crinkled parsley leaves, which lifted a little earth above them, and as yet were only playing bo-peep with life.

And here was a little bed where the lines did not run so evenly and where the small squares seemed to be an experimental map of everything which could be planted or sowed. That was the children's garden.

And Lilliecrona put his violin hastily up to his chin and began to play. The birds began to sing in the big shrubbery which protected the garden from the north wind. It was not possible for any creature that had a voice to be silent, so glorious was the morning. The fiddle-bow moved quite of itself.

Lilliecrona walked up and down the paths and played. "No," he thought, "there is no place more beautiful." What was Ekeby compared with Lövdala. His home had a thatched roof and was only one story high. It lay at the edge of the wood, with the mountain above it and the long valley below it. There was nothing wonderful about it; there was no lake there, no waterfall, no park, but it was beautiful just the same. It was beautiful because it was a good, peaceful home. Life was easy to live there. Everything which caused bitterness and hate in other places was there smoothed away with gentleness. That is how it should be in a home.

In the house the mistress lies asleep in a room which opens on the garden. She wakes suddenly and listens, but she does not move. She lies smiling and listening. Then the musician comes nearer and nearer, and at last it sounds as if he had stopped under her window. Indeed, it is not the first time she has heard the violin under her window. Her husband was in the habit of coming in this way, when they had done something unusually wild there at Ekeby.

He stands there and confesses and begs for forgiveness. He describes to her the dark powers which tempt him away from what he loves best,—from her and the children. But he loves them. Oh, of course, he loves them!

While he plays she gets up and puts on her clothes without quite knowing what she is doing. She is so taken up with his playing.

"It is not luxury and good cheer, which tempt me away," his playing tells her, "not love for other women, nor glory, but life's seductive variety. I must feel that I am encompassed by its sweetness, its bitterness and its riches. But now I have had enough of it, now I am tired and satisfied. I shall never again leave my home. Forgive me; have mercy on me!"

Then she draws aside the curtain and opens the window, and he sees her beautiful, kind face.

She is both good and wise. Her glances bring blessings like the sun's on everything they meet. She directs and tends. Where she is, everything grows and flourishes. She possesses happiness within her.

He swings himself up on to the window-sill close to her, and is as happy as a young lover.

Then he lifts her out into the garden and carries her down under the apple-trees. There he explains to her how beautiful everything is, and shows her the vegetable beds and the children's garden and the funny little parsley leaves.

When the children awake, there is joy and rapture that father has come. They take possession of him. He must see all that is new and wonderful: the bird's-nest in the willow, and the two little foals which were born a few days ago.

Then father, mother, and children take a long walk in the fields. He wants to see how close the rye stands, how the clover is growing, and how the potatoes are beginning to poke up their crumpled leaves.

He must see the cows when they come in from the pasture, visit the new-comers in the barn and sheep-cote, look for eggs, and give all the horses sugar.

The children stick to his heels the whole day. No lessons, no work; only to wander about with their father!

In the evening he plays polkas for them, and all day he has been such a good comrade and playfellow that they fall asleep with a pious prayer that father may always stay with them.

He stays a whole week, and is as happy as a boy all the time. He is enraptured with everything at home; he is in love with his wife and his children, and never even thinks of Ekeby.

He could stand it no longer, it was too much happiness for him. Ekeby was a thousand times worse, but Ekeby lay in the midst of the vortex of events. Oh, how much there was there to dream of and to play of! How could he live away from the cavaliers' exploits and from the long lake of Löven, around which coursed the wild hunt for adventure.

On his own estate everything went on in its calm, wonted way. Everything flourished and grew under the gentle mistress's care. Everyone was happy there. Everything which anywhere else could have caused discord and bitterness passed over there without complaints or pain. Everything was as it should be. If the master of the house longed to live as a cavalier at Ekeby, what then? Does it help to complain of the sun because it disappears every evening in the west, and leaves the earth in darkness?

Who is indomitable without submission? Who can be sure of victory without patience?

CHAPTER 6 *The Witch of Dovre*

The witch of Dovre walks along the shores of Lake Löven. People have seen her there, small and bent, in a leather skirt and a belt with silverwork. How has she come out of the dens of wolves into the world of human beings? What does the old creature from the mountains want in the green valleys?

She comes begging. She is mean, greedy for gifts, although she is so rich. In the clefts of the mountain she hides heavy bars of white silver; and her great herds of black cattle with golden horns feed in the rich meadows far away on the heights. Still she wanders about in birch-bark shoes and greasy leather skirt soiled with the dirt of a hundred years. She smokes moss in her pipe and begs of the poorest. Shame on one who is never grateful, who never gets enough!

She is old. When did the rosy glory of youth dwell in that broad face with its brown greasy skin, in the flat nose and the small eyes, which gleam in the surrounding dirt like coals of fire in gray ashes? When did she sit as a young girl on the mountainside and answer with her horn the shepherd-boy's love-songs? She has lived several hundred years. The oldest do not remember the time when she did not wander through the land. When their fathers were young, they had seen her as an old woman. Nor is she dead yet. I, who am writing this book, have seen her.

She is powerful. She does not bow the knee before anyone. She can summon the hail, she can guide the lightning. She can lead the herds astray and set wolves on the sheep. Though she can do little good, she can cause much evil. It is best to be on good terms with her! If she should beg for your only goat and a whole pound of wool, give it to her; if you don't, the horse will fall, or the cottage will burn, or the cow will sicken, or the child will die.

She is never a welcome guest. But it is best to meet her with smiling lips! Who knows on whose account the bearer of disaster is roaming through the valley? She does not come only to fill her beggar's wallet. She is accompanied by evil omens: foxes bark and owls hoot in the twilight, red and black serpents, which spit venom, crawl out of the wood up to the very threshold.

She can chant incantations and brew philters. She knows all about herbs. What does she, who comes out of the dark forests and the great mountains, think of the people of the valley? For her, who believes in Thor, the slayer of giants, and in the mighty Finnish gods, Christians are like tame farm dogs to a grey wolf. She, who is as untamed as a snowstorm, as strong as a torrent, can never love the dwellers in the plains.

But she always comes down again from the mountains to look at their dwarf-like way of life. Everybody trembles with fear when they see her; but the strong daughter of the wilderness goes calmly on her way among them, protected by their dread. The exploits of her race are not forgotten, nor are her own. As the cat trusts in its claws, so does she trust in her wisdom and in the strength of her divinely inspired prophecies. No king is more sure of his empire than she of the kingdom of fear in which she rules.

The witch of Dovre has wandered through many villages. Now she has come to Borg, and does not fear to go up to the castle. She seldom goes to the kitchen door. Right up the terrace steps she comes. She treads with her broad birch-bark shoes on the flower-bordered gravel-walks as calmly as if she were tramping up mountain paths.

Countess Märta has just come out on the steps to admire the beauty of the June day. Below her two maids have stopped on their way to the store-house. They have come from the smoke-house, where the bacon is being smoked, and are carrying newly cured hams on a pole between them. "Will our gracious Countess feel and smell?" say the maids. "Are the hams smoked enough?"

Countess Märta, at that time mistress of Borg, leans over the balustrade and looks at the hams, but at the same moment the old Finn woman lays her hand on one of them.

The daughter of the mountains is not accustomed to beg and pray! Is it not by her grace that flowers thrive and people live? Frost and storm and floods are all in her power to send. Therefore she does not need to pray and beg. She lays her hand on what she wants, and it is hers.

Countess Märta, however, knows nothing of the old woman's power.

"Away with you, beggar-woman!" she says.

"Give me the ham," says the witch.

"She is mad," cries the countess. And she orders the maids to go to the store-house with their burden.

The eyes of the old woman flame with rage and greed.

"Give me the brown ham," she repeats, "or it will go ill with you."

"I would rather give it to the magpies than to such as you."

Then the old woman is shaken by a storm of rage. She stretches towards heaven her runic-staff and waves it wildly. Her lips utter strange words. Her hair stands on end, her eyes shine, her face is distorted.

"You shall be eaten by magpies yourself," she screams at last.

Then she goes, mumbling curses, brandishing her stick. She turns towards home. She does not go farther south. She has accomplished her errand, for which she had travelled down from the mountains.

Countess Märta remains standing on the steps and laughs at her extravagant anger; but on her lips the laugh will soon die away, for there they come. She cannot believe her eyes. She thinks that she is dreaming, but here they come, the magpies who are going to devour her.

From the park and the garden they swoop down on her, magpies by scores, with claws ready to seize and bills stretched out to peck. They come with wild screams. Black and white wings gleam before her eyes. She sees, as in a fit of delirium, behind this bevy, the magpies of the whole neighbourhood approaching; the whole sky is full of black and white wings. In the bright morning sun the metallic colours of the feathers glisten. In smaller and smaller circles the monsters fly about the countess, aiming with beaks and claws at her face and hands. She has to escape into the hall and shut the door. She leans against it, panting with terror, while the screaming magpies circle about outside.

From that time on she is shut out from the sweetness and green of the summer and from the joy of life. All that remained for her were closed rooms and drawn curtains; her portion was despair, terror, and confusion bordering on madness.

This story may also sound mad; but it must be true nevertheless. Hundreds will recognize it and will bear witness that such is the old tale.

The birds settled down on the balustrade and the roof. They sat there as if they were waiting only until the countess should show herself, to swoop down on her. They took up their abode in the park and there they remained. It was impossible to drive them away. It was only worse if they shot them. For ten new ones came for every one that was shot. Sometimes great flocks flew away to get food, but faithful sentries always remained behind. And if Countess Märta showed herself, if she looked out of a window or only drew aside the curtain for an instant, or tried to go out on the steps,—they came directly. The whole terrible flock whirled up to the house on thundering wings, and the countess fled into her inner room.

She lived in the bedroom at the back of the red drawing-room. I have often heard the room described, as it was during that time of terror, when Borg was besieged by magpies. Heavy quilts before the doors and windows, thick carpets on the floor, softly treading, whispering people.

In the countess's heart there was wild terror. Her hair turned gray. Her face became wrinkled. She grew old in a month. She could not steel her heart to doubt the hateful magic. She started up from her dreams with wild cries that the magpies were eating her. She wept for days over this fate, which she could not escape. She shunned people, lest the flock of birds should follow on the heels of anyone coming in; she sat mostly silent with her hands before her face, rocking backwards and forwards in her chair, low-spirited and depressed in the close air. Sometimes she would start up with cries of lamentation.

No one's life could be more bitter. Can anyone help pitying her?

I have not much more to tell of her now; and what I have said has not been to her credit. It is as if my conscience smote me. She was goodhearted and cheerful when she was young, and many merry stories about her have gladdened my heart, although there has been no space to tell them here.

Although that poor wayfarer did not know it, the soul is ever hungry. It cannot live on frivolity and entertainment. If it gets no other food, it will, like a wild beast, first tear others to pieces and then destroy itself.

That is the meaning of the story.

CHAPTER 7 *Midsummer*

It was Midsummer then, just as it is now while I am writing. It was the most beautiful season of the year. The season when Sintram, the wicked ironmaster at Fors, fretted and grieved. He resented the triumphal procession of the light through the hours of the day, and the overthrow of darkness. He raged at the leafy dress which clothed the trees, and at the many-coloured carpet which covered the ground.

Everything arrayed itself in beauty. The road, gray and dusty as it was, had its border of flowers; yellow and purple midsummer blossoms, wild parsley, and asters.

When the glory of midsummer lay on the mountains and the sound of the bells from the church at Bro was borne on the quivering air even as far as Fors, when the unspeakable stillness of the Sabbath day reigned in the land, then he rose in wrath. It seemed to him as if God and men dared to forget that he existed; and he too decided to go to church. Those who rejoiced in the summer should see him, Sintram, lover of darkness without dawn, of death without resurrection, of winter without spring.

He put on his wolfskin coat and shaggy fur gloves. He had the red horse harnessed to a sledge, and fastened bells to the shining horse-collar. Equipped as if it were thirty degrees below zero, he drove to church. He believed that the creaking under the runners was due to the severe cold. He believed that the white foam on the horse's back was hoarfrost. He felt no heat. Cold streamed from him as warmth from the sun.

He drove over the wide plain north of the Bro church. Large, rich villages lay near his way, and fields of grain, over which singing larks fluttered. Never have I heard larks sing as in those fields.

I have often wondered how he could shut his ears to those hundreds of songsters.

He had to drive by many things on the way which would have
enraged him if he had given them a glance. He would have seen
two bending birches at the door of every house, and through
open windows he would have looked into rooms whose ceilings
and walls were covered with flowers and green branches. The
smallest beggar child went on the road with a bunch of lilacs in
her hand, and every peasant woman had a little nosegay stuck in
her neckerchief.

Maypoles with faded flowers and drooping wreaths stood in
every yard. Round about them the grass was trodden down, for
the merry dance had whirled there through the summer night.

Below on the Löven the floats of timber crowded. The little
white sails were hoisted in honour of the day, although no wind
filled them; and every masthead bore a green wreath.

On the many roads which lead to Bro the congregation were
walking. The women were especially fine in their light summer-
dresses, which had been made ready for that day. All were dressed
in their best.

And the people could not help rejoicing in the peace of the
holiday and in their rest from daily work, in the delicious warmth,
the promising harvest, and the wild strawberries which were beginning to redden at the edge of the road. They noticed the stillness of the air and the song of the larks, and said: "It is plain that
this is the Lord's day."

Then Sintram drove up. He swore and swung his whip over
the straining horse. The sand grated horribly under the runners,
the shrill clang of the sleigh-bells drowned the sound of the church
bells. Under his fur cap his brow was knitted in anger.

The church-goers shuddered and thought they had seen the
evil one himself. Not even to-day, during the midsummer festival
were they permitted to forget evil and cold. Bitter is the lot of
those who wander upon the earth.

The people who stood in the shadow of the church or sat on
the churchyard wall and waited for the beginning of the service,

saw him with calm wonder when he came up to the church door. The glorious day had filled their hearts with joy that they were alive, to roam and enjoy the sweetness of existence. Now, when they saw Sintram, forebodings of strange disaster came over them.

Sintram entered the church and sat down in his seat, throwing his gloves on the pew, so that the rattle of the wolves' claws which were sewed onto the leather was heard throughout the church. Several women, who had already taken their places in the front pews fainted when they saw the shaggy form, and had to be carried out.

But no one dared to drive Sintram out. He disturbed people's devotions, but he was too much feared for anyone to venture to order him to leave the church.

In vain the old clergyman spoke of the bright festival of summer. Nobody listened to him. The people only thought of evil and cold and of the strange disaster which the presence of the wicked ironmaster portended.

When it was over, they saw him walk out on to the slope of the hill where the Bro church stands. He looked down on Broby Sound and followed it with his eyes past the rural deanery and the three headlands on the west shore out into Löven. And they saw how he clenched his fist and shook it over the sound and its green banks. Then looked further south over lower Löven to the misty shores which seemed to shut in the lake. He gazed northward miles beyond Gurlitta Cliff up to Björnidet, where the lake ended. He looked to the west and east, where the long mountains border the valley, and he clenched his fist again. And everyone felt that if he had held a bundle of thunderbolts in his right hand, he would have hurled them in wild joy over the peaceful country and spread sorrow and death as far as he could. For he had now so accustomed his heart to evil that he knew no pleasure except in causing suffering. By degrees he had taught himself to love everything ugly and wretched. He was more insane than the most violent madman, but no one understood that.

Strange stories went about the country after that day. It was said that when the sexton came to lock the church, the bit of the key broke, because a tightly folded piece of paper had been stuck in the keyhole. He gave it to the dean. As was to be expected, it was a letter meant for a being in the other world.

People whispered of what had been written there. The dean had burnt the paper, but the sexton had looked on while the devil's trash burned. The letters had shone bright red on a black ground. He could not help reading them. He read, people said, that Sintram wished to lay waste all the country from which the church-tower at Bro was still visible. He wished to see the forest grow up and conceal the church. He wished to see bears and foxes living in men's dwellings. The fields should lie uncultivated, and no dog or cock should be heard in the neighbourhood. He wished to serve his master by causing every man's ruin. That was what he promised would take place.

And the people looked to the future in silent despair, for they knew that his power was great; that he hated everything living; that he wished to see the wilderness spread through the valley, and that he would gladly take pestilence or famine or war into his service in order to drive away everyone who loved good, joyful work.

CHAPTER 8 *Madame Musica*

When nothing could make Gösta Berling glad, after he had helped the young countess to escape, the cavaliers decided to seek the help of good Madame Musica, who is a powerful fairy and consoles many who are unhappy.

So one evening in July they had the doors of the big drawing-room at Ekeby opened and the shutters taken down. The sun and air were let in, the big, red sun of the late evening, and the cool, mild, misty air.

The striped covers were taken off the furniture, the piano was opened, and the net around the Venetian chandelier taken away. The golden griffins under the white-marble table-tops again reflected the light. The white goddesses danced above the mirror. The variegated flowers on the silk damask glistened in the evening glow. Roses were picked and brought in. The whole room was filled with their fragrance. There were wonderful roses with unknown names, which had been brought to Ekeby from foreign countries. There were yellow roses in whose veins the sap shone as red as the blood in the veins of a human being; and cream-white roses with curled edges, and pink roses with broad petals which were as colourless as water near their edges; and dark red roses with black shadows. They gathered all Altringer's roses, which had come from far distant countries, to rejoice the eyes of lovely women.

The music and music-stands were brought in, and the brass instruments and bows and violins of all sizes; for good Madame Musica shall now reign at Ekeby and try to console Gösta Berling.

Madame Musica has chosen the Oxford Symphony of Haydn, and has got the cavaliers to practise it. Julius conducts, and each of them attends to his own instrument. All the cavaliers can play—otherwise they would not be cavaliers.

When everything is ready Gösta is sent for. He is still weak and low-spirited, but he rejoices in the beautiful room and in the music he is soon to hear. For everyone knows that for those who suffer and are in pain, good Madame Musica is the best company. She is gay and playful like a child. She is fiery and captivating like a young woman. She is good and wise like the old who have lived a good life.

And then the cavaliers began to play, so gently, so softly.

It goes well, it goes brilliantly. From the dead musical notation they conjure up Madame Musica herself. Spread out your magic cloak, dear Madame Musica, and take Gösta Berling to the land of happiness where he used to live.

Alas that it is Gösta Berling who sits there pale and depressed, and whom the old men must amuse as if he where a child. There will be no more joy now in Värmland.

I know why the old people loved him. I know how long a winter evening can be, and how gloom can creep over the spirit in those lonely farm-houses. I understand what it meant when he came.

Ah, imagine a Sunday afternoon, when work is laid aside and thoughts are dull! Imagine an obstinate north wind, whipping cold into the room,—a cold which no fire can relieve! Imagine the single tallow-candle, which has to be continually snuffed! Imagine the monotonous sound of psalms from the kitchen!

Well, and then the sound of bells, eager feet stamp off the snow in the hall, and Gösta Berling comes into the room. He laughs and jokes. He is life, he is warmth. He opens the piano, and plays so that they are surprised at the old chords. He can sing all songs, play any tune. He makes all the inmates of the house happy. He was never cold, he was never tired. The mourner forgot his sorrows when he saw him. Ah, what a good heart he had! How compassionate he was to the weak and poor! And what a genius he was! Yes, you ought to have heard the old people talk of him.

But now, just as they were playing, he burst into tears. He thinks life is so sad. He rests his head in his hands and weeps. The cavaliers are dismayed. These are not mild, healing tears, such as

Madame Musica generally calls forth. He is sobbing like one in despair. At their wits' end they put their instruments away.

And good Madame Musica, who loves Gösta Berling, she too almost loses courage; but then she remembers that she has still a mighty champion among the cavaliers.

It is the gentle Löwenborg, who had lost his fiancée in the muddy river, and who is more Gösta Berling's devoted slave than any of the others. He steals away to the piano.

In the cavaliers' wing Löwenborg has a great wooden table, on which he has painted a keyboard and set up a music-stand. There he can sit for hours at a time and let his fingers fly over the black and white keys. There he practises both scales and studies, and there he plays his Beethoven. He never plays anything but Beethoven.

But the old man never ventures to play on any instrument other than the wooden table. For he holds the piano in awe. It tempts him, but it frightens him even more. The clashing instrument, on which so many polkas have been drummed, is a sacred thing to him. He has never dared to touch it. Think of that wonderful thing with its many chords which could give life to the great master's works! He only needs to put his ear to it, to hear andantes and scherzos murmering there. But he has never played on such a thing. He will never be rich enough to buy one of his own, and on this piano he has never dared to play. Nor was the major's wife very willing to open it for him.

He has heard how polkas and waltzes have been played on it. But for such profane music the noble instrument could only crash discordantly and complain. No, if Beethoven were to come, then it would let its true, clear sound be heard.

Now he thinks the time has come for him and Beethoven. He will take courage and touch the holy thing, and let his young lord and master be gladdened by the sleeping harmonies.

He sits down and begins to play. He is uncertain and nervous, but he gropes through a couple of bars, tries to bring out the right tone, frowns, tries again, and puts his hands before his face and begins to weep.

Yes, it is a bitter thing. The shrine is no longer sacred. There are no clear, pure tones hidden and dreaming in it; there are no mighty thunders, no rushing hurricanes. None of the endless harmonies direct from heaven had remained there. It is an old, worn-out piano, and nothing more.

But then Madame Musica gives the colonel a hint. He takes Ruster with him and they go to the cavaliers wing and get Löwenborg's table, where the keys are painted.

"See here, Löwenborg," says Beerencreutz, when they come back, "here is your piano. Play for Gösta!"

Then Löwenborg stops crying and sits down to play Beethoven for his sorrowful young friend. Now he will certainly be happy again.

In the old man's head sound the most heavenly tones. He cannot but think that Gösta hears how beautifully he is playing. He meets with no more difficulties. He plays his runs and trills with the greatest ease. He would have liked that the master himself could have heard him.

The longer he plays, the more he is carried away. He hears every note with unearthly clearness. He sits there glowing with enthusiasm and emotion, hearing the most wonderful tones, confident that Gösta must hear them too and be comforted.

Gösta sat and looked at him. At first he was angry at this foolery, but gradually his mood became milder. The old man was irresistible, as he sat and enjoyed his Beethoven.

And Gösta began to think how this man too, who now was so gentle and so carefree, had been sunk in suffering; how he too had lost the woman he loved. And now he sat radiantly happy at his wooden table. Nothing more was needed to add to his bliss.

He felt humbled. "What, Gösta," he said to himself, "can you no longer bear and suffer? You who have been hardened by poverty all your life, you who have heard every tree in the forest, every tuft in the meadow preach of resignation and patience, you who have been brought up in a land where the winter is severe and the summer short,—have you forgotten how to endure?"

Ah, Gösta, a man must bear all that life offers with a brave heart and smiling lips, or he is no man. Regret as much as you like if you have lost what you hold dearest, let remorse tear at your vitals, but show yourself a man. Let your eyes shine with gladness, and meet your friends with cheerful words!

Life is hard, nature is hard. But they both give courage and cheerfulness as compensations for their hardness, or no one could endure them.

Courage and cheerfulness! They appear to be the primary duties of life. You have never failed in them before, and you shall not now.

Are you worse than Löwenborg, who sits there at his wooden piano, or than all the other cavaliers? You know well enough that none of them have escaped suffering!

And then Gösta looks at them. Oh, what a performance! They are all sitting there so seriously and listening to this music which nobody hears.

Suddenly Löwenborg is waked from his dreams by a merry laugh. He lifts his hands from the keys and listens as if in rapture. It is Gösta Berling's old laugh, his good, kind, infectious laugh. It is the sweetest music the old man has heard in all his life.

"Did I not say that Beethoven would help you, Gösta," he cries. "Now you are yourself again."

So did good Madame Musica cure Gösta Berling's melancholia.

CHAPTER 9 *The Vicar of Broby*

Eros, all-powerful god, you know well that it often seems that a man should have freed himself from your power. All the tender feelings which unite mankind appear to be dead in his heart. Madness stretches out its claws to seize the wretch; but then you come in all your power; and like the great saint's staff, the dried-up heart bursts into flower.

No one is so mean as the vicar of Broby, no one is more cut off from his fellow-men by malice and uncharitableness. His rooms are unheated in the winter, he sits on an unpainted wooden seat, he dresses in rags, lives on dry bread, and is furious if a beggar enters his door. He lets the horse starve in the stable and sells the hay, his cows nibble the dry grass at the roadside and the moss on the wall. The bleating of the hungry sheep can be heard far along the highway. The peasants throw him presents of food which their dogs will not eat, of clothes which their poor disdain. His hand is stretched out to beg, his back is bent servilely in gratitude. He begs of the rich, and lends to the poor. If he sees a piece of money his heart aches with longing till he gets it into his pocket. Woe betide anyone whose accounts are not in order on the day payment falls due to him.

He married late in life, but it would have been better if he had never done so. His wife died from overwork and exhaustion. His daughter is in service with strangers. He is old, but age grants him no relief in his struggle. The madness of avarice never leaves him.

But one fine day in the beginning of August a heavy coach, drawn by four horses, drives up Broby hill. A delicate old lady arrives in great state, with coachman and footman and lady's maid. She comes to see the vicar of Broby. She had loved him when she was young.

He had been tutor at her father's house, and they had loved one another, although her proud family had separated them. And now she is driving up Broby hill to see him before she dies. All that is left to her in life is to see once again the man she loved when she was a young girl.

She sits in the great carriage and dreams. She is not driving up Broby hill to a poor little parsonage. She is on her way to the cool, leafy arbour down in the park, where her lover is waiting. She sees him; he is young, he can kiss, he can love. Now that she will soon meet him, his image rises before her with singular clearness. He is so handsome, so very handsome! He is capable of adoration; he is ardent; he fills her whole being with rapture.

She is now sallow, withered, and old. She is sixty, perhaps he will not recognize her; she has not come in order to be seen, but to see, to see the beloved of her youth, who has gone through life untouched by time; who is ever young, beautiful, ardent.

She has come from so far away that she has not heard a word about the vicar of Broby.

The coach clatters up the hill, and at the summit the vicarage is visible.

"For the love of God," whines a beggar at the wayside, "a copper for a poor man!"

The noble lady gives him a piece of silver and asks where the vicarage is.

"The vicarage is in front of you," he says, "but the vicar is not at home, there is no one at the vicarage."

The little lady seems to fade away. The cool arbour vanishes, her lover is not there. How could she expect, after forty years, to find him there?

What did the gracious lady wish to do at the vicarage?

She had come to meet the vicar. She had known him in the old days.

Forty years and four hundred miles have separated them. And for every ten miles that she has come nearer to Broby, she has become a year younger and has left behind her the burden of sorrows and memories connected with these years; so that when she now comes to the vicarage she is a girl of twenty again, carefree and without any regrets.

The beggar stands and looks at her, sees her change under his eyes from twenty to sixty, and from sixty back to twenty.

"The vicar is coming home this afternoon," he says. The gracious lady would do best to drive down to the Broby inn and come again later. In the afternoon, the beggar can answer for it, the vicar will be at home.

A moment later the heavy coach with the little wizened lady rolls down the hill to the inn, but the beggar stands trembling and looks after her. He feels that he ought to fall on his knees and kiss the wheel tracks.

Elegant, newly shaven and washed, in shoes with shining buckles, with silk stockings, and with ruffles and frills, the vicar of Broby stands at noon the same day before the dean's wife at Bro.

"A fine lady," he says, "a count's daughter. Do you think that I, a poor man, can ask her to come into my house? My floors are black, my drawing-room is without furniture, the dining-room ceiling is green with mildew and damp. Help me! Remember that she is a noble count's daughter!"

"Say that you have gone away!"

"My dear lady, she has come four hundred miles to see me, a poor man. She does not know my position. I have not a bed to offer her. I have not a bed even for her servants!"

"Well, let her go back again."

"Dear lady! Do you not understand what I mean? I would rather give away everything I possess, everything that I have gathered together by hard work and industry, than that she should go away without my having received her in my house. She was twenty when I saw her last, and it is now forty years ago! Help me, so that I may invite her to my house! Here is money, if money can help, but more than money is needed here."

Oh, Eros, women love you. They would rather go a hundred steps for you than one for other gods.

In the deanery at Bro the rooms are emptied, the kitchen is

emptied, the larder is emptied. Wagons are piled up and driven
to the vicarage. When the dean comes home from the communion service, he will find empty rooms; looking in through
the kitchen door to ask for his dinner, he will find no one there.
No dinner, no wife, no maids! What else could be done?

Eros had willed it.

A little later in the afternoon the heavy coach comes clattering
up Broby hill. And the little lady sits and wonders if any new
mischance will happen; if it is really true that she is now going
to meet the one joy of her life.

Then the coach drives up to the vicarage. Someone is coming;
there he comes. He lifts her out of the carriage, he carries her in his
arms; strong as ever. She is clasped in an embrace as warm as of
old, forty years ago. She looks into his eyes; which glow as they did
when they had only seen five and twenty summers.

A storm of emotion comes over her—more profound than ever.
She remembers that he once carried her up the steps to the terrace.
She, who believed that her love had remained alive all these years,
had, nevertheless, forgotten what it was to be clasped in strong
arms, to look into young, glowing eyes.

She does not see that he is old. She only sees his eyes.

She does not see the black floors, the mildewed ceilings, she
only sees his beaming eyes. At that hour the vicar of Broby is a
fine figure and a handsome man. He becomes handsome when he
looks at her.

She hears his voice, his clear, strong voice; it has a caressing
sound. He only speaks so to her. Why did he need furniture from
the deanery for his empty rooms; why food, why servants? The
old lady would never have missed anything. She hears his voice
and sees his eyes.

Never, never before has she been so happy.

She knows that he has been married, but she does not remember
it. How could she remember such a thing? She is twenty, and he
is twenty-five. This smiling youth, is he to become the mean
vicar of Broby? The wailing of the poor, the curses of the
defrauded, the scornful gibes, the caricatures, the sneers; as yet,

none of these things exist for him. His heart burns only with a pure and innocent love. Never shall that proud youth love gold so that he will crawl for it in the dirt; beg it from the wayfarer, suffer humiliation, disgrace, cold and hunger to get it. Will he starve his child, torture his wife, for that same miserable gold? It is impossible. Such a wretch he can never become. He is a good man like all others. He is not a monster.

The girl he loved in his youth does not walk by the side of a despised creature, unworthy of the vocation he has dared to profess!

Oh, Eros, almighty god, spare him that one evening! Neither that evening nor during the next two days is he the vicar of Broby.

The day after that she left.

What a dream, what a beautiful dream! For these three days there was not a cloud!

Smiling, she travelled home to her castle and her memories. She never heard his name mentioned again; she never asked for him. She wanted to dream that dream as long as she lived.

The vicar fo Broby sat in his lonely home and wept. She had made him young. Must he now be old again? Would the evil spirit return and would he become as despicable and contemptible as he had been?

CHAPTER 10 *Squire Julius*

Squire Julius carried down his red, painted wooden chest from the cavaliers' wing. He filled a green keg with fragrant brandy, which had accompanied him on many journeys, and in the big carved luncheon-box he put butter, bread, and seasoned cheese with its delicious shades of green and brown, fat ham, and pancakes swimming in raspberry jam.

Then squire Julius went about bidding farewell, with tears in his eyes, to all the glory of Ekeby. For the last time he caressed the worn balls in the bowling-alley and the round-cheeked youngsters on the estate. He went to the arbours in the garden and the grottos in the park. He was in the stables and the cow-houses; patted the horses' hind quarters, shook the angry bull by the horns, and let the calves lick his bare hand. Finally, he went with a tearful face to the main building, where the farewell breakfast awaited him.

How can our existence be made up of so much darkness? There was poison in the food, gall in the wine.

Not only his throat, but also those of the cavaliers were tense with emotion. A mist of tears dimmed their eyes. The farewell speech was broken by sobs. How fraught with sorrow is human existence! Henceforth, his life would be a perpetual longing. He would never smile again; his memory of the ballads would die, as flowers die in the autumn ground. He would grow pale and thin, wither like a frost-bitten rose, like a parched lily. Never more would the cavaliers see poor Julius. Heavy forebodings passed through his mind, just as the shadows of wind-swept clouds traverse our newly tilled fields. He would go home to die.

He now stood before them in splendid health and full of well-being. Never again would they see him so. Never more would they jestingly ask him when he last saw his feet; never more would they want to use his cheeks as skittle-balls. His liver and lungs were already affected. The disease was consuming his vitality; he was wasting away. He had been aware of it for a long time. His days were numbered.

Oh, may the Ekeby cavaliers remember the dead! May they never forget him!

Duty called him. There in his home his mother sat and waited for him. For seventeen years she had waited for him to come home from Ekeby. Now she had written a letter summoning him to return, and he would obey. He knew that it would be his death; but he would obey like a good son.

Oh, the glorious feasts! The fair meadows bordering the shores of the lake, the proud waterfalls! The wild adventures, the white, smooth floors, the beloved cavaliers wing! Oh, violins and horns, and life of happiness and pleasure! It was death to be parted from all this.

Then squire Julius went out into the kitchen and bade farewell to the servants of the house. In an excess of emotion he embraced and kissed anybody and everybody, from the housekeeper to the scullery maid. The maids wept and lamented over his fate: that such a kind and merry gentleman was about to die, thet they would never see him again.

Squire Julius ordered that his chaise should be taken out of the carriage-house and his horse out of the stables.

His voice almost failed him when he gave the order. So the chaise was not to moulder in peace at Ekeby; so old Kajsa had to be parted from the well-known manger. He did not wish to say anything hard about his mother; but she ought to have thought of the chaise and Kajsa, if she did not think of him. How would they endure the long journey?

Most bitter of all was the parting from the cavaliers.

Little, rotund squire Julius, who was more apt to roll than to walk, felt his tragic position to his very fingertips. He felt himself the great Athenian, who calmly emptied the poison cup in the circle of weeping disciples. He imagined himself as old King

Gösta, who prophesied to the people of Sweden that some day they would wish to raise him up from the dust.

Finally, he sang them his best ballad. He thought of the swan who dies when it sings. It was thus, he hoped they would remember him,—a kingly spirit, which does not lower itself to complaining, but goes its way, borne on melody.

Finally, the last cup was emptied, the last song sung, the last embrace given. He had his coat on, and he held the whip in his hand. There was not a dry eye about him; his own were so filled with the mist of sorrowful tears that he could not see anything.

Then the cavaliers seized him and lifted him up. Cheers thundered around him. They put him down somewhere, he did not see where. A whip cracked, the carriage seemed to move under him. He was carried away. When he recovered the use of his eyes he was out on the highway.

The cavaliers had really wept and had been overcome by deep regret; still their grief had not stifled all the heart's glad emotions. One of them—was it Gösta Berling, the poet, or Beerencreutz, the card-playing old warrior, or Cousin Christopher who was weary of life?—had arranged that old Kajsa did not have to be taken from her stall, or the mouldering chaise from the coach-house. Instead, a big spotted ox had been harnessed to a hay-wagon, and after the red chest, the green keg, and the carved luncheon-box had been put in it; squire Julius himself, whose eyes were dim with tears, was lifted up, not on to the luncheon-box, or on to the chest, but on to the spotted ox's back.

For man is too weak to meet sorrow in all its bitterness! The cavaliers sincerely mourned their friend, who was going away to die,—that withered lily, that mortally wounded singing swan; yet the oppression of their hearts was relieved when they saw him depart, riding on the big ox's back, while his fat body was shaken with sobs, his arms, outstreched for the last embrace, dropped in despair, and his eyes sought sympathy from an indifferent heaven.

Out on the highway the mist began to clear for squire Julius, and he perceived that he was sitting on the swinging back of an animal. And then people say that he began to ponder on all that can happen in seventeen long years. Old Kajsa was apparently changed. Could the oats and clover of Ekeby cause such a transformation? And he cried—I do not know if the stones in the road or the birds in the bushes heard it, but true it is that he cried—"The devil take me, if you have not got horns, Kajsa!"

After another period of profound thought, he slid down gently from the back of the ox, climbed up into the wagon, sat down on the luncheon-box, and drove on, deep in his thoughts.

After a while, when he had almost reached Broby, he heard singing.

It was the merry young ladies from Berga, and some of the judge's pretty daughters, who were walking along the road. They had fastened their food-wallets on long sticks, which rested on their shoulders like guns, and they were marching on bravely in the summer heat, and kept good time in their singing.

"Wither away, squire Julius?" they cried, when they met him, without noticing the cloud of grief which obscured his brow.

"I am departing from the home of sin and vanity," answered squire Julius. "I will dwell no longer among idlers and malefactors. I am going home to my mother."

"Oh," they cried, "it is not true; you do not want to leave Ekeby, squire Julius!"

"Yes," he said, and struck his wooden chest with his fist. "As Lot fled from Sodom and Gomorrah, so do I flee from Ekeby. There is not a righteous man there. But when the earth gives way beneath them, and fire and brimstone rain down from heaven, I shall rejoice in God's righteous judgment. Farewell, girls; beware of Ekeby!"

He then wished to continue on his way; but that was not at all what they had in view. They meant to climb Dunder Cliff; but the road was long, and they felt inclined to ride in Julius' wagon to the foot of the mountain. In less than two minutes the girls had got their way. Squire Julius turned back and directed his course towards Dunder Cliff. Smiling, he sat on his chest, while the girls filled the wagon. Daisies and buttercups grew along the roadside. The ox had to rest every now and then for a while. Then the girls climbed out and picked flowers. Soon gaudy wreaths hung on Julius' head and the ox's horns.

Further on they came upon bright young birches and dark alder-bushes. They got out and broke off branches to adorn the wagon. It soon looked like a moving grove. It was play and fun the whole day.

Squire Julius became milder and brighter as the day went on. He divided his provisions among the girls, and sang ballads for them. When they stood on the top of Dunder Cliff, with the wide panorama lying below, so proud and beautiful that tears came into their eyes at its loveliness, Julius felt his heart beat violently; words poured from his lips, and he spoke of his beloved land.

"Ah, Värmland," he said, "ever beautiful, ever glorious! Often, when I have seen thee before me on a map, I have wondered what thou mightest represent; but now I understand what thou art. Thou art an old, pious hermit, who sits quiet and dreams, with crossed legs, and hands resting in his lap. Thou hast a pointed cap drawn down over thy half-shut eyes. Thou art a muser, a holy dreamer, and thou art very beautiful. Wide forests are thy dress. Long bands of blue water and parallel chains of blue hills are its borders. Thou art so simple that strangers do not see how beauti-ful thou art. Thou art poor, as the devout desire to be. Thou sittest still, while Vänern's waves wash thy feet and thy crossed legs. To the left thou hast thy fields of ore and thy ironworks. There is thy beating heart. To the north thou hast the dark, beautiful regions of the wilderness, of mystery. There is thy dreaming head.

"When I see thee, gigantic and grave, my eyes are filled with tears. Thou art stern in thy beauty. Thou art meditation, poverty, resignation; and yet I see in thy sternness the tender features of kindness. I see thee and turn to worship. If I only look into deep forest, if only the hem of thy garment touches me, my spirit is healed. Hour after hour, year after year, I have gazed into thy holy countenance. What mystery art thou hiding under lowered eyelids, thou spirit of resignation? Hast thou solved the enigma of life and death, or art thou wondering still, thou holy one, thou who art so great? For me thou art the keeper of great, solemn thoughts.

But I see people crawling on thee and around thee, creatures who never seem to see the majesty of earnestness on thy brow. They only see the beauty of thy face and thy limbs, and are so charmed by it that they forget all else.

"Woe is me, woe to us all, children of Värmland! Beauty, beauty and nothing else, we demand of life. We, children of renunciation, of gravity, of poverty, raise our hands in one long prayer, and ask for the one good: beauty. May life be like a rose-bush, with blossoms of love, wine, and pleasure, and may its roses be within every man's reach! Yes, that is what we wish, and our land wears the features of sternness, earnestness, renunciation. Our land is the eternal symbol of meditation, but we have no thoughts of our own.

"Oh, Värmland, beautiful and glorious!"

So he spoke, with tears in his eyes, and with voice vibrating with inspiration. The young girls heard him with wonder and not without emotion. They had little guessed the depth of feeling which was hidden under that exterior glittering with jests and laughter.

When it drew towards evening, and they once more climbed into the hay-wagon, the girls hardly knew whither squire Julius drove them, until they stopped before the steps at Ekeby.

"Now we will go in here and have a dance, girls," said squire Julius.

What did the cavaliers say when they saw squire Julius come with a withered wreath round his hat, and the hay-wagon full of girls?

"We might have known that the girls had carried him off", they said; "otherwise we should have had him back here several hours earlier." For the cavaliers remembered that this was exactly the seventeenth time squire Julius had tried to leave Ekeby, once every fleeting year. Now squire Julius had already forgotten both this and all his previous attempts. His conscience slept once more its year-long sleep.

He was a doughty man, squire Julius. He was a good dancer, gay at the card-table. He was equally handy with a pen, a pencil or a fiddle-bow. His heart was easily moved. Fair words were ever on his tongue, and he was full of songs. But what would have been the good of all that if he had not possessed a conscience, which made itself felt only once a year, like the dragon-flies, which free themselves from the gloomy depths and grow wings, only to live a few hours in the light of day and in the glory of the sun?

CHAPTER 11 *The Plaster Saints*

Svartsjö church is white both outside and in: the walls are white, the pulpit, the seats, the galleries, the ceiling, the window-sashes, the altar-cloth,—everything is white. In Svartsjö church there are no decorations, no pictures, no coats of arms. Over the altar stands only a wooden cross with a white linen cloth. But it was not always so. Once the ceiling was covered with paintings, and many coloured images of stone and plaster stood in that house of God.

Once, many years ago, an artist in Svartsjö had stood and watched the summer sky and the path of the clouds across the sun. He had seen those white, shining clouds, which in the morning float low on the horizon, pile themselves up higher and higher and raise themselves to storm the heavens. They hoist sails like ships. They raised standards like warriors. They invaded the whole sky. They placed themselves before the sun, those growing monsters, and took on wonderful shapes. There was a devouring lion; it changed into a powdered lady. There was a giant with outstreched arms; he laid himself down as a dreaming sphinx. Some adorned their white nakedness with gold-bordered mantles; others spread rouge over snowy cheeks. There were plains. There were forests. There were walled castles with high towers. The white clouds were lords of the summer sky. They filled the whole blue arch. They reached up to the sun and hid it.

"Oh, how beautiful," thought the gentle artist, "if the longing spirits could climb up on those towering mountains and be carried on those rocking ships ever higher and higher upwards!"

And all at once he understood that the white clouds were the vessels on which the souls of the blessed were carried.

He saw them there. They stood on the gliding masses with lilies in their hands and golden crowns on their heads. Space echoed with their song. Angels circled down on broad, strong wings to meet them. Oh, what a host there were! As the clouds spread out, more and more were visible. They lay on the cloud-beds like water-lilies on a pond; they adorned them, as lilies adorn the meadow. Cloud after cloud rolled up. And all were filled with heavenly hosts in armour of silver, with immortal singers in purple-bordered mantles.

That artist had afterwards painted the ceiling in the Svartsjö church. He had wished to reproduce there the mounting clouds of the summer day, which bore the blessed to the kingdom of heaven. The hand which had guided the brush had been strong, but also rather stiff, so that the clouds resembled more the curling locks of a full-bottomed wig than mountains of soft mist. And the forms the holy ones had assumed in the painter's imagination, he was unable to reproduce; instead, he clothed them in long, red cloaks, and stiff bishops' mitres, or in black robes with stiff ruffles. He had given them big heads and small bodies, and he had provided them with handkerchiefs and prayer-books. Latin sentences flew out of their mouths; and for those whom he meant to be the greatest, he had constructed solid wooden chairs on the backs of the clouds, so that they could be carried, sitting comfortably, to everlasting life.

But everyone knew that spirits and angels had never shown themselves to the poor artist, and so they were not much surprised that he had not been able to give them celestial beauty. The good master's pious work had seemed to many wonderfully fine; and much holy emotion had been aroused. It might also have been worthy, of being looked at by us.

But during the cavaliers' year, Count Dohna had the whole church whitewashed; the paintings on the ceiling were then destroyed, and all the plaster saints were removed.

Alas! the plaster saints!

There was a Saint Olof with a crown on his helm, an axe in his hand, and a kneeling giant under his feet; on the pulpit was a Judith in a red jacket and blue skirt, with a sword in one hand and an hour-glass in the other,—instead of the Assyrian general's head; there was a mysterious Queen of Sheba in a blue jacket and red skirt, with a web-foot on one leg and her hands full of Sibylline books; there was a gray Saint Göran lying alone on a bench in the choir, for both horse and dragon had been destroyed; there was Saint Christopher with the flowering staff, and Saint Erik with sceptre and axe, dressed in a flowing brocaded cloak.

Many a Sunday I have sat in the church at Svartsjö, grieving for the images that were no more, and yearning for them. I should not have looked at them in order to see whether they had lost a nose or a foot; whether the gilt had tarnished and the colour had fallen off. I would have seen them shining in the glory of their legends.

These saints were always losing their sceptres or their ears or hands and had to be mended and cleaned. The congregation wearied of it, and longed to be rid of them. But the peasants would never have done the saints any injury if Count Henrik Dohna had not existed. It was he who had them taken away.

I had hated him for doing this, as only a child can hate. I had hated him as the famished beggar hates the niggardly mistress of the household who denies him bread. I had hated him as a poor fisherman hates an ignorant boy, who has destroyed his net and made a hole in his boat. For did not I suffer hunger and thirst during those long divine services? He had taken away the bread on which my spirit would have fed. Did I not long for infinitude, did I not long to mount to heaven? He had destroyed my vessel; he had torn the net with which I would have caught the holy visions. There is no room in the world of adults for real hatred.

The minister was in the pulpit, speaking perhaps of peace and reconciliation; but from where we sat in church, what he said could never be heard. Oh if only those old plaster saints had been there with me! They would surely have preached to me in a way that I could have both heard and understood.

But as it was, I often sat and wondered what had happened when they had been kidnapped and destroyed.

When Count Dohna had caused his marriage to be declared null and void, instead of seeking out his wife and having it made legal, much indignation had arisen; for everyone knew that his wife had left his house only so as not to be tortured to death. It seemed now as if he wanted to win back God's grace and men's respect by performing a good work; and so he had Svartsjö church repaired. He had the whole church whitewashed and the paintings torn down. He and his men carried the images out in a boat and sank them in the depths of lake Löven.

How could he dare to lay his hand on those mighty ones of the Lord?

Did the hand which struck off Holofernes' head no longer hold a sword? Had Sheba's queen forgotten all her secret knowledge that wounds more deeply than a poisoned arrow? Saint Olof, Saint Olof, old viking, Saint Göran, old dragon-killer, the fame of your deeds is, then, dead! But it was well that the saints did not wish to use force against their destroyers. Since the Svartsjö peasants would not pay for paint for their robes and gilding for their crowns, they allowed Count Dohna to carry them out and sink them in the unfathomable depths of lake Löven. They did not wish to stand there disfiguring God's house.

I thought of that boat with its load of saints gliding over the surface of lake Löven on a quiet summer evening in August. The man who rowed took slow strokes with his oars and threw timorous glances at the strange passengers who lay in the bow and stern; but Count Dohna, who was also there, was not afraid. He took them one by one and threw them into the water. His brow was clear and he breathed deep. He felt like a defender of pure Evangelical religion. And no miracle was performed in the old saints' honour. Silent and dejected they sank down into annihilation.

But the next Sunday morning Svartsjö church stood gleamingly white. No images disturbed the peace of meditation. Only with the eyes of the soul could the virtuous contemplate the glory of heaven and the faces of the blessed.

But the earth, man's beloved dwelling, is green, the sky is blue. The world glows with colours. Why should the church be white? White as winter, naked as poverty, pale as grief! It does not glitter with hoar-frost like a wintry wood; it does not shine in pearls and lace like a white bride. The church stands in white, cold whitewash, without an image, without a picture.

That Sunday Count Dohna sat in an arm-chair decorated with flowers in the choir, so as to be seen and praised by all men. He had had the old pews mended, the disfiguring images destroyed, new glass put in all the broken windows, and the whole church whitewashed; and now he was to be honoured. If he wished to appease the wrath of the Almighty, it was only fitting that he had adorned His temple to the best of his ability. But why did he accept praise for it?

He, who came with implacable sternness on his conscience, ought to have fallen on his knees and begged his brothers and sisters in the church to implore God that he might suffer him to enter his sanctuary. It would have been better for him if he had stood there like a miserable culprit than that he should sit honoured and blessed in the choir, and receive praise because he had wished to make his peace with God.

When the service was over and the last psalm had been sung, no one left the church, for the minister was to make a speech to thank the count. But he did not have time to do so.

For the doors were thrown open; back into the church came the old saints, dripping with water from lake Löven, stained with green slime and brown mud. They must have heard that here the man was to be honoured who had given them over to destruction, who had driven them out of God's holy house and had thrown them in the cold, disintegrating waves; the old saints wished to have their say in the matter.

They do not love the monotonous rippling of the waves. They are used to psalms and prayers. They held their peace and let it all happen, as long as they believed that it would be to the glory of God. But this was not so. Here sits Count Dohna in honour and glory in the choir and wishes to be worshipped and praised in the house of God. They cannot suffer such a thing. Therefore they have risen from their watery grave and have marched into the church; they are readily recognized by all. There is Saint

Olof, with his crown on his hat, and Saint Erik, with gold-brocaded cloak, and the gray Saint Göran and Saint Christopher; that was all; the Queen of Sheba and Judith had not come.

But when the people recovered a little from their amazement, an audible whisper goes through the church,—

"The cavaliers!"

Yes, of course, it is the cavaliers. And they go up to the count without a word, and lift his chair on to their shoulders; carrying him from the church, they set him down on the slope outside.

They say nothing, and look neither to the right nor to the left. They merely carry Count Dohna out of the house of God; and when that is done, they take the nearest way to the lake.

They used no violence, nor did they waste much time in explanations. It was plain enough: "We, the Ekeby cavaliers, have our own opinion. Count Dohna is not worthy to be honoured in God's house. Therefore, we carry him out. Let him who will carry him in again."

But he was not carried in. The minister's speech of thanks was never made. The people streamed out of the church. Without exception, everyone thought the cavaliers had acted rightly.

They thought of the fair young countess who had been so cruelly tortured at Borg. They remember her, for she had been so kind to the poor; she had been so sweet to look at that it had been a consolation for them to see her.

It was a pity to come with wild pranks into the church; but both the minister and the congregation knew that they had been about to play a greater trick on the Omniscient. And they stood ashamed before the misguided old madmen.

"When man is silent, the stones must speak," they said.

But after that day, Count Henrik was not happy at Borg. One dark night in the beginning of August a closed carriage drove right up to the big steps. All the servants stood around it, and Countess Märta came out wrapped in shawls with a thick veil over her face. The count led her, but she trembled and shuddered. It was with the greatest difficulty that they could persuade her to go through the hall and down the steps.

At last she reached the carriage, the count sprang in after her, the doors were slammed to, and the coachman started the horses off at a gallop. The next morning, when the magpies awoke, she was gone.

After this, the Count lived far away in the South of Sweden. Borg was sold and has changed hands many times. No one can help loving it. But few have been happy in its possession.

CHAPTER 12 *God's Wayfarer*

God's wayfarer, Captain Lennart wandered up to the inn at Broby, one afternoon in August. He walked into the kitchen. He was on his way to his home, Helgesäter, which lies a couple of miles northwest of Broby, close to the edge of the forest.

At that time, Captain Lennart did not know that he was to be one of God's wanderers on this earth. His heart was full of joy as he was to see his home again. He had suffered a hard fate; but now he was at home, and all would be well. He did not know that he was to be one of those who may not rest under their own roof, nor warm themselves at their own hearth.

God's wayfarer, Captain Lennart, had a cheerful disposition. As he found no one in the kitchen, he poked about like a wild boy. He threw the cat at the dog's head; and his laughter rang through the house when, in the heat of the moment, two comrades forgot the ties of old friendship, and fought with tooth and nail, their eyes aflame and their hair standing on end.

The innkeeper's wife came in, attracted by the noise. She stopped on the threshold and looked at the man, who was laughing at the struggling animals. She knew him well; but when she saw him last, he had been sitting in the prison-van with handcuffs on his wrists. She remembered it well. Five and a half years ago, during the winter fair in Karlstad, thieves had stolen the jewels of the governor's wife. Many rings, bracelets, and buckles, much prized by the noble lady,—for most of them were heirlooms and presents,—had then been lost. They had never been found. But a rumour spread through the countryside that Captain Lennart at Helgesäter was the thief.

She had never been able to understand how such a rumour had started. He was such a good and honourable man. He lived happily with his wife, whom he had brought home only a few years before; for he had only acquired the necessary means to get married, later in life. Had he not a good income from his pay and his estate? What could tempt such a man to steal old bracelets and rings? It seemed to her still more strange that such a rumour could be believed in to such an extent, and so definitely proven, that Captain Lennart was discharged from the army, lost his Order of the Sword, and was condemned to five years' hard labour.

He himself had said that he had been at the market, but had left before he heard anything of the theft. On the highway he had found an ugly old buckle, which he had taken home and given to the children. The buckle, however, was of gold, and belonged to the stolen things; that was the cause of his misfortune. It had all been Sintram's work. He had accused him, and had given the testimony which had led to his conviction. It seemed that he wanted to get rid of Captain Lennart; inasmuch as a short time afterwards proceedings were started against him, because it had been discovered that Sintram had sold gun powder to the Norwegians during the war of 1814. People believed that he was afraid of the evidence that Captain Lennart could have given against him. As it was, he was acquitted on the ground of insufficient evidence.

She could not stare at him enough. His hair had grown gray and his back bent; he must have suffered. But he still had his friendly face and his cheerful disposition. He was still the same Captain Lennart who had led her to the altar, as a bride, and had danced at her wedding. She felt sure he would still stop and chat with everybody he met on the road and throw a copper to every child; he would still say to every wrinkled old woman that she grew younger and prettier ever day; and he would still sometimes seat himself on a barrel and play the fiddle for those who danced around the Maypole.

"Well, Mother Karin," he began, "are you afraid of looking at me?"

He had come especially to hear how things were going in his

home, and whether they expected him. They must know that he had served his time.

The innkeeper's wife gave him the best of news. His wife had worked like a man. She had leased the estate from the new owner, and everything had gone well for her. The children were healthy, and it was a pleasure to see them. And, of course, they were expecting him. His wife was a hard woman, who never spoke about what she thought, but the innkeeper's wife knew that no one was allowed to eat with Captain Lennart's spoon or to sit in his chair while he was away. This spring, not a day had passed without her coming out to the stone at the top of Broby hill and looking down the road. Moreover, she had put out new clothes for him, home-woven clothes, for which she herself had done nearly all the work. That showed that he was expected, although she said nothing.

"They don't believe it, then?" said Captain Lennart.

"No, captain," answered the peasant woman. "Nobody believes it."

Then Captain Lennart would stop no longer; then he wished to go home.

It happened that he met some dear old friends outside. The cavaliers at Ekeby had just come to the inn. Sintram had invited them there to celebrate his birthday. And the cavaliers did not hesitate an instant before shaking the convict's hand and welcoming him home. Even Sintram did so.

"Dear Lennart," he said, "were you certain that God had any meaning in it all?"

"Do you not think I know," cried Captain Lennart, "that it was not our Lord who saved you from the block?"

The others laughed. But Sintram was not at all angry. He was pleased when people spoke of his compact with the devil.

Yes, then they took Captain Lennart with them to empty a glass of welcome; after that he could go his way. But it went badly for him. He had not drunk such treacherous stuff for five years. Perhaps he had eaten nothing the whole day, and was exhausted by his long journey on foot. The result was that he was quite fuddled after a couple of glasses.

When the cavaliers had got him into such a state that he no longer knew what he was doing, they forced on him glass after glass; they meant no harm by it; it was simply that they wished to recompense him for the five years he had had nothing good to taste.

Otherwise he was one of the most sober of men. It is also easy to understand that he had no intention to get drunk; he was to have gone home to his wife and children. But instead he was lying asleep on the bench in the barroom.

While he lay there unconsious, so tempting an object, Gösta took a piece of charcoal and a little cranberry-juice and painted his face. He gave him the features of a criminal; he thought that most suitable for a man who came direct from jail. He painted the effects of a black eye, drew a red scar across his nose, plastered his hair down on his forehead in matted tangles, and smeared his whole face.

They laughed at it for a while, then Gösta wished to wash it off.

"Let it be," said Sintram, "so that he can see it when he wakes. It will amuse him."

So they left it as it was, and thought no more of the captain. The feasting lasted the whole night. They broke up at daybreak. There was more wine than sense in their heads.

The question was what they should do with Captain Lennart. "We will go home with him," said Sintram. "Think how glad his wife will be! It will be a pleasure to see her joy. I am moved when I think of it. Let us go home with him!"

They were all affected by the thought. Heavens, how glad she would be, that prim woman living up at Helgesäter!

They shook life into Captain Lennart and lifted him into one of the carriages which the sleepy grooms had long since driven up. And so the whole crowd drove up to Helgesäter. Some of them were half-asleep and nearly fell out of the carriage; others sang to keep awake. They looked little better than a company of tramps, with dull eyes and swollen faces.

They arrived at last; left the horses in the backyard and marched

with a certain solemnity up to the steps. Beerencreutz and Julius
supported Captain Lennart between them.

'Pull yourself together, Lennart," they said to him, "you are
at home. Don't you see that you're at home?"

He opened his eyes and was almost sober. He was touched that
they had accompanied him home.

"Friends," he said, and stopped to speak to them all, "I have
asked God, friends, why so much evil has befallen me."

"Shut up, Lennart, don't preach!" cries Beerencreutz.

"Let him go on," says Sintram. "He speaks well."

"Have asked Him and not understood; understand now. He
wanted to show me what friends I had; friends who accompany
me home to see my joy and my wife's joy. För my wife is expecting
me. What are five years of misery compared with that?"

Now hard fists pounded on the door. The cavaliers had no
time to hear more.

There was commotion within. The maids awoke and looked
out. They threw on their clothes, but did not dare to open for
that crowd of men. At last the bolt was drawn. The captain's
wife herself came out.

"What do you want?" she asked.

It was Beerencreutz who answered:—

"We are here with your husband."

They pushed forward Captain Lennart, and she saw him reel
towards her, drunk, with a prize-fighter's face; and behind him
she saw the crowd of drunken, reeling men.

She took a step back; he followed her with outstretched arms.
"You left me as a thief," she cried, "and come home as a vaga-
bond." Whereupon she turned to go in.

He did not understand. He wished to follow her, but she struck
him a blow on the breast.

"Do you think that I intend to have a man like you as master
of my house and my children?"

The door slammed and the key turned in the lock.

Captain Lennart threw himself against the door and began to
shake it.

The cavaliers could not help it, they began to laugh. He had been so sure of his wife, and now she would have nothing to do with him. It was absurd, they thought.

When Captain Lennart heard them laughing, he rushed after them and wanted to beat them. They made off and leaped into their carriages, while he ran after them; but in his eagerness he stumbled over a stone and fell. He got up again, but pursued them no farther. A thought struck him in his bewilderment. In this world nothing happens without God's will, nothing.

"Where wilt thou lead me?" he said. "I am a feather blown by thy Spirit. I am thy plaything. Whither wilt thou send me? Why dost thou shut the doors of my home against me?"

He turned away from his home, believing that it was God's will.

When the sun rose he stood at the top of Broby hill and looked out over the valley. Ah, little did the poor people in the valley know that their rescuer was near. No mothers as yet lifted their children on their arms that they might see him as he came. The cottages were not clean and tidy, with the black hearth hidden by fragrant juniper. As yet men did not work with eager industry in the fields that his eyes might be gladdened by the sight of cultivated fields and well-dug ditches.

Alas, where he stood his sorrowful eyes saw the ravages of the drought; how the crops were burned up; and how the people scarcely seemed to trouble themselves to prepare the earth for the new crops. He looked up at the blue mountains, and the sharp morning sun showed him the blackened stretches where the forest-fires had passed. He understood, by many small signs, by the tumble-down fences, by the small amount of wood which had been carted home and sawed, that the people were not attending to their business; there was destitution; and they sought consolation in indifference and brandy.

Perhaps it was fortunate that he, who was himself so deeply afflicted by great sorrow, found that there were others whom he could console in their poverty. Perhaps it was good for him that times were so hard, that the poorer people were in dire need because of the barrenness of nature, and when many who were better off contributed towards aggravating the situation.

Captain Lennart stood there on Broby hill and began to think that God perhaps needed him.

The cavaliers could not at all understand the part they had played in making Captain Lennart's wife act so harshly. Sintram held his tongue. His wife was much blamed throughout the neighbourhood, because she had been too proud to receive such a good husband. People said that anyone who tried to talk to her about him was immediately interrupted. She could not bear to hear his name mentioned. Captain Lennart did nothing to make her change her mind.

It was a day later.

An old peasant lay on his death-bed. He had been given the last sacrament; his strength has ebbed away and he had to die.

Restless as one who is about to set off on a long journey, he has his bed moved from the kitchen to the bedroom and from the bedroom back to the kitchen. By that they understood more than by the heavy rattling of his breathing and the dimming of his eyes, that his time had come.

His wife, his children, and his servants stood around him. He had been successful, rich, esteemed. He was not forsaken on his death-bed. The old man speaks of himself as if he stood in the presence of God, and with sighs and words of confirmation those standing around him bear witness that he speaks the truth.

"I have been a good worker and a kind master," he says. "I have loved my wife like my right hand. I have not let my children grow up without discipline and care. I have not been a drunkard. I have not moved my boundary marks. I have not driven my horse up the hills. I have not let the cows starve in winter. I have not let the sheep be vexed by their wool in summer."

And round about him the weeping servants repeat like an echo: "He has been a kind master. He has not driven the horse up the hills, or let the sheep sweat in their wool in summer."

But through the door a poor man has come in unnoticed, to

ask for a little food. He also hears the words of the dying man from where he stands silent by the door.

And the sick man continues: "I have cleared the forest, I have drained the meadows. I drove the plough in straight furrows. I built three times as big a barn for three times as large a harvest as in my father's time. I had three silver goblets made of shining silver coins; my father had only one made.

The words of the dying peasant reach the man listening at the door. He hears the old man give an account of himself as if he were in the presence of God. He hears the servants and children repeat in corroberation:

— He drove the plough in straight furrows.

— God will give me a good place in his Heaven, the old man says.

— The Lord will receive our master well, say the servants.

The man by the door hears the words; and terror fills him who for five long years has been God's plaything.

He goes up to the sick man and takes his hand.

"Friend, friend," he says, and his voice trembles, "have you considered who the Lord is, before whose face you must soon appear? He is a great God, a terrible God. The earth is his pasture. The storm his horse. Wide heaven shakes under the weight of his foot. And you stand before him and say: 'I have ploughed straight furrows, I have sowed rye, I have chopped wood.' Will you praise yourself to him and compare yourself to him? You do not know how mighty the Lord is to whose kingdom you are going.

"Do not come before your God with boasting!" continues the wayfarer. "The mighty on the earth are like threshed-out straw in his barn. His day's work is to create suns. He has dug out oceans and raised up mountains. Bow before him! Lie low in the dust before your Lord, your God! Catch like a child at the hem of his garment and beg for protection! Humble yourself before your Creator!"

The sick man's eyes stand wide-open, his hands are clasped, but his face lights up and the rattling ceases.

"Oh human soul, departing human soul!" cries the man, "as surely as you now in your last hour humble yourself before your God, he will take you like a child on his arm and carry you into the glory of his heaven."

The old man gives a last sigh, and all is over. Captain Lennart bends his head and prays. Everyone in the room prays with heavy sighs.

When they look up the old peasant is lying there peacefully. His eyes seem still to shine with the reflection of glorious visions, his mouth smiles, his face is beautiful. He has seen God.

"He has seen God," says the son, and closes the dead man's eyes.

"He saw heaven opening," sob the children and servants.

The old wife lays her shaking hand on Captain Lennart's.

"You helped him over the worst, captain."

It was this experience which compelled Captain Lennart to go out among the people. But for this, he would have gone home and let his wife see his real features; from that hour, however, he believed that God needed him. He became God's wayfarer, who came to help the poor. There was great distress and much suffering which prudence and kindness could help more than gold and power.

One day Captain Lennart came to the poor peasants who lived in the neighbourhood of Gurlitta Cliff. There was great destitution among them. They had no more potatoes, and the rye could not be sown, as they had no seed.

Then Captain Lennart took a small boat and rowed across the lake to Fors and asked Sintram to give them rye and potatoes. He was well received by Sintram, who took him to the big, well-stocked granaries and down into the cellar, where there were still potatoes from last year's crop; he let him fill all the bags and sacks he had with him.

But when Sintram saw the boat, he thought that it was too small for such a load. He had the sacks carried to one of his large boats; and his servant, big Mons, rowed it across the lake. Captain Lennart had only his empty boat to look after.

He could not keep up with Mons however, who was a great oarsman and a giant in strength. Captain Lennart sits and dreams, while he rows across the beautiful lake, and thinks of the wonderful fate of the little seed-corns. They were to be scattered over the black earth among stones and stubble, but they would sprout and take root in the wilderness. He thinks of how the soft, light-green shoots will cover the earth; and in imagination he bends to caress the tender shoots. He then recalls how autumn and winter will pass over these poor, weak little things; and that, nevertheless, they will be fresh and valiant when spring comes, and they may begin to grow in earnest. Then his old soldier's heart is gladdened by the thought that the stiff stalks will stand erect several feet high and crowned with their spikes. The little feathery beards of the pistils will tremble, and despite apparent conflict and anxiety the spiklets will bear the soft, sweet kernels. Then the scythes will cut down the stalks, and the flails will thunder over them, and the mill grind the kernels to flour, and the flour will be baked to make bread,—ah, how much hunger will be satisfied by the grain in the boat in front of him!

Sintram's servant landed at the pier of the Gurlitta people, and many hungry men came down to the boat.

Then the man said, as his master had bidden him:—

"The master sends you malt and grain, peasants. He has heard that you have no brandy."

The people became frantic. They rushed down to the boat and ran out into the water to seize the bags and sacks; but that had certainly never been Captain Lennart's intention. He had now come up, and was furious when he saw what they were doing. He wanted the potatoes for food, and the rye for seed; he had never asked for malt.

He called to the people to leave the sacks alone, but they did not listen to him.

"May the rye turn to sand in your mouths, and the potatoes

to stone in your throats!" he cried; for he was very angry because they had taken the grain.

It looked as if Captain Lennart had worked a miracle. Two women, who were fighting for a bag, tore a hole in it and found only sand; the men who lifted up the potato-sacks, felt how heavy they were, as if filled with stones.

It was all sand and stones, only sand and stones. The people stood in silent terror of God's miracle-worker who had come to them. For a moment, Captain Lennart was himself seized with astonishment. Only Mons laughed.

"Go home, fellow," said Captain Lennart, "before the peasants understand that there has never been anything but sand in these sacks; otherwise I am afraid they will sink your boat."

"I am not afraid," said the man.

"Go," said Captain Lennart with such an imperious voice that he went.

Then Captain Lennart told the people that Sintram had fooled them; but they persisted in believing that a miracle had happened. The story of it soon spread; and as the people greatly loved wonders, it was generally believed that Captain Lennart could work wonders. He acquired great power among the peasants, and they called him God's wayfarer.

It was a beautiful evening in August. Lake Löven lay like a mirror, haze veiled the mountains; it was the cool of the evening.

Colonel Beerencreutz, with white moustaches, short of stature, and as strong as a wrestler, came to the shore of the lake, with a pack of cards in his coat pocket, and sat down in a flatbottomed boat. With him were Major Anders Fuchs, his old companion in arms and little Ruster, the flute-player, who had been drummer in the Värmland *chasseurs*, and for many years had been with the colonel as his friend and servant.

On the other shore of the lake lies the churchyard, the neglected churchyard of Svartsjö parish, with its crooked, rattling iron crosses. It was full of hillocks like an unploughed meadow, overgrown with sedges and striped grasses, which had been sowed there as a reminder that no man's life is like another's, but differs like leaves of grass. There are no gravel walks there, no shady trees except the big linden on the forgotten grave of some old priest. A stone wall, rough and high, encloses the miserable field. Miserable and desolate is the churchyard, ugly as the face of a miser, which has withered as a result of the laments of those whose happiness he has stolen. And yet the dead who rest there are blessed, for they have been buried, with psalms and prayers, in consecrated ground. Acquilon, the gambler, who died last year at Ekeby, had had to be buried outside the wall. That man, who once had been so proud and courtly, the brave warrior, the bold hunter, the gambler who held fortune in his hand, had ended by squandering his children's inheritance; all he had gained himself, and all his wife had saved. His wife and children he had forsaken many years before, to lead the life of a cavalier at Ekeby. One evening last summer he had played away the farm which afforded them their means of subsistence. Rather than pay his debt he had shot himself. But the suicide's body was buried outside the moss-grown wall of the wretched churchyard.

Since he died the cavaliers had only been twelve; since he died no one had come to take the place of the thirteenth,—no one but the devil, who on Christmas Eve had crept out of the smelting-furnace.

The cavaliers had found his fate more bitter than that of his predeccessors. Of course, they knew that one of them must die each year. What harm was there in that? Cavaliers may not become old. If their dim eyes can no longer distinguish the cards, if their trembling hand can no longer lift the glass, what is life for them, and what good are they to life? But to lie like a dog outside the churchyard wall, where the protecting sods may not rest in peace, but are trodden by grazing sheep, wounded by spade and plough; where the wanderer goes by without slackening his pace and the children play without subduing their laughter and jests;—to rest there, where the stone wall prevents the sound from coming when the angel of the Day of Judgement wakes with his trumpet the dead within,—oh, to lie there!

Beerencreutz rows his boat over lake Löven. He passes in the evening over the lake of my dreams, about whose shores I have seen gods wander, and from whose depths my magic palace rises. He rows by Lagön's lagoons, where the pines, growing on low circular shoals, rise straight up from the water, and where the ruin of the Viking castle still remains on the steep summit of the island. He rows under the pine grove on the headland of Borg; here one old tree still hangs by its thick roots over the cleft; a huge bear had been caught there; and the old grave-barrows and grave-mounds were evidence of how ancient this place is.

He rows to the other side of the headland; lands below the churchyard, and then walks over mowed fields, which belong to the count at Borg, to Acquilon's grave.

When he comes there he bends down and pats the turf, as one lightly caresses the blanket under which a sick friend is lying. Then he takes out a pack of cards and sits down beside the grave.

Johan Fredrik is so lonely outside here. He must long sometimes for a game."

"It is a sin and a shame that such a man should lie here," says
the great bear-hunter, Anders Fuchs, and sits down at his side.

But little Ruster, the flute-player, speaks with a broken voice,
while the tears run from his small red eyes.

"Next to you, colonel, next to you, he was the finest man I
have ever known."

These three worthy men sit round the grave and deal the cards
seriously and with zeal.

I look out over the world, I see many graves. There rest the
mighty ones of the earth, weighed down by marble. Funeral
marches thunder over them. Standards are lowered over those
graves. I see the graves of those who have been much loved.
Flowers, wet with tears, caressed with kisses, rest lightly on their
green sods. I see forgotten graves, arrogant graves, mendacious
resting-places; and others which convey nothing. But never
before have I seen the black and white checked "Kille" and the
joker with the bells in his cap offered as entertainment to the
occupant of a grave.

"Johan Fredrik has won," says the colonel, proudly. "Did I
not know it? I taught him to play. Yes, now we three are dead,
and he alone is alive."

Thereupon he gathers together the cards, rises, and goes,
followed by the others, back to Ekeby.

The dead man may well have known and felt that not everyone
has forgotten him or his forsaken grave.

Hearts grown wild will pay strange homage to those whom
they love; but he who lies outside the wall, he whose dead body
was not allowed to rest in consecrated ground, he ought to be
glad that not everyone has rejected him.

Friends, children of men, when I die I shall surely rest in the
middle of the churchyard, in the tomb of my ancestors. I shall not
have robbed my family of their means of subsistence, nor taken
my own life; but I certainly have not won such a love; no one
will do as much for me as the cavaliers did for that transgressor.

It is certain that no one will come in the evening, when the sun sets and it is lonely and dreary in the churchyard, to place between my bony fingers the variegated cards.

No one will even come, which would please me more,—for cards tempt me little,—with fiddle and bow to the grave, that my spirit, which strays amid the mouldering dust, may rock in the stream of melody like a swan on glittering waves.

CHAPTER 14 *Old Songs*

Marianne Sinclair sat one quiet afternoon at the end of August in her room and arranged her old letters and other papers.

Round about her was disorder. Great leather trunks and iron-bound boxes had been dragged into the room. Her clothes covered the chairs and sofas. From attics and wardrobes and from the stained chests of drawers everything had been taken out, glistening silk and linen, jewels spread out to be polished, shawls and furs to be selected and inspected.

Marianne was preparing for a long journey. She was not certain if she should ever return to her home. She was at a turning-point in her life and was, consequently, burning a large number of old letters and diaries. She did not wish to be burdened with records of the past.

As she sits there, she finds a bundle of old verses. They were copies of old ballads, which her mother used to sing to her when she was little. She untied the string which held them together, and began to read.

She smiled sadly when she had read for a while; the old songs spoke strange wisdom.

Have no faith in happiness, have no faith in the appearance of happiness, have no faith in roses.

"Trust not laughter," they said. "See, the lovely maiden Valborg drives in a golden coach, and her lips smile, but she is as sorrowful as if the hoofs and the wheels were passing over her life's happiness."

"Trust not the dance," they said. "Many a foot glides lightly over the polished floor, while the heart is heavy as lead."

"Trust not the jest," they said. "Many a one goes to the feast with jesting lips, while she longs to die because of her sorrow."

In what shall one believe? In tears and sorrow!

He who is sorrowful can force himself to smile, but he who is glad cannot weep.

But joy is only sorrow disguised. There is nothing real on earth but sorrow.

She went to the window and looked out into the garden, where her parents were walking. They went up and down the broad paths and talked of everything they happened to catch sight of; the grass and the birds.

"See," said Marianne, "there goes a heart which sighs with sorrow, because it has never been so happy before."

And she thought suddenly that perhaps everything really depended on oneself; that sorrow and joy depended upon the different ways of looking at things. She asked herself whether she had felt happy or unhappy that year. She hardly knew herself.

She had lived through a bitter time. Her soul had been sick. She had been bowed down to the earth by her deep humiliation. For when she returned to her home she had said to herself, "I will remember no evil against my father." But her heart did not consent. "He has caused me such mortal pain," it said; "he has parted me from the man I loved; he drove me desperate when he struck my mother. I wish him no harm, but I am afraid of him." And then she noticed how she had to force herself to sit still when her father sat down beside her; she longed to be away from him. She tried to control herself; she talked with him as usual and was almost always with him. She could conquer herself, but she suffered beyond endurance. She ended by detesting everything about him: his coarse loud voice, his heavy tread, his big hands. She wished him no harm, but she could no longer be near him without a feeling of fear and repulsion. Her repressed heart revenged itself. "You would not let me love," it said, "but I am nevertheless your master; you shall end by hating."

Accustomed as she was to observe everything which stirred within her, she saw only too well how this repulsion became stronger, how it grew each day. At the same time she seemed to be tied forever to her home. She knew that it would be best for her to go away and be among people; but, since her illness, she could not bring herself to do this. It would never be any better. She would only be more and more tortured, and some day her self-control would give way, and she would break out in reproaches against her father and show him the bitterness of her heart, and then there would be strife and unhappiness.

In this way the spring and early summer had passed. In July she had become engaged to Baron Adrian, in order to have her own home.

One fine forenoon Baron Adrian had galloped up to the house, riding a magnificent horse. His hussar's jacket had shone in the sun, his spurs, sword and belt had glittered and flashed, to say nothing of his own fresh face and smiling eyes.

Melchior Sinclair had stood on the steps and welcomed him when he came. Marianne had sat at the window and sewed. She had seen him come, and now heard every word he said to her father.

"Good-day, Sir Sunshine!" cried Melchior. "How fine you are! You are not out courting?"

"Yes, indeed, Sir, that is just what I am," he answered, and laughed.

"Are you not ashamed my boy? What have you to maintain a wife with?"

"Nothing, Sir. If I had anything, I would never get married."

"Is that what you say, Sir Sunshine? But that fine jacket,—you have had money enough to afford that?"

"On credit, Sir."

"And the horse you are riding, that is worth a lot of money, I can tell you. Where did you get that?"

"The horse is not mine, Sir."

This was more than Melchior could withstand.

"God be with you, my boy," he said. "You do indeed need a wife who has something. If you can win Marianne, take her."

So everything had been arranged between them before Baron Adrian had even dismounted. But Melchior Sinclair knew very well what he was about, for Baron Adrian was a fine fellow.

Then the suitor had come to Marianne and had immediately stated his errand.

"Oh, Marianne, dear Marianne. I have alredy spoken to your father. I should like so much to have you for my wife. Say that you will, Marianne."

She had got at the truth. The old baron, his father, had let himself be cheated into buying some used-up mines again. The old baron had been buying mines all his life, and never had anything been found in them. His mother felt anxious, he himself was in debt, and now he was proposing to her in order to thereby save the home of his ancestors and his hussar's jacket.

His home was Hedeby; it lay on the other side of the lake, almost opposite Björne. She knew him well; they were of the same age and had been playmates.

"You might marry me, Marianne. I lead such a wretched life. I have to ride on borrowed horses and cannot pay my tailor's bills. It can't go on. I shall have to resign, and then I shall shoot myself."

"But, Adrian, what kind of a marriage would it be? We are not in the least in love with one another."

"Oh, as for love, I care nothing for all that nonsense," he had then explained. "I like to ride a good horse and to hunt, but I am no cavalier, I am a worker. If I only could get some money, so that I could take charge of the estate at home and give my mother some peace in her old age, I should be happy. I should both plough and sow, for I like work."

Then he had looked at her with his honest eyes, and she knew that he spoke the truth and that he was a man to depend upon. She became engaged to him, chiefly to get away from her home, but also because she had always liked him.

But never would she forget that month which followed the evening in August when her engagement was announced,—all that time of madness.

Each day Baron Adrian became sadder and more silent. He came very often to Björne, sometimes several times a day, but she could not help noticing how depressed he was. With others he could still jest, but when he was with her he was impossible, a solid mass of silence and boredom. She understood what was the matter: it was not so easy as he had believed to marry an ugly woman. No one knew better than she how ugly she was. She had shown him that she did not want any caresses or love-making; but he was nevertheless tortured by the thought of her as his wife, and it seemed worse to him day by day. Why did he care? Why did he not break it off? She had given hints which were plain enough. She could do nothing. Her father had told her that her reputation would not stand any more adventurous engagements. Then she had thoroughly despised them both, and any way seemed good enough to get away from these two men. But only a couple of days after the great festivities in celebration of their engagement, a sudden and wonderful change had taken place.

In the path in front of the steps at Björne lay a big stone, which caused much trouble and vexation. Carriages knocked against it, horses and people tripped over it; it caused the maids who came with heavy milk cans to spill the milk; but the stone was not removed, because it had already lain there so many years. It had been there in the time of Sinclair's parents, long before anyone had thought of building at Björne. He did not see why he should take it up.

But one day at the end of August, two maids, who were carrying a heavy tub, tripped over the stone; they fell, hurt themselves badly, and the feeling against the stone grew strong.

It was early in the morning. Melchior was out on his morning walk, but as the workmen were in the yard between eight and nine, Madame Gustava had several of them come and dig up the big stone.

They came with iron levers and spades, dug and strained, and at last got the old disturber of the peace out of his hole. Then they carried him away to the back yard. It took six men to do it.

The stone had hardly been removed before Melchior came home. You can imagine how angry he was. It was no longer the same place, he thought. Who had dared to move the stone? Madame Gustava had given the order. Those women had no heart in their bodies. Did not his wife know that he loved that stone?

And then he went direct to the stone, lifted it, and carried it across the yard to the place where it had lain, and there he flung it down. And it was a stone which six men could scarcely lift. That deed was greatly admired throughout the whole of Värmland.

While he carried the stone across the yard, Marianne had stood at the dining-room window and looked at him. He was her master, that terrible man with his boundless strength,—an unreasonable, capricious master, who thought of nothing but his own pleasure.

They were in the midst of breakfast, and she had a carving-knife in her hand. Involuntarily she lifted the knife.

Madame Gustava seized her by the wrist.

"Marianne!"

"What is the matter, mother?"

"Oh, Marianne, you looked so strange! I was frightened."

Marianne looked at her. She was a little, wizened woman, gray and wrinkled already at fifty. She loved as a dog does without any memory of hard knocks. She was generally good-humoured, and yet she made a melancholy impression. She was like a storm-beaten tree by the sea; she never had had sufficient quiet to enable her to grow. She had learned to use mean shifts, to lie when needed, and often made herself out more stupid than she was, in order to escape taunts. In everything she was her husband's tool.

"Would you grieve much if father died?" asked Marianne.

"Marianne, you are angry with your father. You are always angry with him. Why cannot everything be forgotten, since you have got a new fiancé?"

"Oh, mother, it is not my fault. Can I help shuddering at him? Do you not see what he is? Why should I care for him? He is violent, he is uncouth, he has tortured you till you are prematurely old. Why is he our master? He behaves like a madman. Why shall

I honour and respect him? He is not good, he is not charitable. I know that he is strong. He is capable of beating us to death at any moment. He can turn us out of the house whenever he wants. Is that why I should love him?"

But then Madame Gustava had become another person. She had found strength and courage and had spoken with authority.

"You must take care, Marianne. It almost seems to me as if your father was right when he shut you out last winter. You will be punished for this. You must teach yourself to endure without hating, Marianne, to suffer without revenge."

"Oh, mother, I am so unhappy."

Immediately afterwards, they heard in the hall the sound of a heavy fall.

They never knew if Melchior Sinclair had stood on the steps and had heard Marianne's words, through the open dining-room door, or if it was only over-exertion which had been the cause of the stroke. When they came out he lay unconscious. They never dared to ask him the cause. He himself never made any sign that he had heard anything. Marianne never dared to think whether she had involuntarily revenged herself. But the sight of her father lying on the very steps where she had learnt to hate him took all the bitterness from her heart.

He soon regained consciousness, and when he had kept quiet a few days, he was like himself again—and yet not at all the same.

Marianne saw her parents walking together in the garden. It was always so now. He never went out alone, he grumbled at guests and at everything which separated him from his wife. Old age had come upon him. He could not bring himself to write a letter; his wife had to do it. He never decided anything by himself, but asked her about everything and let her make the decisions. Moreover, he was always gentle and kind. He noticed the change which had come over him, and how happy his wife was. "She is well off now," he said one day to Marianne, and pointed to Madame Gustava.

"Oh, dear Melchior," she cried, "you know very well that I would rather have you strong again."

And she really meant it. It was her joy to speak of him as he was in the days of his strength. She told how he held his own in riot and revel as well as any of the Ekeby cavaliers; how he had done good business and earned much money, just when she thought that by his wild ways he would lose house and lands. But Marianne knew that she was happy in spite of all her complaints. To be everything to her husband was enough for her. They both looked old, prematurely broken. Marianne thought that she could see their future life. He would get gradually weaker and weaker; subsequent strokes would make him more helpless, and she would watch over him until death parted them. But the end might be far distant. For some time to come, Madame Gustava might still enjoy her happiness in peace. It must be so, Marianne thought. Life owed her some compensation.

For her too it was better. No fretting despair forced her to marry to get another master. Her wounded heart had found peace. She had to acknowledge that she was a truer, richer, nobler person than before. What could she wish undone of all that had happened? Was it true that all suffering was good? Could everything be turned to happiness? She had begun to consider everything good which could help to develop her so that she could attain a higher stage of humanity. The old songs were not right. Sorrow was not the only lasting thing. She would now go out into the world and look for some place where she was needed. If her father had been in his old mood, he would never have allowed her to break her engagement. Now Madame Gustava had arranged it. Marianne had even been allowed to give Baron Adrian the money he needed.

She could think of him too with pleasure, she would be free from him. With his bravery and love of life he had always reminded her of Gösta; now she would see him happy again. He would again be that sunny knight who had come in his glory to her father's house. She would obtain for him land where he could plough and dig as much as his heart desired, and she would see him lead a beautiful bride to the altar.

With such thoughts she sits down and writes him that she is giving him back his freedom. She writes gentle, pursuasive words, good sense disguised in jests; and yet in such a way that he must understand how seriously she means it.

While she writes she hears a horse's hoofs on the road.

"My dear Sir Sunshine," she thinks, "it is the last time."

Then Baron Adrian enters her room.

"What, Adrian, are you coming in here?" and she looks dismayed at all her packing.

He is shy and embarrassed and stammers out an excuse.

"I was just writing to you," she says. "Look, you might as well read it now."

He takes the letter and she sits and watches him while he reads. She longs to see his face light up with joy.

But he has not read far before he grows fiery red, throws the letter on the floor, stamps on it, and swears terrible oaths.

Marianne trembles slightly. She is no novice in the study of love; still she had not previously understood this inexperienced boy, this great child.

"Adrian, dear Adrian," she says, "have done with this playacting! Come and tell me the truth."

He came and almost overwhelmed her with caresses. Poor boy, so he had cared and longed for her.

After a while she looked out. There was Madame Gustava walking with her husband and talking of flowers and birds; and here she sat and babbled of love. "Life has let us both feel its serious side," she thought, and smiled sadly. "Life wants to comfort us; we have each got a big child to play with."

However, it was good to be loved. It was sweet to hear him whisper of the magical power which she possessed, of how he had been ashamed of what he had said at their first conversation. He had not then known what charm she had. Oh, no man could be near her without loving her, but she had frightened him; he had felt so strangely subdued.

She felt neither happiness, nor unhappiness, but she would try to live together with this man.

She began to understand herself, and thought of the words of the old songs about the turtle-dove. It never drinks clear water, but first makes it turbid with its feet, the better to suit its sorrowful spirit. Similarly, she would never go to the spring of life and drink the water of pure, unmixed happiness. Troubled with sorrow, life pleased her best.

CHAPTER 15 *Death, the Deliverer*

My pale friend, Death the deliverer, came in August, when the nights were white with moonlight, to the house of Captain Uggla. But he did not dare to go direct into that hospitable home, for they are few who love him, and he does not wish to be greeted with weeping, but with quiet joy. For he comes to set free the soul from the fetters of pain; to deliver the soul from the burden of the body, and to let the spirit enjoy the free and beautiful life of boundless space.

Into the old grove behind the house, crept Death. In the grove, which then was young and full of verdure, my pale friend hid himself by day, but at night he stood at the edge of the wood, white and pale, with his scythe glittering in the moonlight.

Death stood there, and the creatures of the night saw him. Evening after evening the people at Berga heard how the fox howled to foretell his coming. The snake crawled up the sandy path to the very house. He could not speak, but they well understood that he came as a harbinger. And in the apple-tree outside the window of the room where the captain's wife was, the owl hooted. For everything in nature feels Death and trembles.

It happened that the judge from Munkerud and his family, who had been at a festival at the deanery at Bro, drove by Berga at two o'clock at night and saw a candle burning in the window of the guest-room. They clearly saw the yellow flame and the white candle; and being surprised, they afterwards told of the candle which they had seen burning in the summer night.

The gay daughters at Berga laughed and said that the judge and his party had seen an apparition, for there were no candles in the house, they had already been burned up in March; and the captain swore that no one had slept in the guest-room for days and weeks; but his wife was silent and grew pale, for that white candle with the clear flame was seen when one of her family should be set free by Death.

Soon after this, Ferdinand came home from his work of surveying in the nothern forests. He was pale and ill and was suffering from an incurable disease of the lungs; as soon as his mother saw him, she knew that her son must die.

That good son who had never caused his parents any sorrow had to be taken from them. He must leave earthly pleasures and happiness, and the beautiful, beloved bride who was waiting for him, and the rich estates which were to have been his.

At last, when my pale friend had waited a month, he took heart and went one night up to the house. He thought how hunger and privation had been met there with cheerful faces, so why should not he too be received with joy?

That night the captain's wife, who lay awake, heard a knocking on the window-pane; she sat up in bed and asked: "Who is knocking?"

And the old people tell that Death answered her:

"It is Death who knocks."

Then she rose, opened her window, and saw bats and owls fluttering in the moonlight, but she did not see Death.

"Come," she said half aloud, "friend and deliverer! Why have you lingered so long! I have been waiting. I have called. Come and set my son free!"

The next day, she sat by her son's sick-bed and spoke to him of the blissfulness of the liberated spirit and of its glorious life.

So Ferdinand died, enchanted by bright visions, smiling at the glory to come.

Death had never seen anything so beautiful. For, of course, there were some who wept by Ferdinand Uggla's deathbed; but the sick man himself smiled at the man with the scythe, when he took his place on the edge of the bed, and his mother listened to the death-rattle as if to sweet music. She trembled lest Death should not finish his work; and when the end came, tears fell from her eyes, but they were tears of joy which wet her son's rigid face.

Never had Death been so fêted as at Ferdinand Uggla's burial.

It was a wonderful funeral procession which passed under the lindens. In front of the flower-decked coffin beautiful children walked and strewed flowers. There was no mourning, no crape; for his mother wished that her son, who died joyfully, should not be taken to the good refuge, followed by a gloomy funeral train, but by a shining wedding procession.

Anna Stjärnhök, the dead man's beautiful, glowing bride, followed the coffin. She had set a bridal wreath on her head, hung a bridal veil over her, and arrayed herself in a bridal dress of white, shimmering satin. So adorned, she went to be wedded at the grave to a mouldering bridegroom.

Behind her came, two by two, dignified old ladies and stately men. The ladies came in shining buckles and brooches, with strings of milk-white pearls and bracelets of gold. Ostrich feathers nodded in their bonnets of silk and lace, and from their shoulders floated thin silken shawls over dresses of many-coloured satin. Their husbands came in their best array, in high-collared coats with gilded buttons, with swelling ruffles, and in vests of stiff brocade or richly-embroidered velvet. It was a wedding procession, as the captain's wife had wished.

She herself walked just behind Anna Stjärnhök, and was accompanied by her husband. If she had possessed a dress of shining brocade, she would have worn it; if she had possessed jewels and a gay bonnet, she would have worn them too to do honour to her son on his festive day. But she only had the black silk dress and the yellowed laces which had adorned so many feasts, and she wore them here too.

Although all the guests came in their best array, there was not a dry eye when they walked to the grave. Men and women wept, not so much for the dead, as for themselves. There walked the bride; there the bridegroom was carried; there they themselves wandered, decked out for a feast, and yet—who is there who walks earth's green pathways and does not know that his lot is affliction, sorrow, unhappiness, and death. They wept at the thought that nothing on earth could save them.

The captain's wife did not weep; but she was the only one whose eyes were dry.

When the prayers were read, and the grave filled in, they all returned to the carriages. Only the mother and Anna Stjärnhök lingered by the grave to bid the dead a last farewell. The older woman sat down on the grave-mound, and Anna sat next to her.

"Anna," said the captain's wife, "I have said to God: 'Let Death, the liberator, come and take my son; let Death take him whom I love most; to the peace of the tranquil courts, and only tears of joy shall come to my eyes; with nuptial pomp I will follow him to his grave, and my red rose-bush, which stands outside the window of my room, I will plant near him in the graveyard.' And now it has come to pass my son is dead. I have greeted Death like a friend, called him by the tenderest names; I have wept tears of joy over my son's dead face, and in the autumn, when the leaves have fallen, I shall plant my red rose-bush here. But do you know, you who sit here at my side, why I have prayed to God like this?"

She looked questioningly at Anna Stjärnhök; but the girl sat silent and pale beside her. Perhaps she was struggling to silence inward voices which already there, on the grave of the dead, began to whisper to her that now at last she was free.

"The fault is yours," said the captain's wife.

The girl crouched as if she had received a blow. She did not answer a word.

"Anna Stjärnhök, you were once proud and self-willed: you played with my son, you accepted him and then you threw him up. But what of that? He had to endure it as others do. Perhaps he and we loved your money as much as we loved you. But you came back, you brought blessings to our home; you were gentle, strong and kind, when you returned. You cherished us with your love; you made us so happy, Anna Stjärnhök; and we, poor people, lay at your feet.

"And yet, and yet I have wished that you had not come. Then I would not have had to pray to God to shorten my son's life. At Christmas he could have borne to lose you, but after he had learnt to know you, such as you now are, he would not have had the strength to do so.

"You know, Anna Stjärnhök, you who to-day have put on your bridal dress to follow my son, that if he had lived you would never have followed him in that attire to the Bro church, for you did not love him.

"I saw that you only came out of pity; for you wanted to relieve our hard lot. You did not love him. Don't you believe that I can recognize love; that I see it when it is there, and can understand when it is lacking. Then I thought: 'May God take my son's life before he has his eyes opened!'

"Oh, if you had loved him! Oh, if you had never come to us and gladdened our lives, when you did not love him! I knew my duty: if he had not died, I should have been forced to tell him that you did not love him, that you were marrying him out of pity. I should have been forced to make him set you free, and then all his happiness in life would have been lost. That is why I prayed to God that he might die; that I might not need to disturb the peace of his heart. And I have rejoiced over his sunken cheeks, exulted over his rattling breath, trembled lest Death should not complete his work."

She stopped speaking, and waited for an answer; but Anna Stjärnhök could not speak, she was still listening to the many voices in her soul.

Then the mother cried out in despair:—

"Oh, how happy are they who may mourn for their dead, they who may freely weep! I must stand with dry eyes by my son's grave, I must rejoice over his death! How unhappy I am!"

Then Anna Stjärnhök pressed her hands against her breast. She remembered that winter night when she had sworn by her love to be these poor people's support and comfort; and she trembled. Had it all been in vain; was not her sacrifice one of those which God accepts? Was it all to become a curse?

But if she sacrificed everything, would not God then give His blessing to the work, and let her bring happiness, let her support and help these people?

"What is needed so that you may mourn for your son?" she asked.

"That I shall not believe the testimony of my old eyes. If I believed that you loved my son, then I should grieve for his death."

The girl rose up, her eyes burning with exultation. She tore off her bridal veil and spread it over the grave, she tore off her wreath and laid it beside the veil.

"See how I love him!" she cried. "I give him my wreath and veil. I dedicate myself to him. I will never belong to another."

Then the captain's wife rose too. She stood silent for a while her whole body was shaking, and her face twitched, but at last the tears came—tears of grief.

CHAPTER 16 *The Drought*

If dead things love, if earth and water distinguish friends from enemies, I should like to possess their love. I should like the green earth not to feel my step as a heavy burden. I should like her to forgive me that for my sake she is wounded by plough and harrow, and I would that she will open to receive my dead body. And I should like the waves, whose shining mirror is broken by my oars, to have the same patience with me as a mother has with an eager child when it climbs up on her knee, careless of the faultlessly smooth silk of her festive dress.

The spirit of life still dwells in dead things. Have you not seen it? When the world is full of strife and hatred, dead things have also to suffer much. Then the waves are wild and ravenous; then the fields are niggardly as a miser. But woe to him for whose sake the woods sigh and the mountains weep.

Memorable was the year when the cavaliers were in power. If everything could be related which happened that year to the people living on the shores of lake Löven a whole world would be astonished. For then old loves were renewed, and new loves were kindled. Old hate blazed up again, and long cherished revenge seized its prey.

This infection of restlessness came from Ekeby; it spread first through the manors and estates, and drove men to ruin and to crime. It made its way from village to village, from cottage to cottage. Everywhere hearts became wild, and brains confused. Never did the dance whirl so merrily at the cross-roads; never was the beer-barrel so quickly emptied; never was so much grain turned into brandy. Never were there so many balls; never was the way shorter from the angry word to the knife-thrust. But the uneasiness was not only among men. It spread through all living things. Never had wolves and bears ravaged so fiercely; never had foxes barked and owls hooted so terribly, and plundered so boldly; never had the sheep gone so often astray in the wood; never had the cattle been so smitten by disease.

Anyone who wishes to see how all things are interdependent must leave the towns and live in a lonely hut at the edge of the forest; then he will learn to observe every sign nature makes and to understand how the dead things depend on the living. He will see that when the whole world is restless, the peace of the dead things is also disturbed. The people know it. It is at such times that the dryads extinguish the fires of the charcoal-kilns, the sea-nymphs break the boats to pieces, the river-sprites send illness and the goblins cause the cows to starve. And so it happened that year. Never had the spring freshets done so much damage. The mill and forge at Ekeby were not the only losses. Never had the lightning been known to create such havoc, already before midsummer—after midsummer came the drought.

During the whole period of the long days, no rain came. From the middle of June till the beginning of September, the country was bathed in continual sunshine.

The rain refused to fall, the earth to give nourishment, the winds to blow. Sunshine alone streamed down on the earth. Oh the beautiful sunshine, the life-giving sunshine, how shall I tell of the evil it has done? For sunshine is like love. Who does not know the evils that love has committed; and yet, who can refrain from forgiving the wrongs he inflicts? The grass was not yet high and could not grow; the rye was without nourishment, just when it should have collected sustenance in its ears; the wheat, from which most of the bread was baked at that time, never came up more than a few inches; the late sowed turnips never sprouted; not even the potatoes could obtain any nutriment from that petrified earth.

At such times, those living far away in the forest huts begin to be afraid; and from the mountains terror descends on the calmer people of the plain.

"There is some one whom God's hand is seeking!" the people say.

And each one beats his breast and says: "Is it I? Is it because of the horror felt for me that the rain holds back? Is it in wrath against me that the stern earth dries up and hardens?—and does the perpetual sunshine come from the cloudless sky in order to heap coals of fire on my head? Or if it is not I, who is it that God's hand is seeking?"

It was a Sunday in August. The service was over. The people wandered in groups along the sunny roads. On all sides they saw burned woods and ruined crops. There had been many forest fires; and what had been saved, insects had destroyed.

The gloomy people had plenty of things to talk about. There were many who could tell how hard it had been in the famine years of 1808 and 1809, and in the cold winter of 1812, when the sparrows froze to death. Famine was no stranger to them; they had seen his grim face before. They knew how to make bread out of bark, and how the cows could be taught to eat moss.

There was a woman there who had tried to make a new kind of bread of cranberries and corn-meal. She had a sample with her, and let people taste it. She was proud of her invention.

But the same question hovered in all their minds. It stared out of every eye; and was whispered by all lips: "Who is it, O Lord, whom Thy hand seeks?"

Oh Thou God of severity, who has denied to thee his prayers and his good deeds, that thou shouldst deprive us of even the bread of poverty?

A man in the gloomy crowd which had gone westward and was struggling up Broby hill, stopped a minute before the path which led up to the house of the miserly vicar of Broby. He picked up a dry stick from the ground and threw it on the path.

"Dry as that stick have the prayers been which he has given our Lord," said the man.

He who walked next to him also stopped. He took up a dry branch and threw it where the stick had fallen.

"That is the proper offering to give that priest," he said.

A third man in the crowd followed the others' example.

"He has been like the drought; sticks and straw are all that he has let us keep."

A fourth said: "We give him back what he has given us."

And a fifth: "To his perpetual disgrace I throw him this. May he dry up and wither away like this branch!"

"Dry food to the dry priest," said the sixth.

The people who came after them saw what they did and heard what they said. This was now the answer to their long questioning.

"Give him what belongs to him! He has brought the drought on us."

And each stopped, said his say, and threw his branch before he went on.

In the corner by the path there soon lies a pile of sticks and straw—a pile to bring shame on the vicar of Broby.

That was their only revenge. No one lifted his hand against the vicar or said an angry word to him. Desperate people cast off part of their burden by throwing a dry branch on the pile. They did not revenge themselves. They only pointed out the guilty one to the God of retribution.

"If we have not worshipped you rightly, it is that man's fault. Be pitiful, Lord, and let him alone suffer! We mark him with shame and dishonour. We are not one with him."

It soon became the custom for everyone who passed the vicarage to throw a dry branch on the pile of shame.

The old miser soon noticed the pile by the roadside. He had it carried away,—some said that he heated his stove with it. The next day a new pile had collected on the same spot, and as soon as he had that taken away a new one was begun.

The dry branches lay there and said: "Shame, shame on the vicar of Broby!"

He soon understood what the people meant. That they pointed at him as the source of their misfortune. It was because God was angry with him that He let the earth languish. He tried to laugh at them and their branches; but when it had gone on a week, he laughed no more. Oh, what childishness! How can those dry sticks injure him? He understood that the pent up hate of years sought an opportunity of expressing itself. What of it?—he was not used to love.

All this did not make him more gentle. He had perhaps wished to improve after the old lady had visited him; now he could not. He would not be forced.

But gradually the pile grew too much for him. He thought of it continually, and the feeling which everyone cherished took root also in him. He watched the pile, counted the branches which had been added each day. The thought of it encroached upon all his other thoughts. The pile was destroying him.

Every day he felt more and more that the people were right. He grew thin and very old in a couple of weeks. He suffered from remorse and indisposition. But it was as if everything depended on that pile. It was as if his remorse would grow silent, and the weight of years be lifted off him, if only the pile would stop growing.

Finally, he sat there the whole day and watched; but the people were without mercy. At night there were always new branches thrown on.

One day Gösta Berling passed along the road. The vicar of Broby sat at the roadside, old and haggard. He sat and picked out the dry sticks and laid them together in rows and piles, playing with them as if he were a child again. Gösta was grieved at his misery.

"What are you doing, pastor?" he says, and leapt out of the carriage.

"Oh, I am sitting here and picking. I am not doing anything."

"You had better go home, and not sit here in the dust."

"It is best for me to sit here."

Then Gösta Berling sits down beside him.

"It is not so easy to be a priest," he says after a while.

"It is all very well down here where there are people," answers the vicar. "It is worse up there."

Gösta understands what he means. He knows those parishes in Northern Värmland where sometimes there is not even a house for the clergyman to live in; where you can go for ten miles and only meet two or three people; and where the clergyman is the only educated man. The vicar of Broby had been in such a parish for over twenty years.

"That is where we are sent when we are young," says Gösta. "It is impossible to endure the life there; and so one is ruined forever. There are many who have gone under there."

"Yes," says the vicar of Broby; "a man is destroyed by loneliness."

"A man comes," says Gösta, "eager and ardent, exhorts and admonishes, and thinks that all will be well, that the people will soon turn to better ways."

"Yes, yes."

"But soon he sees that words do not help. Poverty stands in the way. Poverty prevents all improvement."

"Poverty," repeats the vicar,—"poverty has ruined my life."

"The young clergyman comes up there," continues Gösta, "poor like all the others. He says to the drunkard: Stop drinking!"

"Then the drunkard answers," interrupts the vicar: "Give me something which is better than brandy! Furs in winter, and the fresh cool in summer that's what brandy is. Brandy is a warm house and a soft bed. Give me those, and I will stop drinking."

"And then," resumes Gösta, "the clergyman says to the thief: You shall not steal; and to the cruel husband: You shall not beat your wife; and to the superstitious: You shall believe in God and not in devils and goblins. But the thief answers: Give me bread; and the cruel husband says: Make us rich, and we will not quarrel; and the superstitious say: Teach us better. But who can help them without money?"

"It is true, every word is true," cried the vicar. "They believed in God, but more in the devil, and most of all in the mountain goblin. All the crops were devoured by the still to make brandy. No one could see any way of putting an end to this misery. In most of the gray cottages there was want. Hidden sorrow made the women's tongues bitter. Discomfort drove their husbands to drink. They could not look after their fields or their cattle. They made a fool of their clergyman. What could a man do with them? They did not understand what I said to them from the pulpit. They did not believe what I wanted to teach them. There was no one to advise me; no one who could help me to keep up my courage."

"There are some who have held out," says Gösta. "God's grace has been so great to some that they have not returned from such a life broken men. They have had strength; they have borne the loneliness, the poverty, the hopelessness. They have done what little good they could and have not despaired. Such men there have always been and still are. I regard them as heroes. I will honour them as long as I live. I was not able to hold out."

"I could not," added the vicar.

"The clergyman up there thinks," says Gösta, musingly, "that he will be a rich man, an exceedingly rich man. No one who is poor can struggle against evil. And so he begins to hoard."

"If he had not hoarded he would have taken to drink," answers the old man; "he sees so much misery."

"Or he would become dull and lazy, and lose all his strength. It is dangerous for one not born in those parts, to live there."

"He has to harden himself to hoard. At first, he only pretends, but then it becomes a habit."

"He has to be hard both to himself and to others," continues Gösta; "it is hard to amass. He must endure hate and scorn; he must go cold and hungry and harden his heart: it almost seems as if he had forgotten why he began to hoard."

The vicar of Broby looked at him furtively. He wondered if Gösta sat there and was making a fool of him. But Gösta was only eager and earnest. It was as if he was speaking of his own life.

"It was so in my case," says the old man quietly.

"But God watches over him," interrupts Gösta. "He wakes in him the thoughts of his youth when he has amassed enough. He gives the clergyman a sign when His people need him."

"But if the clergyman does not obey the sign, Gösta Berling?"

"He cannot withstand it," says Gösta, and smiles. "He is so

moved by the thought of the warm cottages which he will help the poor to build."

The vicar looks at the little buildings he had made with the sticks from the pile of shame. The longer he talks with Gösta, the more he is convinced that the latter is right. He had always had the intention of doing good some day, when he had enough, —of course that had been his intention.

"Why does he never build the cottages?" he asks shyly.

"He is ashamed. Many would think that he did what he had always meant to do, through fear of the people."

"He cannot bear to be forced, is that it?"

"He can, however, do much good secretly. Much help is needed this year. He can find someone who will distribute his gifts. I understand what it all means," cries Gösta, and his eyes shone. "Thousands shall get bread this year from one whom they load with curses."

"It shall be so, Gösta."

A feeling of exaltation came to these two men who had failed so utterly in their chosen vocation. They were filled with the desire of their youth to serve God and man. They exulted over the good deeds they would do. Gösta would help the vicar.

"We will get bread to begin with," says the vicar.

"We will get teachers. We will have a surveyor come and divide up the land. Then the people shall learn how to till their fields and tend their cattle."

"We will build roads and open new districts."

"We will make locks at the falls at Berg, so that there will be an open waterway between Löven and Väner."

"All the riches of the forest will become a double blessing when the way to the sea is opened."

"Your head shall be weighed down with the blessings bestowed upon you," cries Gösta.

The vicar looks up. They read in one another's eyes the same burning enthusiasm.

But at the same moment they catch sight of the pile of shame.

"Gösta," says the old man, "all that needs a young man's strength, but I am dying. You see what is killing me."

"Get rid of it!"

"How, Gösta Berling?"

Gösta moves close up to him and looks sharply into his eyes. "Pray to God for rain," he says. "You are going to preach next Sunday. Pray for rain."

The old clergyman sinks down in terror.

"If you are in earnest, if you are not he who has brought the drought on the land, if you meant to serve the Most High with your hardness, pray God for rain. That shall be the token; by that we shall know if God wishes what we wish."

When Gösta drove down Broby hill, he was astonished at himself and at the enthusiasm which had taken hold of him. But it could be a beautiful life—yes, but not for him. Up there they would not accept the service he could render.

In the church at Broby the sermon was over and the usual prayers read. The vicar was just going to step down from the pulpit, but he hesitated, finally, he fell on his knees and prayed for rain.

He prayed as a desperate man prays, with few incoherent words.

"If it is my sin which has called down Thy wrath, let me alone suffer! If there is any pity in Thee, Thou God of mercy, let it rain! Take the shame from me! Let it rain in answer to my prayer! Let the rain fall on the fields of the poor! Give Thy people bread!"

The day was hot; the sultriness was intolerable. The congregation sat as if in a torpor; but at these broken words, this hoarse cry of despair, everyone awakened.

"If there is a way of expiation for me, give rain—"

He stopped speaking. The doors stood open. There came a violent gust of wind. It rushed along the ground; whirled up against the church; and, full of sticks and straws, it brought in a cloud of dust. The clergyman could not continue; he staggered down from the pulpit.

The people trembled. Could that be an answer?

But this gust was only the forerunner of the thunder-storm. It sped with unprecedented swiftness. When the psalm was sung, and the clergyman stood by the altar, the lightning was already flashing, and the crash of thunder drowned the sound of his voice. As the sexton played the concluding hymn the first drops were already pattering against the green window-panes, and the people hurried out to see the rain. But they were not content with that: some wept, others laughed, while they let the torrents stream over them. Ah, how great had been their need! How unhappy they had been! But God is good! God let the rain come. What joy, what joy this was!

The vicar of Broby was the only one who did not come out in the rain. He knelt in front of the altar and did not rise. His joy had been too intense. He died of happiness.

CHAPTER 17 *The Child's Mother*

The child was born in a peasant's house east of the Klar river. The child's mother had come seeking employment one day in early June.

She had been unfortunate, she had said to the master and mistress, and her mother had been so hard to her that she had had to run away from home. She called herself Elizabeth Karlsdotter; but she would not say from whence she came, for then perhaps they would tell her parents that she was there; and if they were to find her, she knew that she would be tortured to death. She asked for no pay, only food and a roof over her head. She could work, weave or spin, and tend the cows,—or do whatever they wanted. If they wished, she could also pay for her keep.

She had been clever enough to come to the farmhouse barefoot, with her shoes under her arm; she had coarse hands; she spoke the country dialect; and she wore a peasant woman's clothes. They believed what she told them.

The master thought she looked sickly, and did not count much on her fitness for work. But somewhere the poor thing had to stay. And so she was allowed to stop.

There was something about her which made everyone on the farm kind to her. She had come to a good place. The people were serious and reticent. Her mistress liked her; when she discovered that she could weave, they borrowed a loom from the vicarage, and the child's mother worked with it the whole summer.

It never occurred to anyone that she needed to be spared; she had to work like a peasant girl the whole time. She liked to have much work to do. She was not unhappy. Life among the peasants pleased her, although she lacked all the comforts she was accustomed to. But everything was done so simply and quietly there. Everyone's thoughts were concentrated on his or her work; the days passed so uniformly and monotonously that one mistook the day and thought it was the middle of the week when Sunday came.

One day at the end of August they had had to hurry with the oat crop, and the child's mother had gone out with the others to bind the sheaves. She had overstrained herself, and the child had been born, but too soon. She had expected it in October.

Now the farmer's wife stood with the child in the living room to warm it by the fire, for the poor little thing was shivering in the August heat. The child's mother lay in a room beyond and listened to what they said of the little one. She could imagine how the men and maids came up and looked at him.

"Such a poor little thing," they all said, and then there invariably followed:—

"Poor little thing, with no father!"

They did not complain of the child's crying: they thought a child needed to cry; and, when everything was considered, the child was strong for its age; had it but a father, all would have been well.

The mother lay and listened and wondered. The matter suddenly seemed to her incredibly important. How would he get through life, poor little thing?

She had made her plans in advance. She would remain at the farmhouse the first year. Then she would hire a room and earn her living by weaving. She meant to earn enough to feed and clothe the child. Her husband could continue to believe that she was unworthy of him. She had thought that the child might perhaps grow to be a better man if she alone brought him up, than if a stupid and conceited father were to rear him.

But now, since the child was born, she could not view the matter in the same light. She now thought that she had been selfish. "The child must have a father," she said to herself.

If he had not been such a pitiful little thing, if he had been able to eat and sleep like other children, if his head had not always sunk down on one shoulder, and if he had not so nearly died when he had had the attack of cramp, it would not have been so important.

It was not so easy to decide, but an immediate decision had to be reached. The child was three days old, and the peasants in Värmland seldom wait longer before they have their children baptized. Under what name should the baby be entered in the church-register, and what would the clergyman want to know about the child's mother?

It was an injustice to the child to let him be registered as fatherless. If he were to be a weak and sickly man, how could she take the responsibility of depriving him of the advantages of birth and riches?

The child's mother had noticed that there is generally great joy and excitement when a child comes into the world. Now it seemed to her that it must be hard for this baby to live, whom everyone pitied. She wanted to see him sleeping on silk and lace, as it behoves a count's son. She wanted to see him surrounded with joy and pride.

The child's mother began to think that she had done his father too great an injustice. Had she the right to keep him for herself? That was out of the question. Such a precious little thing, whose worth it is not in man's power to calculate, should she take that to be her own? That would not be honest.

But she did not wish to go back to her husband. She feared that it would be her death. But the child was in greater danger than she was. He might die any minute, and he was not baptized.

The grievous sin which had dwelt in her heart, and which had driven her from her home, was now gone. She did not love anyone else than the child.

It was not too heavy a duty to try to obtain for him his rightful place in life.

The child's mother had the farmer and his wife called and told them everything. The husband journeyed to Borg to tell Count Dohna that his countess was alive, and that there was a child.

The peasant came home late in the evening; he had not met

the count, for he had gone away, but he had been to the perpetual curate at Svartsjö, and talked with him about the matter.

Then the countess heard that her marriage had been declared invalid, and that she no longer had a husband.

The curate wrote her a friendly letter, and offered her a home in his house.

A letter from her own father to Count Henrik, which must have reached Borg a few days after her flight, was also sent to her. It was just that letter, in which the old man had begged the count to hasten to have his marriage made legal, which had indicated to the count the easiest way of getting rid of his wife.

It is easy to imagine that the child's mother was seized with anger rather than with sorrow, when she heard the peasant's story.

She lay awake the whole night. Over and over again she thought of how the child must have a father.

Next morning the peasant had to drive to Ekeby on her account, in order to fetch Gösta Berling.

Gösta asked the silent man many questions, but could find out nothing. Yes, the countess had been in his house the whole summer. She had been well and had worked. Now a child was born. The child was weak; but the mother would soon be strong again.

Gösta asked if the countess knew that the marriage had been annulled.

Yes, she knew it now. She had heard it yesterday.

And as long as the drive lasted Gösta had suffered from successive cold and hot fits.

What did she want of him? Why did she send for him?

He thought of the life that summer on the shores of lake Löven. They had let the days go by with mirth and laughter and festivities, while she had worked and suffered.

He had never thought of the possibility of ever seeing her again. Ah, if he had dared to hope! He would have then come into her presence a better man. What had he now to look back to but the usual follies!

About eight o'clock in the evening he arrived, and was immediately taken to the child's mother. It was dark in the room. He could scarcely see her where she lay. The farmer and his wife came in also.

Now it must be realized that she whose white face shone in the dim light was always the noblest and the purest beeing he knew; the most beautiful soul that had ever animated an earthly body. When once again he felt the bliss of being near her, he longed to throw himself on his knees and thank her for having again appeared to him; but he was so overpowered by emotion that he could neither speak nor act.

"Dear Countess Elizabeth!" was all that he could say.

"Good-evening, Gösta."

She gave him her hand, which seemed once more to have become soft and transparent. She lay silent, while he struggled with his emotion.

The child's mother was not shaken by the up surging of any violent feelings when she saw Gösta. It only surprised her that he seemed to consider her of chief importance, when he ought to understand that it now only concerned the child.

"Gösta," she said gently, "you must help me now, as you once promised. You know that my husband has abandoned me, so that my child has no father."

"Yes, countess; but that can certainly be changed. Now that there is a child, the count can be forced to make the marriage legal. You may rest assured that I shall help you!"

The countess smiled. "Do you think that I will force myself upon Count Dohna?"

The blood surged up into Gösta's head. What did she wish then? What did she want of him?

"Come here, Gösta," she said, and again stretched out her hand. "You must not be angry with me for what I am going to say; but I thought that you who are—who are—"

"An unfrocked priest, a drunkard, a Cavalier, Ebba Dohna's murderer; I know the whole list—"

"Are you already angry, Gösta?"

"I would rather that you did not say anything more."

But the child's mother continued:—

"There are many, Gösta who would have liked to be your wife out of love; but it is not so with me. If I loved you I should not dare to speak as I am speaking now. For myself I would never ask such a thing, Gösta; but I can do it for the sake of the child. You must understand what I am asking of you. Of course, it is a great degradation for you, since I am an unmarried woman who has a child. I did not think that you would be willing to do it because you are worse than others; although, yes, I did think of that too. But mainly I thought that you might be willing, because you are kind, Gösta, because you are a hero and can sacrifice yourself. But it is perhaps too much to ask. Perhaps such a thing would be impossible for a man. If you despise me too much, if it is too loathsome for you to give your name to another man's child, say so! I shall not be angry. I understand that it is too much to ask; but the child is ill, Gösta. It is cruel to be unable to give the name of his mother's husband at his baptism."

As he heard her speak he experienced the same feeling as he had had on that spring day when he had put her on land and had left her to her fate. Now he had to help her to ruin her life, the whole of her future life. He who loved her had to do this.

"I will do everything you wish, countess," he said.

The next day he spoke to the dean of Bro, for it was there that the banns had to be published.

The good old Dean was much moved by his story, and promised to take full responsibility for giving her away.

"Yes," he said, "you must help her, Gösta, otherwise she might become insane. She thinks that she has injured the child by depriving him of his position in life. She has indeed a most sensitive conscience."

"But I know that I shall make her unhappy," cried Gösta.

"That you must not do, Gösta. You must be a sensible man now, with wife and child to care for."

The Dean had to go down to Svartsjö and speak to both the clergyman and the judge. The end of it all was that the next Sunday, the first of September, the banns were published in Svartsjö for Gösta Berling and Elizabeth von Thurn.

Then the child's mother was carried with the greatest care to Ekeby, and there the child was baptized.

The Dean talked to her, and told her that she could still retract her decision to marry such a man as Gösta Berling. She ought first to write to her father.

"I do not regret what I am doing," she said; "think if my child should die before he had a father."

By the time the banns had been published three times, the child's mother was well and had been up several days. In the afternoon the Dean came to Ekeby and married her to Gösta Berling. But no one thought of it as a wedding. No guests were invited. They only gave the child a father, nothing more.

The child's mother was radiant with a quiet joy, as if she had attained a great aim in life. The bridegroom was in despair. He thought of how she had thrown away her life by marrying him. He saw with dismay that he scarcely existed for her. All her thoughts were concentrated on her child.

A few days later the father and mother were mourning the death of the child.

Many thought that the child's mother did not show the violent and profound grief that they had expected; she had a look of triumph. It was as if she rejoiced in the fact that she had thrown away her life for the sake of the child. When the little one joined the angels, he would still remember that on earth he had had a mother who had loved him.

All this happened quietly and remained unnoticed. When the banns were published for Gösta Berling and Elizabeth von Thurn in the church at Svartsjö, most of the congregation did not even know who the bride was. The clergyman and the gentry who knew the story said little about it. It was as if they were afraid that someone who had lost faith in the power of conscience might misinterpret the young woman's action. They were so afraid, lest someone should come and say: "You see, she could not conquer her love for Gösta; she has married him under a plausible excuse." The old people always took great care of the young woman! They could never bear to hear anything said against her. They would scarcely acknowledge that she had sinned. They would not admit that any fault of her's had stained that soul which was so afraid of evil.

Another reason why Gösta's marriage was not much discussed was that another important event occurred just then.

Major Samzelius had met with an accident. He had become more and more strange and misanthropic. His chief intercourse was with animals; and he had collected a small menagerie at Sjö.

He was dangerous too; for he always carried a loaded gun, and shot it off time after time without paying much attention to what he aimed at. One day he was bitten by a tame bear which he had shot unintentionally. The wounded animal attacked him, and succeeded in giving him a terrible bite in the arm. The beast escaped and took refuge in the forest.

The major was put to bed and died of the wound, but not until just before Christmas. If his wife had known that he was lying ill, she could have resumed her sway over Ekeby. But the Cavaliers knew that she would not come before their year was out.

CHAPTER 18 *Amor vincit omnia*

Under the stairs leading to the gallery in the church at Svartsjö
there is a lumber room filled with the grave-diggers' worn-out
spades, with broken benches, with discarded tin signs and other
rubbish.

In there, where the dust lies thickest and seems to hide it from
every human eye, is a chest, inlaid with mother-of-pearl in the
most perfect mosaic. If the dust is removed, the chest seems to
shine and glitter like a mountain-wall in a fairy-tale. The chest
is locked, and the key is in good keeping; it may not be used.
No mortal man may cast a glance into that chest. No one knows
what is in it. First, when the nineteenth century has reached its
close, may the key be placed in the lock, the cover lifted, and the
treasures which it has guarded be seen by men.

This is what the owner of the chest had prescribed.

The inscription on the brass-plate of the lid reads: "Labor
vincit omnia." But another inscription would be more appro-
priate: "Amor vincit omnia". For the chest in the lumber-room
under the gallery stairs is a testimony of the omnipotence of
love.

O Eros, all-conquering god!

Thou, O Love, art indeed eternal! Men have dwelt on the
earth since very ancient times, but thou hast followed them
through the ages.

Where are the gods of the East, the strong heroes who used
thunder-bolts as their weapons, who on the banks of holy rivers
received offerings of honey and milk? They are dead. Dead is
Bel, the mighty warrior, and Thot, the hawk-headed champion.
Dead the glorious ones who rested on the cloud banks of Olympus; dead are also the mighty who dwelt in wall-engirdled Val-

halla. Dead are all the old gods except Eros, Eros, the all-powerful!

His work is in everything you see. It is he who sustains the human race. He is seen everywhere! Where can you go without finding his footprints? Have you ever heard anything of which the key-note is not the sound of his wings? He lives in the hearts of men and in the sleeping germ. See with trembling his presence in inanimate things!

What is there that does not yearn, that does not know desire? What can escape from his dominion? All the gods of revenge shall fall, and all the power that is based on strength and violence shall come to an end. Thou, O Love, art eternal!

Old Uncle Eberhard is sitting at his writing-desk,—a splendid piece of furniture with a hundred drawers, white marble top and mountings of blackened brass. He works with eagerness and diligence; all alone in the Cavaliers' wing.

Oh, Eberhard, why do you not roam about the woods and fields in these last days of departing summer as the other Cavaliers do? No one, you know, worships with impunity the goddess of wisdom. Your back is bent with sixty odd years; the hair which covers your head is not your own; a mass of wrinkles cover your brow, which arches over hollow eyes; and the decay of old age is depicted in the thousand lines about your empty mouth.

Oh, Eberhard, why do you not roam about the woods and fields? Death will only take you all the sooner from your writing-table, because you have not allowed life to entice you from it.

Uncle Eberhard draws a thick line in ink under the last few words. From the innumerable drawers of the desk he takes out the yellowing, closely scribbled manuscripts; all the different parts of his great work,—that work which is to preserve Eberhard Berggren's name for all time. But just as he has piled up bundles of manuscript, and is staring at them in silent rapture, the door opens, and in walks the young countess.

There she is, the old men's young mistress,—they wait on her and adore her more than grandparents wait on and adore the first grandson. They had found her in poverty and sickness; and now they had bestowed upon her all the worlds' glory, just as the king in the fairy tale had done for the beautiful beggar girl he had found in the forest. It is for her that the horn and violin now sound at Ekeby,—that everything moves, breathes, and works on the great estate.

She is well again, although still very weak. Time passes slowly for her alone in the big house; and as she knows that the Cavaliers are away, she wishes to see what it looks like in the Cavaliers' wing, those notorious premises.

So she comes softly in and looks up at the whitewashed walls and the yellow striped bed-curtains, but she is embarrassed when she sees that the room is not empty.

Uncle Eberhard goes solemnly towards her, and leads her forward to the great pile of papers.

"Look, Countess," he says; "now my work is ready. Now what I have written shall go out into the world. Now great things are going to happen."

"What is going to happen, Uncle Eberhard?"

"Oh, Countess, it is going to strike men like a thunderbolt, a bolt which both enlightens and kills. Old Jehovah has sat secure ever since Moses dragged him out of the thunder-cloud on Mount Sinai and put him on the throne of grace in the innermost sanctuary of the temple. But now men shall see what he is: Imagination, emptiness, exhalation, the still-born child of our own brains. He shall sink into nothingness," said the old man, and laid his wrinkled hand on the pile of manuscript. "It stands here; and when people read this, they will have to believe. They will rise up and acknowledge their own stupidity; they will use crosses for kindlingwood, churches for storehouses, and priests will plough the earth."

"Oh, Uncle Eberhard," says the Countess, with a slight shudder, "are you really such a dreadful person? Are such dreadful things written there?"

"Dreadful!" repeated the old man, "it is only the truth. But we are like little boys who hide their faces in a woman's skirt as

soon as they meet a stranger: we have accustomed ourselves to
hide from the truth, from the eternal stranger. But now he shall
come and dwell among us, now he shall be known by all."

"By all?"

"Not only by philosophers, but by everybody; do you understand, Countess, by everybody."

"And so Jehovah is to die?"

"He and all the angels, all the saints, all the devils, and all the lies."

"Who will then rule the world?"

"Do you believe that anyone has ruled it before? Do you
believe in that Providence which looks after sparrows and the
hair of your head? No one has ruled it, no one shall rule it."

"But we, we human beings, what will become of us?"

"We shall be the same as we have been—dust. That which
has been burned up cannot burn again; it is dead. We are merely
fuel consumed by the flickering flames of life. The sparks of
life fly from one person to another. We are lighted; we flame
up, and die out. That is life."

"Oh, Eberhard, is there no life of the spirit?"

"None."

"No life beyond the grave?"

"None."

"No good, no evil, no aim, no hope?"

"None."

The young woman walks over to the window. She looks out at
the autumn's yellowing leaves, at dahlias and asters which hang
their heavy heads on broken stalks. She sees the Löven's black
waves, the autumn's dark storm-clouds, and for a moment she
inclines towards repudiation.

"Uncle Eberhard," she says, "how ugly and gray the world is;
how futile everything is! I should like to lie down and die."

But then she hears a murmur in her soul. The vigour of life and
its strong emotions cry out for the happiness of living.

"Is there nothing," she exclaims, "which can give life beauty
since you have taken from me God and immortality?"

"Work," answers the old man.

But she looks out again, and a feeling of scorn for that impoverished wisdom comes over her. The unfathomable rises before her; she feels the immanent spirit in everything; she is sensible of the power latent in seemingly dead matter, but which can develop into a thousand forms of shifting life. Her whirling thoughts seek to find a name whereby to call the presence of God's spirit in nature.

"Oh, Eberhard," she says, "what is work? Is it a god? Has it any meaning in itself? Give it some other name!"

"I know no other," answered the old man.

Then she finds the name she is seeking,—a poor name which is often sullied.

"Uncle Eberhard, why do you not speak of love?"

A smile glides over the empty mouth where the thousand wrinkles cross.

"Here," says the philosopher, and strikes the heavy packet with his clenched fist, "here all the gods are slain, and I have not forgotten Eros. What is love but the lust of the flesh? In what is he superior to the other needs of the body? Make hunger a god! Make fatigue a god! They are just as worthy. Let there be an end to such absurdities! Let the truth live!"

The young Countess sinks her head. It is not so; all that is not true; but she cannot contest it.

"Your words have wounded my soul," she says; "but still I do not believe you. You may be able to kill the gods of revenge and violence but no others."

But the old man takes her hand, lays it on the book, and swears in the fanaticism of unbelief.

"When you have read this, you must believe."

"May it never happen to me," she says, "for if I were to believe that, I could not live."

And she goes away sadly from the philosopher. But he continued to sit and ponder for a long time after she had gone.

Those old manuscripts, scribbled over with heathenish confessions, have not yet been tested by the world. Uncle Eberhard's name has not yet reached the heights of fame.

His great work lies hidden in a chest in the lumber-room under the gallery stairs in the church at Svartsjö; it shall first see the light of day at the end of the century.

But why has he done this? Was he afraid not to have proved his case? Did he fear persecution? You little know Uncle Eberhard.

Let the reason now be clearly understood; he loved the truth, not his own glory. So he sacrificed the latter and not the former, in order that a deeply loved child might die retaining the belief in that which she has cherised most.

O Love, thou art indeed eternal!

CHAPTER 19 *The Broom-Girl*

No one knows the place in the lee of the mountain where the pines grow thickest and deep layers of moss cover the ground. How should anyone know it? No man's foot has ever trodden it before; no man's tongue has given it a name. No path leads to that hidden spot. It is the most solitary tract in the forest, and now thousands of people are looking for it.

What an endless procession of seekers! They would fill the church at Bro—not only at Bro, but also at Löfviks and Svartsjö.

All who live near the road rush out and ask, "Has the country suffered misfortune? Is the enemy upon us? Where are you going? Tell us where."

"We are searching," they answer. "We have been searching for two days. We shall go on to-day; but afterwards we can do no more. We are going to search the Bjärne forest and the fir-clad heights west of Ekeby.

It was from Nygård, a poor district far away among the eastern mountains, the procession had first started. The beautiful girl with the heavy, black hair and the red cheeks had disappeared a week before. The broom-girl, to whom Gösta Berling had wished to become engaged, had been lost in the great forests. No one had seen her for a week.

So the people started from Nygård to search the forest. And everybody they met joined in the search.

Sometimes one of the newcomers asks,—

"You men from Nygård, how has it all happened? Why do you let that beautiful girl go alone in strange paths? The forest is deep, and God has taken away her reason."

"No one molests her," they answer; "she does not interfere with anyone. She goes as safely as would a child. Who is safer than one whom God himself must care for? She has always come back before."

Thus, the search parties have gone through the eastern woods which separate Nygård from the plain. Now on the third day they pass by the church at Bro on the way to the woods west of Ekeby.

But wherever they go, they arouse people's wonder; and a man from the crowd has constantly to stop and answer questions:

"What do you want? What are you looking for?"

"We are looking for the blue-eyed, dark-haired girl. She has lain down to die in the forest. She has been gone a week."

"Why has she lain down to die in the forest? Was she hungry? Was she unhappy?"

"She has not suffered want, but she had a misfortune last spring. She has seen that mad priest, Gösta Berling, and has loved him for many years. She knew no better. God had taken away her wits."

"Last spring the misfortune happened,—before that, he had never looked at her. Then he said to her that she should be his sweetheart. It was only in jest; he let her go again, but she could not be consoled. She kept coming to Ekeby. She followed him wherever he went. He tired of her. When she was there last, they set their dogs on her. Since then no one has seen her."

To the rescue, to the rescue! A human life is at stake! A human being has lain down to die in the forest! Perhaps she is already dead. But may be she is still wandering there with out finding the right way. The forest is wide, and her reason is with God.

Come everybody, men and women and children! Who can dare to stay at home? Who can know if God does not intend to use just him? Come all of you who need mercy, that your soul may not some day wander helpless in dry places, seeking rest and finding none! Come! God has taken her reason, and the forest is wide.

It is wonderful to see people unite for some great purpose. But it is not hunger, or the fear of God, or war which has caused these people to set forth. They will receive nothing for all the trouble they take, they will have no reward for their striving; they are only out to find a fool. It all costs so much sweat, so much walking, so much anxiety, so many prayers; and yet their only possible recompense is to find a poor, misguided girl, whose reason is with God.

Those anxious searchers fill the highway. With earnest eyes they scan the forest; they proceed on their way sadly, for they realize that more probably, they are searching for the dead than the living.

Ah, that black thing at the foot of the cliff, it is not an ant-hill after all, but a fallen tree. Praised be Heaven, only a fallen tree! But they cannot see distinctly, the pines grow so thick.

It is the third day of the search; they are used to the work. They search under the sloping rock, on which one's foot can slip, under fallen trees, where an arm or leg could easily have been broken, under the thick growing pine branches trailing over soft moss, inviting one to rest.

The bear's den, the fox's hole, the badger's deep burrow, the red cranberry slope, the silver fir, the mountain, which the forest fire laid waste a month ago, the stone which the giant threw,— all these they have found, but not the place under the rock where the black thing is lying. No one has been there to see if it is an ant-hill, or a tree-trunk, or a human being. Alas! it is indeed a human being, but no one has been there to see her.

The evening sun is shining on the other side of the wood, but the young woman is not found. What should they do now? Should they search through the wood once more? The wood is dangerous in the dark; there are bottomless bogs and deep clefts. And what could they, who had found nothing when the sun was shining, find when it was gone?

"Let us go to Ekeby!" cries one in the crowd.

"Let us go to Ekeby!" they all cry together.

"Let us ask those cavaliers why they let the dogs loose on one whose reason God had taken; why they drove a fool to despair. Our poor, hungry children weep; our clothes are torn; the potatoes rot in the ground; our horses are running loose; our cows are untended; we are nearly dead with fatigue—and the fault is theirs. Let us go to Ekeby and investigate this matter.

"During this cursed year we have had to suffer everything. The winter will bring us starvation. Whom does God's hand seek? It was not the clergyman at Broby. His prayers could reach God's ear. Who, then, can it be, if not these Cavaliers? Let us go to Ekeby!

"They have ruined the estate, they have driven away the major's wife to beg on the highway. It is their fault that we have no work. The famine is their doing. Let us go to Ekeby!"

So the dark, embittered men crowd down to Ekeby, hungry women with weeping children in their arms follow them; and last come the cripples and the old men. And the bitterness spreads like an ever-increasing storm from the old men to the women, from the women to the strong men at the head of the train.

It is the autumn-flood which is coming. Cavaliers do you remember the spring-flood?

A cottager who is ploughing in a pasture at the edge of the wood hears the people's mad cries. He throws himself on one of his horses and gallops down to Ekeby.

"Disaster is coming!" he cries; "the bears are coming, the wolves are coming, the goblins are coming to take Ekeby!"

He rides about the whole estate, wild with terror.

"All the devils in the forest are let loose!" he cries. "They are coming to take Ekeby! Save yourselves who can! The devils are coming to burn the house and to kill the Cavaliers!"

And behind him can be heard the din and cries of the rushing horde. Does it know what it wants, that raging stream of bitterness? Is it out for fire, or murder, or plunder?

They are not human beings; they are wild beasts. Death to Ekeby, death to the Cavaliers!

Here brandy flows in streams. Here gold lies piled in the vaults. Here the storehouses are filled with grain and meat. Why should the honest starve, and the guilty have plenty?

But now your time is out, the measure is overflowing, Cavaliers. In the forest lies one who condemns you; we are her deputies.

The Cavaliers stand in the big building and see the people coming. They know already why they are denounced. For once they are innocent. If that poor girl has lain down to die in the forest, it is not because they have set the dogs on her,—they never did that—but because Gösta Berling, a week ago, was married to Countess Elizabeth.

But what is the good of speaking to that mob? They are tired, they are hungry; revenge drives them on, plunder tempts them. They rush down with wild cries, and before them rides the cottager, whom fear has driven mad.

The Cavaliers have hidden the young Countess in their inner-most room. Löwenborg and Eberhard are to sit there and guard her; the others go out to meet the people. They are standing on the steps before the main building, unarmed, smiling, as the first of the noisy crowd reach the house.

And the people stop before that little group of quiet men. They had wanted to knock them down and to trample them under their iron-shod heels, as the people at the Sund ironworks had done to the manager and the inspector fifty years ago; but they had expected closed doors, raised weapons; they had expected resistance and fighting.

"Dear friends," say the Cavaliers; "dear friends, you are tired and hungry; let us give you a little food and first a glass of Ekeby's own home-distilled brandy."

The people will not listen; they scream and threaten. But the Cavaliers are not discouraged.

"Only wait," they say; "only wait a second. See, Ekeby stands open. The cellar doors are open; the store-rooms are open; the dairy is open. Your women are dropping with fatigue; the children are crying. Let us get them food first! Then you can kill us. We will not run away. The attic is full of apples. Let us go after apples for the children!"

An hour later the feasting is in full swing at Ekeby. The biggest feast that the large house has ever seen is celebrated there that autumn night under the shining full moon.

Woodpiles have been lighted; the whole estate flames with bonfires. The people sit about in groups, enjoying warmth and rest, while all the good things of the earth are lavishly bestowed upon them.

Resolute men have gone to the farmyard and taken what was needed. Calves and sheep have been killed, and even one or two oxen. The animals have been cut up and roasted in a trice. Those starving crowds are devouring the food. Animal after animal is led out and slaughtered. It looks as if the whole barn would be emptied in one night.

They had just baked that day. Since the arrival of young Countess Elizabeth, work was once more being done in the house. It seemed as if the young woman never remembered for an instant that she was Gösta Berling's wife. Neither he nor she acted as if it were so; but on the other hand she made herself the mistress of Ekeby. As a good and capable woman must always do, she tried most zealously to remedy the waste and the negligence which reigned in the house. And she was obeyed. The servants felt a certain pleasure in again having a mistress over them.

But of what avail was it now that she had had the kitchen stores filled with bread; that there had been cheese-making, churning and brewing during the month of September?

Let the people have everything there is, so that they may not burn down Ekeby and kill the Cavaliers! Let them have bread, butter, cheese! Roll out the beer-barrels, take out the hams from the storehouse, out with the brandy-kegs, out with the apples!

How can all the riches of Ekeby suffice to mitigate the people's anger? We can be glad if we succeed in getting them away before any evil deed is done.

All this is done for the sake of the woman who is now mistress at Ekeby. The Cavaliers are brave men; they would have defended themselves if they had followed their own will. They would have preferred to drive off the marauders with a few sharp shots, if it had not been for her sake, who is gentle and begs for the people.

As the night advances, the crowds become placid. The warmth and the rest, the food and the brandy have assuaged their terrible excitement. They begin to jest and laugh.

As it draws towards midnight, it looks as if they were preparing to leave. The Cavaliers stop bringing food and wine, drawing corks and pouring ale. They sigh with relief, feeling that the danger is over.

But just then a light is seen in one of the windows of the big house. All who see it utter a cry. It is a young woman who is carrying the light.

It had only been for a second. The vision disappeared; but the people think they have recognized the woman.

"She had thick black hair and red cheeks!" they cry. "She is here! They have hidden her here!"

"Oh, Cavaliers, is she here? Have you got our child, whose reason God has taken, here at Ekeby? What are you doing with her? You let us grieve for her a whole week, search for three whole days. Away with wine and food! Shame on us, that we accepted anything from your hands! First, let her out! Then we shall know what we have to do to you."

The people are quick; but quicker still are the Cavaliers. They rush in and bar the door. But how could they resist such a mass? Door after door is broken down. The Cavaliers are flung aside; they are unarmed. They are wedged in the crowd, so that they cannot move. The people are determined to enter and to find the broom-girl.

In the innermost room they find her. No one has time to see whether she is light or dark. They lift her up and carry her out. She must not be afraid, they say. They are here to save her.

But they who now stream from the building are met by another procession.

In the most lonely spot in the forest the body no longer rests of a woman who had fallen over a high cliff and had been killed by the fall; a child had found her. Searchers who had remained in the forest had lifted her on their shoulders. Here they come.

In death she is even more beautiful than in life. Lovely she lies with her long, black hair. Fair is the form since eternal peace rests upon it.

Lifted high on the men's shoulders, she is carried through the crowd. With bent heads all do homage to the majesty of death.

"She has not been dead long," the men whisper. "She must have wandered in the woods until to-day. We think that in trying to escape from us, who were looking for her, she fell over the cliff."

But if this is the broom-girl, who is the one who has been carried out of Ekeby?

The procession from the forest meets the procession from the house. Bonfires are burning all over the yard. The people can see both the women and recognize them. The other is the young Countess from Borg.

"Oh! what is the meaning of this? Is this a new crime? Why is the young Countess here at Ekeby? Why have they told us that she was either far away or dead? In the name of holy justice, ought we not to throw ourselves on the Cavaliers and trample them to dust under our iron-shod heels?"

Then a ringing voice is heard. Gösta Berling has climbed up on the balustrade and is speaking. "Listen to me, you monsters, you devils! Do you think there are no guns and powder at Ekeby, you madmen? Do you think that I have not wanted to shoot you like mad dogs, if she had not begged for you? Oh, if I had known that you would have touched her, not one of you would have been left alive!

"Why are you raging here to-night and threatening us with murder and fire? What have I to do with your crazy girls? Do I know where they run off to? I was kind to that girl; and this is the result. I ought to have set the dogs on her,—it would have been better for us both—but I did not. Nor did I ever promise to marry her; I never did that. Remember that!

"But now I tell you that you must let her go, whom you have dragged out of the house. Let her go, I say; and may the hands that have touched her burn in everlasting fire! Do you not understand that she is as much above you as heaven is above the earth? She is as delicate as you are coarse; as good as you are bad.

"Now I will tell you who she is. First, she is an angel from heaven—secondly, she was married to the Count at Borg. But her mother-in-law tortured her night and day; she had to stand at the lake and wash clothes like an ordinary maid; she was beaten and tormented as none of your women have ever been. Yes, she was almost ready to throw herself into the river, as we all know, because they were torturing the life out of her. I wonder which one of you was there then to save her life. Not one of you was there; but we Cavaliers, we did it.

"And when afterwards she gave birth to a child in a distant farmhouse, and the count sent her the message: 'We were married in a foreign land; we did not comply with the law and the regulations. You are not my wife; I am not your husband. I care nothing for your child!'—yes, when this happened, and she did not want the child to be entered in the church register as being fatherless; then you would have been proud enough if she had said to one of you: 'Come and marry me! I must have a father for the child!' But she chose none of you. She took Gösta Berling, the penniless priest, who may never speak the word of God. Yes, I tell you, peasants, that I have never done anything harder; for I was so unworthy of her that I did not dare to look her in the eyes, nor did I dare refuse, for she was in despair.

"And now you may believe what evil you like of us Cavaliers; but to her we have done what good we could. And it is thanks to her that you have not all been killed to-night. But now I tell you: set her free, and go away yourselves, or I think the earth will open and swallow you up. And as you go, pray God to forgive you for having frightened and grieved one who is so good and innocent. And now be off! We have had enough of you!"

Long before he had finished speaking, those who had carried out the Countess had put her down on one of the stone steps; and now a big peasant came thoughtfully up to her and stretched out his great hand.

"Thank you, and good-night," he said. "We wish you no harm, Countess."

After him came another and shook her hand. "Thanks, and good-night. You must not be angry with us!"

Gösta sprang down and placed himself beside her. Then they took his hand too.

So they came forward slowly, one after another, to bid them good-night before they went. They were once more subdued; they were again human beings, as they had been when they left their homes that morning, before hunger and revenge had made them into wild beasts.

They looked in the Countess's face, and Gösta saw that the innocence and gentleness they saw there brought tears into the eyes of many. There was in all of them a silent adoration of the noblest they had ever seen.

They could not all shake her hand. There were so many, and the young woman was tired and weak. But they all came and looked at her, and could take Gösta's hand,—his arm could stand a shaking.

Gösta stood as if in a dream. That evening a new love sprang up in his heart.

"Oh, my people," he thought, "oh, my people, how I love you!" He felt how he loved all that crowd who were disappearing into the darkness with the dead girl at the head of the procession, with their coarse clothes and evil-smelling shoes; those who lived in the gray huts at the edge of the wood; those who could not write, and often not even read; those who had never known the fulness and richness of life, only the struggle for their daily bread.

He loved them with a painful, burning tenderness which forced the tears from his eyes. He did not know what he wanted to do for them, but he loved them, each and all, with their faults, their vices and their weaknesses. Oh, Lord God, if the day could come when he too should be loved by them!

He awoke from his dream; his wife laid her hand on his arm. The people were gone. They were alone on the steps.

"Oh, Gösta, Gösta, how could you!"

She put her hands before her face and wept.

"It is true what I said," he cried. "I never promised the broom-girl that I would marry her. 'Come here next Friday, and you shall see something funny!' was all I ever said to her. It is not my fault that she cared for me."

"Oh, it was not that; but how could you say to the people that I was good and pure? Gösta, Gösta! Do you not know that I loved you when I had no right to do it? I was ashamed, Gösta! I was ready to die of shame!"

And she was shaken by her sobs.

He stood and looked at her.

"Oh, my friend, my beloved!" he said quietly. "How happy you are, who are so good! How happy to have such a beautiful soul!"

CHAPTER 20 *Kevenhüller*

Kevenhüller, who was subsequently to become a learned and accomplished man, was born in the year 1770 in Germany. He was the son of a count, and could have lived in lofty palaces and ridden at the Emperor's side if he had so wished; but this was not to his liking.

He would have liked to fasten windmill sails to the highest tower of the castle, to turn the hall into a locksmith's workshop, and the boudoir into a watch-maker's room. He would have liked to fill the castle with whirling wheels and working levers. But when he could not do this, he left all the pomp and apprenticed himself to a watch-maker. There he learned everything there was to learn about cog-wheels, springs, and pendulums. He learned to make sun-dials and star-dials, clocks with singing canary-birds and horn-blowing shepherds, chimes which filled a whole church-tower with their wonderful machinery, and clockwork so minute that it could be kept in a locket.

When he had received his master's diploma, he donned his knapsack, took his stick in his hand, and wandered from place to place to study everything that ran on rollers and wheels. Kevenhüller was no ordinary watch-maker; he wished to be a great inventor and reformer.

When he had wandered in this way through many countries, he turned his steps towards Värmland, with the intention of studying there mill-wheels and mining. One beautiful summer morning he happened to be crossing the market-place of Karlstad. But that same beautiful summer morning it had pleased the wood-nymph to extend her walk as far as the town. The noble lady also came across the market-place from the opposite direction, and so met Kevenhüller.

That was a meeting for a watch-maker's apprentice. She had shining, green eyes, and a mass of light hair, which almost reached the ground, and she was dressed in green, shimmering silk. She was the most beautiful woman Kevenhüller had ever seen.

He stood as if he had lost his wits, and stared at her as she came towards him.

She came straight from the deepest thicket of the wood, where the ferns are as high as trees, where the giant firs shut out the sun, so that it can only fall in golden drops on the yellow moss.

I should like to have been in Kevenhüller's place, to see her as she came with ferns and pine-needles tangled in her yellow hair and a little black snake about her neck.

How the people must have stared at her! Horses bolted, frightened by her long, floating hair. The street boys ran after her. The men dropped their meat-axes to gape at her.

She herself was calm and majestic, only smiling a little at the excitement, so that Kevenhüller saw her small, pointed teeth shine between her red lips.

She had hung a cloak over her shoulders so that none should see who she was; but as ill-luck would have it, she had forgotten to cover her tail. It dragged along the paving-stones.

Kevenhüller saw the tail; he was sorry that a noble lady should make herself the laughing-stock of the town; so he bowed and said courteously:—

"Would it not please your Grace to lift your train?"

The wood-nymph was touched, not only by his kindness, but by his politeness. She stopped before him and looked at him, so that he thought that shining sparks passed from her eyes into his brain. "Kevenhüller," she said, "hereafter, with your two hands you will be able to accomplish whatever piece of work you desire, but only one specimen of each kind."

She said it and she could keep her word. For who does not know that the wood-nymph has the power to bestow genius and wonderful qualities to those who win her favour?

Kevenhüller remained in Karlstad and hired a workshop there. He hammered and worked night and day. In a week he had made a wonder. It was a carriage, which went by itself. It went up hill and down hill, went fast or slow, could be steered and turned, and stopped and started, just as one wished.

Kevenhüller became famous. He was so proud of his carriage that he journeyed up to Stockholm to show it to the king. He did not need to wait for post-horses nor to scold ostlers. He proudly drove in his own carriage and was there in a few hours.

He drove right up to the palace, and the king came out with his court ladies and gentlemen and looked at him. They could not praise him enough.

The king then said: "I should like you to give me that carriage, Kevenhüller." And although he did not acquiesce, the king persisted and wished to have the carriage.

Then Kevenhüller saw that in the king's train stood a lady in waiting with light hair and a green dress. He recognized her, and he understood that it was she who had advised the king to ask him for his carriage. He was in despair. He could not bear that anyone else should have his carriage, nor did he dare to refuse the king's request. Therefore he drove it with such speed against the palace wall that it was broken into a thousand pieces.

When he came home to Karlstad he tried to make another carriage. But he was unable to do so. Then he was dismayed at the gift the wood-nymph had given him. He had left the life of ease in his father's castle to be a benefactor to many, and not to create marvels which only one person could use. What good was it to him to be a great master, yes, the greatest of all masters, if he could not reproduce his marvels so that they could be used by thousands of people.

And he so greatly longed for quiet, sensible work that he became a stone-cutter and mason. It was then he built the great stone tower down by the west bridge, and he meant to build walls and portals and courtyards, ramparts and turrets, so that a veritable castle should stand by the Klar River.

And there he should realize his childhood's dream. Everything which had to do with industry and handicraft should have a place within the castle halls. White millers, blacksmiths, watchmakers with green shades before their strained eyes, dyers with stained hands, weavers, turners, filers,—all should have their workshops in his castle.

And everything went well. He built the tower himself of the stones he had hewn. He had fastened the sails of a windmill to it,—for the tower was to be a mill,—and now he wanted to begin on the smithy.

But one day he stood and watched how the light, strong wings were made to revolve by the wind. Then his old longing came over him.

He shut himself in in his workshop, tasted no food, took no rest, and worked unceasingly. At the end of a week he had made a new marvel.

One day he climbed up on the roof of his tower and began to fasten wings to his shoulders.

Two street boys saw him, and they gave a cry which was heard through the whole town. They started off; panting, they ran up the streets and down the streets, knocking on all the doors, and screaming as they ran:—

"Kevenhüller is going to fly! Kevenhüller is going to fly!"

He stood calmly on the tower-roof and fastened on his wings, and in the meantime crowds of people came running through the narrow streets of old Karlstad. Soon the bridge was black with them. The market-place was packed, and the banks of the river swarmed with people.

Kevenhüller at last got his wings on and set out. He gave a couple of flaps with them, and then he was up in the air. He lay and floated high above the earth.

He drew in the air with long breaths; it was strong and pure. His breast expanded, and the old knights' blood began to seethe in him. He tumbled like a pigeon, he hovered like a hawk, his flight was as swift as the swallow's, as sure as the falcon's. If he had only been able to make such a pair of wings for everyone! If he only could give them all the power to raise themselves in this pure air! He could not enjoy it alone. Ah, that wood-nymph, —if he could only meet her!

Then he saw, with eyes which were almost blinded by the dazzling sunlight, how someone came flying towards him. Great wings like his own, and between the wings floated a human body. He saw floating yellow hair, billowy green silk, wild shining eyes. It was she, it was she!

Kevenhüller did not stop to consider. With furious speed he threw himself upon her to kiss her or to strike her,—he was not sure which—but at any rate to force her to remove the curse from his existence. He did not look where he was going; he saw only the flying hair and the wild eyes. He came close up to her and stretched out his arms to seize her. But his wings caught in hers, and hers were the stronger. His wings were torn and destroyed; he himself was swung round and hurled down, he knew not whither.

When he regained consciousness he was lying on the roof of his own tower, with the broken flying-machine by his side. He had flown right against his own mill; the sails had caught him, whirled him round a couple of times, and then thrown him down on the roof of the tower.

So that was how it ended.

Kevenhüller was again a desperate man. He could not bear the thought of honest work, and he did not dare to use his magic power. If he could make another wonder and then destroy it, his heart would break with sorrow. And if he did not destroy it, he would certainly go mad at the thought that he could not do good to others with it.

He got his knapsack and stick; let the mill stand as it was; and decided to go out and search for the wood-nymph.

In the course of his travels he came to Ekeby, a few years before the major's wife was driven out. There he was well received; and there he remained. The memories of his childhood came back to him, and he allowed them to call him Count. His hair grew gray and his brain became dormant. He was so old that he could no longer believe in the feats of his youth. He was not the man who could work wonders. It was not he who had made the automatic carriage and the flying-machine. Oh, no,—tales, tales!

But then it happened that the major's wife was driven from Ekeby, and the Cavaliers became masters of the great estate. Then a mode of life began which had never been worse. A storm passed over the land; men fought on earth, and even the spirits made war in heaven. Wolves came from Dovre with witches on their backs, and the wood-nymph came to Ekeby.

The Cavaliers did not recognize her. They thought that she was a poor and distressed woman whom a cruel mother-in-law had hunted to despair. So they gave her shelter, revered her like a queen, and loved her like a child.

Kevenhüller alone saw who she was. At first he was dazzled like the others. But one day she wore a dress of green, shimmering silk, and when she had that on, Kevenhüller recognized her.

There she sat on silken cushions, and all the old men made themselves ridiculous in waiting on her. One was a cook and another a footman; there was also a reader, a court-musician and a shoemaker; they all had their occupations.

They said she was ill, the odious witch; but Kevenhüller knew what that illness meant. She was laughing at them all.

He warned the Cavaliers against her. "Look at her small, pointed teeth," he said, "and her wild, shining eyes. She is the wood-nymph,—all evil is afoot in these terrible times. I tell you she is the wood-nymph, she has come here to bring about our ruin. I have seen her before."

But when Kevenhüller saw the wood-nymph and had recognized her, the desire for work came over him. It began to burn and seethe in his brain; his fingers ached with longing to grasp hammar and file; he could hold out no longer. With a bitter heart he put on his working-blouse and shut himself up in an old smithy, which was to be his workshop.

A cry went out from Ekeby over the whole of Värmland:— "Kevenhüller has begun to work!"

A new wonder was to see the light. What was it to be? Will he teach us to walk on the water, or to raise a ladder to the stars?

One night, the first or second of October, he had the wonder ready. He came out of the workshop and had it in his hand. It was a wheel which turned incessantly; as it turned, the spokes glowed like fire, and it gave out warmth and light. Kevenhüller had made a sun. When he came out of the workshop with it, the night grew so light that the sparrows began to chirp and the clouds to burn as if at dawn.

There would never again be darkness or cold on earth. His head whirled when he thought of it. The sun would continue to rise and set, but when it disappeared, thousands and thousands of his fierewheels would burn all over the land, and the air would quiver with warmth, as on the hottest summer-day. Harvests would ripen in midwinter; wild strawberries would cover the hillsides the whole year round; the ice would never close the waterways.

His fire-wheel would create a new world. It would be like providing furs for the poor and a sun for the miners. It would supply power to the mills, life to nature, and a new, rich, and happy existence to mankind. But at the same time he knew that it was all a dream and that the wood-nymph would never let him reproduce his wheel. And in his anger and longing for revenge, he thought that he would kill her, and then he no longer knew what he was doing.

He went to the main building, and in the hall under the stairs he put down his fire-wheel. It was his intention to set fire to the house and burn the witch in it.

Then he went back to his workshop and sat there silently listening.

There was shouting out in the courtyard. Now they could see that a great deed had been accomplished.

Yes, run, scream, sound the alarm! But she is burning in there, the wood-nymph whom you laid on silken cushions.

May she writhe in torment, may she flee before the flames from room to room! Ah, how the green silk will blaze, and how the flames will play in the torrents of her hair! Courage, flames! courage! Catch her, set fire to her! Witches burn! Fear not her magic, flames! Let her burn! There is one who must burn throughout the whole of his life for her sake.

Bells were ringing, wagons came rattling, pumps were brought out, water was carried up from the lake, people came running from all the neighbouring villages. There were cries and wailings and commands; that was the roof, which had fallen in; there was the terrible crackling and roaring of fire. But nothing disturbed Kevenhüller. He sat on the chopping-block and rubbed his hands.

The he heard a crash, as if the heavens had fallen, and he started up in triumph. "Now it is done!" he cried. "Now she cannot escape; now she is crushed by the beams or burned up by the flames. Now it is done.

And he thought of the honour and glory of Ekeby which had had to be sacrificed to get her out of the world,—the magnificent halls, where there had been so much happiness, the tables which had groaned under dainty dishes, the precious old furniture, silver and china, which could never be replaced—

And then he sprang up with a cry. His firewheel, his sun, the model on which everything depended, had he not put it under the stairs to cause the fire?

Kevenhüller looked at himself, paralyzed with terror.

"Am I going mad?" he said. "How could I do such a thing?"

At the same moment the door of the workshop opened and the wood-nymph walked in.

She stood on the threshold, smiling and fair. Her green dress had neither hole nor stain, no smoke darkened her yellow hair. She was just as he had seen her in the market-place at Karlstad in his young days; her tail hung between her feet, and she had all the wildness and fragrance of the woods about her.

"Ekeby is burning," she said, and laughed.

Kevenhüller had the sledge-hammer lifted and meant to throw it at her head, but then he saw that she had his fire-wheel in her hand.

"See what I have saved for you," she said.

Kevenhüller threw himself on his knees before her.

"You have broken my carriage, you have rent my wings, and you have ruined my life. Have grace, have pity on me!"

She climbed up on the bench and sat there, just as young and mischievous as when he saw her first.

"I see that you know who I am," she said.

"I know you, I have always known you," said the unfortunate man; "you are genius. But set me free! Take back your gift! Let me be an ordinary person! Why do you persecute me? Why do you destroy me?"

"Madman," said the wood-nymph, "I have never wished you any harm. I gave you a great reward; but I can also take it from you if you wish. But consider well. You will repent it."

"No, no!" he cried; "take from me the power of working wonders!"

"First, you must destroy this," she said, and threw the fire-wheel on the ground in front of him.

He did not hesitate. He swung the sledge-hammer over the shining sun; sparks flew about the room, splinters and flames danced around him, and then his last wonder lay in fragments.

"Now I will take from you what I have given you," said the wood-nymph. As she stood in the door and the glare from the fire streamed over her, he looked at her for the last time. She seemed to him more beautiful than ever, and no longer malicious, only stern and proud.

"Madman," she said, "did I ever forbid you to let others copy your works? I only wished to protect the man of genius from a mechanic's labour?"

Whereupon she left him. Kevenhüller was insane for a couple of days. Then he became an ordinary man again.

But in his madness he had burned down Ekeby. No one was hurt. Still, it was a great sorrow to the Cavaliers that the hospitable home, where they had enjoyed so many good things, should suffer such damage in their time.

CHAPTER 21 *Broby Fair*

On the first Friday in October the big Broby Fair begins, and
lasts one week. It is the great festival of the autumn. Slaughtering
and baking take place in every house; the new winter clothes are
then worn for the first time; the brandy rations are doubled;
and men rest from their work. There is feasting on all the estates.
The servants and labourers draw their pay and hold long con-
ferences over what they shall buy at the Fair. People from a
distance come in small companies with knapsacks on their backs
and staffs in their hands. Many people drive their cattle before
them to the market. Small, obstinate young bulls and goats stand
still with their fore legs stretched out in front of them, thus
causing much vexation to their owners and much amusement to
the by-standers. The guest-rooms at the manors are filled with
guests; items of news are exchanged, and the prices of cattle discussed.

And on the first day of the Fair what crowds swarm up Broby
hill and over the wide market-place! Booths are set up, where the
tradespeople spread out their wares. Rope-dancers, organ-
grinders, and blind violin-players are everywhere, as well as
fortune-tellers, vendors of sweetmeats and of brandy. Beyond
the rows of booths, vegetables and fruit are offered for sale by
the gardeners from the big estates. Wide stretches are taken up
by ruddy copper-kettles. It is plain, however, by the business
transacted at the Fair, that there is want in Svartsjö, Bro, Löfvik
and in the other Lövsjö parishes: trade is poor at the booths;
and most lively in the cattle-market, for many have to sell both
their cow and its calf, so as to be able to live through the winter.

It is a gay scene. If one only has money for a glass or two, one
can keep up one's courage. And it is not only the brandy which

is the cause of the merriment; when the people from the lonely wood-huts come down to the market-place with its seething masses, and hear the din of the screaming, laughing crowd, they become, as it were, delirious with excitement.

Everybody who does not have to stay at home to look after the house and the cattle has come to the Broby Fair. There are the Cavaliers from Ekeby and the peasants from Nygård, horse-dealers from Norway, Finns from the Northern forests, vagrants from the highways.

Sometimes the whole surging sea will concentrate into a whirlpool which revolves about a central point. No one knows what is at the centre, until a couple of policemen force their way through the crowd to stop a fight or to right an overturned cart.

Towards noon the great fight began. The peasants had got it into their heads that the tradespeople were using too short yardsticks. It began with quarrelling and rowdiness around the booths; and then it developed into violence.

Everyone knows that for many who for days had known nothing but want and suffering, it was a pleasure to be able to hit out, no matter at whom or what. And as soon as they see that a fight is going on they come rushing up from all sides. The Cavaliers meant to break through in order to make peace after their own fashion; and the tradesmen ran to help one another.

Big Mons from Fors is the most eager for a fight. He is drunk, and he is angry; he has knocked down a tradesman and has begun to beat him; but hearing his calls for help his comrades hurry to his assistance and try to make Mons let go of him. Then Mons sweeps the rolls of cloth from one of the counters, and seizes the counter itself, which is a yard wide and five yards long and made of thick planks, and begins to brandish it as a weapon.

A terrible man is big Mons. It was he who kicked down a wall in the Filipstad jail. He who could lift a boat out of the water and carry it on his shoulders. When he begins to hit about him with the heavy counter, everyone runs away from him. But he follows people, striking right and left. For him it is no longer a question of friends or enemies; he only wants someone to hit, now that he has got a weapon.

The people scatter in terror. Men and woman scream and run. But how can the women escape when many of them are leading their children by the hand? Booths and carts stand in their way; oxen and cows, maddened by the noise, prevent their escape.

In a corner between the booths a group of women are wedged, and towards them the giant rages. He thinks that he can see a tradesman in the midst of the crowd? He raises the plank and lets it fall. He prepares to attack the pale, shuddering, terror-stricken women who huddle together under his deadly blow.

But as the board descends whistling over them, its force is broken by a man's upstretched arms. One man has not crouched down, but has raised himself above the crowd. One man has voluntarily accepted the blow so as to save many other people. The women and children are uninjured. One man has broken the force of the blow, but he now lies unconscious on the ground.

Big Mons does not lift up his board again. He has caught the man's eye, just as the counter struck his head; and the sight has paralyzed him. He lets himself be bound and taken away without resistance.

But the report spreads throughout the Fair that big Mons has killed Captain Lennart. They say that he who had been the people's friend died to save the women and defenceless children.

A silence falls on the great square, where life had just lately surged at fever heat: trade ceases, the fighting stops, the people leave their dinners.

Their friend is dead. The silent throngs stream towards the place where he has fallen. He lies stretched out on the ground quite unconscious; no wound is visible, but his skull seems to be flattened.

Some of the men lift him up carefully on to the counter which the giant has let fall. They think that they can detect signs that he is still alive.

"Where shall we carry him?" they ask one another.

"Home," answers a harsh voice in the crowd.

Yes, good men, carry him home! Lift him up on your shoulders and carry him home! He has been God's plaything, he has been blown like a feather before his breath. Carry him home!

That wounded head has rested on the hard prison beds, on sheaves of straw in barns. Let it now come home and rest on a soft pillow! He has suffered undeserved shame and torment, he has been hunted from his own door. He has been a wandering fugitive, following God's ways where he could find them; but his promised land was that home whose gates God had closed to him. Perhaps his house stands open for one who has died to save women and children.

Now he does not come as a malefactor, escorted by reeling boon companions; he is followed by sorrowing people, in whose cottages he has lived while he helped their sufferings. Carry him home!

And so they do. Six men lift the board on which he lies on their shoulders and carry him away from the fair. Wherever they pass, the people move to one side and stand quiet; the men uncover their heads, the women courtesy as they do in church when God's name is spoken. Many weep and dry their eyes; others begin to tell what a fine man he had been,—so kind, so gay, so resourceful and so religious. It is wonderful to see that, as soon as one of his bearers grows tired, another quietly comes and puts his shoulders under the board.

In this manner, Captain Lennart also passes the place where the Cavaliers are standing.

"I must go and see that he comes home safely," says Beeren-creutz, and leaves his place at the road-side to follow the procession to Helgesäter. Many follow his example.

The fair is deserted. People follow Captain Lennart to his home.

When the procession reaches Helgesäter, the house is silent and deserted. Again the colonel's fist beats on the closed door. All the servants are at the Fair; the captain's wife is alone at home. It is she again who opens the door.

And she asks, as she asked once before,—

"What do you want?"

Whereupon the colonel answers, as he answered previously,—
"We have brought your husband."

She looks at him, where he stands stiff and calm as usual. She looks at the bearers behind him, who are weeping, and at all that mass of people. She stands there on the steps and looks into hundreds of weeping eyes, which gaze anxiously at her. Finally, she looks at her husband, who lies stretched out on the bier, and she presses her hand to her heart. "That is his true face," she murmurs.

Without asking anything more, she bends down, draws back a bolt, opens the hall-doors wide, and then precedes the others into the bedroom.

The colonel helps her to drag out the big bed and shake up the pillows, and so Captain Lennart is once more laid on soft down and white linen.

"Is he alive?" she asks.

"Yes," answers the colonel.

"Is there any hope?"

"No. Nothing can be done."

There was silence for a while; then a sudden thought comes to her.

"Are all those people weeping for his sake.

"Yes."

"What has he done?"

"The last thing he did was to let big Mons kill him to save women and children from death."

Again she sits silent for a while and thinks.

"What kind of a face did he have, colonel, when he came home two months ago?"

The colonel started. Now he understands; now at last he understands.

"Gösta had painted his face."

"So it was on account of one of your pranks that I shut him out of his home? How will you answer for that, colonel?"

Beerencreutz shrugged his broad shoulders.

"I have much to answer for."

"But I think that this must be the worst thing you have done."

"I have never had a harder road to walk than that up to Helge-säter today. Moreover, there are two others who are to blame in this matter."

"Who?"

"Sintram is one; and you are the other. You are a hard woman. I know that many have tried to speak to you of your husband."

"It is true," she answers.

Then she begs him to tell her all about that evening at Broby.

He tells her all he can remember, and she listens silently. Captain Lennart lies still unconscious on the bed. The room is full of weeping people; no one thinks of shutting out that mourning crowd. All the doors are open, all the rooms and the stairs and the hall are filled with silent, anxious people; far out in the yard they stand in a dense crowd.

When the colonel has finished, she raises her voice and says,—

"If there are any Cavaliers in here, I ask them to go away. It is hard for me to see them when I am sitting by my husband's death-bed."

Without another word the colonel rises and goes out. So do Gösta Berling and several of the other Cavaliers who followed Captain Lennart. The people move aside for the little group of humiliated men.

When they are gone the captain's wife says: "Will some of those who have seen my husband during this period tell me where he lived, and what he did?" Then they begin to tell his wife about Captain Lennart, for she had misjudged him and in her strictness had hardened her heart against him.

It was a long time before they had all finished. All through the twilight and the evening they stood and spoke; one after another stepped forward and spoke of him to his wife, who would not hear his name mentioned.

Some tell how he found them on a sick-bed and cured them. There are wild brawlers whom he has tamed. There are mourners whom he has cheered; drunkards whom he had led to sobriety. Everyone who had been in unbearable distress had sent a message to God's wayfarer, and he had helped all of them, or at least he had awakened their hope and faith.

Out in the yard the crowd stands and waits. They know what is going on inside: what is said aloud at the death-bed is whispered from man to man outside. Anyone who has something to say pushes gently forward. "Here is one who can bear witness," they say, and let him pass. And they step forward out of the darkness, give their testimony, and disappear again into the darkness.

"What does she say now?" those standing outside ask when someone comes out. "What does she say?"

"She is radiant like a queen. She smiles like a bride. She has moved his arm-chair up to the bed and laid on it the clothes which she herself had woven for him."

But then a silence falls on the people. No one says it; but all know it at the same time: "He is dying."

Captain Lennart opens his eyes and sees everything.

He sees his home, the people, his wife, his children, the clothes; and he smiles. But he has only waked to die. He draws a rattling breath and is gone.

Then the narratives cease; but someone begins to sing a hymn for the dead. All join in, and, carried by hundreds of strong voices, the hymn rises on high.

It is earth's farewell to the departing soul.

CHAPTER 22 *The Forest Cottage*

It was many years before the Cavaliers reigned supreme at Ekeby.

The shepherd's boy and girl played together in the wood, built houses with flat stones, and picked cloud-berries. They were both born in the wood. The wood was their home and their mansion. They lived in peace with everything there.

The children looked upon the lynx and the fox as their watch-dogs, the weasel was their cat, hares and squirrels their cattle, owls and grouse sat in their bird-cage, the pines were their servants, and the young birch-trees guests at their feasts. They knew the hole where the viper lay curled up for his winter rest; and when they had bathed they had seen the water-snake come swimming through the clear water; but they feared neither snake nor wild creature; they belonged to the wood and it was their home. There nothing could frighten them.

Deep in the wood lay the cottage where the boy lived. A steep path through the woods led to it; mountains closed it in and shut out the sun; from a bottomless swamp that lay near by an icy mist rose up all the year round. Such a dwelling seemed far from attractive to the people living in the plains.

The shepherd's boy and girl were to marry some day; they would live there in the forest cottage, and support themselves by the work of their hands. But before they were married, the ravages of war passed over the land, and the boy enlisted. He came home again without being wounded or injured physically; but he had been changed for life by the campaign. He had seen too much of the world's wickedness and man's cruelty to man. He could no longer see the good.

At first no one saw any change in him. He went with the girl whom he had loved in his childhood to the clergyman and had the banns published. The forest cottage above Ekeby became their home, as they had planned long before; but it was not a happy home.

To his wife her husband appeared a stranger. Since he had come from the wars, she no longer recognize him. His laugh was harsh, and he spoke but little. She was afraid of him.

He did no harm, and worked hard. Still he was not liked, for he thought evil of everybody. He felt that he was a hated stranger. The forest animals were now his enemies. The mountain, which shut out the sun, and the swamp, from which the mist rose, were his foes. The forest is a terrible place for one who has evil thoughts.

He who intends to live in the wilderness should have bright memories. Otherwise he will see only murder and oppression among plants and animals, just as he saw it before among men. He expects evil from everything he meets.

The soldier, Jan Hök, could not explain what was the matter with him; but he felt that nothing went well with him. There was little peace in his home. His sons who grew up there were strong, but wild. They were hardy and brave men, but they too lived at enmity with all men.

His wife was tempted by her sorrow to probe the secrets of the wilderness. In swamp and thicket she gathered healing herbs. She could cure illness and give advice to those who were crossed in love. She won fame as a witch; and was shunned, although she did much good.

One day the wife tried to speak to her husband of his trouble.

"Ever since you went to the war," she said, "you have been so changed. What did they do to you there?"

Then he rose up, and was ready to strike her; and that was what happened every time she spoke of the war; he became mad with rage. From no one could he bear to hear the word war; and this soon became known. So people were careful to avoid the subject.

But none of his brothers in arms could say that he had done more harm than others. He had fought like a good soldier. It was only all the dreadful things he had seen which had frightened him so much that since then he saw nothing but evil. All his trouble came from the war. He thought that nature hated him, because he had had a share in such things. Those who knew more could console themselves that they had fought for their country and their honour. What did he know of such things? He only felt that everything hated him because he had shed blood and done much injury.

When the major's wife was driven from Ekeby, he lived alone in his cottage. His wife was dead and his sons were away. During the fairs his house was always full of guests. Black-haired, swarthy gypsies put up there. They like those persons best whom others avoid. Small, long-haired horses climbed up the forest path, dragging carts loaded with children and bundles of rags. Women, prematurely old, with features swollen by smoking and drinking, and men with pale, sharp faces and sinewy bodies followed the carts. When the gypsies came to the forest cottage, there was a merry life there. They indulged in brandy and cards and loud talking. They had much to tell of thefts and horse-dealing and bloody fights.

The Broby Fair began on a Friday, and then Captain Lennart was killed. Big Mons, who dealt the fatal blow, was son to the old man in the forest cottage. When the gypsies on Sunday afternoon sat together there, they handed old Jan Hök the brandy bottle oftener than usual, and talked to him of prison life and prison fare and trials; for they had often experienced these things.

The old man sat on the chopping-block in the corner and said little. His big lack-lustre eyes stared at the crowd which filled the room. It was dusk, but the wood-fire lit up the room.

The door was softly opened and two women entered. It was the young Countess Elizabeth followed by the daughter of the vicar of Broby. Lovely and radiant, she came into the circle of light. She told them that Gösta Berling had not been seen at Ekeby since Captain Lennart died. She and her servant had searched for him in the forest the whole afternoon. Now she saw that there were men here who had wandered much and knew all the paths. Had they seen him? She had come in to rest, and to ask if they had seen him.

It was useless to inquire of them, for none of them had seen him.

They gave her a chair. She sank down on it, and sat silent for a while. There was no sound in the room. All looked at her and wondered at her. At last she grew frightened at the silence; she gave a start, and tried to speak of trivial things. She turned to the old man in the corner. "I think I heard that you have been a soldier," she said. "Tell me something of the war!"

The silence grew still deeper. The old man sat as if he had not heard.

"It would be very interesting to hear about the war from some one who had been there himself," continued the Countess; but she stopped short, for the vicar's daughter shook her head at her. She must have said something that was inappropriate. Everybody was looking at her as if she had offended against the simplest rules of propriety. Suddenly a gypsy woman raised her sharp voice and asked: "Were you not the Countess at Borg?"

"Yes, I was."

"That was something different from running around the forest after a mad priest."

The Countess rose and bade them farewell. She was quite rested. The woman who had spoken followed her out of the room.

"You understand, Countess," she said, "I had to say something; for it does not do to speak to the old man of war. He can't bear to hear the word. I only meant well."

Countess Elizabeth hurried away, but she soon stopped. She saw the threatening forest, the dark mountain, and the reeking swamp. It must be terrible to live here for one whose soul is filled with evil memories. She felt compassion for the old man who had sat there with the dark gypsies for company.

"Anna Lisa," she said, "let us turn back! They were kind to us, but I behaved badly. I want to talk to the old man about pleasanter things."

And happy to have found some one to comfort, she went back to the cottage.

"I think," she said, "that Gösta Berling is wandering here in the forest and means to take his own life. Consequently, it is most important that he should be found as soon as possible and prevented from doing so. I and my maid, Anna Lisa, thought we saw him sometimes, but then he disappeared. He keeps to that part of the mountain where the broom-girl was killed. It strikes me that there is no necessity for me to go down to Ekeby to get help. Here are many active men who could easily catch him."

"Go along, boys!" cried the gypsy woman. "When the Countess does not feel above asking a service of the forest people, you must go at once."

The men rose immediately and went out to conduct a search.

Old Jan Hök sat still and stared before him with lustreless eyes. The gloom and hardness of the man were terrifying as he sat there. The young woman could think of nothing to say to him. Then she saw that a child lay sick on a sheaf of straw, and noticed that a woman had hurt her hand. Instantly she began to care for the sick. She was soon friends with the gossiping women, and had them show her the smallest children.

In an hour the men came back. They carried Gösta Berling bound into the room. They laid him down on the floor before the fire. His clothes were torn and dirty, his cheeks sunken, and his eyes wild. Terrible had been his life during those days; he had lain on the damp ground; he had burrowed with his hands and face in bogs, he had dragged himself over rocks, and had forced his way through the thickest underbrush. Of his own free will he would never have come with the men; but they had over-powered him and bound him.

When his wife saw him thus, she was angry. She did not free his bound limbs; she let him lie where he was on the floor. With scorn she turned from him.

"What you look like!" she said.

"I had never meant that you should see me again," he answered.

"Am I not your wife? Is it not my right to expect you to come to me with your troubles? In bitter sorrow I have waited for you these two days."

"I was the cause of Captain Lennart's misfortunes. How could I dare to show myself to you?"

"You are not often afraid, Gösta."

"The only service I can do you, Elizabeth, is to rid you of myself."

She looks down at him with unspeakable contempt flashing from beneath her frowning brows.

"You wish to make me a suicide's wife!"

His face was distorted.

"Elizabeth, let us go out into the silent forest and talk."

"Why should not these people hear us?" she cried, speaking in a shrill voice. "Are we better than any of them? Has anyone of them caused more sorrow and injury than we? They are the children of the forest, and of the highway; they are hated by every man. Let them hear how sin and sorrow also follow the lord of Ekeby, the beloved of all, Gösta Berling! Do you think your wife considers that you are better than any of them—or do you think you are?"

He raised himself with difficulty on to his elbow, and looked at her with sudden defiance. "I am not such a wretch as you think."

Then she heard the story of those two days. The first day Gösta wandered about in the forest, driven by remorse. He could not bear to meet any one's eye. But he did not think of dying. He meant to journey to far distant lands. On Sunday, however, he came down from the hills and went to the Bro church. Once more he wished to see the people: the poor, hungry people whom he had dreamed of serving when he had sat by the old vicar's pile of shame, and whom he had learned to love when he saw them disappear into the night with the dead broom-girl.

The service had begun when he came to the church. He crept up to the gallery, and looked down on the people. He had felt bitter agony. He had wanted to speak to them, to comfort them in their poverty and hopelessness. If he had only been allowed to speak in God's house, hopeless as he was, he would have found words of hope and salvation for all of them.

Then he left the church, went into the sacristy, and wrote the message which his wife already knew. He had promised that work should be renewed at Ekeby, and grain distributed to those in greatest need. He had hoped that his wife and the Cavaliers would fulfil his promises when he was gone.

As he came out, he saw a coffin standing before the parish public-rooms. It was a plain coffin, rough-cut in haste, but covered with black crape and wreaths. He knew that it was Captain Lennart's. The people had begged the captain's wife to hasten the funeral, so that all those who had come to the Fair could be at the burial.

He was standing and looking at the coffin, when a heavy hand was laid on his shoulder. Sintram had come up to him.

"Gösta," he said, "if you want to play a regular trick on a person, lie down and die. There is nothing more cunning than to die, nothing which so deceives an honest man who suspects no harm. Lie down and die, I tell you!"

Gösta listened with horror to what he said. Sintram complained of the failure of well-laid plans. He had wanted to see the shores of the Löven laid waste. He had made the Cavaliers lords of the place; he had let the vicar of Broby impoverish the people; he had called forth the drought and the famine. At the Broby Fair the decisive blow was to have fallen. Excited by their misfortunes, the people were to have turned to murder and robbery. Then there would have been lawsuits to beggar them. Famine, riot, and every kind of misfortune would have ravaged them. Finally, the country would have become so odious and detestable that no one could have lived there, and it would all have been Sintram's doing. It would have been his joy and pride, for he was evil-minded. He loved desert and uncultivated fields But this man who had known how to die at the right moment had spoiled it all for him.

Then Gösta asked him what would have been the good of it all.

"It would have pleased me, Gösta, for I am bad. I am the grizzly bear on the mountain; I am the snow-storm on the plain; I like to kill and to persecute. Away, I say, with people and their works! I don't like them. I can let them slip from between my claws and cut their capers,—that is amusing too for a while; but now I am tired of play, Gösta, now I want to strike, now I want to kill and to destroy."

He was mad, quite mad. As a joke, he had begun a long time ago with those devilish tricks, and now his maliciousness had got the upper hand; now he thought he really was a spirit from the lower regions. He had fed and fostered the evil in him until it had taken possession of his soul. For wickedness, as well as love and brooding, can drive people mad.

He was furious, and in his anger he began to tear the wreaths off the coffin; but then Gösta Berling cried: "Let the coffin be!"

"Well, well, well, so I am not to touch it? Yes; I shall throw my friend Lennart on the ground and trample on his wreaths. Do you not see what he has done to me? Do you not see in what a fine gray coach I am riding?"

And Gösta then saw that a couple of prison-vans with the sheriff and constables of the district stood and waited outside the churchyard wall.

"I ought to convey Captain Lennart's wife my thanks for having sat down yesterday and read through old papers in order to find proof against me in that matter of the powder, you know? Shall I not let her know that she would have done better in occupying herself with brewing and baking, than in sending the sheriff and his men after me? Shall I have nothing for the tears I have wept to induce Scharling to let me come here and say a prayer by my dear friend's coffin?"

And he began again to drag at the crape.

Then Gösta Berling came close up to him and seized his arms.

"I will give anything to make you leave the coffin alone," he said.

"Do what you like," said the madman. "Call the others if you like. I shall always manage to do something before the sheriff can get here. Fight with me, if you like. That will be a pleasing sight here by the church. Let us fight among the wreaths and palls."

"I will buy rest for the dead at any price. Take my life, take everything!"

"You promise much."

"You can put me to the test."

"Well, then, kill yourself!"

"I will; but first let the coffin be safely in the earth."

That is how it came about. Sintram took Gösta's oath that he would not be alive twelve hours after Captain Lennart was buried. "Then I shall know that you can never become a good fellow," he said.

It was easy for Gösta Berling to promise. He was glad to be able to give his wife her liberty. Remorse had made him long for death. The only thing which troubled him was, that he had promised the major's wife not to die as long as the daughter of the vicar of Broby was a servant at Ekeby. But Sintram said that she could no longer be considered to be a servant, since she had inherited her father's fortune. Gösta objected that the old clergyman had hidden his treasures so well that no one had been able to find them. Then Sintram laughed and said that they were hidden up among the pigeon's nests in the church tower. Thereupon he went away. And Gösta went back to the forest again. It seemed best to him to die where the broom-girl had been killed. He had wandered there the whole afternoon. He had seen his wife in the forest; and then he had not had the strength to kill himself.

All this he told his wife, while he lay bound on the floor of the cottage.

"Oh," she said sadly, when he had finished, "how well I know it all! Heroic display! Heroic feats! You are always ready to thrust your hands into the fire, Gösta, always ready to throw yourself away! How noble such things seemed to me once! How I now value calmness and good sense! What good did you do the dead by such a promise? What did it matter if Sintram had overturned the coffin and torn off the crape? It would have been picked up again; there would have been new crape and new wreaths. If you had laid your hand on that good man's coffin, there before Sintram's eyes, and sworn to live to help those poor people whom he wished to ruin, that I should have commended.

If you had thought, when you saw the people in the church: 'I will help them; I will make use of all my strength to help them,' and not laid that burden on your weak wife, and on old men with failing strength, I should also have commended that."

Gösta Berling lay silent for a while.

"We Cavaliers are not free men," he said at last. "We have promised one another to live for pleasure, and only for pleasure. Woe to all of us if one breaks his word!"

"Woe to you," said the Countess, indignantly, "if you become the most cowardly of the Cavaliers, and slower to improve than any of them. Yesterday afternoon all the eleven sat in the Cavaliers' wing; they were very sad. You were gone; Captain Lennart was gone. The glory and honour of Ekeby were gone. They left the toddy tray untouched; they would not let me see them. Then the maid, Anna Lisa, who stands here, went up to them. You know she is an energetic little woman who for years has struggled desperately against neglect and waste.

" 'To-day I went home again and looked for father's money,' she said to the Cavaliers; 'but I found nothing. All the debts are paid and the drawers and closets are empty.'

" 'We are sorry for you, Anna Lisa,' said Beerencreutz.

" 'When the major's wife left Ekeby,' continued Anna Lisa, 'she told me to look after her house. And if I had found father's money, I would have rebuilt Ekeby. But as I did not find anything else to take away with me, I took father's pile of shame; for great shame awaits me when my mistress comes again and asks me what I have done with Ekeby.'

" 'Don't take so much to heart what is not your fault, Anna Lisa,' said Beerencreutz again.

" 'But I did not take the pile of shame for myself alone,' said Anna Lisa. 'I took it also on your account, good gentlemen. Father is not the only one who has been the cause of shame and injury in this world.'

"And she went from one to the other of them, and laid down some of the dry sticks before each. Some of them swore, but most of them let her go on. At last Beerencreutz said, calmly:—

" 'You have done well. We thank you. You may go now.' When she had gone, he struck the table with his clenched fist till the glasses rang.

" 'From this hour,' he said, 'I'll be absolutely sober. Brandy shall never again bring me to such shame.' Thereupon he rose and went out.

"Gradually all the others followed him. Do you know where they went, Gösta? Well, down to the river, to the point where the mill and the forge had stood, and there they began to work. They began to drag away the logs and stones and clear the place. The old men have had a hard time. Many of them have experienced sorrow. Now they can no longer bear the disgrace of having ruined Ekeby. I know only too well that you Cavaliers are ashamed to work; but now the others have accepted that disgrace. Moreover, Gösta, they mean to send Anna Lisa up to the major's wife to bring her home. But you, what are you doing?"

He still found an answer to give her.

"What do you want of me, an unfrocked priest? I am rejected by men, and hateful to God?"

"I too have been in the church at Bro to-day, Gösta. I have a message for you from two women. "Tell Gösta,' said Marianne Sinclair, 'that a woman does not like to be ashamed of the man she has loved.' 'Tell Gösta,' said Anna Stjärnhök, 'that all is now well with me. I manage my own estates. I do not think of love, only of work. At Berga too they have overcome the first bitterness of their sorrow. But we all grieve for Gösta. We believe in him and pray for him; but when will he be a man?'

"Do you hear? Are you rejected by men?" continued the Countess. "Your misfortune is that you have been met with too much love. Women and men have loved you. If you only jested and laughed, if you only sang and played, they have forgiven you everything. Whatever it has pleased you to do has seemed right to them. And you dare to call yourself an outcast! Or are you hateful to God? Why did you not stay and attend Captain Lennart's burial?

"As he had died on a fair-day, the news had spread far and wide. After the service, thousands of people came up to the church.

The funeral procession started from the town hall. They were only waiting for the old Dean. He was ill and had not preached; but he had promised to come to Captain Lennart's funeral. And at last he came, with head sunk on his breast, and dreaming his dreams, as he is wont to do now in his old age, and placed himself at the head of the procession. He noticed nothing unusual. He took the familiar path and did not look up. He read the prayers, and sprinkled earth on the coffin, and still he noticed nothing. Then the sexton began a hymn. Hundreds and hundreds of voices joined in. Men, women, and children sang. It was then that the Dean awoke from his dreams. He passed his hand over his eyes and stepped up on the mound of earth to look round. Never had he seen such a crowd of mourners. All were singing; all had tears in their eyes,—all were mourning.

"Then the old Dean began to tremble. What should he say to these people? He must say something to comfort them.

"When the hymn had ended, he stretched out his arms over the people.

" 'I see that you are mourning,' he said; 'and grief is harder to bear for one who has long to live than for me who will soon be gone.'

"He stopped dismayed. His voice was too weak, and words failed him.

"But he soon began again. His voice had regained its youthful strength, and his eyes glowed.

"Firstly, he told us all he knew of God's wayfarer. Then he reminded us that neither outward polish nor great ability was the cause of Captain Lennart's being so highly honoured as he now was, but only the fact that he had alway followed God's ways. And now he asked us to do the same. Each should love and help the other. Each should think well of the other. And he explained everything which had happened this year. He said it was a preparation for the time of love and happiness which now was to be expected.

"And we all felt as if we had heard a prophet speak. All wished to love one another; all wished to be good.

"He lifted up his eyes and his hands and proclaimed peace in the neighbourhood. "In God's name," he said, "may perturbation of mind cease! May peace dwell in your hearts and in all nature! May the dead things and the animals and the plants know peace and cease from doing harm!"

And it was as if holy peace had descended upon the whole district. It was as if the heights were radiant and the valleys smiled and the autumn mist had assumed a rosy tint. Then he prayed for a deliverer to succour the people. 'Some one will come,' he said. It is not God's will that you shall perish. God will find some one who will feed the hungry and lead you in His ways.'

"Then we all thought of you, Gösta. We knew that the Dean spoke of you. The people who had heard your message went home talking of you. And you wandered here in the wood and wanted to die! The people are waiting for you, Gösta. In all the cottages they are sitting and saying that, as the mad priest at Ekeby is going to help them, all will be well. You are their hero, Gösta.

"Yes, Gösta, it is certain that the old man meant you, and that ought to make you want to live. But I, Gösta, who am your wife, I say to you that you shall go and do your duty. Do not dream of being sent by God,— the call may come to anyone, you know. You are to work without striving after any heroic feats. You are not to endeavour to shine and to astonish people; you must behave in such a way that your name is not too often heard on the people's lips. But think well before you retract your promise to Sintram. You have now got a certain right to die, and life is not likely to offer you many attractions in the future. There was a time when my wish was to go home to Italy, Gösta. It seemed too much happiness for me, a sinner, to be your wife, and to be permitted to be with you throughout life. But now I shall stay. If you dare to live, I shall stop; but do not expect any joy from that. I shall force you to follow the weary path of duty. You need never expect words of joy or hope from me. Can a heart which has suffered like mine love again? Tearless and joyless I shall walk beside you. Think well, Gösta, before you choose to live. We shall go the way of penance."

She did not wait for his answer. She nodded to Anna Lisa and went. When she came out into the forest, she began to weep bitterly, and wept until she reached Ekeby. When she was there, she remembered that she had forgotten to talk of more cheerful things than war to the soldier Jan Hök.

In the cottage there was silence when she was gone.

"Glory and honour be to the Lord God!" said the old soldier, suddenly.

They looked at him. He had risen and was looking eagerly about him.

"Wicked, wicked has everything been," he said. "Everything I have seen since I got my eyes opened has been wicked. Bad men, bad women! Hate and anger in forest and plain! But she is good. A good woman has stood in my house. When I am sitting here alone, I shall remember her. She shall be with me when I am in the forest."

He bent down over Gösta, untied his fetters, and lifted him up. Then he solemnly took his hand.

"Hateful to God," he said and nodded. "That is just it. But now you are not so any more; nor am I either, since she has been in my house. She is good."

The next day old Jan Hök came to the bailiff Scharling. "I will carry my cross," he said. "I have been a bad man, therefore I have had bad sons." And he asked to be allowed to go to prison instead of his son; but that could not be.

The best of old stories is the one which tells of how he followed his son, walking beside the prison van; how he slept outside his cell; how he did not forsake him until he had suffered his punishment.

"It has been God's storm," she said,—"God's storm. I know now that is has all been for the best!"

Then the door to the sick-room closed, and they never saw her again.

There is so much to say to one who is dying. The words throng to the lips when one knows that in the next room lies one whose ears will soon be closed for ever. "Ah, my friend, my friend," one wants to say, "can you forgive me? Can you believe that I have loved you in spite of everything! Ah, my friend, I thank you for all the joy you have given me!"

That is what one wishes to say, and much more, so much more.

But the major's wife lay in a burning fever, and the voices of the Cavaliers could not reach her. Would she never know how they had worked, how they had taken up her work?

After a little while the Cavaliers went down to the forge. There all work was stopped; but they threw new coal and new ore into the furnace, and made ready to smelt. They did not call the smith, who had gone home to celebrate Christmas, but worked themselves at the forge. If the major's wife could only live until the hammer got going, it would tell her their story.

Evening came and then night, while they worked. Several of them thought, how strange it was that they should again celebrate Christmas Eve in the forge.

Kevenhüller, who had built the mill and the forge, and Christian Bergh stood by the forge and attended to the melting iron. Gösta and Julius were the stokers. Some of the others sat on the anvil under the raised hammer, and others sat on coal-carts and piles of pig-iron. Löwenborg was talking to Eberhard, the philosopher, who sat beside him on the anvil.

"Sintram dies to-night," he said.

"Why just to-night?" asked Eberhard.

"You know that we made an agreement last year. Now we have done nothing which has been ungentlemanly, and therefore he has lost."

"You who believe in such things know very well that we have done a great deal which has been ungentlemanly. First, we did not help the major's wife: second, we began to work; third, it was not quite right that Gösta Berling did not kill himself, when he had promised."

"I have thought of that too," answered Löwenborg; "but my opinion is, that you do not rightly comprehend the matter. To act with the thought of our own mean advantage was forbidden us; but not to act as love or honour or our own salvation demanded. I think that Sintram has lost."

"Perhaps you are right."

"I tell you that I know it. I have heard his sleigh-bells the whole evening, but they are not real bells. We shall soon have him here."

And the little old man sat and stared through the door of the forge, which stood open, at the bit of blue sky studded with stars, which showed through it.

After a little while he started up.

"Do you see him?" he whispered. "There he comes creeping. Do you not see him in the doorway?"

"I see nothing," replied Eberhard. "You are sleepy, that's all."

"I saw him so distinctly against the sky. He had on his long wolfskin coat and fur cap. Now he is over there in the dark, and I cannot see him. Look, now he is up by the furnace. He is standing close to Christian Bergh; but Christian seems not to see him. Now he is bending down and is throwing something into the fire. Oh, how wicked he looks! Take care, friends, take care!"

As he spoke, a tongue of flame burst out of the furnace, and covered the smiths and their assistants with cinders and sparks. No one, however, was injured.

"He wants to be revenged," whispered Löwenborg.

"You too are mad!" cried Eberhard. "You ought to have had enough of such things."

"Do you not see how he is standing there by the prop and grinning at us? Indeed I believe that he has unfastened the hammer."

He jumped up and dragged Eberhard with him. The second after the hammer fell thundering down on to the anvil. It was only a clamp which had given way; but Eberhard and Löwenborg had narrowly escaped death.

"You see that he has no power over us," said Löwenborg, triumphantly. "But it is plain that he wants to be revenged."

And he called Gösta Berling to him.

"Go up to the women, Gösta. Perhaps he will show himself to them too. They are not so used as I to seeing such things. They may be frightened. And take care of yourself, Gösta, for he has a special grudge against you, and perhaps he has power over you on account of that promise."

Afterwards they heard that Löwenborg had been right, and that Sintram had died that night. Some said that he had hanged himself in his cell. Others believed that the ministers of justice had had him killed secretly, for the trial seemed to be going well for him, and it would never do to let him out again among the people in Lövsjö. Still others thought that a dark visitor had driven up in a black carriage, drawn by black horses, and had taken him out of prison. And Löwenborg was not the only one who saw him that night. He was also seen at Fors and in Ulrika Dillner's dreams. Many told how he had shown himself to them, until Ulrika Dillner had his body moved to the churchyard at Bro. She also had the evil servants sent away from Fors and introduced good order there. After that it was no longer haunted.

It is said that before Gösta Berling reached the house, a stranger had come to the wing and had left a letter for the major's wife. No one knew the messenger, but the letter was carried in and laid on the table beside the sick woman. Soon after she became unexpectedly better; the fever decreased, the pain abated, and she was able to read the letter.

The old people believe that her improvement depended on the influence of the powers of darkness. Sintram and his friends would profit by the reading of that letter.

It was a contract written in blood on black paper. The Cavaliers would have recognized it. It had been written on the previous Christmas Eve in the forge at Ekeby.

And the major's wife lay there now and read that since she

had been a witch, and had sent the souls of Cavaliers to hell, she was condemned to lose Ekeby. That and other similar absurdities she read. She examined the date and signatures, and found the following note beside Gösta's name: "Because the major's wife has taken advantage of my weakness to tempt me away from honest work, and to keep me as a Cavalier at Ekeby, because she has made me Ebba Dohna's murderer by betraying to her that I am an unfrocked priest, I sign this."

The major's wife slowly folded the paper and put it in its envelope. Then she lay still and thought over what she had learned. She understood with bitter anguish that this was what people thought of her. She was a witch and a sorceress to all those whom she had served, to whom she had given work and food. This was her reward. They could not believe anything better of an adulteress.

Her thoughts raced. Wild anger and a longing for revenge flamed up in her fever-racked brain. She had Anna Lisa, who with Countess Elizabeth tended her, send a message to Högfors to the manager and overseer. She wished to make her will.

Again she lay thinking. Her eyebrows were drawn together, her features were terribly distorted by suffering.

"You are very ill," said the Countess, softly.

"Yes, more ill than ever before."

There was silence again, but then the major's wife spoke in a hard, harsh voice:—

"It is strange to think that you, too, Countess, you whom every one loves, are an adulteress."

The young woman started.

"Yes, if not in deed, yet in thought and desire, and that makes no difference. I, who lie here, know that it makes no difference."

"I know it too!"

"And yet you are happy now. You may possess him whom you loved without sin. That black spectre does not stand between you when you meet. You may belong to one another before the eyes of the world, love one another, go side by side through life.

"Oh, madame, madame!"

"How can you dare to stay with him?" cried the old woman, with increasing violence. "Repent, repent in time! Go home to your father and mother, before they come and curse you. Do you dare to look upon Gösta Berling as your husband? Leave him! I shall give him Ekeby. I shall give him power and glory. Will you dare to share that with him? Do you dare to accept happiness and honour? I did not dare to do so. Do you remember what happened to me? Do you remember the Christmas dinner at Ekeby? Do you remember the cell in the bailiff's house?"

"Oh, madame, we sinners go here side by side without happiness. I am here to see that there shall be no joy by our hearth. Do you think I do not long for my home? Oh, I long with bitter longing for the protection and support of home; but I shall never again enjoy them. Here I shall live in fear and trembling, knowing that everything I do leads to sin and sorrow, knowing that if I chance to help one, I shall ruin another. Too weak and foolish for the life here, and yet forced to live it, bound by an everlasting penance."

"With such thoughts we deceive our hearts," cried the major's wife; "it is only weakness. You do not want to leave him, that is the only reason."

Before the Countess could answer, Gösta Berling came into the room.

"Come here, Gösta," said the major's wife at once, and her voice grew still sharper and harder. "Come here, you whom everybody praises. You shall now hear what has happened to your old friend whom you allowed to wander about the country, despised and forsaken.

"I will first tell you what happened last spring, when I came home to my mother, for you ought to know the end of that story.

"In March I reached the iron-works in the Älvdal forest, Gösta. Little better than a beggar I looked. They told me that my mother was in the dairy. So I went there, and stood for a long while silent at the door. There were long shelves all round the room, and on them stood shining copper pans filled with milk. And my mother, who was over ninety years old, took down pan after pan and skimmed off the cream. She was active enough, the old woman; but I saw clearly how hard it was for her to stretch up in order to reach the pans. I did not know if she had seen me; but after a while she spoke to me in a curious, shrill voice.

" 'So everything has happened to you as I wished,' she said. I wanted to speak and to ask her to forgive me, but it was a waste of words. She did not hear a word of it,—she was stone-deaf. But after a while she spoke again: 'You can come and help me,' she said.

"Then I went in and skimmed the milk. I took down the pans in the proper order; and put everything in its place, and skimmed just deep enough; and she was pleased. She had never been able to trust any of the maids to skim the milk; but I knew of old how she liked to have it done.

" 'Now you can take charge of this work,' she said. And then I knew that she had forgiven me.

"And afterwards, it seemed, all at once, as if she could not work any more. She sat in her arm-chair and slept almost the whole day long. She died two weeks before Christmas. I should have liked to have come before, Gösta, but I could not leave her."

She stopped. She began to find breathing difficult; but she made an effort and went on:—

"It is true, Gösta, that I wished to keep you near me at Ekeby. There is something about you which makes every one rejoice to be with you. If you had shown any desire to settle down, I should have given you much power. I always hoped that you would find a good wife. At first, I thought that it would be Marianne Sinclair, for I saw that she already loved you, when you lived as wood-cutter in the wood. Then I thought that it would be Ebba Dohna, and one day I drove over to Borg and told her that if she would marry you, I would leave you Ekeby in my will. If I did wrong in that, you must forgive me."

Gösta was kneeling by the bed with his face hidden in the blankets, and was moaning bitterly.

"Tell me, Gösta, how you mean to live? How will you support your wife? Tell me that. You know that I have always wished

you well." And Gösta answered her smiling, while his heart
was almost breaking with grief.

"In the old days, when I tried to be a labourer here at Ekeby,
you gave me a cottage to live in, and it is still mine. This autumn
I have put it quite in order. Löwenborg has helped me, and we
have whitewashed the ceilings and papered the walls and painted
them. The little inner room Löwenborg calls the Countess's
boudoir, and he has searched the neighbouring farm-houses
for furniture bought at manorhouse auctions. He has bought
some of this furniture; and we have now high-backed armchairs
and chests of drawers with shining mountings. But in the big
outer room stands the young wife's weaving-loom and my
lathe. Household utensils and all kinds of things are there, and
Löwenborg and I have already sat many evenings and talked of
how the young Countess and I will arrange things in the cottage.
But my wife has only heard of it now. We wanted to tell her when
we left Ekeby."

"Go on, Gösta."

"Löwenborg was always saying that a maid was needed in the
house. 'In the summer it is lovely here in the birch grove,' he
used to say; 'but in winter it will be too lonely for the young
wife. You will have to have a maid, Gösta.'

"And I agreed with him, but I did not know how I could
afford to keep one. Then one day he came and brought his music,
and his table with the painted keyboard, and put it in the cottage.
'So it is you, Löwenborg, who are going to be the maid,' I said to
him. He answered that he would be needed. Did I intend the
young Countess to cook the food, and to carry wood and fetch
water? No, I had not meant her to do anything at all, as long as I
had a pair of arms to work with. But he still thought that it would
be best if there were two of us, so that she might sit the whole
day on her sofa and embroider. One could never know how much
waiting on such a little woman needed, he said."

"Go on," said the major's wife. "It eases my pain. Did you
think that your young Countess would be willing to live in a
cottage?"

He wondered at her scornful tone, but continued:

"No, I did not dare to think it; but it would have been so wonderful if she had been willing. It is thirty miles to the nearest doctor. She, who has a light hand and a tender heart, would have had work enough to tend wounds and allay fevers. And I thought that everybody in trouble would find the way to the fine lady in the forest cottage. There is so much distress among the poor, which kind words and a gentle heart can help."

"But what about you, Gösta Berling?"

"I shall have my work at the carpenter's bench and lathe. I shall in future live my own life. If my wife will not accompany me, I cannot help it. If some one should offer me all the riches of the universe, it would not tempt me. I want to live my own life. I shall be a poor man now, and remain a poor man, among the peasants, and help them with whatever I can. They need some one to play the polka for them at weddings and at Christmas; they need some one to write letters to their sons who are far away,—I will be that some one. But I must be poor."

"It will be a gloomy life for you, Gösta."

"Oh, no, it would not be if we were but two who kept together. The rich and happy would come to us as well as the poor. It would be gay enough in our cottage. Our guests would not care if the food was cooked in their presence, or be shocked that two must eat from the same plate."

"And what would be the good of it all, Gösta? What praise would you win?"

"Great would be my reward if the poor would remember me for a year or two after my death. I should have done some good if I had planted a couple of apple-trees at the house-corners, if I had taught the country fiddlers some of the old tunes, and if the shepherd children had learnt a few good songs to sing along the forest paths.

"You can believe me, I am still the same mad Gösta Berling that I was before. A country fiddler is all I can be, but that is enough. I have many sins to atone for. To weep and to repent is not for me. I shall give the poor pleasure, that is my penance."

"Gösta," said the major's wife, "it is too humble a life for a man with your ability I will give you Ekeby."

"Oh," he cried in terror, "do not make me rich! Do not lay such duties upon me! Do not part me from the poor!"

"I will give Ekeby to you and the Cavaliers," repeated the major's wife. "You are a capable man, Gösta, whom the people bless. I say like my mother, 'You shall take charge of this work!' "

"No, we could not accept it,—we who have misjudged you and caused you such pain!"

"I will give you Ekeby, do you hear?"

She spoke bitterly and harshly, without kindness. He was filled with dismay.

"Do not tempt the old men! It would only make them idlers and drunkards again. God in Heaven, rich Cavaliers! What would become of us!"

"I will give you Ekeby, Gösta; but then you must promise to set your wife free. Such a delicate little woman is not for you She has had to suffer too much here in the land of the bears. She is longing for her bright native country. You shall let her go. That is why I give you Ekeby."

But then Countess Elizabeth came up to the major's wife and knelt by the bed.

"I do not long any more. My husband has solved the problem, and found the life I can live. No longer shall I need to go strict and cold beside him, and remind him of repentance and atonement. Poverty and want and hard work will do that. The paths which lead to the poor and the sick I can follow without sin. I am no longer afraid of the life here in the north. But do not make him rich; for then I do not dare to stay."

The major's wife raised herself in the bed.

"You demand happiness for yourselves," she cried, and threatened them with clenched fists,—"happiness and blessing. No, let Ekeby be the Cavaliers', that they may be ruined. Let man and wife be parted, that they may be ruined! I am a witch, I am a sorceress, I shall incite you to evil-doing. I shall be what my reputation is."

She seized the letter and flung it in Gösta's face. The black paper fluttered out and fell on the floor. Gösta knew it too well.

"You have sinned against me, Gösta. You have misjudged one who has been a second mother to you. Do you dare to refuse your punishment? You shall accept Ekeby, and it shall ruin you, for you are weak. You shall send home your wife, so that there will be no one to save you. You shall die with a name as hated as mine. Margareta Celsing's obituary is that of a witch. Yours shall be that of a spendthrift and an oppressor of the poor."

She sank back on the pillows, and all was still. In the silence were heard muffled blows, now one and now another. The sledge-hammer had begun its far-echoing work.

"Listen," said Gösta Berling, "that is the sound of Margareta Celsing's obituary! That is not a prank of drunken Cavaliers; that is the song of the victory of labour, raised in honour of a good, old worker. Do you hear what the hammer says? 'Thanks,' it says; 'thanks for good work; thanks for bread, which you have given the poor; thanks for roads, which you have opened; thanks for districts, which you have cultivated! Thanks for pleasure, with which you have filled your halls!'—'Thanks,' it says 'and sleep in peace! Your work shall live and continue. Your house shall always be a home for happy labour.'—'Thanks,' it says, 'and do not judge us who have sinned! You who are now starting on the journey to the regions of peace, think gentle thoughts of us who still live.'"

Gösta ceased, but the sledge-hammer went on speaking. All the voices which had ever spoken kindly to the major's wife were mingled with the ring of the hammer. Gradually her features relaxed, as if the shadow of death had fallen upon her.

Anna Lisa came in and announced that the gentlemen from Högfors had come. The major's wife let them go. She did not wish to make a will.

"Oh, Gösta Berling, man of many deeds," she said, "so you have conquered once more. Bend down and let me bless you!"

The fever returned with redoubled strength. The death-rattle began. The body toiled through dreary suffering; but the spirit

soon knew nothing of it. It began to gaze into the heaven which
is opened for the dying.

So an hour passed, and the short death-struggle was over. She
lay there so peaceful and beautiful that those about her were
deeply moved.

"My dear old friend," said Gösta, " I have seen you once
before like this. Now Margareta Celsing has come back to life.
Now she will never again give way to the major's wife at Ekeby."

When the Cavaliers came in from the forge, they were told of
Margareta Celsing's death.

"Did she hear the hammer?" they asked.

She had done so, and they could be satisfied.

They heard, too, that she had meant to give them Ekeby; but
that the will had never been made. That they considered a great
honour, and rejoiced over it as long as they lived. And no one
ever heard them lament over the riches they had lost.

It is also said that on that Christmas night Gösta Berling stood
by his young wife's side and made his last speech to the Cavaliers.
He was grieved at their fate now that all of them had to leave
Ekeby. The ailments of old age awaited them. The old and
worn-out would receive a cold welcome.

And so he spoke to them. Once more he called them old gods
and knights who had risen up to bring pleasure into the land of
iron. But he lamented that the pleasure garden where butterfly-
winged pleasure flits is filled with destructive caterpillars, and
that its fruits are withered.

Well he knew that pleasure was a good thing for the children of
this world and that it must exist. But, like an enigma that was
difficult to solve, the world was burdened by the question how
a man could be both happy and good. He called it the easiest
thing and yet the hardest. Hitherto they had not been able to
solve the problem. Now he believed that they had learned it,
that they had all learned it during that year of joy and sorrow, of
happiness and despair.

You dear old people! In the old days you gave me precious gifts. But what have I given you?

Perhaps it may gladden you that your names will be heard again in connection with the dear old places? May all the brightness which belonged to your life illumine again the regions where you have lived! Borg still stands; Björne still stands; Ekeby still lies by lake Löven, surrounded by waterfalls and the lake, by park and smiling meadows; and when one stands on the broad terraces, legends swarm about one like the bees in summer.

But, speaking of bees, let me tell one more old story. Little Ruster, who went as a drummer at the head of the Swedish army, when in 1813 it marched into Germany, could never weary of telling stories of that wonderful land in the south. The people there were as tall as church towers, the swallows were as big as eagles, the bees as geese.

"Well, but the bee-hives?"

"The bee-hives were like our ordinary bee-hives."

"How did the bees get in?"

"Well, that was their concern," said little Ruster.

Dear reader, must I say the same? The giant bees of fancy have now swarmed about us for a year and a day; but how they are to return into the bee-hive of fact, they really must find out for themselves.